Hillcity Press

Edited by Monica Wanat

Cover art by Damián V.

Cover design by Mibl Art

Map by Maarten de Wekker

SCEPTER

— OF —

FIRE

• SCEPTER AND CROWN BOOK THREE •

HILLCITY
PRESS

For Xan, in honor of Windsong.

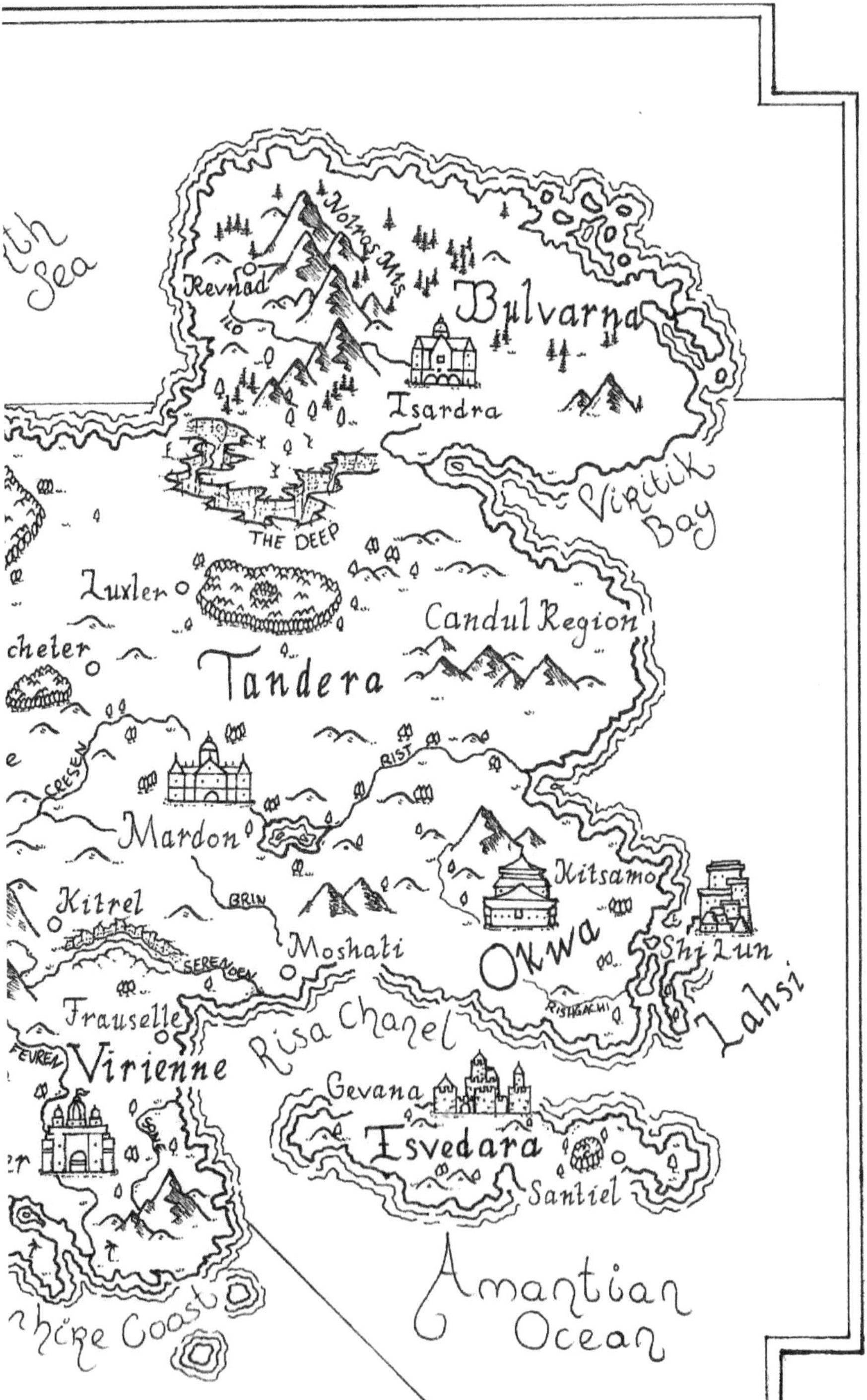

th
Sea
Notres Mts
Revnad
ILO
Bulvarna
Isardra
Viritik
Bay
THE DEEP
Luxler
Candul Region
cheter
Tandera
CRESEN
RIST
Mardon
Kitsamo
Kitrel
BRIN
Moshati
Okwa
Shi Lun
Lahsi
SERENDEN
Frauselle
Risa Chanel
RISHGACHI
FEUREN
Virienne
Gevana
Esvedara
Santiel
Amantian
Ocean
hore Coast

Sign up for my VIP reader newsletter and get exclusive access to free stories, giveaways, first looks at covers, and sneak peeks of new projects.

Vip.cfeblack.com/join

1

ALY

Alyana Barron stood atop the palace roof, gazing out at the capital city of Mardon, which twinkled with bright windows and the warm glow of a multitude of Truthwells. The stars strewn across the night sky mirrored the world of light and shadow in Aly's mind. Fires crackled in chimneys with a particular spark to them that Aly had always found intriguing, but she passed over the energy of the flames, still searching. Her mind touched the flowing power of the Cresen River as Aly pushed her awareness farther out into the sleeping city.

Red wasn't in the barracks. The former king, yanked from his throne so suddenly, was not doing a very good job obeying his orders. In one week, he'd been caught twice sneaking from the barracks down the road that led to the palace.

He was trying to come to her, like he'd promised. They'd beaten him both times.

One. Two. Three. Aly counted the murky energy signatures of three Canyon beasts lurking in the city.

In the week since Alexander's coronation, the number of

beasts sneaking past the city's defenses had surged. She marked their location and uttered three quick spells, careful to direct her magic with the words of truth and the focused intentions of her mind. She kept her eyes closed until the dim light of each beast's Well snuffed out.

A sigh of relief breezed from her mouth and mingled with the warm night air. Aly was pleased her magic had still been strong enough to split into three directions at once. Such an action would have been easy with Red as her source, but King Benedict Alexander's Truthwell was like a murky pond compared to Red's ocean of energy. And Alexander's Well was suffering from a tangle of lies planted there by Queen Kassia herself.

Aly rubbed her temples, absently massaging the tension there, as she once again pressed her mental awareness outward, sweeping the city for one familiar light.

Her magical gaze swept over thousands of people, some of whom were congested with lies, others who were as clear as a mountain stream, with only the faintest hints of darkness in their depths. No single Well was truly void of shadows—it was what marked a human Well from that of an animal. The light inside of a human was ten times brighter, but it was also tainted by evil.

At times like this, when Aly beheld so many Wells at once, she trembled a little at the amount of darkness that surrounded her. So many people believed lies, and they didn't have the ability to *see* them for what they were, like Aly could, like all sorcerers could. It didn't quite seem fair, but it was the way the Maker had created the world. Only a few gifted people could *see* the power of truth and the ugliness of lies.

And yet, many of those who could see the darkness still desired it. Her father had been one of them.

She found Red's light quickly, his bright Well still the Beacon it had always been. As soon as her magic touched his energy, she let out a small sigh, as if admiring a stunning sunset. Then reality crushed this sentiment as reality hit.

He leaves tomorrow.

His company's departure had been moved up, thanks to the news of the growing debacle at Caridan, the army camp at the Canyon's edge. It had been decimated by a recent attack and beasts were flooding into the country at alarming rates. Despite this danger, Alexander was hoarding most of his troops in the capital, after hearing of the group of Zealots marching their way from the Candul region, their motivation unknown but their threat quite clear.

Red, the rightful King of Tandera, was being taken from her, ordered to the Canyon's edge as a death sentence. It was unfair, after all they had been through, after all he had done to prove how much he cared for Tandera's wellbeing.

Despite the late hour, Red wasn't asleep. His Well moved along a distant street. She tensed, ready to leap off the roof and fly to him, but a quick tightening in her stomach delayed her action.

Alexander had not enjoyed Aly's little display after the coronation. She'd left bruises across his middle from the royal scepter. She hadn't meant to hit that hard.

Despite the fact that her magic had eased his pain, in retaliation for her insubordination, Alexander had ordered what he knew would hurt Aly the most. Quietly and in private, Red had been beaten with a stick to mimic the scepter.

Aly had screamed when Alexander had told her.

Her arms fell flat against her sides. Alexander could kill Red if Aly angered him too much.

"No. I won't allow that," she declared into the night, her mind made up. She had to see Red before his company departed. Alexander wouldn't need to find out she'd left the palace.

As she crafted a flight spell, something odd tripped her concentration.

A voice.

In her head.

She stilled, ready to receive a mental message for the king. The voice was hard to hear, as if the person were whispering. She squinted in confusion.

"He's attempting another escape. Even now he's left the barracks. You cannot tolerate this behavior." It was a woman's voice, almost familiar but too faint to pinpoint.

Aly couldn't figure out why the messenger didn't announce herself or use names. Mental messages between sorcerers had rules and, unless they were direct replies, they required the sender's name.

But this voice was speaking as if from behind a door, as if Aly wasn't the intended recipient, and the speaker uttered the word *he* like whoever was listening would know the person in question without clarification.

The voice added one last line. *"Command his death at dawn."*

Then an icy realization struck Aly: This voice *was* familiar. Kassia, errant Queen of Bulvarna, was speaking into Aly's mind.

Aly shivered despite the warm night. After the coronation, Aly had sensed Alexander's mind was Bound to a second sorcerer, and she'd then discovered Kassia's hold on Alexander.

Aly had watched Kassia's twisted Truthwell blink out of sight as Kassia had fled the cathedral a week ago. Since then, Aly hadn't heard a word about Kassia or sensed her tampering with Alexander's thoughts.

Aly knelt atop the palace roof to keep from falling into the gardens below as she poured every ounce of concentration into her Binding with Alexander's Well. Aly listened intently for more hushed words. Kassia must not know Aly's Binding to Alexander permitted her to hear what the Bulvarnan queen whispered to Alexander as he slept. This connection would prove advantageous, albeit a bit horrifying, if Kassia's commands to the king were shared with Aly as well. And Aly couldn't be certain if her words to Alexander were being shared in Kassia's mind. It was a risk, and Aly would need to remember not to say anything to Alexander's mind that she didn't want Kassia overhearing.

When silence continued for several more seconds, Aly leaped up.

Kassia was somewhere close. Few sorcerers could send mental messages over long distances; instead, they used chains of trusted sorcerers to relay information.

Here was the source of Alexander's wickedness these past months. He may never have fully approved of Gevar's marriage to Isabelle, or the children born from that union, but the man had never seemed capable of such subterfuge as he'd displayed since their trip to Bulvarna.

Kassia was playing some grand game that Aly still did not fully understand. All she knew was that Kassia wanted to separate the Beacon and Beholder, by whatever means possible.

Aly staggered as she recalled her father's legacy: ripping entire towns apart to find sorcerer children who hadn't registered with the palace. Kassia had been hunting the Beholder for decades. Somehow, although she had failed to kill Aly and Red earlier in the year, Kassia's plan had worked—she had wrenched them apart, destroying the power they could only wield together.

Now Kassia had found another pawn, and this time she'd planted a crown on his head.

Kassia's whispered words replayed in Aly's mind. *Command his death at dawn.* Kassia could only mean Red. He was, after all, not in the soldiers' barracks, as ordered.

Aly had a choice: chase Kassia, who would likely be impossible to find considering her ability to shroud herself and her Well, or find Red and warn him to return to the barracks before his absence was noted.

Her heart fluttered madly as she hurled herself from the rooftop, arms out, and dove toward the meandering Well of Tandera's rightful king.

2

RED

Red increased his pace, sensing someone following him, but his sore muscles protested. His ribs still ached from the beatings he'd taken, and his back split with a sharp pain every time his left foot hit the pavement. After a few more hurried steps, a spell hit him from behind, sending him sprawling to the cobblestones faster than his hands could catch his fall. His knees slammed the stones, followed quickly by his wrists and chest.

Groaning, he struggled to breathe under the binding spell.

He'd made it farther this time, but only because Seb's distractions had improved. His friend had swallowed a cup full of saltwater, all in service to Red's plan to escape the barracks. Red wondered what they'd do to Seb when they found out he wasn't really sick. He couldn't take another beating, not with the wounds on his back from the flogging only barely starting to heal.

As soon as the binding spell lifted, someone was jerking Red's hands behind his back and slapping on cuffs. The cuffs pinched against his already sore wrists.

Would they beat him again for trying to escape? Or was there a worse punishment headed his way. Images of Seb's whip-torn back flashed in his mind.

Red looked out across the midnight streets of Mardon toward the direction of his home. *I'm trying, Aly.* He'd promised to come to her, and his efforts had all failed. A week ago, he'd been a king protected by magic, now he was a prisoner caged by it.

Alexander, smartly, had separated most of Red's men from him, sending them out in the first company to deploy to the Canyon. Red's company would depart in the morning, and his chances of seeing Aly diminished with each passing hour.

The soldier yanked him to his feet, as if Red were a common deserter, not a king trying to return to his stolen crown and his stolen love.

Alexander had taken everything from him.

Red's mother had been quickly sent away to the summer palace on the Gulf of Eseda, not to return to Mardon. He would likely not see his mother again once he departed for Caridan, and the thought stung deep in Red's chest. His sisters had been allowed to remain in the palace, a wonder given their former royal status.

Carolyn had fallen in love with Alexander's nephew and, while at only sixteen she was still too young to marry, this romance had secured her place in the household of the usurper. Red understood that love could change a person's allegiances, but it pained him to know Carolyn remained by Alexander's side.

Then there was Elise. Even the thought of her name brought a wave of anger. She had been his closest companion, closer even than Seb. He still held out hope that her betrayal had been coerced rather than chosen. He couldn't stomach the idea that she had sided with Alexander over her own brother. However, if Elise was anything, she was resolute. Whatever her choices, she clung to them with fervor, as if afraid to admit mistakes. She'd chosen to betray Red and Seb, and if watching Seb's public whipping hadn't changed her mind, she'd likely not turn from that path now.

Red grunted as his captor, one of his commanding officers, dragged him back down the street toward the barracks. Red ignored the man's comments, his mind drifting toward Aly when his feet could not. He had not known how difficult it would be to reach her when he had no magic and no weapons and very few allies.

The officer manhandling Red approached the intersection that would take them back to the barracks. Beside them a Protector materialized, likely the one who'd cast the binding spell.

Red sensed the sorcerer's tension, his masked face looking away at something neither Red nor Captain Mitchell could see. He'd watched Aly enough to know when a sorcerer was detecting danger, searching through the world of shadow and light for threats.

"What is it?" Captain Mitchell asked before Red could say anything.

The Protector's elaborate goat's mask turned slowly from left to right, an eerie sight in the dim glow of the gas lamps lining the street. "Woodwolf. Return to the barracks at once."

With that, the Protector rushed down the street and dropped from sight as his magic enveloped him.

Captain Mitchell nodded, though the Protector was already gone. The army had precious few Protectors, and those they did have had been ordered not to leave Mardon. With the approaching Zealot army, Alexander was collecting every possible Master Sorcerer to defend the city. As soon as Red's company departed, they would be on their own, save for the magic of a few Comforters among the enlisted men.

Mitchell jerked Red's hands, eliciting another annoyed grunt from Red, then released the cuffs and stepped back.

Red shook his wrists and shot the captain a puzzled expression.

"You've got one hour. And don't go after *her*." Mitchell rushed through his words, gaze darting left and right. "Go to the New Moon Tavern." The cuffs in his hands clinked slightly as Mitchell fidgeted, his agitation apparent in his pinched brow and pursed lips. He cleared his throat, adding, "That's a direct order." He marched off before Red could say a word.

The New Moon Tavern was Weston Grey's secret lair—or at least it had been earlier this summer. His gang of spies operated out of a back room in the tavern, and Red wasn't sure if it was good news or bad news that he'd been summoned there.

Red fisted his hands at his sides, recalling the cool tip of Grey's pistol against his forehead and the surreptitious way the spy had mentioned the tavern. Red had trusted Grey, more because of Aly than anything else. *Whose side is Grey really on?*

Mitchell had appeared unhappy when he'd uncuffed Red. Red wondered if Grey had threatened someone Mitchell loved. Red wouldn't put anything past the master spy.

He turned back toward the palace, even took a few steps in that direction.

But he knew Grey didn't leave things to chance. He paused and shook his head. The woodwolf that had distracted the Protector...could even that be Grey's doing? If Grey had orchestrated this hour of freedom for Red, there was little likelihood Red could stray from the desired path without another of Grey's hounds coming to flush him out.

Red sighed. Going to Aly wouldn't change their present circumstances. She couldn't simply walk away from her duty to

Alexander—her vows forbade it. Besides, if she really wanted to find Red, her magic could lead her to him.

Red had conjured a dozen reasons why she hadn't visited him yet. It didn't make the truth any less painful: The woman he loved was out of his reach.

Grinding his jaw in frustration, Red changed course, heading down the road that would take him to the New Moon Tavern.

The tavern bustled with activity, despite the late hour.

Raking a hand through his hair, Red's fingers snagged on a stubborn piece of cabbage, deposited there during the disaster that was Alexander's final coronation parade earlier this morning. Red had never imagined his own people would throw rotten produce at him. It turned his blood into fuel, and he ached to show these Mardonians what he'd wanted for Tandera, and yet he had nowhere to direct his burning energy. He'd even failed again at finding Aly.

He had done everything in his power to make this country a better place to live, but everything he had tried had failed, almost as if his failure had been planned. Now he faced life as a soldier and would be leaving for the Canyon, heading farther from Aly and into the jaws of the most dangerous place on the continent. His good intentions hadn't helped anyone.

When he snaked through the wide dining room, a memory bombarded him of sitting across from Aly when they had decided to travel to the Crescent Forest. What if they had made a different decision? Would he have found a way to keep his crown, to provide the food and the wood his people needed?

He shrugged off the thought and wove past the tables toward a back hallway, to the door decorated with a crescent moon.

At a nearby table, a beefy man with a skeptical frown half-stood, then a look of recognition crossed his face as he resettled in his chair. Red lifted his shoulders and exhaled.

He knocked on the door marked with the moon symbol. No

one answered. He wasn't sure how long he should wait. He knocked again. Minutes later, he tried the knob, but of course the door was locked. This was pointless.

As he walked back out into the tavern's main dining hall, a hand on his chest stopped him. It was the surly man Red had noticed earlier. The man smelled of alcohol. Red shoved the man aside, not caring that he was twice Red's size.

"Excuse me," Red said.

The man grabbed Red's arm. "I'm not supposed to let you leave."

"Pardon?" Red turned. The man's large face and shaved head were pink with the effort he was exerting to hold Red.

"I'm to keep you here until he shows up."

"Who?"

"Bishop."

Red had no idea who Bishop was. "Sorry, but I don't know him."

The other man frowned. "You're the former king, ain't you? Well, he said you'd show up, and he said to delay 'til he could get here."

Red sighed. He suddenly felt a bit like fly who'd stumbled into a spider's web. He wondered briefly if this man were one of Grey's employees who had been tasked with keeping Red here until Grey could arrive. Though if Grey had planned this meeting, it was strange that he wasn't here already.

The large man rested a hand on the hilt of a small revolver at his waist.

Red decided to order a drink. He sat down at a table and sipped an ale, wondering what Aly was up to and if she yearned for him half as much as he did for her. He had been the one to kiss her, and though she'd kissed him back, she'd maintained a shield around herself, keeping Red always at a distance. She claimed it was for the sake of her magic, that Red's presence distracted her and thus endangered him and anyone she meant to protect. After what happened at the Crescent Forest, he knew she was right, but her commitment to her duty hadn't tamed his feelings for Aly—it had merely inflamed his admiration for her.

After some time, the large man stood, walked behind Red, and mumbled, "I thought you should'a won."

Red, blindsided by this comment after so many minutes of silence, stared at the back of the man as he walked away, ambling drunkenly into a serving woman. The woman brushed past the large man and headed straight for Red.

"He'll see you now," she singsonged, never stopping in her trajectory around the noisy room.

Bewildered at this covert operation, Red stood and walked back to the room at the end of the hall. Immediately it opened, revealing a smiling Grey.

"I'm disappointed you never came," Grey said, a sly tilt to his mouth. "I had to arrange this all on my own."

Red gave the man a flat, hard expression before surveying the room.

"You're wondering if you can trust me."

"The last time I saw you, you held a pistol to my face."

"And I invited you here."

"But for what reason?" Red crossed his arms with a scowl.

Grey waved a hand toward an armchair. "Sit. Have a drink." He moved into the room and plopped down into one of the chairs beside the hearth. There was a fire burning, despite the heat outside. Gray leaned over and tossed something into it. "Nobody will bother us when the smoke's rising." He leaned back into his chair and crossed his legs. "I'm glad you came."

Red took the other seat, forcing himself not to grimace or groan in pain. "I'm still not sure it even was a choice."

Grey's smirk deepened. "Oh, it was a choice. You finally had your moment to run to her, and instead, you're sitting here, with me."

Red bristled, ready to argue, but Grey cut him off.

"You might have encountered a Canyon beast had your path taken you a different direction, but I am glad that was not the case."

Red snorted. It sounded almost as if Grey were boasting of knowing where the Canyon beasts would be and who they would attack. The man knew much of Mardon's dangerous happenings, but no one could claim control over the beasts of the Deep. "Is that a threat?" asked Red, wanting to know under what pretenses he was here.

Grey only smiled and sipped his glass. "There's something you should know about serving at the Canyon," Grey said, ignoring Red's question. "I'll keep this quick because I don't want anyone to know I've been talking to you here. And people are watching me closer now than ever before." He took another sip of something clear. "But I know how to avoid people well enough."

The heat from the fire was uncomfortable, but Red was grateful for the reminder that most Tanderans lived without the comforts of magic. He'd had a taste of the less comfortable life these past weeks, and it had been good for him. Growing up in a palace had prevented him from truly knowing his people. He had to keep reminding himself that plenty of Mardonians managed without magic. He could embrace such a life too.

Grey set down his glass and slapped both hands on his knees. "All right. How good are you at killing Canyon beasts, Your Majesty?"

Red blinked.

"Foxbloods? Woodwolves? The elusive garland cat?" Grey tapped a finger on his glass. "How do you expect to live more than a week in Caridan if you aren't prepared to fight them?"

Red had fought them. In the Canyon, with Aly. He avoided these memories, but now they clearly flooded into his mind. The woodwolves had nearly killed Veeter Yin that day, but Aly's cloak had lifted him to safety where he could receive treatment. In the end, it had been Red who'd killed Yin—Red's failure to secure his own crown. Red blinked hard and pushed the guilt away. Yin was a warrior, sworn to protect the crown. He'd died still believing Red would wear it once again.

"You assume I have never fought these creatures," Red stated.

Grey's brow barely twitched. "No, I assume you have had little success killing them."

In the Canyon, after Aly had healed him, he'd fought off a foxblood with his belt, and he'd only stopped fighting when he'd slipped on the wet rocks and knocked himself into a daze.

Grey continued, as if reading Red's thoughts. "I have a secret to killing Canyon beasts, and I'm going to tell it to you because I want you to live."

Red's brows lifted. He had little choice but to keep listening.

"Though Canyon beasts are wicked creatures, they're still animals, and they like meat. Here's what you do to stay alive: Kill a lot of squirrels."

"Squirrels?" asked Red, confused.

"I always took one with me when I was on patrol, and if a beast came toward me, I tossed that squirrel—or sometimes it was a frog or a mouse. It takes their attention away from you, just for a second. A second is all you get, but it's enough if you can aim a gun."

"Why don't all the soldiers know this?" Red asked.

"A lot of them do. It's not really that much of a secret. People saw me do it many times. But a lot of people don't like carrying dead squirrels around, and there's the fact that one needs to allow the beasts near for this trick to work."

Red tried to process what it would be like to toss a dead

squirrel toward a charging woodwolf. "If you're that good of a shot, can't you shoot the beasts without bothering with the squirrels?"

Grey stared at him with hard eyes. "It takes more than one bullet to kill a Canyon beast, unless that bullet hits them right between the eyes. If you hit them anywhere else, they'll keep coming." He scratched absently at a scar on his hand. "They're hungry. They're always hungry. If you can get them to eat something besides you, then you have a chance."

"Interesting," Red said, leaning back. "Squirrels, huh?"

"They are plentiful in the forest around the Canyon. I recommend that you become proficient at killing them."

A moment passed as Red stared at the crackling fire. The heat in the room grew oppressive, or perhaps it was his nerves, twisting tighter. In the week since Alexander's coronation, he'd tried to think of all the ways he could escape and return to the palace, embrace Aly, and reclaim his rightful throne. But it wasn't that simple. This wasn't a story for children, and he wasn't going to manifest some hidden strength that could transform the hearts of his entire nation towards desiring him as their king. At least not overnight.

Coming here, Red had harbored a small hope that Grey had some secret plan for stealing back the throne. He had been foolish to dream of such things.

In the morning, he really would be leaving for Caridan. The time for miraculous wings of fate were over.

Grey studied him with a small tilt to his bearded face. "You're wishing you'd taken this hour to go to her. You feel this was a waste of your time."

Red bristled, but his mind was made up. "I'm not going to run away from my people." He leaned forward, his stare matching Grey's. "And the best way I can protect them is as a soldier."

"How noble of you." Grey leaned back. "You know, to gain this crown back, you might need to do a few things you never thought you'd do."

"What is that supposed to mean?"

"You might have to get your hands dirty," replied Grey.

"If I can't win the crown by honest methods, why win it at all?"

Grey smiled, as if Red had said something amusing. "I like you. You want to do everything the right way. Aly would like that."

Red glanced toward the door, as if Aly might somehow be hiding beyond it, the way she used to hover nearby but out of sight. But she couldn't simply run away from the man she was now Bound to protect. She hadn't run from Red when a death curse nearly stifled her own magic. "She must protect Alexander now," Red said, a sinking feeling in his gut.

"Just because she's standing next to him doesn't mean she wants to be," muttered Grey.

"Oh, you think you know what she wants?"

"I think it's quite obvious what she wants."

A moment of silence passed, then another knock at the door broke the tension in the room.

"Ah, here we are," Grey said, standing. "It is time for me to leave, but you have another visitor."

Red stood, turning toward the door. "Another visitor?"

Grey offered a small nod, back to his pristine manners and inscrutable expression. "I called him to come only after I knew you were here. I wasn't sure if he could break away from the cathedral."

Grey opened the door to reveal Arthur Ondorian donned not in his priestly robes but a gentleman's suit complete with a tall hat.

"Glad you could come," Grey said, shaking hands with the

high priest. "I'll leave you two to it, then." He walked back and tossed something in the fire that made a puff of white smoke. "That should give you a few minutes. When you leave, exit through separate doors." Before leaving, Grey turned back to them, "And do not worry, the room is protected from eaves-droppers."

Red accepted an eager handshake from Ondorian. His aching back protested the vigorous shake, but Red kept his face pleasant.

"To what do I owe this honor?" asked Red, carefully taking a seat once more.

The priest, still sprightly for his age, moved quickly to the chair opposite Red's. "I have much to tell you about my travels," he began, voice urgent and low despite Grey's assurances that spies couldn't be listening at the keyhole. "After you and Aly descended into the Canyon and *lived*, I took it upon myself to conduct my own research. Under the guise of study, I ventured north to the libraries of Excheter and Luxler, then on to the Black River by way of Bulvarna."

"You *what?*" Red balked. The man he'd listened to every week in the cathedral had appeared so soft, so scholarly. He couldn't imagine this man in the depths of the Deep.

Ondorian's bald forehead crinkled as his brows lifted slowly. "I went to the river."

"How did you descend?" Memories of leaping off the cliff's edge sent a shudder down Red's spine.

The priest shrugged. "There are paths on the Bulvarnan side, traveled by the villagers in the Forgotten Cities." He nodded at Red's shocked expression. "I did not want to pass through Cari-dan, as I wished no one other than my traveling companions to know my mission, especially considering the way your descent affected your reputation." He lifted two hands. "No offense, Your Majesty."

Still shaking his head in disbelief, Red asked, "How did you get *out?*"

Chuckling softly, Ondorian said, "My Protector. Now, sire, I must continue or we will run out of time."

"Of course, go on." Red lifted a hand.

Ondorian settled back in his chair. "I travelled to the Canyon seeking answers. I knew that you had touched the water and yet you lived. That piqued my interest, and I started digging to learn everything I could about the Black River." He glanced at the fire, still smoking white. "I found some interesting facts buried deep in our histories. There are poems and personal accounts that speak of the water as having *affections*. Many of the accounts of the river have been destroyed, so it is only the ones that mention it in a more allegorical or metaphorical way, especially a negative way, that still exist. And then there are the few remaining banned texts, like Kanto's poems that you read. However, books can only teach us so much." He smiled. "I tested the theory myself and touched the water."

Red lurched forward, immediately regretting the quick movement. "You touched it?"

"Of course I did," the priest replied. "I'm Theod's man, through and through, and I know that no water here or there on the Maker's good earth can have the power of life and death."

"But everyone believes it does. Or rather, that it has the power of death, at least."

Ondorian nodded but narrowed his eyes. "That they do. But do *you?*"

Red held the priest's stare a moment, then sat back. "No, I suppose I don't."

A broad, knowing smile broke across Ondorian's face. "Because your experience taught you a new truth, one that history has forgotten. I knew the water itself couldn't be wicked."

"It's the source of death curses. It *reached* for me, sir."

"Ah," Ondorian whispered, raising a hand as if he were preaching. "The water itself, I said. But there is something *in* the water that is the source of its wickedness."

Red's eyes widened. He'd always wondered how water could lie. Once, as a child, he'd questioned his tutor about it, and he'd been thoroughly reprimanded for such thoughts. Now, the high priest himself was stating the very thing Red had been chastised for thinking. He stared at the priest's lifted hand. The skin was withered in a strange way on two fingers.

"This was the only part of me that touched the water. I didn't die, nor was I cursed, but unlike you, I didn't come away unscathed. Something in the water did not like me." At Red's worried expression, he added, "It does not hurt."

Red ran a hand through his curls. The high priest of Tandera had gone into the most dangerous place on earth, the place that had ruined Red's reputation and triggered events that lost him his crown. But it was also the place that had given him a chance at life again by eliminating the curse that would have killed him.

Ondorian shifted forward, as if to stand. "I want to know more about that river, and I need you to learn from it for me. It is paramount that we learn the truth of its evils, and it would raise some eyebrows if I were to continue to visit that place. Not to mention that the trip was rather taxing on my old bones. I must say, it is rather convenient, from my point of view, that you are heading back to Caridan." His bushy brows waggled, drawing a surprised chuckle from Red. "I know you did not desire this, Your Majesty, but perhaps there is more to recent events than you or I know. Theod is not asleep, nor is he blind. I sense that we have greater changes ahead of us than we have behind us." His gaze narrowed, mirroring Red's. "Strange things are at work in Mardon. I sense a deluding influence has taken the minds of some of the people, and I can't understand it." The priest shook his head. "Do this for me, and let us uncover the lost truths about the river. I fear we may be missing something that will lead to our downfall if we do not recover it."

Red blinked at the weakening fire, turning Ondorian's words over in his mind. *Perhaps there is more to recent events than you or I know.* He was telling Red that losing the crown was all part of a divine plan. Could heading back to the Canyon be part of that plan too?

When he'd lost his crown, he'd lost his home, his family, and his love, all at once. He'd never pictured a future as bleak as the one he now faced. Alexander could strip him of his title, but he couldn't bleed Tandera out of him. As long as he could, Red would serve Tandera. It was all he had left.

At Ondorian's words, hope kindled within Red, alive with new purpose.

Not only would Red defend his country from the threat of the Canyon, but he would discover this lost truth about the river.

He would once again descend into the Deep.

3

ALY

The moon had risen over the city, its dull glow dimmed by hasty clouds that whispered of rain. The city's darkened windows looked like deep, empty holes.

As Aly's mind honed in on Red's Truthwell, she blinked in surprise. Grey was with him.

She pulled from Alexander's Truthwell and shaped the air around her body, using her cloak as a sail as she tore through the night. Heart hammering, Aly soared over rooftops and chimneys, wind whipping under her clothing like a thousand tiny wingbeats.

Her stomach knotted and flipped, but she laughed out loud with the freedom of flight. Aly enjoyed the sensation of being on the cusp of disaster, held back by mere words. Flying made her feel more alive than anything else—until she'd felt Red's hand on her cheek, his lips against hers.

She needed to feel alive tonight, not chained to her role as Royal Sorcerer to a usurper. She needed to see Red alive before his march to Caridan. She needed to see his face.

She had ached to go to him every day since the coronation.

But seeing him would only remind her how very far away he truly was, that his Truthwell was no longer her source of power, his face no longer one she would see in the palace halls.

He said he'd fight to come back to me.

She stopped these thoughts before they spiraled out of control once again. He was watched and guarded; he could no more reach her than a fish could reach the stars.

But here he was, in conversation with Lord Weston Grey, of all people.

She sat on the rooftop until Red exited the tavern. She'd wanted to see Red, not Grey, and not even Ondorian, though his arrival had been most surprising. Grey was plotting something.

Aly drifted down toward Red's bright Truthwell as he walked alone down a deserted street. She dropped to the pavement behind him, still shrouded, and watched him walking in his soldier's uniform. Her heartbeat tripled.

The dethroned king shuffled close to the buildings, as if hiding in the shadows of the dark night, away from the glow of the street lamps. Her entire body leaned toward him, the magic inside of her dancing toward his Well and her heart yearning for the safety of his embrace. His steps were shorter than usual, as if careful. *He's in pain.* She clutched her hand to her chest, but it could do nothing to push down the ache inside of her.

"Red," she whispered.

He spun around, eyes wildly searching back and forth across the dark street. When he saw her, his face brightened.

The doubts that had welled up when he hadn't come to her now melted off her like a spring snow as he pulled her into his chest, reminding her of the way that he always brought her close whenever she felt most alone. His nearness had become a balm, the antidote to her life of solitude. She squeezed him a little tighter, afraid this could be their last embrace.

He groaned.

"Oh, I'm sorry!" She pulled away but kept her hands on his arms. Alexander had been pleased when he'd told her of Red's beatings. She scowled at the memory and flashed a quick healing spell at Red.

The tension fled from Red's face and his eyes closed momentarily in relief. "Thank you."

When he opened his eyes, his gaze held an intensity that rivaled the inferno at the Crescent Forest. She wanted to kiss him, but she had too much to say.

"Red, I discovered—"

His hand found the side of her face, his fingers slipping under her hair.

The words evaporated off her tongue.

His kiss was like lightning. She did not want to cut it short.

"What are you doing here?" he finally asked, a little breathless.

"I had to see you."

"We leave in the morning," he said, stroking the skin beside her ear with his thumb. His tone said what they couldn't admit: He was marching toward an early grave, and she wasn't going to be there to protect him.

"I will set some spells to protect you," she murmured.

He pulled her hands from where she gripped his arms, twisting his palms to lock with hers. "That isn't your job anymore."

Her lungs deflated, and he caught her head against his chest as she tipped forward. "I'm so sorry, Red."

Stroking her back, he said over her head, "I just spoke to Grey and Arthur Ondorian."

Aly looked up at him.

"Ondorian wants me to go into the Canyon."

"Are you serious?"

Red nodded. "That's where he's been. He descended into the

Canyon, and he thinks there is something about the river that we've misunderstood. He wants me to continue his research."

Aly pressed a hand to her mouth, trying to try not to laugh and cry out in protest. It was too absurd to think of the high priest going down into the Canyon, and even more absurd that he'd asked Red to return to the Black River, but Red's face was frighteningly serious.

"It was convenient that he missed the coronation," Aly mused.

"I think that was planned," Red replied with a smirk.

She reached up and ran a hand across Red's forehead, dragging some of his sweaty hair out of his face. She missed the coronet that used to rest there. "Where's the crown I made you?"

"Officers took it."

"I'll make you another one."

Red chuckled, a joyless sound. "It's a crown of dust—no one bows to that."

The ache growing inside Aly's chest burst like a soap bubble, and she bit her lip to keep from moaning at their pathetic reality. Instead, she pushed up on her tiptoes and kissed him. "I do. And one day, they will too."

His eyes remained closed as she lowered down off of her tiptoes. She wanted to look at him forever when he wore that expression on his face.

"Promise me that you won't do anything stupid," she demanded.

His smile faded. "What does that mean?"

"I mean stay alive until we can figure this out."

"Ondorian thinks the river holds some secret, something big. It's almost like I was meant to go there, to find this lost truth, Aly." His eyes sparked with a flash of mad hope. "I want to defend my country from the Canyon, and what better way than to uncover the secret to the Canyon's evil?"

She bit her lip, suppressing a worried smile. Here was the rightful king, a man so committed to his people's wellbeing that he didn't retreat from serving them, even when he'd lost so much. The hope that drove him was so much a part of him that she couldn't help but smile to see it once again lighting his face.

But this time he wouldn't have her magic to protect him. She shivered at the thought.

He raked his fingers through his red hair. "You always told me to fight the lies with truth. Perhaps I will discover something that will help us defeat the lies of that wicked place."

Us. She inhaled sharply. "Red, how can we..." Her words trailed off. Though it looked like nothing more than a death sentence, Red wasn't accepting defeat by going willingly to Caridan. He was embracing this death sentence and somehow still managing to find within it a mad hope. But Beacon and Beholder had been torn apart, and their days of battling the darkness together were over. Aly could see no positive outcomes in Red descending into the Deep.

It wouldn't be mad hope if it made sense, she told herself, smiling up at him. "How do you do it?"

"Do what?"

"Stay so optimistic?"

His smile melted into a stare that flamed heat into Aly's cheeks. "Because I can't accept a world where you are not by my side. I said I would conquer the world to have you." He tipped his forehead against hers. "If I have to start by conquering the very seat of evil, I will do it. If I need to tear the entire world apart and then piece it back together, just to be with you, then I will find a way."

Aly couldn't speak for several moments. Instead, she kissed him again, holding nothing back.

After a moment, she stepped away, knowing it would not be long before one of their absences was noticed. She hadn't yet told him what she discovered on the rooftop. "When Kassia speaks her lies into Alexander's mind, I can hear her."

Red blinked at her for several seconds, absorbing this new information. "Can you use it to find her?"

Aly looked at her hands. "No."

"But this is an advantage. You will know what she's planning."

She met his gaze. "She doesn't exactly spell it all out to him. I've only heard her voice once since the coronation. Tonight. She wants Alexander to order your death in the morning, for leaving the barracks."

"Does she now?" Red's jaw worked. He spun away, a hand absently scratching his chin.

"You should return before they notice."

"Sounds like they'll know anyway." He faced her with lifted brows. "Kassia must be in Mardon, if she's watching me that closely."

Aly stared into Red's deep brown eyes, aching to know if she would see them again after tonight. "I will find her. Somehow. She'll let something slip."

Red nodded. "I know you will."

Aly bit her lip, wondering if she should voice what was on her mind. But given this might be her last chance to talk to Red, she didn't want to hold back. "What is it all about, do you think? Why go to such lengths to separate us?" Aly asked.

Red stared over her shoulder a moment, deep in thought. "She's planning something. Has been for years, likely. She wanted to wait to do it until she was certain Beacon and Beholder couldn't thwart her."

Aly had come to a similar conclusion, though she couldn't imagine what Kassia might attempt. "Well, she's pulled us apart now, so she's won."

"No," Red said, dipping his head so his eyes were level with hers. "No, she hasn't. You can still change the world. You've already changed mine."

Aly let out a pitiful chuckle, her insides thrilling at his last statement. "It was supposed to be *us*, not just me. And why send an army of Zealots to Mardon? Why continue to manipulate Alexander?"

Red pulled her into another hug and said over her head, "I have no idea. But you're the one person who can find out."

After another quick kiss, he backed away, the corner of his mouth curling up. "You're the scepter, Aly. You can still defeat Kassia at her game. You have the power to burn the world if you so please."

She rolled her eyes. "And then I'd be no better than my father. Than Kassia. I *do* need you, Red."

His mouth softened but his gaze turned electric. "Then I will stay alive until I can be exactly what you need."

4

ELISE

The palace hallways smelled of the wrong kind of pipe smoke, and every mirror reflected a face Elise didn't want to see, a face of treason. Elise could barely stomach the walk through the mirrored halls to the breakfast room, knowing she'd be dining alongside her brother's usurper. She kept her gaze forward, ignoring the reflection that walked with her down the long, carpeted hall.

For Tandera, she repeated in her mind, pouring herself into the premise that spying would eventually serve her country, her brother, her heart.

Grey's warnings circulated in her head like goldfish in a pond, but the memory of Seb's broken, bleeding body was the first thing she saw every morning and the last thought she shoved away at night. Would she even learn information critical enough to make amends for *that*? To make up for the way she'd betrayed her own brother?

If Grey can spy, so can I.

This prospect, however thin, was her only path forward, so she clung to it.

Already in the breakfast room sat Alexander, his wife, his nephew, and Carolyn. Elise swallowed, pasted a pleasant expression on her face, and sat across from her sister.

Carolyn's smile was brighter than the chandelier. Sitting beside Edward Alexander had this effect on her younger sister. At only sixteen, Carolyn was convinced she'd found her forever love. Elise had thought the same thing, with Lordan.

Life wasn't always so kind.

Elise reached for her just-filled cup of tea when she heard a faint rustle of fabric, and a moment later the queen consort gasped and dropped her tea all over her lap.

Alexander half stood in surprise and yelled at the attendants to clean up the mess.

"Dear me," whimpered Queen Alexander. Her title had recently altered as she assumed the role of sovereign's wife. "Something brushed my arm and rather startled me," she said, trying to level her tone.

Aly popped into view rounding the corner of the table behind the queen, wearing her phoenix mask that covered her entire face. No part of Aly's expression was visible, but her eyes burned into Elise as she moved. As she had each time Aly scrutinized her this past week, Elise kept her face unmoved but averted her eyes.

Carolyn tracked Aly's movements with a surprised expression. Elise quietly brushed butter on a warm biscuit and imagined the biscuit was the queen consort's face. She could feel Aly's gaze but still couldn't return it, so she smiled up at her sister instead as the queen bustled from the room to change her stained dress

Aly stopped right behind the king's chair.

Alexander looked uncomfortable as he tried to turn to look back at her. "Come 'round here where I can see you," he barked.

When Aly didn't move, he spun the other way and said, "By the Deep, child, you are obstinate."

Aly's unseen smirk was palpable as she replied, "I need only protect your life, sire. I can do that better from here."

Alexander huffed. "There are no threats in the breakfast room. Sit down."

The king missed Aly's grunt of disagreement and the hard stare she was drilling into Elise over the king's head. Elise wished Aly could know why she'd chosen to befriend the Alexanders, but spies never revealed their true allegiances. Elise would find Grey soon, hoping to learn if he had any more assignments for her. There *had* to be something for her, some task that could rectify these feelings of rot growing inside her.

Aly finally stepped around the table and sat down in the queen consort's vacant seat.

"That is my wife's seat," Alexander snapped.

Aly broke about ten rules of etiquette and reached across the table for an unused coffee cup. She accepted the napkin handed her by a server, shook it out, and placed it in her lap.

Alexander scoffed, as if about to protest, but Aly raised her hand, fingers poised to direct magic, and the entire room fell silent in fear. Aly's hand continued to move and pushed her mask up, settling it behind her head.

A smile crept across Aly's lips.

A server stepped forward with a pot.

Alexander glared at Aly. "I have asked you to keep the mask on. Masters are supposed to be hidden from sight. That is the way of things."

Aly raised her eyebrows at Alexander. "Oh, and who made that rule?" Aly grinned as a hot plate of breakfast was set in front of her.

His tone darkening, Alexander said, "I was informed that Frederick once again attempted desertion last night."

Everyone in the room tensed. Aly paused, her hand over her fork.

"I must set an example with him, a warning to all deserters. I believe his death will be the example I need."

A small puff of air escaped Aly's open mouth. A weight sank in Elise's chest, threatening to crush her to the floor.

Aly lifted her gaze slowly to Alexander's. Her eyes blazed with anger. "You promised."

The king responded by taking a sip of tea.

A half-second later, the teacup shot out of the king's hand and shattered on the floor. Elise jumped in surprise. Carolyn covered her mouth.

Alexander leaned toward Aly, his mustache dripping. "You forget who holds his life now. Do not deign to threaten me. Your power is entirely mine."

For a moment, Aly studied him with a tilted head. Her silence grew so uncomfortable that Elise had to look away.

Finally, Aly said, "My power belongs to no one. It is mine to use as I will. If you desire my protection, you will let Frederick live."

The two stared at one another for a moment as Carolyn and Elise pretended to keep eating.

"Any news of the Zealots?" Edward asked, breaking the strained silence.

Everyone in the room looked at Alexander for his answer.

After coronation, scout reports had informed the city that a large group of armed Zealots had left the Candul region, intent on attacking Mardon. Their reasons remained a complete mystery, though the scouts had ascertained that the Zealots had been marshalled by none other than Queen Kassia of Bulvarna. Short of outright revenge for killing her Royal Sorcerer, neither Elise nor the members of court could discern why Kassia would send untrained sorcerers to attack Tandera's capital. It was an act of war, but Kassia had not shown herself since fleeing Isardra after the disastrous peace summit. There were too many unknowns for Tandera or the other sovereign nations to create a definitive plan regarding the Zealots. So far, Alexander's strategy involved trying to convince anyone with a Protector to remain in the city.

The king pulled at his mustache, as he often did when he wished to delay his answer. Elise had surmised that these delays had two main purposes: one, he wished to increase the tension in his audience, or two, because he did not know what to say. She assumed this time it was the latter, considering the Zealots heading toward Mardon were already starting to cause panic in the streets, despite the new king's attempts to show the power and prosperity of the *new* Tandera.

Alexander's eyes flickered in tiny, rapid motions for no more than two breaths. Elise narrowed her eyes at him. She'd seen her father react in similar ways when receiving mental messages from his sorcerer—from Aly, though Elise hadn't known Aly then. She'd also observed members of court develop a similar far-off look in their eyes for brief moments, perhaps when their own Protectors were communicating silently. Aly, however, was busy slathering a biscuit with jam and appeared entirely too engrossed in the act to be sending a mental message to the king. Elise didn't know how magical messages worked, but for all other spells, Aly had to concentrate, and she almost always used her hands.

Could someone else be speaking to Alexander's mind? Was that even allowed? Elise studied the king, but his eyes were already still. He looked at her and frowned.

"The Zealots make slow progress, marching on foot. They are leaderless, and few can ascertain their aim. They will disband before they reach the city. We need not worry." Alexander coughed quietly, as if uncomfortable with his answer or the fact that no one in the room likely believed him. Perhaps there was yet more bad news he was hiding.

Edward nodded slowly, but Carolyn jumped into the conversation.

"Where exactly are they now—sire?" She *almost* always forgot to add these honorifics, but managed to cram them in and finish them off with her winning smile.

"They will arrive at the Rist within the week."

Carolyn inhaled, a worried look on her face. "Will they sail to Mardon in ships?"

"They have no ships," snapped Alexander. "They march with spears and rudimentary bows." He took a delicate bite of biscuit.

"And wild magic," Carolyn grumbled, settling down lower in her chair. She tossed a quick grimace at Elise, who returned it by mouthing, *Everything will be okay.*

Despite all the people Elise had betrayed, Carolyn still loved her. Elise wanted so badly for her little sister to be happy, to be forever free from painful mistakes and the ache of heartbreak. Elise glanced at Edward. He was young and handsome in a bookish way, and he believed in Carolyn. He'd even dragged Carolyn's trebuchet out of storage and set it up in the back gardens, near the river, where he and Carolyn were known to launch everything from watermelons to old crates to watch them explode into pieces. He may be the usurper's nephew, but he loved Carolyn.

Elise only hoped he was a better man than Lordan.

"She's right," Aly said, looking up from her breakfast. "Their magic is dangerous. You cannot discount this army. I've seen what Zealots are capable of."

Whispers of what happened at the Crescent Forest had circulated through Mardon. Elise had heard at least five versions of it, every version mentioning fire. Elise, through careful questioning and observation, had discerned that her brother had been attacked and that all the wood they'd planned to bring to Mardon had burned. She understood that the Zealots hated outsiders, but burning the lumber didn't make sense. Neither did a group of Zealots attacking Mardon.

Red had kept his promise to the people, even if he'd returned without the needed wood.

With a low voice, Aly added, "They do not march without purpose. You know who sent them. You are *well* acquainted with her."

Elise sat up straighter. She'd heard more in the past week about the Candul region, that bleak desert on Tandera's eastern shore, than she had in her entire life.

Alexander glared daggers at Aly, who seemed unconcerned. When Aly caught Elise's stare, the sorcerer frowned.

Aly thinks I'm a traitor. Elise couldn't blame the sorcerer. She hated the way that felt, considering Aly had been so friendly on the train from Bulvarna. *If only we could return to that train ride. I would tell myself never to talk to Lordan again.* Elise sighed. She was entrenched in this role now, and there was little sense relinquishing it before she'd truly ascertained anything of value. She'd already accomplished Grey's first request; she had gained the king's trust. Now, it was up to Grey to give her the chance she'd hoped for: the chance to spy on Lordan.

Elise looked apologetically at Aly, but the sorcerer's attention was again on the king. By the way her face was set and the tiny flickering of her closed mouth, Elise assumed Aly was speaking silently to Alexander.

Sure enough, Alexander's eyes darted rapidly. *So he had been receiving a mental message earlier, but not from Aly.* Something for Elise to remember.

Alexander leaped up, startling Elise. "How dare you!" he bellowed at Aly.

Aly stood, her hands on the table. "You know I am not lying."

The entire room fell silent as the two stared at one another, arguing over whatever Aly had told him privately.

Alexander suddenly realized people were watching him. He straightened his ascot and cleared his throat. "I believe we can discuss this another time."

Aly lifted a brow. "Sir, you can't possibly avoid—"

"You are dismissed!" The air in the room shook.

With a look that could smelt steel, Aly stepped away from the table, then offered a mocking bow before vanishing from sight.

After a tense moment of silent eating and sipping, Carolyn nudged Edward.

Edward coughed. "Sire, if I may, have you considered my proposal?"

"What proposal? Ah, yes." His eye snapped to Elise. "As you all know, we are short one palace ambassador, after the recent removal of those loyal to Isabelle Windon. My nephew suggested you become the new ambassador in her place."

Elise's cheeks flared with blush at the sudden weight of every gaze. Carolyn beamed beside Edward. *Edward suggested it, did he?* Edward loved Carolyn, but he hadn't spoken more than a dozen words to Elise that weren't direct replies or common courtesies. There was something strange to this request, and it smelled of Lord Weston Grey.

Elise bobbed her head, hiding a slim smile. "I am humbled, sire." *This could be my ticket to Vona.* Maybe all her pain would not be for nothing. She could finally strike Lordan back—though, admittedly, revenge sounded rather childish now that an army might attack her city and her people. But Seb's body, beaten and bleeding, and her brother's look of utter betrayal stood behind her now. She'd come too far; she'd dived too deep.

She would help Tandera by collecting secrets, and at the right time, they would expunge the awful guilt gnawing at her for her sins.

"I told him it was a preposterous idea. You are too young." Alexander sipped his coffee, oblivious to Elise's deepening frown. "But I do have several messages that need to be sent to a few men of great rank, and I feel sending a letter in person will produce my desired response."

Elise's mind filled with memories of Vona's shores.

"What say you to delivering one of these messages?" He peered at Elise with a flash of venomous triumph in his eyes. It chilled Elise to the bones.

"I will happily go, Your Majesty." Elise inclined her head.

"Excellent." Alexander smiled at Edward. "She will deliver a message to Lord Chesterton in Luxler."

"Luxler?" asked Elise, embarrassed at her sudden outburst. A spy should never have outbursts.

Alexander's mustache twitched as his lips curled into a nasty grin. "Yes. It is so close to the Canyon that I am afraid none of my other trusted messengers wish to travel there, considering the countryside's current state. And you must not fail to procure an agreeable response. Mardon's very survival may depend on it."

A messenger rushed into the breakfast room, offered a quick bow, and waited for the king's permission to speak.

"Well?" Alexander asked.

"There's been an attack, sire. Largest pack of woodwolves ever reported in the city."

5

ALY

As the last man filed in to the king's council chamber, Alexander pounded the royal scepter on the stone floor and stalked to the head of the long table. He had taken to carrying the phoenix-topped staff around with him; a visual reminder that he held Aly's magic in the palm of his hand. As the king's closest advisors took their seats, all other attendants and sorcerers were dismissed, shuffling from the room in perfect silence.

Aly sulked in the corner, her wide-shouldered cloak carelessly open, her mask hanging around her neck. Under her shroud, she didn't need these disguises, and Alexander had bid her remain invisible for this meeting.

She had made him angry at breakfast when she'd told him, for the third time, that Kassia was controlling his mind. She'd told him the day of his coronation, and he'd blamed her words on the ravings of a broken-hearted girl. Trying a gentler tone the next day, she had told him again when he'd forbidden her from leaving the palace unless accompanying him. He'd warned her that her claims were treasonous, and that she should stop them if she cared for Red's wellbeing.

Red's company should already be on the road, and Aly hoped Alexander wouldn't send someone after Red to spite Aly for her offence. The king's denial verged on madness. It would take more than truth to convince that man his mind was not his own.

Some of the faces in the council room were new to Aly. Wyndall she knew. Riode Liere had been replaced by another Referen consul, his position denoted by his pale blue sash and trident pin.

Among the familiar faces at the king's council table was Lord Weston Grey's. Aly stared hard at his bearded face, wishing her eyes alone could bore holes into his complacent brow. The man was a two-sided mask. Neither side was his authentic self. She wanted to hate him for how he played both sides, but she realized that to some it looked as if she now supported Alexander rather than Red. Appearances could indeed be deceiving.

"May the Maker guide us," Alexander called out from the king's chair, voice gruff and impatient.

"And his means provide us," Ondorian uttered, his booming voice smaller than usual.

Aly smiled from her invisible position, pleased with the familiar sight of the high priest and the pleasant memories of her early days in Mardon. Arthur Ondorian had returned rather suddenly the day after coronation, carrying a pile of texts he'd collected from the libraries of Luxler and Excheter, claiming he'd attempted to return in time for the ceremony but had been delayed unexpectedly. He hadn't offered any clarity when Alexander had asked for it, to which Aly had been smugly grateful. She would speak to Ondorian later and hear of the Priest Reckoner's trip into the Deep.

"The attack," Alexander barked, drawing every eye back to him. "Tell me what happened. Why were those beasts not contained before they reached the square?" Beside his mouth, his mustache waved like two flapping arms. "We have Protectors watching the perimeter of the city, for Theod's sake!"

Wyndall coughed and leaned forward. "The attack, Your Majesty?"

"Woodwolves, man!" Alexander slammed the table with his free fist. The scepter wobbled in his other hand. "In the middle of Mardon!"

Wyndall shrank back. "I was unaware, sire."

Living in his comfortable world while the poor die in the streets, Aly mused.

Ondorian held up a hand, his gaze dark as he silently reprimanded the king for his curse. "Perhaps there is an explanation, sire." He waited until the other men turned expectant gazes upon him. "I sense that in the time I was away, a deluding influence has settled upon this place."

Aly gasped, her sound masked by her shroud, but she wasn't the only one to hear what Ondorian was truly saying. Did he know of Kassia's control over the king?

Alexander twisted the scepter, its heavy shaft scraping out a dull shriek. "What, pray, do you mean, priest?" the king questioned through clenched teeth.

"The attack in the square, while quite public, was hardly attended by even the closest Protectors or soldiers. The Protector I sent from the cathedral, fortunately, arrived in time to save what would have been several more victims. For a puzzling reason, few people appeared concerned with the presence of the woodwolves, as if they couldn't see them at all." Ondorian turned piercing eyes on the king. "I believe a blindness has come upon our people that is perhaps preventing them from seeing and hearing what is right before them."

Aly trembled, nervous that Ondorian would say something to cause Alexander to banish him as well.

Wyndall cut in. "He is right. I did not hear any mention of it at all." He lifted a hand as if the priest's words exonerated Wyndall from a great crime.

"We do not have the time to discuss such nonsense," Alexander replied. "I called this meeting so we could determine how to prevent more attacks and how in Theod's name we will deal with that army of Zealots!" He reined in his stampeding words and added, "As king, I must protect my people."

Confined to invisibility, Aly pursed her lips and rolled her eyes. Though making faces while under her shroud was normal for her, it no longer felt right. In recent months, she'd learned to hold her brow smooth, to press back her frowns. Now that she had no reason to display her newfound control, she chafed against the freedom like a trained show horse turned loose in the forest.

The new Referen consul spoke up, his accent as rhythmic as the sea that bordered his country. "Your Majesty, if that Zealot army was indeed launched by Queen Kassia, this means war. She may not be dispatching her own troops, but she is responsible for mobilizing those Zealots. They will not turn back. If I may, you must arm your people with Protectors. Line the city streets with them."

"Noted, Nars," coughed Alexander.

Nars had been chosen as consul to the Tanderan king, which meant he likely knew as much about Tandera as any foreign dignitary was allowed to know. He would know, then, that Tandera lacked a plethora of unemployed Protectors, save the Zealots who refused to subject their magic to the whims of employers. Master sorcerers were rare, and this man would know that. Aly crossed her arms, ready to hear the king's rebuttal.

Wyndall shifted in his chair, cupping his mouth with a folded finger. Grey sat stone still, eyes occasionally grazing the corners of the room.

Aly bit her lip. Nothing was lining up. There were beasts in the streets that some people couldn't even see—or refused to acknowledge. There was an army of *Tanderan* sorcerers marching on their capital—though historically the Candul region operated apart from the rest of Tandera. If Kassia had entered the Candul region and mobilized an entire force of people who had once been happy to remain aloof from the rest of society, something was amiss. She could have sent her own soldiers. Why the Zealot sorcerers?

There's something strange going on, Aly mused. She needed to speak to Ondorian.

Wyndall broke the strained silence. "We would be most wise to use sorcerers, I agree."

Where do you plan to procure these sorcerers? Aly asked into Alexander's mind. He might not accept her advice out loud, but she wouldn't remain silent. He couldn't force her not to share her thoughts with him.

The king startled so violently that he dropped the scepter. It clanged to the stone floor, a sound so ugly and sharp that every man in the room cowered or shook. Aly chuckled.

Grey hopped up and collected the scepter, handing it reverently back to Alexander. "Sire," he said quickly, his voice low. "I would like to return to Caridan. Our troops need support, and I am more than willing to go."

Alexander's mustache twitched as he stared down at Grey for a several heartbeats. "No. We require your Protector here."

As Grey's body rose from his kneeling position, he snapped his eyes behind the king to the corner where Aly stood. He couldn't possibly see or hear her, but apparently nothing passed his notice. His body angled away from everyone else, he offered the smallest possible wink and slid back into his heavy chair.

Alexander, attempting to recover his dignity, cleared his throat and announced, "We will do it. We will defend the city with Protectors."

Wyndall nodded. Grey's expression darkened.

"Sire, with whose Protectors?" asked Ondorian, ever the pragmatist.

Aly grinned at the honest priest.

"With—with our own Protectors! We have them."

"Our friends will not give up their Protectors," Grey noted, a slight edge to his voice. "They've all raised their sorcerers' wages and insured their contracts. Those Protectors will not be leaving their posts."

Aly covered a smirk, though no one could see her. Grey had just tossed Alexander's response back in his face—if Grey wanted to take his sorcerer to Caridan, he would do it. Sorcerers worked for their employers, not the king. Aly's chest lightened to think that perhaps Grey would take his Protector to the Canyon's edge. She swallowed, a little taken aback by how quickly she wished Grey to walk into danger, if it meant added protection for Red.

She wished she could convince Grey to go, but the man would do what he felt best for Tandera. If that meant staying in Mardon, he would remain.

Grey continued, unphased by the glower on Alexander's face. "Many nobles with holdings to the east have already sent their Protectors home to defend their estates. Others have left the city with their Protectors, fleeing the possibility of an attack."

Nars scoffed. "Then demand their return, or risk your people's safety."

Alexander whirled toward Aly's hidden position, turning toward the wrong corner. He spoke to the wall when he said, "Are there more of you lurking in small towns like Kitrel? We must find more unemployed sorcerers!"

Aly remained shrouded, not gratifying him with her visible presence. Into his mind, she said, *The only place I know of that has more sorcerers is the Crescent Forest.*

Alexander turned back to his men. "My sorcerer will protect the entire city."

Aly barked out a laugh, dropping her shroud and storming forward. "I will do no such thing, *sire*. My duty is to protect you, and you alone. I will fulfill my duty. I will not allow harm to come to those near me, if I can see a way to prevent it. But to protect the entire city at all times from all threats is absurd, and you know it. To do so would, after all, leave you vulnerable." As an afterthought, she shoved her mask down over her face.

Alexander scrambled to rise, his tall frame assuming a position of authority as he looked down at Aly. "There must be something you can do! You are supposed to be the strongest sorcerer in the country!"

Aly held his stare, seeing past his derision to the desperation lurking beneath. This man might be under the influence of Kassia's lies, but he still desired to protect Mardon from the threat of an attack. At least the wicked queen hadn't blackened his mind enough to ignore the impending attack altogether. He was trying to show strength and create a plan, but his pinched eyes and the near-constant flickering of his mustache belied his unease. He had taken the throne, yet it appeared he hadn't the faintest idea how to defend his people.

Shaking her head slightly, Aly said, "There is, perhaps, something I can do." Her mind flashed to Naia, who'd been shoved in a sorcerer's prison cell—an underground room guarded by Masters—for her conspiratorial work with Red at the coronation. "I've trained one Zealot to control her magic. I could try to train more, to bolster our number of sorcerers." She omitted including a regal honorific in her response, but no one seemed to notice, as they were fixed on her with bewildered expressions.

"Pah, we have no time for that!" spat Alexander.

"Naia learned quickly. Perhaps others would as well."

Grey knocked on the table, nodding as if he toyed with an idea. "We all saw that woman's magic. It was impressive—more so given she learned that kind of control in a matter of weeks. If Aly can take a Zealot, with no training and no knowledge of the *Verad*, and have her flying through cathedral windows in less than a month, than I think we should consider this as an option, Your Majesty."

Alexander looked back at Aly, his bushy mustache twitching. "I will not allow my personal Protector to *leave*," he snapped. Though Aly thought she could read a small victory in his expression, as if being Bound to her magic was all he really desired, and her *presence* he could do without.

Grey maintained his smooth, unaffected expression. "You will be satisfied with the dwindling number of sorcerers in the city, then."

Nars lifted a hand in agreement. "If the Royal Sorcerer can aid you in defending your country, Your Majesty, I see little reason why you should deny her this opportunity. There is surely another Master willing to protect you while she is away."

Wyndall spilled his next words eagerly. "Indeed, sire. I have three in my family's employ. I will send one to you immediately to replace *her*," he offered with a nod towards Aly.

Ondorian stole at glance at Aly as the king paced, deliberating. The Reckoner offered her the tiniest nod, barely perceptible. Then to the king, he said, "Send her, Your Majesty. If anyone can do this, it is Tandera's Royal Sorcerer. But might I suggest you send her former student with her as well, as a means of showing to the other Zealots what their magic can achieve when trained by our book? An example of sorts."

Aly smiled under her mask. She'd already asked for Naia's release twice and had been denied both times.

Alexander huffed and *thunked* the scepter on the floor. "Fine! You will go to the Crescent Forest and train me an army. You have six weeks!"

Three days later, Aly stood at the exit to the sorcerer's prison in Mardon, bouncing on her toes as she waited.

The heavy door opened and out walked Naia, striding into the bright sun. Her friend blinked, spotted Aly, then rushed to her.

"How'd you do it?" Naia asked.

Aly wanted to throw her arms around her friend, but Naia had never been one for physical touch. Instead, Aly smiled and swallowed, steeling herself for the answer. "He's agreed to let you go on one condition. You must come with me to the Crescent Forest to—"

"No." Naia lifted a hand and turned to walk away.

The prison guard, in his white cloak and crow's mask, lurched forward. Naia screamed and was on the ground in an instant, her face pressed to the stones. She snarled, twisted around, and lifted a hand as if to cast a spell of her own.

"Wait!" Aly yelled, her arms out. Aly jerked her head toward the guard. "They won't let you say no." Aly's heart pinched a little at the look of panic on Naia's freckled face. Her wild hair was slightly matted from days without bathing, and she was in desperate need of clean clothes.

Naia glared up at the prison guard. "I see that." She stood without accepting Aly's extended hand. Tipping her head into one hand, Naia let out an exasperated sigh. "I won't go back there."

Aly wasn't sure if Naia meant prison or the forest where she grew up.

Naia lifted her arms in dramatic fashion at the white-cloaked

Protector watching her. "See? See this? I'm going with her." Naia marched off, brushing Aly's shoulder as she passed.

Aly jogged to catch up, her heart leaping with excitement. "I'm so glad to see you."

Naia grunted. "Only reason I am coming is because I hate the way that place feels. It's like continuous suffocation down there in the dark. Never thought I'd *miss* magic. But don't think for a minute I'm going back to the light-forsaken forest."

Aly glanced sideways at her friend. The sorcerer's prison was deep underground, a place where Truthwells were too distant for even most Masters to Pull from. The only sources would be the rocks lining the cells, which had all been Stripped of whatever light they contained, and the dirt, which provided very little fuel for escaping chains and locks.

Aly shivered, unnerved at the thought of being buried and separated from all Truthwells. She quickly told Naia of events that had occurred since her incarceration.

Naia scratched her head almost incessantly as Aly spoke. "You really think I'm going to go with you."

Aly lifted her brows expectantly, though she read the horror on her friend's face. Her friend's past haunted her, and she didn't want to return to the one place she hated most. Aly wished there was another option, but she would be glad to have her friend beside her again. "It's that or prison, Naia."

"Fine."

Aly exhaled. "Excellent. We leave in the morning."

6

RED

The army's progress was glacial compared to a carriage propelled by magic, but to make up the difference, the officers pushed the men hard, marching for twelve or more hours a day. Only the officers rode on horseback. Red was stuck walking with the rest of the enlisted men, and he vastly underestimated how badly one's feet could hurt after days of marching. The trip took eight days, and by the time they passed through Luxler, the last town before Caridan, the men were road worn and hungry.

Luxler had changed in the few short weeks since Red had last passed through. People hurried and carriages barely missed colliding as drivers whipped the horses to move faster. Windows in several buildings had shattered, giving the streets a hollow, abandoned feeling.

"What happened here?" Red asked Captain Mitchell as they crossed the city.

Mitchell glanced down from his saddle. "A pack of wood-wolves tore through the city a few days ago. With news of the army marching on Mardon and the increase in attacks, many of the city's wealthy citizens have fled to the capital, taking their Protectors with them."

Red grunted. "If the Zealot army is heading *toward* Mardon, why flee to it?"

Mitchell huffed. "People flee to the seat of power, especially those with a little power of their own. Might have something to do with the fact that the king has demanded his courtiers to return to the city so as to collect as many sorcerers there as possible. They're worried he'll strip their titles if they refuse."

Red had the urge to spit on the ground but held himself back. Mitchell was trying to goad him by reminding Red of how little power he had now. Ahead of him, Seb marched with a noticeably slumped posture. After the whipping, he hadn't stood straight or walked right. The long hours of marching hadn't helped his healing, which was slow and unaided by magic.

Red missed the days when the country's happenings were reported to him over breakfast; he'd not realized how privileged this was until he'd been required to gather all intelligence on his own. Seeking more news, he ventured one more question. "What steps has Alexander taken to protect the city?"

Mitchell's leather gloves squeaked as he tightened his fists on the reins. Instead of answering, he tapped his horse with his heels and trotted ahead, barking at Seb to stand up straight.

If Luxler was in such a state, it did not bode well for what awaited them in Caridan.

It was late afternoon by the time they arrived at the tent city on the Canyon's edge, and it was nothing like Red remembered.

Caridan had been ravaged.

The mist of the Canyon crept farther into the camp than it had before, stretching its cool white fingers between the tents. The Protectors who had vanished weeks ago had not yet been replaced, and the camp had remained in one place, rather than moving frequently, hoping the shield-like spells cast by the absent Protectors would remain intact. But that hope was fading with the thinning shield spells, allowing the mists to leak into the air and muddy the minds of men.

Around the camp stood the pathetic remains of what had once been an ice wall built by the camp's Comforters to keep out the beasts of the Deep. The grass was wet and riddled with deep footprints. Some of the tents were falling in.

The soldiers stood at attention as General Daniels, the commander at the Canyon's edge for the past eight years, walked along the line of fresh faces. Only a few months ago, Red had been welcomed here as king. Now he stood among the ranks of the enlisted, shoulders erect, face stern.

Daniels paused as he stood in front of Red. His hand moved almost as if to salute his king, and then he recognized Red's uniform and lowered his arm. Red stiffened and instead saluted his general.

Daniels moved on to address the soldiers. "I need six men to replace my current scouts." He looked at Red's commanding officer, Captain Mitchell, to supply the names.

Mitchell rattled off five names, then said with an air of excited condescension, "Private Frederick Windon."

Red didn't even blink at hearing his name. Despite the way Mitchell had turned aside that final night in Mardon, allowing Red to visit Grey, the captain was in no way Red's ally. His behavior toward Red since that night had proven his distaste of his former sovereign. Red knew Mitchell would volunteer him for every possible assignment, every possible danger. After all, Alexander had sent Red here to die.

He squared his shoulders and nodded. Mitchell narrowed his eyes a fraction, as if waiting for Red to argue. But Red wouldn't.

Serving at Caridan was, after all, the best way he could protect his country now, and he wouldn't shy away from opportunities to do just that.

As Mitchell proceeded down the line of soldiers, Red glanced out through the thin mist in the direction of the Canyon. Though fear prickled his skin at the memories of the beasts, anticipation danced in his blood. He needed to descend into the Canyon, but scouts didn't travel past the rim. Ondorian was counting on him, and in a way, all of Tandera was too, if Red could uncover a way to truly defeat the Canyon's evil once and for all.

It was perhaps a step beyond mad hope, a step into true fantasy, but he couldn't shake the idea now that it had taken root.

A soldier rattled on about nightly preparations and the routine for ensuring everyone lived until dawn. "The ramifications for ignoring these protocols will be fatal."

Red's mind snagged on one word: *ramifications*.

He bristled every time he thought of how his choices had spiraled into something he had never intended. It wasn't his trip into the Canyon that had ruined him and snatched his throne and family away—it was Kassia. He had only wanted to fulfill his father's last wish, to secure a peace between Tandera and Bulvarna to keep their people safe from the Deep.

Like planting a tree beside your house, his father used to say, *some things may seem like a pleasant idea at the time, but as the days unfold, and the tree roots begin to buckle the foundation of your house, you begin to see that even good ideas can ruin what matters most.*

Red's good intentions had ruined much.

The soldier addressing the new arrivals continued, "At sundown, you can expect the mist to thicken and the beasts to rise. Prepare, gentlemen. You've just stepped into hell."

With that, Daniels dismissed the men.

Red found Seb after the meeting. A look of horror brimmed in his friend's eyes, a look that mirrored his own feelings of unease.

"What happened here?" muttered Seb, all humor gone from his normally chipper voice.

"Death," said a man from nearby.

Red looked up. General Daniels walked toward them.

"Good to see you, sir," Red said.

Daniels nodded. His beard was bushier, his eyes glassier. He took out a flask and took a sip from it. That at least hadn't changed. "How was the journey?"

"Miserable," answered Seb.

Daniels stuffed his flask back in an inside pocket. "We've been taking too many turns scouting at night. We are glad for the relief." He nodded at Red. "You'll leave after the evening meal. When you do, I suggest you travel in that direction." He flicked only his eyes to the left, a subtle motion with no flare or humor. It was the direction away from the Canyon's edge.

"Sir, I am here to serve my country and defend my people."

Daniels frowned. "I will keep that in mind, soldier. You are dismissed." He barely waited for their salute before he turned and drifted away between the tents.

The air was cooler than it should be for late summer. Everything about this place was wrong: the air, the smells, the broken-down tents. In one of the abandoned tents, a pole had pierced the dark fabric. The mist swirled in a sudden breeze.

"This place gives me the creeps," Seb muttered as they picked their way through the mud toward a tent marked with the number seven, their assigned quarters. When they peeked inside, there was a man lying facedown in one of four cots. He lifted up on one elbow and looked at them with wild eyes, then flopped back down.

"Hey, what's your name?" asked Seb as he stormed in.

The man mumbled from his cot.

"What was that?" Seb prodded.

"Vincent Jakes," the man repeated, lifting his face from the pillow to speak.

"Nice to meet you," Red said over the man's blanket.

Jakes rolled over, bringing his drab, tan blanket around with him and tucking it around his body like a crepe.

"Okay, then," Seb wheezed, making a dramatic face at Red.

Amos Johnson strode into the tent behind them and nodded at Seb and Red. "Looks like I make four."

There was a small aisle between the cots and two central poles holding up the damp canvas. A single, burning light hung on one pole, and an abandoned-looking small iron stove sat against the other pole.

Seb picked up the lid of the lonely kitchen pot atop the stove and peeked in. He immediately recoiled and set the lid back down. "Somebody needs to wash that."

"Be my guest," retorted the man on the cot.

Red sat down on one cot, plopping his bag down beside him. The bed creaked and sank a little deeper into the ground. "Excellent."

"Can you tell us what it's like?" Amos asked, shuffling over to sit across from the man named Jakes.

Jakes grunted from under the covers.

"Look, man, we only arrived. We're here to help," Seb said.

Jakes peeled the covers down and stared at them. "You're here to die, just like the rest of them," he said.

"Hey, thanks for the encouragement, man," snapped Seb, slinging his bag down so hard one end of the cot buckled and crashed to the ground. "Perfect." He bent down to straighten out the legs, his careful movement evidence of his lingering pain. "Does anything work here?"

"Ever since the Protectors left, not really," Jakes replied, finally emerging from beneath his blanket.

It was oddly cold. Red eyed the thin blankets rolled up at the end of his bed. He couldn't imagine winter in a place like this. Grey had spent six years here. How could anyone be here for six years? He'd been here for six minutes and already hated the place.

Jakes stood and stretched, cracking all of his knuckles above his head. He grabbed a towel from a hook beside his bed and walked towards the door of the tent.

"Where are you going?" Seb asked. The man disappeared behind the tent flap without answering. "He's fun," mumbled Seb.

Red looked at the tent wall behind Jakes's bed, where a small board had been propped. He pointed at rows of tally marks.

Seb walked over and bent forward to examine the tally marks. "Days he's been here?"

"Days 'til he leaves?" suggested Red.

"People who've died?" Amos added.

Silence filled the tent for a dark moment.

"Look, you need to win your crown back and get us out of here," Seb said.

Amos nodded. "You heard him—we're all here to die."

Red sighed and stood up. "We're not here to die. We're here to protect our country."

"How can you have any hope in this place?" Amos asked, eyes wide.

Aly's face popped into Red's mind. She had been his mad hope when there'd been nothing but death ahead of them. But she wasn't here now. He must have something else to hope in—something greater.

He closed his eyes. There was one thing he could depend on, hope in, against all odds and in the face of all danger—the truth.

Maker, help us.

The evening meal was served in the giant mess tent. A heavy rain had settled in, and every so often, the men took turns standing up from the table to push the canvas ceiling where it drooped with heavy puddles. Beetles the size of sugar cubes buzzed around the lamps in the tent, occasionally diving for the table.

Seb snapped his napkin at a passing bug. The dead beetle bounced onto Red's plate.

"Thanks," Red mumbled. With two fingers he flicked it away.

The food was bland, but it filled his growling stomach. He would be leaving for his first scouting trip in less than an hour. He was grateful for the squirrel he'd killed and stowed in his pack earlier, despite Seb's strange looks. Maybe he'd be able to keep his promises to Aly and Ondorian.

At the close of the meal, General Daniels stood up at the end of the table to address the men. "Another soldier has gone missing," he said, adding no introductory remarks or cushioning statements. A few of the soldiers blinked and looked around at their friends. "This is the ninth man to have gone missing, Captain Missio."

Beetles rudely dove into plates as the men stared at Daniels. Red heard the word *Comforter* whispered up and down the table.

The general continued in his flat, even voice. "With the arrival of the newest soldiers, we have also received new orders from the king. We must find the missing sorcerers and return them to Mardon." Daniels let these words settle by taking a long swig from his flask. With this casual action, the man was displaying what he thought of this ridiculous order without disobeying a direct command from the king. He set his flask down a little too hard. "I need a brave group of men to descend into the Canyon in search of our missing soldiers."

One man lifted his voice over the rain. "You think they're still alive?"

"It's madness," muttered another.

General Daniels glowered. "I will not let these men continue to vanish without at least attempting to bring them back."

Red mentally applauded the man, who was taking ownership of this ludicrous plan, making it appear like his own idea. This small change in the presentation of this order instantly brought about nods of assent from around the tables. Red took note of that tactic, should he ever need to sway a crowd.

"Now," Daniels continued, "I need four men, volunteer only. The team will depart when the weather clears. You are dismissed."

The men started to peel away from the table. Red stared at his hands. His nightmares still replayed the strangeness of the Canyon almost every night. But Ondorian had said there was something to be discovered about the river, something buried under years of misunderstandings, or even lies. This was his opportunity.

But to descend without a Protector was foolish indeed.

Red stood, and before Daniels had picked up his flask, he called out, "I will go."

The General eyed him with what might have been pity, but it was quickly replaced with a nod of respect. After Red, Amos volunteered. Seb cleared his throat, but Red leveled a pointed glare at his best friend. He wouldn't allow Seb to endanger himself in the Canyon, not after having suffered so recently from a Canyon beast's infection. Two more men spoke up before Seb could protest.

"That makes four," Daniels announced. "But you should at least have a Comforter with you. Jakes! Take Carter's place."

The gruff man from Red's tent saluted General Daniels, his hand trembling as he did so.

"We're supposed to have two Protectors coming in next week. I've no mind to disobey our king, but I've no mind to lose four soldiers to the Deep, if I can help it. You four will descend with one of them as soon as they arrive." Daniels turned to leave the tent.

Then a scream tore through the camp.

7

ALY

ly peered through the window of the carriage at the gates of the old Crescent Forest lumberyard. Her heart froze.

This was the scene of her nightmares.

The entire camp was scarred black. The giant piles of wood that they had once hoped would save Mardon were now piles of ash the size of houses. The massive stumps that marked the felled trees looked like empty, rough-hewn tables for a party of giants.

Aly paused the carriage inside the entrance to the camp as wagons behind her jostled through the gates.

In the seat across from Aly, Naia rubbed her hands together, bit her lip, and alternately rocked or swayed.

Aly offered her friend a weak smile. Ondorian had been the one to convince Alexander to free Naia for the sole purpose of aiding Aly in this endeavor, but the fear and hatred on Naia's face as they wheeled into the camp confirmed that Naia wasn't any happier here than she'd been in her cell in Mardon.

"Why did I let you talk me into this?" Naia hissed.

Aly only shrugged, unsure what to say. How was Naia reacting to being back here? It pained Aly to see this place again, and she'd only been here a short time. Naia had lived her entire life in this forest and had witnessed many atrocities. Aly was glad to be away from the usurper, but part of her wished they hadn't had to come here. She wondered if she'd still be able to hear Kassia's whispered lies from here, or if that advantage was now gone.

"Ondorian told me we might be able to learn from the Zealots."

Naia scoffed. "Like how to self-combust."

Shaking off the memory of the man who had died by that method, Aly continued, "The Zealots have lived apart from our society for so long that they may have alternate versions of history. Ondorian wants me to search these out, learn their versions of the Canyon's creation."

Naia's eyes darkened. "You never asked me about that."

Aly dropped her gaze. "I didn't think you'd want to talk about it. You said you never wanted to talk about your past."

When Aly peeked back at Naia, an appreciative smile played at the edge of Naia's mouth. "You're right, I don't."

Aly glanced back out at the lumberyard, flashes of that awful night replaying in her head. "Ondorian told me one more thing: If I train these Zealots to be soldiers, they will likely answer to me."

Now Naia sat up and leaned toward Aly, a disbelieving smirk flickering across her face. "You, *not* Alexander."

Aly nodded. "I have a feeling that whoever agrees to train with us will be a bit like you. They'll be ready to leave their dangerous magic behind and learn a different way. If I'm right, whoever we train here won't care about distant battles and kings they've never met."

Naia caught on to this line of thinking and said, "They'll be your army, not his."

Aly tilted her head. "I don't need an army, but I'm hopeful I can gain a few more friends, ones who will fight beside me when the time comes." She inclined her head toward Naia, recalling the way Naia had agreed to go to battle with Aly and Red.

Naia gnawed her lip and nodded. Then, she wrapped her arms around her chest and shrank down low in the seat, looking almost as frightful as she had the day she arrived at camp, asking to be cured of her magic.

"I know you never wanted to come back," Aly said. "But I'm glad he let you go. And I'm glad you're with me."

Naia grumbled, "I hate this place."

"At least it isn't a cell."

Naia's brows rose. "The past is a prison few people ever escape."

Overcome with a wave of emotion, Aly slid next to her friend, careful to leave a sliver of space. "You are stronger now. Your magic is no longer a threat to anyone. You escaped this place long before we left it."

Eventually, Naia nodded. Sucking in a loud breath, she scooted around Aly for the carriage door. Over her shoulder she whispered, "These people are dangerous. To you, to me, to these men. They proved it last time by killing some of our friends. Are you willing to take that risk again?"

Aly swallowed. The deaths of those men rested on Aly's shoulders. If she hadn't let her feelings for Red distract her, she might have foreseen the attack and prevented it. However, Red wasn't here to distract her this time.

When she set foot on the blackened earth, she turned to the men descending from the carriages. "We will not stay here."

Even with her magic, she couldn't make this place livable.

Not again. Men had died here, men that she had laughed with and dined with, men who had saluted Red as their king.

The crew sent by Alexander to support Aly's efforts assembled in front; they were a rag-tag bunch, compiled of anyone who was not expressly needed in Mardon as war approached. Though they wore the official livery of palace staff, these men reminded her of Red's band of lumberjacks—except these men lacked purpose here. They stared idly about, swatting mosquitoes and grimacing at the state of the ruined camp.

Naia's wild curls barely moved in the hot summer air as she slowly shook her head. "I know a good place."

Aly nodded, grateful they had the advantage of Naia's familiarity with the forest. More to herself than to those listening, Aly added, "I will keep you all safe. There will not be another disaster here."

Naia marched toward the old logging road. "This way."

To live in the forest meant to intrude on the Zealots' territory. However, this time, they weren't here for the trees—they were here for souls.

One of Alexander's soldiers who accompanied them spoke up in an annoyed tone. "You want us to travel *into* the forest?"

"To make ourselves more approachable to these people," Aly replied, "we should move into the forest and live among them. Show them that we value their way of life."

"Value their way of life?" Naia said, brows lifted as she spun on her heel.

"Value their life, at least," Aly amended.

"These people are crazy," scoffed the soldier.

Naia scowled at him.

He didn't appear to notice. Perhaps he didn't know she had recently been among the Zealots. "Crazy and unpredictable," he rambled on.

"You're wrong in one aspect," Naia snapped, stepping toward

him, fists clenching at her waist. "They are predictable. They hate anyone who conjures magic in a controlled way or who attempts to exercise control over them." She snarled her words.

"We are here to show them that control can be good, that it can make them safer," Aly said, stepping up to put a calming hand on Naia's shoulder.

Her friend recoiled from Aly's touch, but she dropped her shoulders and loosened her fists.

Aly pressed her lips into a small smile as she thought of Red and how he always pulled her close when she was angry or afraid. Like Naia, Aly had been cut off from society despite her nearness to it these past six years. She had craved friendship and the touch of another person's skin. But assuming Naia craved the same was foolish and self-centered.

Stepping away from Naia, Aly closed her eyes and briefly thought of Red. She yearned for his nearness now but swallowed back such feelings and set her mind to being the friend and teacher Naia needed. Aly had taught Naia to follow the *Verad*; she could teach others.

"Come, Naia will lead the way. Leave the wagons."

With Aly's magic encircling them and her mind searching for threats, Naia led the small party down the old logging road, then took a turn down a path so narrow most would have missed it. It was likely an animal trail, or perhaps a trail taken by one or two people. They picked their way into the woods until the camp and the stumps and the logging road could no longer be seen. They arrived at a small natural clearing.

"Here," Naia said. "We will build here."

Aly smiled and nodded, swatting away a gnat storm with a pulse of magical breeze. There were no Zealots nearby.

The man who'd spoken earlier made an indignant little sound. "How will we get the wagons back here, m'lady?" His term of respect dripped with disdain.

"I will bring the supplies," Aly quipped.

"You will, eh?" The soldier flashed Aly a mockingly impressed look. "So why did the king ship you out to the middle of nowhere to train some crazies, then?"

She ignored the man. With the flick of her wrist and the utterance of a single spell, all of the supplies and the carriages lifted from where they sat at the edge of the forest, up over the enormous trees, to the clearing where Aly and Naia and the soldier now stood.

Aly, arms lowering slowly, gently set the entire caravan down in the clearing. Only one travel trunk toppled free of its bindings and clunked to the ground. The soldiers and servants gaped at Aly's cloaked form. Some stepped backward or angled their bodies away from her.

She quirked her brow at the soldier who'd spoken to her, whose mouth still hung open.

As the men unloaded supplies, Aly cast protective enchantments, more perhaps than would ever be necessary, but she wasn't going to have another mishap. Red wasn't here to distract her—a fact that hurt as much as it comforted her. She had let him in, behind the walls she'd constructed after her disastrous ending with Weston Grey, and her magic had faltered.

She'd known it would happen.

She'd let it.

She'd *wanted* it. Her desire to be known and loved had overruled the truth about magic. The price she paid for that would haunt her forever.

Her hands shot out in violent gestures as she mumbled her spells. Naia stood nearby, casting less complex spells. And true to Naia's private nature, she didn't ask Aly about her strange grumblings.

Even now, when plagued with guilt over the way Red captivated her, Aly couldn't help but search for him. She pressed her mental awareness outward, roaming over vast fields and dozens of villages, searching for the light that called to her, the light she'd lost. And for once she was jealous of the men and women in the world who could fall in love with total abandon—without the burden of a weighty gift holding back the tidal wave of their affections.

Red would be nearing Caridan, or already there, surrounded by danger from which she could no longer protect him.

Drawing from Alexander's Well, which her mind never fully released despite the distance, she walked around the perimeter of what was to be their new camp, sensing both the Wells of what surrounded her in the forest and the distant Wells she passed as she pressed her magic toward the Canyon's edge.

It took longer than she'd expected and, for a moment, a sense of dread pooled in her stomach. She always thought that his light would be accessible to her. But what if she couldn't find him? What if Alexander's Well wasn't strong enough to send her magic as far as it needed to go?

As her awareness stretched farther and farther away, her eyes drifted shut, but she could still hear the buzz of a hungry mosquito and the hammering of tent pegs behind her.

Aly's mind crossed over cities and forests and farmland, until she sensed the shadowy presence of the Canyon. Only then did she sharpen her focus, honing in on the brightest light she could see, the light she knew so well.

She exhaled at the sight of Red's Well. It was almost like being close to him. There were no dark shadows licking at the edges of his light. There were no twisting tendrils of inky darkness like those that existed in Alexander's mind. Red's Truthwell burned so bright that even the dark spots that represented the lies he believed were almost imperceptible. She knew they were there—every human believed something that wasn't true. The difference was, Red's areas of light were mesmerizing in contrast. He truly was rare—or rather, his light was, as was the energy it could supply.

Her magic yearned for his Well, for its power. She ground her teeth against the strength of this desire. He was no longer her Beacon—she would no longer change the world with his light.

They would simply need to find other ways to change the world.

She wondered, briefly, if Grey had decided to travel to Caridan, with or without the king's approval. To reject Alexander's authority would be risky for Grey, but he lived his entire life on a chessboard full of risky options.

Satisfied Red had not been harmed, she severed her magical connection and surveyed the dismal scene before her. In comparison to Red's light, everything around her appeared dark.

At that moment she sensed the Well of another, one standing directly outside the small clearing in the forest.

"Naia," she whispered, pointing in the direction of the Truthwell. Naia must have sensed his presence too, for they walked quietly to the edge of the clearing.

A white-haired man stood at the edge of Aly's magical shield. He was bent at the waist, as if age weighed him down. He stared around the clearing, wide-eyed and mouth ajar.

Aly glanced at Naia, whose face was set with a hard scowl as she watched the man.

"Naia," Aly hissed, gaining her friend's attention. "If we're going to recruit these people, to train them to defend us, we should probably try to smile."

Naia peeled back her lips, appearing more feral than friendly. "Is that better?"

Shaking her head, Aly walked toward the man. Her blood pumped faster as all her internal warning bells rang.

The man eyed her and stepped back. "Who are you? What are you doing here?"

"I'm Aly. This is Naia. We're here to...meet some of the people who live in the forest." She really should have thought through how to explain her presence here.

Her magical shield sparkled between them, a thin haze of pale golden light. The older man raked his gaze over the towering wall that stretched across the space before him. His facial muscles relaxed, then tightened as his mouth curled into a smile.

"This is a shield, isn't it?" He reached out to touch it.

"I wouldn't," Aly warned, jerking a half-step forward. Her shield was cast to ward off threats, and she didn't know yet if this man qualified.

He jerked his hand back. "How do you make it so precise? So...thin?"

Excitement leaped within Aly's chest, making her smile back at the man. "You want to learn how?"

He tilted his head, then a wave of emotion swept over his face as he grimaced. "No. I better not." He lifted two hands, which Aly noted were speckled with age and scars. "I will find another way around." The man turned and slipped away faster than Aly expected for his age.

Aly's heart sank a little. Naia, on the other hand, crossed her arms and made a satisfied grunting sound. After a moment, Aly was left alone, staring out at the forest.

Training these Zealots would be no easy task.

8

RED

Red leaped up. Guns fired before they had so much as moved toward the exit. Adrenaline flaring, Red and the others scrambled out of the tent.

Seb drew his pistol as soon as they stepped into the fog. Red clutched the ash blade in his left fist and his revolver in the other. To the left, sounds of a fight grew louder.

Snarls swirled among the howls of men in pain. Red and his company had been here less than one day. Ready or not, the beasts were here for blood.

One man ran toward them from the direction of the fight, his face pale.

Panic rose inside of Red, then he remembered what it had been like in the Canyon, when reality had twisted and spun like a windmill.

"Stay calm," he said aloud as they jogged toward the awful sounds.

"Easier said than done, mate," Seb snapped. Seb's hands trembled so hard the gun in it was rather a hazard.

Ahead, two giant woodwolves darted around a tent, loping in enormous strides directly toward them.

Red fired in the dim light.

The first wolf whimpered but kept coming. Grey wasn't wrong—these beasts weren't easy to kill. More pistols fired off to his right, near the camp entrance.

How many beasts were there?

Nearby, canvas ripped as a knife stuck through a tent. A large, bulky shape flopped against the fabric wall, snarls and human grunts mingling in a sickening sound.

Behind him, Amos raced toward the tent as the two beasts kept charging toward them. Seb fiddled with his trigger and dropped the gun in the mud, cursing as he bent to retrieve it.

"Move!" Red yelled. He fired again, steadying his hand with the one holding the ash blade, which glowed a strange, hungry orange. He missed.

The beasts moved too fast, their loping gait making a hard target. They had only seconds.

Leaving his pistol in the mud, Seb hopped up and launched a blade, which flew over one wolf's head. The wolf lunged straight for Seb, as if sensing Seb was the easier target. Red took aim and fired one more time, hitting the beast in the shoulder right as it connected with Seb's throat.

A guttural scream ripped from Red's mouth as he dove at the beast, falling with it and Seb. He pressed the revolver right to the wolf's head behind the ear and pulled the trigger.

A mist of dark blood sprayed Seb's face. The wolf shuddered under Red's body before falling still. He shoved it aside, but its jaws were still clamped to Seb.

The blood—a river.

Red's screamed and grabbed the beast's fangs, prying with all his might as blood drenched his knuckles.

Choking, gurgling sounds burbled from Seb's open mouth.

The second wolf took a bullet from Amos, but it barely slowed.

And then the beast inside the tent clawed its way through the torn canvas, its white fur streaked with red. It limped toward Seb's prone form.

Two more men materialized, firing at the wolves. Another wolf, black as a starless night, lurked between the tents behind Amos.

"Behind you!"

Amos spun and pulled the trigger before realizing he was out of bullets.

The wolves were coming from different directions and pretty soon the bullets started flying close over Red's head.

"Hold your fire!" barked Red.

This battle would have to be fought with blades.

He bit his lip, closed his eyes, and lunged away from Seb toward the next wolf. He grabbed the beast by the tail and used all his strength to pull it off Amos. Red would not see his friends die today. The wolf curled around and snapped at Red, biting his hand.

The pain raged like fire through his hand. He kicked with his foot, snapping the beast's jaw shut so hard that the beast whimpered. With another lunge he had his ash blade in the beast's flank. Its flesh sizzled on contact, and immediately the wound grew to an alarming size and the beast wriggled, flopped, and lay still.

With one more quick lunge, Red yanked the ash blade free. It drew a line of blood with it, darker than he expected, as if it had been cooked by the heat of his ash blade. A strange smell turned his stomach as he wiped the blade on the grass. The grass didn't singe, nor did his hand when he tapped the glowing steel with his finger. He lifted his brows at his blade and then dove on his hands and knees towards Seb. He tore his jacket off and tucked it around Seb's neck, pressing as hard as he dared.

He had no idea how to treat a wound. He was no doctor.

"Seb," he said, over and over again, not knowing what else to say. "Stay with me, brother."

In minutes, the snarls of the wolves and the sound of pistol fire fell silent. Four beasts lay dead on the ground. The faint smell of woodsmoke and gunpowder filled the air.

"Over here!" shouted Red. "We need a Comforter!"

With his forearm, Red wiped Seb's forehead free of red splatters, then moved his thumb to rub the blood from beside his friend's eyes. Seb's dark eyes rolled around, frantically searching and not seeing. The only sound that left his mouth was a bubbling murmur.

"No!" Red grunted. He leaped up. "We need help here!" He ran through camp shouting, looking for the medic's tent. Finally, he saw the medic's uniform ahead through the pale fog. "Over here!" He swung his arm and pivoted back toward where Seb lay on the ground.

The Comforter followed him and descended upon Seb, already whispering spells. Within minutes, the blood stopped seeping out of Seb's neck, but the wound was still there.

"Can't you heal him?" he snapped. *We need Aly!*

The Comforter looked at Red with a hard, almost sad, expression. With a small cough, he jumped up and ran off to the next victim.

Red couldn't look at Seb. There was nothing more he could do right now. He must help the others. He knelt beside the ripped canvas tent where Amos was attempting to extract the man inside. The Comforter was already gone. That meant only one thing: The man inside the tent no longer had a glowing Truthwell.

"Get him up," Amos said, reaching down to collect the dead man's legs.

Red's hand bled from the bite mark and pulsed with the evil that was now coursing through his veins.

He was cursed—again. Not the same kind of curse, but still his body was poisoned and he needed to extract it before it spread to his heart.

When he lifted the man's limp shoulders, Red grunted as more blood squished out of the tear in his hand. His wound, however, was nothing compared to Seb's or this man's. Red cringed and looked away as they hefted the soldier out of the demolished tent and onto the soft ground.

"Oy," Amos said, eyes on Red's hand. "Get that seen to, sire. I'll see to Sebastian. Go."

The burning pain was reaching for Red's heart even now. "I'm not leaving him." Kneeling beside Seb, Red forced his gaze to assess the damage. He swallowed hard, ignoring the searing pain creeping up his arm.

There were only three Comforters in the camp, but there were also two physicians trained at the university and a handful of nurses. Red flagged one of the nurses down. He marched over with a look of steel resolve on his pale face and flipped open a small satchel.

Even though magic could heal better than medicine, stitches and ointments could still be effective. It would have to be enough. The Comforters were all out attending the other wounded soldiers.

As the nurse removed Red's jacket from Seb's neck, a small curse hissed from his cracking lips.

Seb's eyes closed, and Red feared they might not open again.

9

ELISE

A cushioned carriage from the palace rumbled toward Luxler, carrying Elise on her first solo ambassadorial mission for the king. The journey, made longer without a Protector to propel the carriage, had drained Elise of the will to keep her posture firm even as the wheels bounced over uneven roads. Considering the need for caution as she neared the Canyon, Elise elected to confine their journeys to the middle of the day, avoiding the hours before dawn and after dusk, thus extending their trip but decreasing her fear.

As Luxler's squat skyline finally came into view, she sighed with relief, ready for a hot meal and a bath.

Red lasted weeks without a routine, without attendants or Comforters. For some reason, thinking of what her brother endured during the weeks leading up to the rather shocking coronation ceremony gave Elise more reasons to be thankful for her own situation—almost thankful enough to douse the sting of guilt that threatened to choke her every single day.

Red and Seb should be in Caridan by now; their company likely had arrived a day or two ago. Her chest tightened with the fear that even one day in Caridan could bring disaster. Grey had survived at the Canyon's edge for six years, but Seb and Red were not hardened soldiers. They, like her, had grown up away from danger.

It was odd to think how close she was to them once again. When Red's company had departed for Caridan, a twang of sadness had knotted her nerves. He and Seb were traveling so far away and to such a dangerous place. But despite how near she was to them, a chasm still stood between them, would always stand between them. Elise could no more to reach out to those she'd betrayed than she could Lordan or Queen Kassia.

She'd been so blinded by heartbreak that spying on Lordan had seemed like a goal worth achieving, at any cost. Foolishly, she'd presumed her brother and Seb would see her as valiant for her unbridled efforts to gather intelligence for Tandera.

Now, however, she needed to prove that her choice to enter into Grey's employ a wise one. She would make Seb's pain worth it—if possible. She would make Red's and Aly's loss worth it. The only way to achieve this was to rise higher in the Alexanders' estimation, to simultaneously sink deeper into the mire of information gathering.

Across from Elise sat her new attendant, a young, quiet woman named Greta, who was Josephine's replacement. Alexander had dismissed anyone he assumed to be loyal to the old Tandera, including the royal family's personal attendants. Greta had an uncanny ability to sleep despite the constant bumping and rocking of the carriage.

A single guard rode outside the carriage. His presence somewhat mollified Elise's fears of Canyon beasts.

Beside Elise sat her valise, which contained the king's sealed letter. She still didn't understand why this message couldn't be sent via the more direct and efficient sorcerer networks, but the king had said a personal delivery might improve his odds at a desirable response. What that really meant was that the king would blame Elise if he didn't receive the answer he wanted. It was a clear message. If Elise failed here, her tenure in the palace might be short-lived—and if she could no longer gather intelligence for Grey, to utilize however he chose, what would be her role?

She couldn't allow herself to be *cast aside*. Lordan had done so to her twice now, and the thought of being useless and unwanted stabbed shards of pain into Elise's chest.

Elise closed her hands around the handle of the valise. As instructed, she had not let the letter out of her possession since leaving Mardon over a week ago. This trip was Elise's last and final test, her way of proving her worth to the king's government.

The carriage trundled down the road, and Elise's hair was a mess from bouncing against the back of the seat for so many hours. She didn't know how she would she look presentable upon arriving at Lord Chesterton's estate.

As the largest city near the Canyon, Luxler had been bleeding citizens for days. Many of the wealthy families had fled to their other properties in safer cities, but many of the nobles in Luxler had homes in Mardon, and the capital wasn't as safe as everyone wanted to believe.

The carriage rolled all the way through Luxler, bumping down its cobbled roads toward the eastern edge. What Elise saw chilled her bones. The abandoned homes had been burgled, their windows broken and doors either missing or ajar. Other windows had been barricaded with wooden planks. People hurried everywhere they went. A few men walked with white-cloaked Protectors at their heels. Elise passed two abandoned and ransacked carriages in the street.

This once grand city had been brought to its knees by the fear of the Deep.

Elise was glad to leave the main city behind, though it meant she was traveling that much closer to the Canyon. Eventually, the Chesterton estate peeked out from behind long rows of tall oaks. The warm-colored bricks were half-covered with ivy, giving the house a quaint, garden-like feel.

Elise's carriage rolled up to the front of the house on tiny gravel. Only then did Greta awake. Cedar trees hugged close to the house, their smell brightening Elise's senses. She clutched the valise containing the letter, not trusting it in anyone else's hands. She would not fail this first assignment from the king.

She was awkwardly helped out of the carriage as a footman offered to take her valise, which she politely refused.

A butler in bright livery bowed to her. "Lady Elise, welcome, welcome. Lord Chesterton is most pleased you have come," he said.

Lord Chesterton was a widower. His wife had died some time ago and he had never remarried. But his three daughters, one of whom was grown and married, still lived on the estate.

Elise straightened her back and nodded politely.

The man swept an arm behind him. "Come, I am certain that you are quite tired from your journey. My name is Jameson and I will gladly show you inside. Would you like to rest before meeting the lord of the house?"

She noted the oddness of Chesterton meeting her so quickly. Most important men were inclined to make guests wait, especially lowly female couriers, even ones sent directly from the king. She nodded again, careful to appear composed.

"Very well. We have a room prepared for you. We have other guests as well, but there is plenty of room at Chesterton Estate." He started toward the house.

Other guests? Elise shook away her amused expression. She supposed wealthy men almost always had guests in their home, and this was nothing out of the ordinary. Perhaps his daughters had company, despite the location so near the Deep.

She followed the man inside the house, enjoying the smell of pine and cedar that followed her all the way through the main corridor, with walls a deep honey color. Everything inside the house was made of wood, creating a cozy atmosphere. There were red and gold tapestries and warm-toned rugs. Frames were painted with a gilded hue and all of the furnishings and lamps had bronze accents. Magic cooled the house, and yet there was such a happy warmth inside of it.

Elise smiled as the man led her and Greta to a small bedroom. Pink curtains tucked up against the latticed windows. Gold and pink drapes framed the bed that sat squarely in the middle of the room beneath a large chandelier made of antlers. It was certainly an odd décor, but one that invited comfort.

Elise dropped her valise on the bed and longingly glanced at the covers. But now was no time for a nap.

If Lord Chesterton was truly going to meet her as soon as she was ready, she would ready herself quickly. The butler excused himself, and Greta bustled into the room, immediately tending to Elise's belongings.

After a bath and a change of clothes, Elise sat down in a chair before a tryptic mirror and allowed Greta to rearrange her hair into a more presentable fashion.

"Lord Chesterton will see you now," said the butler as she descended the main stair a short while later.

Elise held the large letter bearing the king's wax seal as she walked into a large room walled on one side with floor-to-ceiling shelves. Tall windows lined the other side and warm, angled light hit the dust like gold flecks. A large man in a dark suit stood by one window with an open book in his hand.

"Ah." The book snapped shut as he spun around. "My dear Lady Elise, welcome to my home," said the man, spreading his arms wide. His oversized frame exploded from a buttoned vest and waistcoat, and his ascot was buried somewhere beneath a fold of flesh. On his pink face was a broad smile that appeared perplexingly genuine.

Elise smiled. Some men would feel insulted at a woman of no rank coming to do business. "Most delighted to be here, sir. Your home is lovely."

"Yes, my wife made it so. I have not changed a thing since she left us," he said, as if speaking of his dead wife were as conversational as speaking of the weather. "She truly made this place home, and I certainly would have ruined that if I changed anything, don't you think?"

It was odd he asked her opinion so boldly. "I think this place would be lovely no matter how it was decorated," she replied, looking around at the warm wooden tones everywhere.

The man smiled broadly at her, a twinkle in his eye. "Come, sit. Have some tea. Or do you prefer coffee? Water? Perhaps something stronger? Vodka?" He offered her a sly wink.

"Just tea, thank you."

"Good girl. Oh, my apologies, Ambassador. I have three daughters, and I still call them girls, though they are all older than twenty and five."

He fluttered about to offer her tea. Two footmen stood at the door, not even moving to take over this particular job. Lord Chesterton was an odd person if he poured his guests' tea and spoke to them as if they were friends upon meeting them. Elise didn't feel like correcting him on her title. She was no official ambassador, but she liked the way it sounded.

She sat on the edge of the sofa and accepted the clinking teacup from her host. She nodded at him and took a sip, barely holding back her strained face as she tasted the warm brew.

Chesterton chuckled. "You are not a fan of the tea, I see. I should have warned you it is Bulvarnan tea."

"You drink Bulvarnan black tea?" asked Elise. Then, taking a risk, she added in a friendly tone, "How treasonous of you." A good ambassador knew how to befriend people and ease into the good graces of their hosts. She hoped she'd aptly judged this man's sense of humor.

His eyebrows rose, then he chortled. He sat so heavily onto the opposing sofa that it bounced and made a horrible screeching sound where perhaps one of the springs had broken. Chesterton ignored the sound. "I find that it tastes better. Recognizing when another way is better than yours is how progress is made. Is that not right, Ambassador?"

There was something charming about this older gentleman, and a flash of grief sprang to her throat as she thought of her beloved father. What would he say of her recent choices? Snapping herself out of her guilt, she glanced at the letter in her lap. "Sir?"

"Of course." He reached out a hand and took the extended letter from her. "To business, to business." He popped open the seal, slid the letter out with three small jerking motions, and held the letter in his lap without reading it. "This will contain something I do not want to read. Can we speak plainly first?"

Elise lifted her brows. "Certainly, sir. Whatever you please."

His eyes narrowed in a playful way. "You are the picture of propriety, Ambassador. But you know what I think? I think you have many more thoughts than you ever allow yourself to vocalize." He shook his head, jiggling his chin. "My daughters would be appalled if they knew I was saying this to you, who will report back to our king. However, they would not expect anything else from their dear old father."

She suppressed a small smile.

"You see, the reason I am a little hesitant about this letter is because of you, Ambassador," Chesterton continued. "If this contained something that I would agree to easily, he would have sent me a message directly to one of my Protectors. Instead, he sent you all this way. Either he greatly dislikes you, or this contains a query I am unlikely to receive well." He flipped the letter open and glanced at it. After a moment, he eyed Elise. "Curious?" he asked.

She blinked at him. It was not her place to know what was in that letter, though curiosity burned within her.

"If you are anything like my daughters, you *need* to know what is in this letter. They would come and snatch it from my hands, but I do not expect that from you, of course." He chuckled softly. "I will tell you what it says." He stood. "The king wishes for me to send my Protectors to Mardon."

"Your Protectors, sir?"

"Technically, he offered for me to move there, but he knows I am never going to leave this place. This was my wife's home. This is my family's home. I will not be leaving." He glanced again at the letter. "He said that if I do not wish to relocate that I should send two of my Protectors to Mardon. He is trying to collect an army, you see. An army of sorcerers."

Elise shivered at the thought, and yet an army of Zealots marched toward Mardon even now. She could understand the king's desperation.

Lord Chesterton inhaled sharply. "He shall have my reply, and he will receive it with the same efficiency with which he sent my letter. No offense, my dear." He offered her a small flourished bow. "I will write out my refusal, and you will return it to him. However," he added, "I recommend that you do not remain in his presence when he opens it."

Memories of Seb's bleeding body flashed into her mind and panic gripped her. *What if Alexander deems me responsible for this?* She groped for anything she might say to change Chesterton's mind. She liked this man, but she feared the king.

"Sir," she said as he turned to pick up the book he'd held earlier. "Would it not be best to honor your king's wishes?"

He studied her through narrow eyes for a moment. "Likely it would be good, but a man must care for his own home too. And I am not leaving my children here with only one Protector for the lot of us. We are too close to the Canyon...too close indeed." His expression darkened, and his eyes traveled across the room as if looking for something not there.

"Sir?" Elise asked, breaking his strange moment of distraction.

He blinked and peered over at her. "My apologies. We had a disruption last night. Some of our guests have recently returned from the Canyon. They arrived in rather poor condition." He lifted both hands. "All the more reason I must keep my Protectors here, where they are needed."

Elise's heart shrank. Red and Seb were at the Canyon. "Was there an attack?"

Chesterton nodded, his attention already down on the book in his lap, so he missed the flash of fear on her face. Before she could open her mouth to respond, he waved a hand and continued. "Dinner will be served in half an hour. We will eat in the main dining room, in honor of you, our special guest."

With that, he picked up his book and effectively dismissed Elise.

Red's company had been attacked. Her heart thundered as she exited the library.

She left the room trying not to worry about her brother or Seb or what would happen to her when she returned to Mardon with an unfavorable answer from Chesterton. No matter if she could procure a better answer from the lord by the time she left, it was apparent that everything around her was falling apart.

What could she now do in the face of a world falling apart?

· · ·

The dining room at Chesterton's estate was vast and buttressed with exposed wooden beams. Two massive iron chandeliers hung over a grand table strewn with magnolia leaves and cedar boughs that smelled sweet and crisp as the forest. Elise took the honored seat beside Lord Chesterton, and his three daughters sat across from her. A twang of jealousy resounded in Elise's heart as she saw this happy family come to dine together in their home. She had been part of such a happy family only a few short months ago.

Everything had shattered since then: her heart, her family, her home, her country.

Stomach rumbling, she shook away those feelings as the first course descended in front of her.

"How do you like it?" Chesterton asked after a moment.

"Excellent," Elise answered. She had few chances to change his mind about the king's request, and she must act quickly. "Sir, if I may, I fully understand the need to protect your family from harm." She coughed, hating herself for the way she'd harmed her own family and friends. "Perhaps you would all be safer in Mardon?" Many nobles believed as much, and if she could convince him to take his family to the capital, the king would not only receive one Protector, he would receive three.

Chesterton eyed her over his lifted glass. "I understand the threats here. We have fought them off for many years. I do not, on the other hand, understand a rag-tag group of untrained sorcerers. *That* is a foe I am not willing to face." He glanced toward the window at the back of the room. "I respect your diligence in the matter, Ambassador, but—"

The massive glass window at the end of the room shattered.

Screams broke out. Elise dropped her fork and pushed back from the table so quickly she toppled her chair.

A shape leaped through the window. It landed on four feet and immediately shifted into the shape of a man.

10

ELISE

lise's scream disappeared among the mayhem as everyone in the room dove for the exits. Elise scrambled from her toppled chair and shuffled for the exit on her hands and knees. She had to escape.

Three white-cloaked Protectors leaped into action, sucking heat from the room. Light flashed against the walls, silhouetting a leaping figure that might have been a bear. Fear strangled Elise, and her muscles grew sluggish. Gulping air, she stared at her hands on the floor, and with a purposeful inhale, she hopped to her feet and ran, not looking back.

Lord Chesterton let out a snarl of rage. "Not my daughters! Protect the girls!" he yelled to his Protectors.

Someone grabbed Elise by the shoulders and tugged her through the door, shoving her down the hall. Elise ran heedlessly, her dress tangling between her legs. She grabbed it with her fists and pulled, not caring that her ankles and half her calves were showing as she sprinted down the hall and around the corner.

She kept running. Up the stairs. Down the hall.

She tried the first knob. Locked. The next opened, and she slammed herself inside, her back to the door, her body on fire with panic and terror.

A groan sounded from the direction of the bed. She darted her gaze toward the covers and noticed a dark, familiar face among the burgundy sheets.

Sebastian Thorin.

She jolted, slamming against the door in unladylike fashion. The door rattled behind her, and she stumbled for the knob, then remembered what was behind this door.

Instead, she shot forward into the room, searching for another exit.

Seb wheezed and the sickly sound slowed Elise's motion. She stumbled when she truly caught sight of him. A thick bandage wrapped around his entire neck. His eyes were bloodshot. He looked awful.

"What are you doing here?" she asked.

He hadn't moved other than to trace her movements with his eyes. He opened his mouth but only a small, rasping croak came out.

She was still breathing heavily, and her chest was sweating. As she opened her mouth to speak again, she realized he was not in a position to protect himself. She couldn't very well haul him to safety if the lyth should find them. Half-panicked, she hurried back and locked the bedroom door.

The door suddenly seemed very thin and very breakable. She spied a trunk at the foot of the bed and shoved it in front of the door.

Panting as quietly as she could, she stood back and stared at the barricade.

The Protectors would take care of the beast. They were safe in here.

She must calm down, think sensibly. Here was the man who

she had betrayed, injured yet again. She couldn't allow him get hurt, not when she had stumbled into *his* room, of all the rooms in this enormous house.

"There's a lyth in the house," she said finally.

Seb raised his eyebrows. After another hoarse cough, he said, "And here I thought you were trying to lock me in a bedroom." He grimaced in pain.

"Don't speak," she hissed, snapping out the command. "And don't be ridiculous." He was feeling good enough to crack a joke, at least.

A pang of guilt pierced her chest. The last time they had seen one another, he had been tied to a post in Mardon's main square, a whip tearing at his back. Thanks to her. She turned and walked toward the window.

"What happened at Caridan?" She couldn't bring herself to ask directly about Red.

"Your brother is alive," Seb answered, understanding exactly what she hadn't asked.

She heard noises and pressed her face to the window to peer into the yard below. Light flashed off of shattered glass on the grass below. A puff of dust-like magic billowed out over the yard, and a dark shape emerged from the gloom. She backed away from the window, but not before the lyth, in its human form, had glanced up.

"*No,*" she whispered, stumbling against the four-poster bed. "No, no, no."

Within seconds, a creature landed on the window sill. It was a bat, wings spread wide, its fuzzy body pressed against the glass.

Elise shrieked. Seb hollered out in his hoarse voice.

She bolted for the door, attempting to shove the trunk out of the way right as the lyth slammed against the glass. A horrible cracking sound filled the room.

Then she looked back at Seb. Her eyes pressed shut as the window shattered. As the glass fell to the floor and a dark shape flapped toward her, she lunged in front of the bed, spreading her arms out wide. The beast flew toward her. Now it had four furry legs and a spotted coat. The lyth lunged for Elise, appearing not to notice Seb buried in the covers.

Too afraid to scream, Elise's shoulder banged the bedpost as she stumbled.

Something flashed behind her.

Elise closed her eyes as the beast, now a leopard, leaped.

A small *swish* by her ears, and the leopard's body collapsed to the floor beside her with a sickening clunk, a dagger hilt in its neck. Its manic eyes stared at her and bubbles of saliva dripped from his open mouth.

She was frozen in fear, heart beating fast enough to burst.

In an attempt to save its life, the leopard tried to shift into a smaller housecat, but the knife that was protruding from its flesh remained lodged in deep. As the animal shrank, its wound worsened, hitting more organs as its body compressed.

The door burst open and banged into the trunk. A moment later, the trunk slid across the room and a white-cloaked Protector speared a quick spray of blue magic at the beast. It twitched and stilled.

When it finally stopped moving, Elise tilted her head against the bedpost and stared at the ceiling, breathing in rapid, shallow gasps.

Then Seb was standing beside her, shirtless again, collared with white bandages. He caught her as she fainted.

All of the residents and guests of Lord Chesterton's estate had congregated in the library as the grounds were searched for any remaining threats. One of Chesterton's Protectors informed her that her guard, Maurice, had died in the attack. Though she didn't know the man, she had been grateful for his presence on her trip, and his death felt cold and unfair.

Elise sat on a small wooden chair near the shelves. Chesterton sat cradling one of his weeping adult daughters and his other two daughters occupied the sofa. The eldest's husband stood behind her, hand working over his beard.

Seb, now fully dressed, lounged on a settee as one of the Protectors tended to his bandages and administered a few additional healing spells. The only other person to sustain injury in the attack was one of the three Protectors, who had promptly healed himself and was out leading the patrol of the grounds. A fortunate outcome, given the nature of their attacker.

Elise's hands still trembled, even as she pressed them into her lap. Her eyes kept cutting to Sebastian. The first few times he caught her staring, she glanced away, but soon she found she couldn't take her eyes from him, and welcomed his return gaze, which quickly morphed into a stare so intense she felt her cheeks growing hot.

He'd saved her life. Wounded and weak, he had come to her aid, even after she'd betrayed him.

One of the Protectors, a man in a white cloak and golden horse mask, walked up to Elise. "His Majesty needs a report of what happened here—from you, Lady Elise," he said in his crisp, plain voice.

Elise nodded. Her eyes flickered back to Seb, who now lay in a rather comfortable-looking position, no more bandages encasing his neck. "A lyth attacked Lord Chesterton's estate. None are wounded—anymore." She snapped her eyes back to the Protector. "If it had not been for one man, I would now be dead. Sebastian Thorin saved my life."

The Protector lifted a finger as he sent her message. Elise wondered if this man's message would be sent to Aly or someone else, now that Aly was likely already in the Crescent Forest on another of Alexander's crazed errands.

Alexander had successfully removed from Mardon all those in power who were loyal to Red, even Aly. He'd garnered her magic, then shipped her away. Elise had assumed he'd keep Aly close. Elise needed to do better when it came to reading Benedict Alexander. Her future depended on it.

The Protector nodded when he was finished. "Also, as you will be needing a replacement guard for your return journey, Captain Mitchell, the officer who traveled here with the injured soldiers, believes Sebastian Thorin would be better suited to that kind of work than serving in Caridan." He inclined his head at a uniformed man in crimson standing by one of the large windows.

Elise's brows peaked almost at her hairline. Seb, too, had sat up and was leaning forward, elbows on knees, staring not at the Protector, but at Elise.

Her stomach flipped. Seb was a traitor, labeled so by her own actions. What would he say to being assigned to protect her? He'd saved her life today, but surely he hated her for what she had done.

She must say something quickly, something that would make it appear like she wasn't pleased with this arrangement. "Very well, it will serve him right to be forced to protect someone he hates."

The sorcerer nodded and walked out of the room.

Seb leaned back and crossed his arms, an inscrutable expression on his brow. A minute later, he rose and left the library.

Elise huffed, wondering what was on his mind. Curiosity overcame her, and after a moment, she stood, brushed imaginary wrinkles out of her skirts, and walked toward the door.

"Powder room?" she asked one of the estate's staff stationed at the exit.

The man nodded and stepped into the hall. "There's one right across the hall," he said.

Elise offered a polite nod and forced herself to not reveal her annoyance on her face. She employed her best princess walk to cross the small space, taking her sweet time so she could glance up and down the hall.

At the end of the hall, Seb's retreating form spun around. Their eyes met briefly. The man behind Elise was still watching her, so she pushed her way into the powder room and shut the door behind her. She leaned back and exhaled, unsure why her pulse was rising.

Where is he going? A spy should know where all the important players were, right? She turned and grasped the door handle again, then she shook her head. A spy wouldn't compromise discretion for the sake of burning curiosity.

She'd talk to Seb later, find out how he really felt at being assigned to her personal guard. If this Captain Mitchell thought Seb wasn't suited for Caridan, it was surely an insult. How would Seb take that? At least if Seb was to travel all the way to Mardon with her, she could ask more about Red, and that was a small comfort. But she would need to maintain her feigned indifference to him, or Seb would call her bluff.

Elise looked around the small room—and smiled. The powder room had two doors.

The other one exited into a bedroom, a guest room by the looks of the untouched bed and bare dresser. She strode to the double doors that opened onto the lawn but hesitated before turning the knob. The lyth was gone. The Protectors had swept the entire household by now.

She grasped the handle and cracked the door, but a flicker of panic briefly stalled her motion. As she hesitated, the door pushed open.

Seb walked in, his face and body only a step from hers. His

closeness sent her pinwheeling backward until she bumped into an overstuffed ottoman. She stepped to the side, trying not to trip over the rug without taking her eyes off of Seb's intense brow.

He strode toward her, not allowing any space to breathe. "Looks like I will have you all to myself now," he grunted in a menacing, un-Seb-like tone.

Elise bristled, guilt stabbing into her composure. "I can send you straight back to Caridan, if that's where you prefer to be, but your commanding officer doesn't want you."

His broad chest pressed upon her, but she kept her chin lifted. She would not back down. Unlike the other women he may have known, she was not intimidated by his handsome looks.

This close to him, she needed to force her eyes from roaming the edges of his jaw and the lines of his neck, where a tiny scar lingered from his recent wound. Her blood hammered in her ears.

No, don't, she scolded herself, eyes flitting back up to his dark eyes. She'd been deceived by good looks once before. *Never again.*

He stared hard at her, as if waiting for her to break. Perhaps most women crumbled after he looked at them this long, but she would not. Finally, he stepped back and exhaled. His arm raised to scratch the back of his neck, and Elise's traitorous gaze fell on his muscles, which were visible beneath the thin fabric

"Why did you betray me?" he asked, leaning against one of the massive posts in the bed and adopting his typical cavalier demeanor.

After a deep, leveling breath, she said, "Because you were a traitor to the king." Her heart rate betrayed her lie, but perhaps he assumed the blush in her cheeks was merely a result of her recent stumble across the room.

"Elise Windon, friend of the usurper? I don't buy it," Seb replied. "Tell me the truth."

Inside, Elise's fractured heart burned with an intense desire to tell him exactly what he wanted, but she'd made promises to Grey. An informant could never reveal her true role to anyone.

She understood now why Grey pushed away all the women at court, why he crafted a persona few women desired. It was easier that way, easier than standing in front of someone who begged for the truth and knowing she could never truly let that person in.

"Fine," he mumbled. Without warning, he reached up and ripped his shirt over his head in one fluid motion.

Elise gasped. "What are you—?"

He spun around. On his back were five raised scars.

A jolt coursed through Elise. She stared at the wounds, recalling the way the whip had rocked his entire body.

"Is it worth it?" he inquired over his shoulder. "Is the lie you're defending really worth it?"

He couldn't see her swallow down a wave of nausea and guilt. *Don't give in. Don't back down.*

The crinkled skin along his still-healing scars screamed at her.

Who have I become?

She had agreed to serve Tandera, and she wouldn't give up now. Grey had secured her this ambassadorial mission, which meant he was likely to keep giving her tasks.

Tandera is worth it, she told herself as he whirled back around. A knot in her throat made it hard to swallow for several seconds. Nevertheless, she stiffened her neck and squared her shoulders.

He slipped the shirt back over his head, tugging it down to mask—*thank Theod*—what lay hidden beneath fabric. It was the third time she'd seen him shirtless, and she remembered each time vividly. Elise blinked and looked away.

"You really won't talk, will you?" he said, eyes narrowing. At Elise's continued silence, his scowl relaxed. He stepped forward. "Whatever your reason—and I know you have one—I accept."

Elise shook her head, confused. "Accept what?"

"A position in your personal guard." His lip quirked.

"It is not for you to decide."

He leaned forward. "I realize that. But I'll take a ruthless princess over bloodthirsty woodwolves any day. Mitchell's right. Caridan isn't for me."

"Ruthless?" Her brows lifted, half-amused at this term. *More like worthless.* How could he choose to be around her when the scars on his back still pained him? Even so, a long breath whooshed from her lungs at his statement. It was mercy, after all, to be removed from Caridan, and she hoped he could see it. She hoped he *couldn't* see her pulse trembling in her temples.

Her grand plan to repay Lordan for breaking her heart was starting to ruin her more than mend her. Grey had been right to warn her against this path.

She'd been a fool not to listen.

Seb stalked closer. "I wonder what Red will think when he learns I've been assigned to *you.*" The last word came out with the intensity of a curse. His hand reached for the doorknob as he offered one of his winning grins, a sharp contrast from his biting tone. "I will go where you command, Princess," he said with a small, mocking nod.

"No more arguments?" she blurted, drawing his attention back. She couldn't account for her outburst.

He looked at her with the tiniest glint of mischief back in his eyes. "I can argue if you'd like me to."

Elise realized how pathetic she looked, trying to extend this conversation. "No, I simply thought that you would put up a fight. I assumed it would disgust you to have to work for me."

He lifted one arm and leaned onto the door. "I don't hate you."

Why not? She yearned to ask.

It must have been obvious on her face because before he left, he said again, "I could never hate you."

11

ALY

Their first morning in the Crescent Forest, Aly awoke with a strange feeling in the pit of her stomach.

Staring at the sloped ceiling of her and Naia's tent, Aly's mind immediately shot to Red. Something was wrong. She squeezed her eyes shut and searched out Red's Well, her hands knotting across her stomach as she tensed for bad news.

Guilt stung her chest. Last night, she'd been so mentally exhausted from casting powerful protective enchantments and helping set up camp that she'd fallen asleep even as her mind had reached for Red's Well one last time. If something had happened to him, and she'd missed it due to exhaustion, she wasn't sure how she would handle that.

She honed in on his Well much more quickly this time. Red's light was nearly on top of the blackness of the Deep.

"Please be okay," she muttered, losing her focus on the real world and sinking entirely into the space only her magic could see, the world where light and darkness battled for men's souls.

She grasped for the light of Red's Well as it rushed into her mind's eye. Even though it was across the country, it was still bright, albeit smaller, like a distant star.

Longing for his beautiful light—and for him—leapt inside of her. As her mind settled again on his Well, she noted that the dance of shadow and light writhed in a way she had only seen twice before: when he'd been infected with a Canyon Beast's bite.

Her eyes popped open.

"No," she whispered, sitting up on her cot. Now that she had a grasp on Red's Well, she wouldn't release it. "I shouldn't have let him go," she grumbled, flipping off her blankets and groping for her boots.

Naia groggily peeked at her. "Giving up so soon?"

Aly quickly tugged her hair into a tight braid. "Red. He's been bitten, I think. I have to go to him." Aly spun in small circles as she finished her hair. "He's tainted with Canyon magic but hasn't been healed. There aren't any Protectors in Caridan, and the healing ointments won't cure a bite, only slow the poison."

Naia sat up, her curls a wild mess. "You're going?"

Aly dropped her arms and nodded. When she'd changed into her traveling pants and shirt and grabbed her canteen, she ran to the edge of the camp, Naia at her heels. "What am I doing?" she blurted, looking around. She pressed her hands to her forehead. "I must protect these people."

Naia stopped her with a lifted hand. "I'll protect them. You go."

Aly hesitated, then nodded. She trusted Naia, but her friend was not yet powerful enough to save all of these men, should the Zealots attack. "Give me a minute? I'll add some more spells."

Aly closed her eyes and spun in a circle, swinging her arms. She cast spell after spell, protecting the people in the camp. She cast a spell to herd all wildlife on a route around the camp—she didn't want the men frightened for no reason. She cast another spell to send any wandering sorcerers in a different direction, making it appear from the outside as if this place had no Wells to offer for magic. She cast one that would prevent any spoken spells from descending upon the camp.

The only attacks she couldn't defend against from afar were from the sorcerers themselves—their very bodies could be weapons. She had to hope they wouldn't target the camp while she was gone. It would only be a few days, and it wasn't like they'd be chopping trees down this time.

Memories of men falling, dead, at the lumberyard pricked her conscience.

But this was *Red*. She had to go.

By the time she was finished casting enchantments, her still-spinning cloak slapped against her legs. She opened her eyes.

Naia twisted one side of her mouth in what was either a forced smile or a restrained grimace. "I'll make sure they finish setting up camp and don't leave until you return. We have plenty of food, and the creek over there will be a fine water source. But do try to hurry. I'm not you, Aly. I'm no savior."

Haste was the only thought in Aly's mind, and then she was gone.

She leaped into the air, soaring straight up. For a little extra push, she drew energy from the trees as well as Alexander's small and muddied Well. The trees had deep, rich Wells, though dim in comparison to any human's. She'd take what they could offer. Aly needed all the power she could gather.

This would be the farthest she'd ever flown, and the fastest.

Please live, she commanded Red silently, fearing the effects of his untreated bite and dreading the possibilities of the disaster she was tempting by leaving Naia alone in the Crescent Forest.

But her decision had been made and her hand played.

I'm coming.

. . .

Two days later, dawn light peeked over the horizon, with its first gray tones powdering the night sky.

Aly charged forward, wind whipping through her hair. No matter how tightly she braided her hair, it always slipped loose with the wind. Alexander's Well wasn't the deep, rich source she needed for this kind of magic, so she fueled her flight with the energy from every tree, rock, and blade of grass within reach. She soared over houses, over fields, over trees.

Her stomach growled angrily. She hadn't eaten much since leaving the Crescent Forest. Red's Truthwell still roiled with something sinister that she couldn't pin down. He was in danger, and she wasn't there. There wasn't time to stop and eat, and she only slept a few hours, barely enough time to revive her weary mind.

Had he already descended into the Canyon? Was he being sucked in by the river's influence? Was something else happening to him?

These thoughts tortured her mind as she attempted to focus on her magic despite her growing exhaustion.

She pushed harder, knowing every second away from Red meant his pain and the spread of that poison. It was also dangerous to be this far from the king she had sworn to protect, but the spells she'd cast over him before she'd left for the Crescent would hold—they had to.

The truth was, despite what her vows demanded, part of her still was loyal to Red.

Theod, forgive me, she murmured between spells, hoping her actions weren't tipping toward violating her sacred vows to protect the king to whom she was Bound.

Caridan materialized out of the murky fog below. Dropping the spells for speed and enhanced aerodynamics, she angled downward. In seconds, she slammed into the middle of camp, her feet sinking into mud. The early morning mist swirled around her.

Her shroud kept her hidden, but her feet squelched in the mud as she stomped toward the tent with the red medic's symbol on it. Inside the tent burned Red's troubled Well.

She ripped the tent flap open and stormed inside. There he was, the rightful king, wearing a soldier's uniform and lying on a cot.

"Red!" she shouted, dropping her shroud and running toward him.

His eyes popped open. It took him several seconds to register who he was seeing. She knelt beside him on the ground.

"Aly." He tried to roll toward her, but his body lurched against something. Then she noticed the straps holding him down. She gasped. One of his arms was bandaged to the elbow.

"What happened to you? What's wrong?" she said, gently lifting his injured hand.

Before he could answer, she removed the bandage with a spell and cringed. Black streaks reached up his forearm.

Her eyes pressed shut. *If I hadn't Bound myself to Alexander, Red wouldn't be in pain right now. He wouldn't even be here!* Magic poured from her lips as she spoke the Maker's words, shaping the power with the precision of unchanging truth.

"How long has this been in you?" Aly asked as her magic sank into his arm. She Pulled from everything nearby, including the ground beneath her feet, but still the evil inside of him resisted. The temptation to Pull from Red's mesmerizing Well was almost too strong to ignore.

"Three days," he said.

It had taken her two days to reach him…and the delay had caused him great pain. She glanced around the tent. The dirt floor that had been spared from the rains, but boots had tracked in mud and created little grooves in the aisles. This was no pristine medic's tent. It was a disgrace. Several other men lay tied to their cots. Infections of the Canyon's dark magic could spread easily, as Red and Aly knew from Seb's experience only weeks ago.

"I'm so sorry," she whispered. She scooted closer to the cot, her knees sliding underneath the wool blanket hanging off the edge.

A feeling of despair weighed heavily on Aly as she stared down at Red in the dimly lit space. With another quiet spell, she protected Red from further infection, both the magical kind and the natural kind. She would do the same for the others in the tent before she left.

"Seb was attacked... They took him to Luxler," Red told her, his voice strained.

Her mouth opened in shock. "There are Protectors in Luxler. He'll be fine." She hoped it was true. "Elise was sent to Luxler," she added. "Alexander sent her as a courier to a Lord Chesterton."

Red frowned. "That's where they took Seb. I hope she doesn't betray him again while she's there."

Aly wished she could say something helpful about Red's sister, but the former princess was an enigma to Aly. There must be a reason for Elise's bizarre behavior of late, but Aly wasn't sure it would be sufficient to excuse her actions.

"You need a Protector here," Aly hissed, changing the subject back to the present situation. This place wouldn't last much longer without one.

Red's eyes fluttered shut as the healing magic mingled with his pain. "We were expecting two Protectors to arrive in a few days, but they aren't coming. That army heading toward Mardon—it has changed the king's priorities. The Canyon isn't enemy number one anymore. He's hoarding all the sorcerers in the capital."

Aly pinched her lips. "He sent me to train an army from the Crescent Forest," she admitted, watching as the black streaks faded from Red's arm.

Red grunted. After a moment, he said, "Was that Kassia's idea?"

Aly shook her head. "I don't think so. His mind is fragile, at best, but not all his ideas are from her. Grey thought it would be best if I was away from Alexander, and he—and Ondorian—convinced him to send me to the Crescent." She shrugged. "I only just arrived when I realized you were injured."

Red closed his eyes and lay back. As she held his hand and arm, she linked her fingers with his. He squeezed her hand and peeked up at her. "We've lost several men to the Canyon lately. Some of the men hold out hope that they may still be alive. I volunteered to search for them." At her bewildered expression, he added, "It's the perfect opportunity to examine the river again."

Aly pressed her fear down and let her forehead fall against his hand. His skin was hot as her magic pushed the infection out. Their trip into the Canyon had been a critical event, not only for themselves—it had been a small match laid against a well-oiled pyre. Because they had survived, the high priest had descended into the Canyon, and now the rightful king was planning to descend once more to the river. Tandera was shifting, ever so slightly, toward that dark abyss, and Aly sensed it was an inescapable slope.

When she looked at his skin again, black streaks lingered in his veins. "If I could simply Pull from your Well..." she grumbled.

"You're still powerful, even without me."

She looked away.

Red's eyes squinted in pain as he spoke. "Remember your

strength, Aly. You lost sight of my light once, and you still saved me."

She spied the ash blade glowing faintly on the ground beside his cot. The black vines of poison drained down into his fingers, but the toxins had been in him so long now that removal required more than a simple healing spell. She was extracting the poison from his blood, but poison from a Canyon beast's bite, when left to fester, resisted.

"I need more energy," she declared, snatching up the ash blade and staring at its flickering orange embers.

They'd practiced and practiced, trying to replicate her creation of this blade and of those irises in the palace garden that night. She had succeeded only once, when she made the peony outside of Lordan's palace. She'd thought it was something she'd done differently, but it was *him*. He was the difference. The blade in her hands pulsed with vestiges of magic.

There was a new brightness to the blade that she hadn't noticed before, almost like a lone firefly on a moonless night.

She inhaled and closed her eyes. *Please*, she pleaded with the Maker as she explored the energy of the blade with her magical awareness.

As her mind touched the energy there, she let out a muffled gasp. Like the peony she'd created in Vona, the blade's energy signature mirrored Red's own. She reached deeper into its energy and realized there was more power there than what a knife should hold. It was almost like a small bit of Red's energy had been captured in the item they had created.

She shouted out a triumphant laugh and ripped every bit of energy from the knife and drove the magic into Red's hand.

His hand glowed orange at first, then bright white. Light leaked out from the closed wound beneath his stitches. He howled in pain, and she pressed a hand to his chest to keep him down. The darkness funneled down to the wound, then with a final, pained exhale, the last of the poison evaporated from Red's body.

It was over.

The light in his skin faded, and he collapsed against the cot. The blade in her hand crumbled into white ash and drifted to the floor.

Aly kept her hand on his as he lay there a moment in a silence. Within seconds, they were breathing together in a steady rhythm. He twisted his hand and clasped hers, then drew it to his lips and pressed his mouth against her skin. Delighted heat bubbled up inside of Aly.

He glanced at the ash tumbling across the ground. "What happened to the blade?" he asked.

"I don't know." She stood, propped her chin on two fingers, and paced. "The knife...it's like it contained a small part of your Well. I don't know how, but it acted a bit like the box I created to contain your father's voice, only it contained a small bit of your energy."

Red tugged at his restraints, and Aly flicked them away with a quick spell. He sat up.

"And you could Pull it for your magic?"

The side of her mouth curled into a smile. "Yes." It wasn't as satisfying as Pulling from his bright Well, but it was the most she'd felt of his light since the coronation. "But I Stripped it. The blade is gone."

"Interesting," he said, rubbing his chin where a beard had grown. He hadn't shaved in a long time. It made his smooth, kingly face entirely different—more rugged and, somehow, even more attractive. "Did you just find a way around your vows?"

She blinked at him, pressed one hand to her forehead, and once again paced beside his cot, overwhelmed with this possibility. "This is...this is *incredible*, Red! I can bottle your Truthwell.

That's never been done before." She grabbed his wrists as he stood, her enthusiasm building.

Her face was close to his, especially once he leaned closer. He reached his hand up to the back of her neck. She wasn't ready for this intimacy, not with the excitement boiling inside her and the other injured men nearby, so she spun away. His hand trailed down the outside of her arm as it fell.

"You can't bottle it anymore, Aly."

She stopped short and spun back to face him. He was right. She'd made that blade *with* his Well. Now that blade was gone. How could they have had this amazing, unprecedented power at their disposal and *missed it?* Aly fisted her hand and knocked it against her forehead, groaning loudly.

The ability to bottle a Truthwell was undocumented magic, novel and innovative. People had tried and failed for centuries, yet somehow Aly had accidently accomplished it. If anything, magic was stronger when controlled and directed by truth. So, how could she have unintentionally managed this with her magic? With the ash blade, she'd needed a weapon to defeat her father. The knife had presented itself.

But was it truly an accident? She'd been trying to draw Red's light, to hurl his energy at her father in a way that would stop his attack. The knife had accomplished that, and it had preserved some of Red's energy within it.

What did I say that night? Aly tried to recall her exact words when the knife had materialized, but no part of her brain could remember the specifics of that spell. The peony had materialized when Red had fired rather unexpectedly at her head. She'd been reciting a simple line, over and over: *To some, truth appears as a fool's lie; to those in darkness, light is madness.* Fueled by magic, the Maker's words had reformed the bullet into a flower. It was certainly a foolishness she couldn't quite explain, but at least it hadn't been accidental.

Perhaps Theod had more to show her about magic than she'd ever expected.

"I've missed my chance," she whispered. "Even if I could do it again, I can't even Pull from you anymore. What a waste."

"What about those flowers at the palace? You made those with my energy."

She dropped her fist. "Alexander's wife cut them all for a display at a party." She sighed. "I can't believe I didn't figure this out *before*. We could have changed the world with that power."

He grabbed her hand. "We will still change the world. Even if not as Beacon and Beholder."

Aly frowned. "I'm sorry, but—"

"Ondorian said things happen for a reason. The *Verad* also says as much. If we really believe that, then we're both where we need to be. Maybe I'm supposed to visit the river. Maybe I really will find some hidden truth that will change everything." His hopeful eyes only reminded her that he wasn't hers to protect anymore. She couldn't very well zip away from the Crescent Forest every other day, especially once they engaged the Zealots. Red was planning to descend into the world's most dangerous place, without a Protector.

Aly tipped her head against his chest and, to her delight, he enveloped her with his strong arms. "I won't be able to protect you when you go down there."

With a finger, he tipped her chin up. "I know." Then he kissed her once, slowly.

When he pulled away, she had a hard time drawing her next breath. A low whistle sounded from somewhere in the tent, and Aly's blush deepened to a shade darker than Red's crimson coat.

She lowered her voice so the other soldiers couldn't hear them. "You can't travel into the Canyon without a Protector." An idea popped into her mind. "I could send Naia." Red lifted a brow, but Aly blazed on, consumed with the flicker of hope at her new idea. "She doesn't even want to be in the Crescent Forest. As soon as I return, I'll send her here to protect you." She glanced around. "All of you!"

"Aly, General Daniels said I was to leave as soon as I was healed. Already we've postponed the descent."

"Can you not delay a little longer? Only until Naia arrives?" *If she agrees to come, that is.*

Red sighed and shook his head. "I can try, but it's unlikely. The men down there, if they're still alive, don't have long."

Determined not to appear dismayed, Aly spun and marched toward the nearest injured man, touching his head and dousing him with healing magic. She did the same for the next and the next, wondering all the while how Naia could arrive in Caridan before Red entered the Canyon. When she finished healing everyone, a round of applause broke out.

One man started a chant of *long live the king,* and the others quickly joined in. Red's face beamed as he nodded appreciatively at the soldiers. They bowed and filed out of the tent, leaving Aly alone with Red.

"See," she whispered as he took her hand again. "They are loyal to you. You will win this nation back."

He pulled her to his chest. "I haven't given up that hope." After another short kiss, he added, "Thank you for saving us today. Now go, before Alexander discovers what you're up to." She hugged him, relishing the feeling of his arms around her, then followed him out of the medic's tent, where a small crowd had gathered in the small spaces between the tents. More applause greeted them. Every soldier bowed. Her face fell. She couldn't be their savior. She had orders from Alexander to train Zealots in the Crescent. These soldiers were looking at her and Red as if their danger had been erased and all was well in Caridan.

All was far from well.

Aly prepared her spells for flight and squeezed Red's hand one more time. She had to leave, but she wouldn't let these men continue on without hope or protection. She only prayed Naia would agree to come.

She *had* to, or these men would die.

12

ALY

Aly, half-starved and exhausted, collapsed in their clearing in the middle of the Crescent Forest. She rested her head on the grass a moment, trying to find the energy to stand. Her mind was so spent, she couldn't form the words of a spell to lift her off the ground.

Naia burst from a nearby wooden structure that hadn't existed four days ago. The entire camp appeared complete, aided by magic and many hands. "Aly!"

"Food, water," Aly muttered. She'd never gone this long without a proper meal, especially while expending so much energy and maintaining such intense concentration. Keeping her body level in the air required a lot of balance and core strength, and the mental focus necessary to keep up the spells—not only for her own flight but for the protection of the people here *and* the king's protection—left her brain in a dense fog.

Naia rushed to Aly to prop her head in her lap. "Water!" Naia shouted over her shoulder. Then she palmed herself in the forehead and snapped her fingers. It began to rain. "Oops." Naia shook her head and waved her hands. "Not that." She shot a hand toward a tent and within seconds, something bumped against the canvas, then ripped right through.

A cup soared into Naia's outstretched hand, sloshing its contents to the ground. She peered down into the mostly empty cup and grunted. "I'm still not good at this," she said. "Let's get you inside."

A man ran toward them with a canteen. He glanced at the wet ground and the cup in Naia's hand. Then he noticed the slit in the tent beside them. He rolled his eyes and handed Aly the canteen.

The lukewarm water trickled down like a healing tonic. But when Aly tried to sit up, her head reeled. Naia steadied her. The man who'd brought the canteen helped Aly stand.

Once she was upright, however, she shook them both off. "I'm fine," she said and stumbled toward the wooden building, Pulling gently on Alexander's distant Well to keep from collapsing again. Her mind yearned for a break from the myriad spells she'd been sustaining and the buzzing anxiety she felt at leaving Red and those soldiers in death's shadow.

She let out a deep sigh and sat at one of the newly constructed wooden tables inside the small room. She accepted a cup of water that was handed to her.

"Soup will be ready soon," Naia said hopefully, taking a seat across from Aly. "But here." She offered Aly an apple.

Aly gnawed on it, without concern for manners.

After three bites of apple, her vision started to blur. Suddenly, the table looked like a fantastic place to take a nap. She lowered her cheek to the table and closed her eyes.

She had made it back in two days, not allowing herself to stop.

Naia gently took the apple from Aly's hand before it fell to the ground. "What did you do?" she asked, stroking Aly's damp hair from her face.

Aly rolled her head so that she could see her friend. "I didn't stop."

Naia pursed her lips. "You didn't trust me to manage this camp?"

"No, you I trust. It's them." Aly lifted a hand and waved it in the general direction of the forest. "But...Red." Her voice trailed off. "Red needs a Protector. They all do." She again rested her head on the table. Before she could ask Naia to be the Protector Red needed, Naia spoke first.

"We have three," Naia said with an eager smile.

"Three what?" asked Aly, her mind trying to latch onto Naia's words.

"Three recruits. I found them myself." Naia sat back, proud.

Aly pried her face off the wood and yawned. "That's wonderful."

"I can tell you're thrilled."

"I am. I just need to sleep." Aly's eyelids drooped. "Oh, I also told Red I'd...send you to the Canyon."

"Oh, you did?" Naia balked. "Glad I was invited to that discussion."

"They need a Protector. Desperately." Aly stood, one hand braced on the table. "Seb almost died because they didn't have one."

"I thought you wanted me here, to help you train the Zealots?"

Aly nodded slowly. "I do. Or I did. But they need you more than I do. Red plans to enter the Canyon again." Aly didn't have the energy to discuss this, but her concern for Red kept her pressing for a response. "Please do this, Naia."

Shaking her head, Naia asked, "Do I have a choice?"

"You always have a choice. We can talk in the morning. Now, I really need to sleep."

Her friend watched her go. "Want me to bring you some soup?" she called.

Aly nodded and walked out.

From inside the small hut, Naia's voice rang out. "Of course I'll save your bonnie lad. I'll take any reason to get out of here."

The next morning, Aly's head throbbed when she opened her eyes. She whispered a spell and the pain evaporated.

"That's better," she mumbled, sitting up on her small cot. Already the nights this far north had a crisp chill, and Aly was grateful for the magic that instantly warmed her body. With renewed strength flowing through her rested body, she stretched and pushed her magical awareness outward, quickly checking in on Red, then scanning the surrounding forest for any threats.

Her mind snagged on three burning Wells right outside the enchanted border around their camp.

"Naia," Aly hissed, snapping her fingers at her sleeping friend.

Naia peeked one eye open. "What?"

"There are three Zealots, right out there!" Aly pointed.

"I know," groaned Naia, rolling over. "I told you I recruited them."

Aly paused, her hands in midair as she thought up another protective spell. "Right." She vaguely recalled last night's conversation. Her mind had been in a haze. Naia had agreed to travel to Caridan, which meant Aly would be left to train the Zealots all on her own. She'd wanted Naia by her side—the proof that a Zealot could master control, that Aly's teaching was effective.

Instead, she would have to accomplish this alone. Red's safety was more important than Naia's companionship.

Aly hadn't even removed her boots last night, but they were

on the ground beside her cot. She smiled over at Naia, who was exhuming herself from a heap of blankets.

"Thank you," Aly muttered.

"For what?" Naia's voice came out muffled.

"For agreeing to go to Caridan."

Naia rubbed her face with both hands. "Canyon beasts are preferable to this place."

Aly's skin prickled with anxiety as she considered Naia's words. The Zealots hated controlled magic. To train several at once could welcome disaster. She would be foolish to think nothing bad would happen. *It's a mad hope*, she thought with a small smile.

"Red has orders to descend as soon as possible."

Naia caught her meaning and frowned. "I can't fly as fast as you. I've only ever been able to fly over short distances."

Aly nodded passively. At least Naia was going, and that was all Aly could ask. She only hoped Red would be successful in delaying his departure a few more days.

"They are eager to meet you," Naia offered, switching back to the topic of the recruits.

"Food first." Aly's stomach rumbled.

Minutes later, they walked toward the small kitchen hut. "So, who are they?" Aly asked as they crossed the dew-dampened clearing.

Naia cracked her knuckles before responding. "There's Igor. He's the one who spoke to us the other day. He came back. Seems ready to learn. Then there are the other two." She let out a slow breath. "Rainbow and Zoraiya."

"Rainbow? That's really a name?"

Naia tilted her head at Aly. "It's Zoraiya you need to worry about. She's terrifying. Killed her entire family."

Aly stopped walking, mouth agape. "And she wants to train?"

Naia shrugged. "Says she does, but I wouldn't be surprised if she wants to kill us all."

"That's comforting."

"You're the one who agreed to come here and train these people."

Aly sighed. Even if she thought Alexander's dreams of a well-ordered Zealot army were far-fetched, she couldn't very well hide from the opportunity to help these people learn to safely conjure magic. "We can't leave them to continue killing each other, when we can show them a safer way to live. That would indeed be wicked."

In the kitchen hut, Aly downed an entire stack of griddle cakes slathered with jam. She gulped a cup of coffee before setting it down with a *thunk*.

"Feeling better?" Naia asked, twisting her big hair into a knot on top of her head.

"Yes. Let's meet the new recruits. And after that, you should leave for Caridan."

Naia's eyes widened. "I can't fly for two straight days. You know I can't concentrate that hard for that long."

She smiled at Naia, hiding her fears for Red's safety and the safety of the other soldiers. "They will appreciate your help whenever you arrive."

They walked into the clearing, passing through her enchantments and into the forest. Bugs leaped away from Aly's feet and spiderwebs crossed their path like tiny barricades that tickled their skin as they crashed through them. Excitement riddled with apprehension swirled inside of Aly as they rounded a massive tree trunk and saw three faces.

One woman sat on a rock, taking bites out of a leg of meat. The older man Aly'd seen the other day struggled to stand from his seat beside a tree. A tall, slender woman glanced over her shoulder at them from a few paces away. Magic crackled in the air. Instantly, a shield erupted around Aly and Naia just in time. Sparks burst toward them in angry explosions, sizzling off the pale magical shield Aly had erected.

"All right, then," Aly mumbled.

"That's Zoraiya." Naia stared at the woman shooting sparks at them.

The figure before them resembled a willow tree, long limbs arcing in graceful movements as the woman lifted both arms above her head, like a bizarre dancer.

Aly disliked having to meet her first students from behind a shield, so she stepped out from behind the magical barrier and stared directly at Zoraiya. Her actions established that she didn't fear this woman and that she believed her own magic strong enough to deter any direct attacks.

A few more sparks danced up into the branches overhead, but none aimed for Aly. "Apologies," Zoraiya cooed in a singsong voice edged with razor sharpness. "You startled me."

"Careful, Zor, you'll set the whole forest on fire," replied the man. He was wrinkled like a sun-dried mushroom.

That must be Igor. Aly's eyes traveled to the other person. *And that must be Rainbow.* Her eyes widened as she took in Rainbow's appearance. A woman as gnarled as tree trunks perched on a small rock, nibbling on her breakfast of roasted meat. Grease dripped down her chin, and her hair hung in matted dreadlocks. A small fire smoked near her feet and a few bones littered the ground.

Rainbow appeared to have skipped bathing for a very long time. A small drape of torn fabric hung across her chest and around her waist. She had scars up and down her arms: round, wrinkled scars and long, scratch-like scars. Despite a stab of pity, Aly tried not to recoil at the sight of this woman.

"This is Rainbow, Zoraiya, and Igor," Naia announced.

Igor finally pried himself off the ground with a few grunts, and brushed his hands down his sides.

"Nice to meet you," Aly said with a smile.

Zoraiya frowned and lowered her arms. Rainbow snarled into her leg of meat. Aly tried not to watch. Igor alone nodded at her greeting.

Zoraiya pointed at Naia as she spoke to Aly. "You changed her into one of you. Look at her now, all dressed and fancy."

"At least I'm not a murderer," Naia snapped at Zoraiya.

The woman's dark eyes narrowed. "My magic did it, so it wasn't murder. It was eliminating those who needed to be eliminated."

Aly's throat constricted. How could she combat lies *this* twisted? Was truth powerful enough to change a person who thought murder was acceptable?

She contemplated throwing up her hands and turning around to run. But even now, an army of these misguided people marched toward Mardon. Perhaps if she learned a little more about these people and their ways, she could discover a way to defend her city against them. Ondorian believed something could be learned from the Zealots, something critical. She couldn't give up before even starting.

Naia balled her fists. "What if I decide *you* need to be eliminated? Do you agree that wouldn't be murder?"

Aly flinched at Naia's words. She'd underestimated how being here would affect Naia's mental state. The woman was already relapsing into the fidgety, snappish person she'd been when she first arrived at the lumberyard.

Zoraiya sniffed and looked at her dirty fingernails. "You and your pathetic *chained* magic couldn't hurt me."

Naia raised a hand and sliced through the air. A precise line of flames danced around her legs, then snaked around Zoraiya's feet, finishing up by making a perfect heart shape in the dead leaves. With a *snap*, Naia put out the spell. "What you see as chained is actually free. You think of control as a hindrance, when it provides more power than you've ever known."

Everyone stared at the ground where the flames had been. Aly caught a flicker of fear on Zoraiya's face. Perhaps that was a step toward respect.

Igor, who couldn't stand perfectly straight, placed his hands on his hips, neck craned up to look at Naia. "You can take the madness out of us," he said, voice shaking.

Naia gestured to Aly. "She can. Not me." She lifted both hands. "I'm no teacher."

"I can teach you how to apply your magic in safe ways," Aly agreed. "I can teach you its full potential." As the words left her mouth, she knew she had gone too far. The first statement was fine to say, the second was too much.

Zoraiya turned around and smashed her fist into the broad tree trunk behind her. Splinters of wood pelted out in all directions, one of which entered Zoraiya's neck. She stuck her hand to her skin and yanked out a large splinter. Blood oozed down her collarbone, and she let out a string of curses. She flung the splinter down and kept her other hand pressed to her neck.

Aly flicked a finger at her side, uttering a healing spell.

Zoraiya lifted her palm. Her neck was no longer wounded. She grunted at Aly, which must have been her particular way of saying *thanks*.

Training an army for Alexander was going to be even more difficult than Aly imagined.

"Why are you here?" Naia asked, voice low and edged with anger. "Why, if you don't want to *learn* what she has to teach?"

"I'm curious. That's all," Zoraiya replied. She looked at her hands innocently. "I'm not here to be converted or to change my ways. I merely like knowing what happens in my forest."

Naia crossed her arms. Rainbow sucked the last of the juice

off of the bone she was chewing and tossed it to the side. Aly blinked down at her. Naia had begged Aly to take away her magic—she'd wanted so badly to change. These people didn't seem to have the same urgency to change. There was so much that they needed to be unlearn before she could start to teach them what she knew about magic.

But to do so, Aly needed to understand what they had been taught. What originally prompted the belief that magic should never be controlled or contained with disciplined thoughts?

To Naia's mind, Aly whispered, *Go. Red and the others need you. I will be all right here.* Naia scratched the side of her head and shot Aly a skeptical look. *It'll be fine. When you fly, don't forget the spells for aerodynamics.*

Naia laughed. "You're using big words again," she said aloud. "You know I have no idea what you're talking about."

Zoraiya lifted a brow. Rainbow picked at something on the ground.

"Oh," said Aly. She was constantly forgetting Naia's lack of formal education. The woman was smart but had never read a book in her life. She was learning to read, but it was coming along slowly, considering the interruption of prison and her general distaste of study.

"It means traveling faster with less resistance," Aly muttered, unsure why they were having this conversation out loud, but hoping it showed the three Zealots that Naia was still learning, that she still *wanted* to learn more.

"Ah." Naia nodded. "I think I can finesse a few spells to do that."

"Good, because if you don't, you'll be exhausted just from the wind pushing you all day."

Igor cleared his throat. "Traveling a long distance? You could try burning. It worked for me once."

Aly and Naia pinned startled gazes on him.

"I think I'll pass on burning, but thank you," Naia replied, already marching out of the clearing.

Igor shrugged. "The fire didn't hurt me. Only the landing."

Aly didn't know how to respond to that. Before her friend vanished from sight, Aly shouted, "I will check in with you in the morning!" *Theod, keep her safe.*

Igor tilted his head as he examined Aly. "If she is traveling a long way away, how will you check in with her?"

Aly blushed. Perhaps it would be good for her students to know the power of controlled magic, even if it was something only she could do. "I can see...energy signatures across large distances." She wasn't sure if these people were ready to call energy sources by their proper name: Truthwells.

Zoraiya's mouth twitched in an impressed but annoyed way. "Fancy," she snarled.

Looking at Zoraiya, Igor, and Rainbow, Aly realized training them would be different than training Naia. Naia had come to her desperate for a change. These three possessed a curiosity about her abilities, but it was unclear if they had the drive needed to discard their old philosophies about magic.

And something else burned deep inside of Aly, a tiny, nagging fear that perhaps *she* wasn't ready to learn from the Zealots. What if they revealed a lie behind something that Aly had believed her entire life?

If she expected them to see the falsehoods in their own beliefs, she must be willing to do the same.

Aly cleared her throat and sat down, tucking her skirts around her legs. Forcing away her worries about Red and her concern for Naia's safe arrival, she focused on the people right before her. "Before we do anything else, I want to learn from you three," she said, ignoring Zoraiya's crisp laugh. "Tell me what you know of magic."

13

RED

The morning of their descent dawned slowly, blanketed beneath another day of steady rain. Canyon winds whipped against the tent and woke Red long before the reveille.

General Daniels had agreed to wait until the weather cleared, but after four days of incessant rain and unusually heavy fog, Daniels had told them their time was up, no matter that the beasts grew bolder when the mists never lifted. The general was under pressure from the king to carry out this rescue, and even with his liberty to arrange the mission according to his best judgment, they were pressing into delinquency if the soldiers delayed much longer.

Red couldn't wait any longer for Naia's arrival, if she was even coming. Messages from Mardon spoke of the impending attack and increased sightings of Canyon beasts. Hearing about his city from Captain Mitchell's rather dry daily announcements left Red with more questions than answers. Apparently, Kassia had dispatched Bulvarnan troops, who had joined forces with the Zealots, making the coming attack most certainly an act of war on Kassia's part. Mardon would likely be in an uproar, demanding the king rectify the troubling situation.

As he dressed for the descent, Red thought of his home. He was certain the people of Mardon blamed the soldiers here at Caridan for the number of beasts slipping into the country. It had always been that way, only now Red was one of these soldiers. He also knew the usurper had crafted this dangerous rescue mission for two reasons: to appear like he had some semblance of control over the situation in Caridan, and to punish Red by sending him back into the Deep. Though Red had volunteered, Alexander would have ordered his participation in this mission one way or the other.

Red stared at Seb's vacant cot as he buckled his belt. He trailed his fingers over the empty hilt at his waist where the ash blade used to sit, its absence a tangible reminder that Aly was gone and likely couldn't return any time soon. Nearby, Amos dressed quietly. Neither one had said a word. They were descending into the most dangerous place in the world today, the very seat of evil, and they did not have a Protector with them. Their time for delaying was over, and Red's hope wavered as he pulled on his crimson jacket.

Jakes had apparently had another night of little sleep, as his cot was already empty, his boots and pack missing.

When Red finished lacing his boots, he stood. Amos saluted him.

"I'm glad you're coming with me, but I also wish you weren't," Red said.

"To the death, sire," Amos said with a nod.

Red offered his man a close-lipped smile, and they filed out into the damp, gray morning. Canyon mist hung thick as pudding in the morning air. Thunder rumbled in the distance.

They found Jakes in the mess tent, huddled over an empty tin cup. His red eyes confirmed his lack of sleep, and his posture conveyed he'd tossed expectation to the wind in the face of their looming mission.

Red patted him on the back as he took a seat beside the Comforter. He was grateful Daniels had insisted on a Comforter descending with them. It was better than going without any magic at all.

Jakes flicked a few crumbs off the table. "Why me?" he asked.

"Why not you?" Red asked, sipping his coffee that tasted little better than black ash mixed in hot water. It was nothing like the coffee served in the palace, and it was a shame that these men, fighting to their deaths to protect their country, couldn't enjoy a decent cup of coffee in the mornings. But Red discarded these thoughts as he looked at Jakes. This man needed to believe in himself if he was to have any chance of helping them all survive the Canyon.

"There are twelve Comforters in Caridan," Jakes replied. "Daniels should have picked one of them."

Red had seen Jakes perform magic. The fierceness with which the man moved his arms when he conducted his spells suggested that he believed in those spells more than the other Comforters did. There was a gusto to his movements, an intensity to his gaze, whenever he cast a spell, even if it was only to warm the men's tents at night or cool them during the heat of day. Jakes pushed away the mist of the Canyon like it was an enemy only he could fight.

"Do you know why Daniels chose you?"

Jakes shrank into himself. He seemed embarrassed by the biscuit crumbs still on his lap and brushed them off quickly. "Because I'm expendable."

"No," scoffed Red. "He chose you because he sees something in you that he doesn't see in the others."

Jakes' brows lifted, but he remained silent.

"You care about magic. And you care about the people you

protect." Red needed to light a fire under Jakes to motivate him. As long as Jakes believed he was worthless, his magic wouldn't fulfill its greatest potential.

"I'm not that great of a fighter," Jakes said.

"You have magic."

"So do the others."

Red leaned forward, resting his elbows on the table. "Your spells are more effective. When you cool the camp during mealtime, it works faster, and I feel it more deeply inside of me than when the other men do it. When you push the mist away in the morning, it withdraws from you like it fears *you*. It cannot come through your spell. I've seen it. It hits a wall and rolls right around the camp."

Jakes' cheeks darkened at the compliments. "You've been here a week."

"And in that time, I've noticed that your magic is different. It's that noticeable."

Neither spoke for a moment, then Jakes asked, "What if I can't do this?"

"You will," said Red. He leaned in. "There's more to what we're about to do than what I can tell you. Your mission in the Canyon is not only to protect us, but to *get out*, no matter what happens. Watch. Listen. Make absolutely certain that you bring back the truth of what you see down there. The rest of us will be more likely to see what isn't real, what isn't true, but because you have the advantage of *seeing* truth and lies, you're less susceptible to the Canyon's evils." This was only partially true, as many sorcerers had succumbed to the darkness of the Deep, but he wanted Jakes to believe it, to hold fast to the light. "Do you understand?" He fixed him with his most commanding stare.

Jakes nodded. "Yes, sir."

After a quick cup of coffee and a cold biscuit, Amos and Jakes followed Red out of the mess tent. They collected their

fourth team member, a soldier named Private Gibbs, a silent
and imposing figure. They then walked to the edge of camp,
where the Comforters' spells ended, where the four men
paused. At the top of the walls, summer gave way to the
eternal cold of the Canyon as chilled air wafted up from the
Deep.

"Let's go," Red said, and stepped beyond the camp's border.

As soon as they passed through the enchantments, freezing
gusts bit at Red's face. Only weeks ago, when he and Aly and
Veeter Yin had descended, it had been nowhere near this cold,
the wind nowhere near as violent. In that short amount of time,
the Canyon had changed, and not simply due to the season. The
Deep didn't want him to return.

Red stopped walking as unbidden memories slammed into
him. Tilting walls, black water, pain, madness.

A slap on his back brought him back to the present. Amos
smiled and pressed Red forward. Red nodded appreciatively and
ignored the knot of tension in his stomach. He'd only made it
out last time because of Aly. But this time he must stay strong
and in his right mind.

They soon reached the small path along the top of the walls,
created by both beasts and soldiers alike. As Caridan moved
periodically, the soldiers on scouting duty needed a way to stay
oriented, should the mist become too thick to see. They'd taken
the same trails the animals used and turned them into small
footpaths along the Canyon's walls.

The men began the short trek to the long, white bridge that
spanned the eerie depths. The first village on the Bulvarnan side
was a few hours' walk. If the paths created by these villagers
were truly as worn as Ondorian had said, they could reach the
bottom by midday, if they made good time. Still, that wouldn't
leave long to search and ascend before nightfall.

Red looked at the other men and offered a thin smile.

"Things change down there, gentleman," he said, staring down in to the murky depths. "Don't trust what you see."

Jakes shifted his weight. "Then how are we supposed to find our men?"

Red hitched up the pack on his shoulders. To everyone else, this might feel like a death mission, but not to Red. The Canyon would not be the end of him. He would find out its secrets and, somehow, bring those back to Ondorian—and to Aly. His first descent had been to save his own life. This time, he was descending to save everyone else. Whatever Ondorian sensed about the Canyon, Red was determined to find it, and with it he would bring an end to the poisonous corruption leaking from this place.

He blinked at Jakes. "If you think you are going mad, start speaking truth."

"That's too simple," Jakes muttered.

"It worked for me."

Jakes shot him a skeptical look but gave a curt nod.

"Any room for one more?" called a familiar voice from behind them.

Red turned and gave a short, shocked laugh as Lord Weston Grey strode toward them through the mist. He wore soldier's attire and a smirk on his face.

"Grey," Red said, stepping up to shake his hand. "What brings you out here?"

Grey shook hard. "Let's just say I know a number of the king's couriers, and I caught wind of a ridiculous mission to send soldiers down into the Canyon. Somehow, I knew you would be one of them." He winked at Red. "I couldn't let you have all the fun."

"Fun?" asked Jakes. "And who are you?"

"Weston Grey, pleased to meet you, Private." Grey leaned

forward and whispered to Red, "And a holy man we both know mentioned you might need a Protector."

Another man walked from between the trees and stood beside Grey with crossed arms and a stern face. He wore huntsman's clothes and carried a pack.

Grey grinned. "I'm not sure if you've met Antony, my Protector."

Amos let out a whoop that mirrored Red's relief. "Look, boys, we ain't gonna die!"

A wide grin spread across Red's face. He wouldn't question further why Grey was here or how he'd found out about their mission. The important thing was that they were no longer descending without the aid of a Protector. He should have trusted Grey from the beginning.

"Oh, and Private Gibbs," Grey said, turning to the tall man who had said nothing at all since leaving the camp. "I'm your replacement. Report back to Daniels. It's good to see you."

Gibbs nodded, then rather unexpectedly saluted both Red and Grey before departing.

"Good man," Grey said, watching Gibbs depart. "Saw some pretty awful things in his day. Doesn't talk much anymore."

"Does Alexander know you are here?" asked Red.

"Alexander knows what he needs to know. Nothing more. Nothing less."

After that, Amos and Jakes walked with a new lift in their step, and Red also couldn't help but hope their mission would be a success. But even with a Protector, finding lost men in the Canyon wouldn't be easy.

The first skittering sound of claws on stone shattered the men's veneer of confidence.

"Form up!" Grey shouted, his pistol in his hand before Red had even reached for his.

Red drew his gun and mirrored Jakes' motions, putting his

back to Grey and his weapon toward the thick fog. Amos fumbled into position as well, neither of them having been properly trained for this before being dumped out at Caridan, as if they were offerings to the Deep.

Antony stood beside Red, his hands lifted to perform magic. He pushed his palms outward and the fog dissipated all around them.

The black fur of a woodwolf darted among the nearby trees.

"There," Red called, alerting the men.

Antony chopped a flat hand through the air, skewering a tree branch through the wolf's back. The animal yelped, raged against its binding, then went still.

Red shivered as the chill from Antony's magic breezed across his shoulders. Amos and the others turned to look at the dead animal.

"Thanks," Grey said, slapping a hand on Antony's shoulder.

Antony merely nodded.

"But toss it, man, it's already freezing up here," Grey continued. "My fingers are so numb, I'd be no good with my knife if he'd gotten that close."

Antony frowned at Grey. "He didn't get that close."

Grey's face was paler than usual, and he rubbed his hands together at his waist to warm them. Antony strode ahead, leading the way to the bridge.

"Be thankful for Aly," Grey muttered to Red. "She never made me cold. Well, not unless she meant to."

Grey fell in behind Antony and marched off into the swirling fog. Red stared at Aly's former tutor. He was right, not many sorcerers were as skilled as Aly at extracting energy from a person's Truthwell. Red recoiled at the memory of being partially Stripped once. He'd felt awful for an entire day, until Aly had healed him from afar. That was before he'd even known she existed.

Then a thought occurred to Red: When and if Naia arrived, she wouldn't have anyone to Pull from. She'd been training on Truthwells supplied by nature, but to truly become a Master, she would need a human Truthwell to fuel her magic. Aly had almost paired Naia with a young man from the lumber yard before he'd died that awful night.

Either way, Naia's arrival would only be added protection for them, and he hoped she had no trouble in her journey.

The rest of the trek to the bridge was blissfully uneventful. They were still on schedule to reach the Canyon bottom and have several hours of thin daylight left to search for the missing men.

Their feet made hollow sounds on the long, white bridge. Suspended over the eerie depths, memories of Aly siphoning his death curse plagued his mind. It was in those moments that he'd discovered how much he truly needed her. He missed her constant presence, but he shoved down the feeling and scanned the mists for any signs of flying lyths.

They passed the halfway mark. Then the trees on the Bulvarnan side could be seen vaguely through the fog.

Amos stopped walking so abruptly that Red bowled into him, knocking him to the stones. As his body rolled over, wide, distant eyes stared out of Amos' face.

"Amos!" Red knelt beside his friend.

"Step away," Antony intoned, descending in one swift motion to hover over Amos.

As Red leaned back, not yet ready to abandon his man, Antony placed two hands on Amos' chest and muttered snippets of the *Verad*.

Amos gagged and sat up. "Oy, what happened?"

"It is no matter," Antony responded before Red could speak. "Let us proceed."

"I thought I was bleeding to death," Amos admitted, rubbing his hands down his front, as if searching for a wound.

Red helped the soldier stand and patted him on the back, offering an encouraging smile. The lies of the Deep did not always play by the rules of logic. Though Antony had saved the man quickly, Amos continued to be jumpy and became progressively more irritable as they walked across the bridge.

When they set foot on solid ground once again, Red breathed a sigh of relief. Amos bent down and patted the earth with a trembling hand.

"I didn't miss this gloom," Grey grumbled, looking up at the sky, where the sun barely shone through dense clouds.

A shape darted out of the mist, straight at them. It was a man, blade lifted.

Red drew his pistol, but something pushed the man aside. A block of ice *thunked* to the ground beside the stumbling man, and Jakes whooped as if pleased with his strike. In seconds, the man had regained his balance and was running at them again, snarling like a mad dog. Then he changed.

The knife sailed through the air as the beast dropped to all fours and took the form of a bear. It lumbered toward them at incredible speed.

Antony leaped into the air and snatched the knife as it tumbled end over end. As he dropped back down, he hurled the blade back at the bear. It sank into fur that quickly shifted into scales.

The bear was a snake before Antony's feet hit the ground. The blade dropped away, but the wound from the knife left a flopping gash in the snake's side.

Red aimed and fired. The snake's entire body blasted sideways at the shot. It wriggled, and one more bullet from Grey's gun ended the lyth.

Silence hung over the men as they glanced around, weapons ready.

When no more attacks appeared imminent, the group fell into line once more. No one put away their weapons this time.

Red stared at the back of Antony's cloak, grateful for the man's presence. Without him, their chance of survival was almost non-existent.

Two hours and another dead foxblood later, they stood at the top of a small footpath that hugged the steep Canyon walls and dropped off quickly into the mist.

"I will lead," Red declared, stepping forward, ignoring the spike in his heartrate.

"No, you will not." Grey stuck his arm out to halt Red's movement. "I brought Antony here so you wouldn't get yourself killed, Your Majesty. Let him lead."

Red wanted to refuse, but Amos placed a hand on his shoulder. Antony bowed politely and stepped once again ahead of Red.

The descent was slow. Scree littered much of the path, and every few steps, someone was stumbling, sliding toward the precipice. The sounds of small stones bouncing down into the gloom reminded them how far they would fall should they slip. Soon, the men walked close enough to each other to reach out a hand should they lose their footing.

"Some path," Jakes grumbled.

The adrenaline and fear pumping through Red's veins made the trek even more exhausting than it might have been. Every step presented a threat, every rustle of fabric sounded like the approach of a beast.

Red took a small swig of his canteen, careful to replace the lid without dropping it.

Behind him, Jakes said, "Good idea." Sounds of a cap

unscrewing preceded the loud sound of gravel crunching. Amos, who brought up the rear, yelled.

The entire group turned, careful not to lose their balance. A squirrel leaped off of Amos' shoulders and alighted on Jakes'. Instantly, it clawed its way to the top of Jakes' head.

Amid his screams of surprise, Jakes lost balance. Amos and Red lunged for him at the same time. Red caught his arm and Amos, with one solid swipe, knocked the furious squirrel into the abyss.

When they'd pulled Jakes back onto the trail, he sat against the rock wall and hugged his knees. "Was that a lyth?"

Grey shook his head. "I don't think so. It would have tried to change if it was."

"I've never seen a squirrel attack before," Jakes said, brow pinched. He was sweating and breathing heavily.

Antony whispered a short healing spell and the scratch marks faded off Jakes' head.

"I have," Red said. Everyone looked at him. "In the Crescent Forest, there are strange beasts affected by the magic of the Zealots."

Grey nodded, as if that made perfect sense.

"I hate this place," Jakes admitted, shivering despite his sweat. "You should have picked someone else to come."

Red squatted beside Jakes. "I hate it too. But we owe it to the men we lost to search for them." *And we owe it to the world to uncover whatever the river is hiding.*

"Men you don't even know," muttered Jakes.

"No," Red agreed, "but if they were brave enough to fight for Tandera, then I know them well enough to know they are good men."

Jakes accepted Red's hand and stood. "Not all who fight this war are noble and good." He looked at Grey. "Some come here to die or to forget."

At that moment, the telltale sound of claws climbing bare rock met their ears. It sounded like a stampede, rising from the depths of the earth to swallow them whole.

Red and Grey exchanged a glance. Weapons drawn, the men pressed their backs into the rock wall and watched as innumerable dark shapes surged toward them from the darkness below.

14

ELISE

Sebastian Thorin snored from the seat across from Elise, his slumber uninterrupted by the gentle rocking of the carriage. Seb's horse, the one that had belonged to her deceased guard Maurice, had vanished into the night. Large paw prints were found by the stables at the inn where they had stayed the previous night.

Greta had been in near hysterics when she'd found out. Her earlier stress had drained her energy, leaving her in a deep sleep as they rode home. The return journey had been faster, given their need to make haste to return to Mardon well before the large army that approached the capital.

As they neared Mardon, they'd learned from other travelers that the Zealot army had not turned back or disbanded, as Alexander had hoped. Instead, Mardon's situation had taken a decided turn for the worse: Bulvarnan soldiers had joined the Zealots, creating an imposing force.

In fact, Elise still didn't understand *why* the Zealots were marching on Mardon. They chose to live apart, to remove themselves from the cares of society.

But now Bulvarna had joined the Zealots, Elise assumed it had something to do with the fact that Red and Aly had killed the Royal Sorcerer of Bulvarna. They had traveled north to search out peace, but the army marching toward the capital proved Red's actions had backfired.

Elise understood well that good intentions didn't always produce good results.

Carriages lined the road into Mardon, causing an unusual slow-down.

When their carriage didn't move for several minutes, Elise leaned her head out the window, curiosity pinching her brow. These people assumed it would be safer in the city, where more Protectors lived. But Elise knew enough about magic to know that Protectors couldn't save every soul in the capital if the army attacked.

We need Aly here. She stared out the carriage window as people on foot streamed by, carrying bushels or baskets or children. Elise's heart ached at the sight. She wanted to open the door and tell them all to turn around, to seek safety elsewhere. But hope was often the only safety people really needed. She couldn't take that from them, and her words would do little but add fear.

She knocked her head against the cushioned seat, ignoring the way it tousled her hair.

"What are you doing?" Seb asked, sitting up. He wiped a hand across his chin, a brief look of embarrassment flashing on his handsome face. He spied Greta's still-closed eyes and seemed relieved the other woman hadn't noticed his drool.

"Look at them," Elise replied.

Seb leaned toward the window, his shoulders close to Elise as he craned his neck to peer back toward Mardon. The carriage lurched forward again, tipping Seb's off-balance body into Elise's lap.

One of his arms caught his weight against the seat behind her, putting his face a mere handsbreadth from her own. His knees tangled with her skirts.

A single moment was all it lasted, but heat blazed up Elise's skin, flushing her pale face. A curl of a smirk toyed at Seb's mouth, then he was leaning away, taking his warmth with him as he resumed his seat.

"Sorry, Princess," he muttered, with a glint in his eye that said he was anything but sorry.

Greta had woken with Seb's tumble and now kept her eyes decidedly averted out her window, for which Elise was grateful.

Elise watched Seb for a moment. His expressions alternated between playful and more serious, hoping to make her flinch or smile or look away, but Elise had forged her expression like iron.

Eventually, he gave up and looked back out the window. "Anything new since Red and I were banished?"

Arrows shot from Elise's eyes, but her mouth never moved. Her heart trilled and her blood heated with the shame she still felt at the memory of all she'd done to him, the memory of the wounds he'd shown her.

Elise never expected she would *feel* again, not after what Lordan had done. Her heart had died and she'd chosen what had looked like the only path forward—a path that led her deeper into the dark.

But the way her heart pounded now, the way her cheeks flamed when he'd fallen into her, proved her heart was far from dead.

And that terrified her. A heart that lived could again be broken.

"You knew the risk for helping my brother."

His eyes narrowed. He'd been expecting her to say something else. "Why, Elise? I have yet to discover what caused such a change in you."

"You never knew me, Sebastian Thorin. You cannot speak to how I have changed."

He leaned back and crossed his arms. "Fair enough. But as a member of your personal guard, I *will* know you. I will riddle you, Princess, if it is the last thing I do."

Her cheeks blazed, and she hated that her skin always belied her deepest emotions, the ones she couldn't bury with skilled composure. "Your myriad devotees will not approve," she quipped, chin lifted. She must remember who he was, *what* he was. *Never again*, she told herself, *will I let a man cast me aside*.

"You assume I can maintain *devotees* now that you've effectively labeled me a traitor?"

"Do you not?" she spat without so much as a blink.

"I thought you didn't want to get to know me?"

She scowled. "I don't." Was that a tiny laugh from Greta? Elise deepened her frown.

"You only let your grammar slip when you are truly ruffled. Have I *ruffled* you?"

Her every muscle ached to turn away, to look out the window, but that would show defeat. Instead, she held his agonizing gaze. "Not in the slightest, soldier."

To Elise's great relief, Alexander apparently wasn't going to throw her out of the palace for failing to garner one of Chesterton's Protectors. Maybe it was Carolyn's influence, as funneled through Edward, that prevented it. Whatever the cause, Elise was grateful as the palace gates opened to admit her once again.

As they drove up to the residential wing's entrance, Carolyn darted down the palace steps, skirts in her hands.

Elise poured herself out of the carriage, ignoring Seb's hand as he offered it to her, and embraced her sister.

"Guess what?" Carolyn blurted, before even returning a greeting.

Elise pulled back from Carolyn, holding her by the shoulders and leveling a hesitant, curious gaze at her.

"Lordan has returned!"

Air escaped from Elise's open mouth, and her eyes inadvertently flicked toward Seb, who was watching her. "Why?" she spat a little too loudly. She swallowed and clasped her hands in front of her waist, her heart thumping madly against her ribs.

"Alexander asked for his aid. He has six Protectors with him!"

Elise missed everything that was spoken next. Things were never so simple. Weeks ago, Lordan had dodged Red's plea for help with a feeble attempt at sending aid, which was essentially useless for how slowly it would arrive in Caridan. No, the King of Refere was here to *gain* something.

A chill traveled down Elise's spine as she wondered what Lordan could stand to gain from this arrangement. She would discover what it was.

The palace hummed with the frenetic energy that typically accompanied royal visitors, but this time it was quadrupled by the efforts to fortify the palace from the oncoming attack. Enchantments hung like glowing tapestries over every external door and window. The palace grounds sparkled with the addition of so much magic in the air.

As the thinly attended evening meal concluded and the guests meandered toward the ballroom, King Alexander approached Elise with clipped steps. He rather gruffly offered Elise his elbow, which she took with a hesitant smile.

"In your absence, I have secured for you a most advantageous match." His voice sounded anything but pleased, though a gleam of satisfaction twinkled in his brown eyes. "You will wed King Lordan and be forever out of my way."

Inhaling sharply, Elise opened her mouth to reply as her

stomach flipped upside down. Grey had said he could arrange such a match, but she'd assumed he had been overstating his influence. Had Grey planted this idea in Alexander's mind?

"You will accept his proposal tonight," Alexander added, startling her from her thoughts.

She blinked as the king walked away. She hadn't even said a word.

In some ways, this was what she'd wanted. This marriage would provide the perfect opportunity to enact revenge on Lordan while providing Tandera with crucial intelligence from a foreign court. But her insides whirled like a ballet dancer. As she took in the ballroom, her eyes landed on Seb. Since he was a member of her personal guard, would he accompany her to Refere?

The knots in her stomach twisted tighter.

Carolyn danced up to grab Elise's arm. "What was that about?"

Elise couldn't bring herself to speak, so she shook her head.

The ballroom was bedazzling, so much so that one might forget an army of untrained sorcerers would reach the city within days. Streamers of pure golden light crisscrossed the ceiling between the chandeliers. Magic also wrapped the room in walls of suspended white flower petals.

Carolyn allowed Edward to steal her away to the dancefloor, where the first dance commenced, leaving Elise alone at the edge of the room.

Walking along the perimeter, Elise scanned the attendees until she spotted Lordan in the nearest corner, chatting with Lord Wyndall. Meeting her eye, he lifted his glass to her. She spun angrily away, slamming into Seb's chest.

"Oy there, Princess."

She shuffled backward. "Pardon me." She tried to step around him, but he matched her pace.

"Dance with me."

"Never."

"Toss it all, Elise, war is headed our way. I'd like to dance with *you*."

The way he said her name brought her eyes finally to his. There was no humor there. No smirk at his lips. Only the most surprising emotion imaginable: desperation. Why on earth would he want to dance with the woman who betrayed him?

Still burning with anger, fear, and confusion at Alexander's arrangement, she boldly stepped closer to Seb. "Fine."

His brows lifted. "Fine."

Taking her hand, he led her to the dancefloor, where they bowed to one another. He lifted her hand like a king might lift a queen's and placed his other on her waist, firm and strong. With a step forward, he moved her across the dancefloor with well-practiced agility. Within seconds, her breath came faster. Dancing with Seb was like dancing with a summer brook: all fluid motion, quick but never rushed, perfectly timed and elegant at every step.

She smiled as he released her into a fast spin. Catching her waist again, he held her closer, the warmth of his palm bleeding through her thin dress. She could see how one dance with him would be enough to melt most women.

She wrenched her eyes away and spotted Lordan watching her. *Perfect.*

At the next spin, she stopped almost against Seb's chest, ignoring the way his hand tried to press her farther away, to the respectable distance. Rebellion and joy and fear and hope twined within her as she longed to enjoy the dance without the fear of war or marriage to a man she hated.

"Princess," Seb whispered in her ear, "while I normally would not oppose a beautiful woman trying to press closer, I wonder if you are only trying to make a particular acquaintance of ours jealous. If so, you're doing a marvelous job. He's staring at you like you're tonight's roast duck to be consumed."

Elise's eyes partially closed at the warmth of his breath on her cheek. "There is no need for me to make him jealous. Not when Alexander has taken it upon himself to arrange our betrothal."

Seb's arms stiffened as he missed a step, jostling them in the middle of the dancefloor.

After the song ended, they stepped apart. She curtsied and he bowed. When she looked up at him again, his eyes searched the room, then stopped. His face hardened into a frown, and Elise spun to see that he was glaring at Alexander. In that moment, Seb looked ready to return the king's whippings, or worse.

When he marched away, Elise stared after him, tracing his movement along the ballroom wall until he slipped out of an external door and disappeared into the night.

"My lady, may I have a word?" Lordan's silky voice sent shivers down Elise's spine—or maybe it was the knowledge that the man she hated most was about to propose.

She forced a smile as she curtsied politely and accepted his arm.

Lordan led her out of the ballroom. Following the mirrored hall, they made the short walk to the grand palace library. The library opened up onto a terrace that connected back to the ballroom, and the lights and music of the party could be seen from the tall windows lining the back wall. Elise kept her eyes on the double glass doors that offered a chance of escape, if only in her mind.

When Lordan gestured for her to sit, she steeled herself to face him and turned. She did not sit.

"You look lovely, my darling," he began.

How dare you call me 'your darling'. Elise clamped her hands together at her waist as her insides roiled, but she managed a demure smile. If her time as a spy had led to this moment, she would not let this opportunity for revenge pass her by, no matter how much her mind and body rebelled at the idea of marrying this man.

His handsome face disgusted her now. He'd had two decent chances to offer her his hand, and both times she would have taken it happily.

"Alexander has communicated to you his wishes?" he asked in a honeyed tone.

Through clenched teeth, she said, "Yes. I have been waiting for this for some time."

She could see the countless possibilities for subtle, slow revenge the way she could visualize a scene she wanted to paint before she began. But her chest ached with disappointment. Hers would be a lonely life, devoid of love, if she travelled to Vona. Now that she faced this reality, she couldn't bring herself to want it. It had sounded good in theory—now her palms were sweating as she tried to think of any way out of this.

Lordan's jawline flickered, as if he were grinding his teeth.

"You seem nervous," she cooed, trying to drown out her own fears. "In Vona, you vowed you wanted me." *Admit it, you fool. You never did love me.* Her cheeks blazed with anger, but she hoped he saw it as the blush of a flattered princess.

He grabbed onto the back of a tall chair, the skin around his knuckles losing color.

"So where is this promised proposal?" asked Elise, coyly stepping toward him. She would draw this out, make him squirm a little.

Elise saw light flickering at the glass doors leading outside. A surprised guest shouted an apology and shut the door with a rattling clang. They both stared at it a moment, and though it didn't move again, Elise heard another small click. Perhaps the surprised guest had shut another door nearby.

Lordan's throat bobbed as he looked at her. "Fine, Elise. Will you do the honor of becoming my queen?"

Elise stared at him, ignoring the part of her that raged at the injustice of his tardy proposal. In truth, it was a blessing from Theod that he had not proposed when she would have accepted. "I do not wish to rule Refere." It was all she could think to say as her mind whirled.

"Of course, it is merely an honorary title. You know this." He stepped over to her, his hand gripping her upper arm. "Do not think to refuse me."

Rattled by his sudden aggression, she spat out the words screaming inside of her head. "I—do—not—love—you." She tried to jerk her arm away, but his grip was strong.

"Yes, you do." Arrogance laced his tone.

Elise stumbled backward in shock as he leaned forward to kiss her. She shoved him hard in the chest. "What is wrong with you?"

Rage flashed on his face and he grabbed her arm, pulling her close.

Something inside of her had snapped, and all her rage at his dual rejections blazed out of her. "I *hate* you. I hate you for almost killing my brother. I hate you for the way you discard people you do not need. I hate you for how much I cried over you. I hate you for using me like a tool to accomplish your ends. I hate you for making me *believe* you a second time. And I hate you for how much *hate* you've brought out in me."

"You can't refuse me now, mad or not." As Lordan's lips crushed hers, hurting her face, something yanked him away.

"You will not touch her!" yelled a deep, familiar voice.

Elise watched in amazement as Seb hurled the King of Refere across the sitting space like he was a child's ragdoll. Lordan stumbled into another reading chair, toppling it. On the floor by the entrance to one of the adjacent reading rooms was a discarded book, splayed spine-up on the floor.

"Are you okay?" Seb asked, rushing to her. His hands fluttered out, as if to touch her, then dropped back to his sides.

"I'm fine," she breathed. She wasn't, but she would be. For some reason, she couldn't look at Seb or Lordan, so she stared at the patterned rug.

"Come on," Seb begged as Lordan stood.

"You will both be punished," the Referen king said flatly.

"We do not need to be the ones to leave," Elise said. "He will leave." She lifted her chin.

"Yes, I will. And you will be wishing you had accepted my offer when those Zealots attack and you are left to witness a slaughter in the streets."

Elise swallowed. "We will win without your help."

Lordan stormed out of the library, leaving Seb staring at Elise, shoulders rising with his rapid breaths. Elise held his gaze, her pulse beating at breakneck speed.

"Thank you," she muttered, still in shock.

He walked toward her, and her skin growing hotter at his nearness. Her hands trembled at her sides, so she clasped them, fumbled her grip, then clamped them together at her middle. They were still shaking as Seb reached out and took one hand, then the other, gently, as if she might shatter.

The heat of his hands on hers consumed her thoughts. He brought her hands up to his chest. She was shaking now for an entirely new reason, and her heart beat so violently she was certain he could feel her pulse.

"Elise," he whispered. "Are you all right?"

"I'm fine."

His face was as serious as she'd ever seen it. "Did he hurt you?"

"No." *Not exactly.*

He must have sensed the hesitation in her answer, because he pressed forward, allowing their clasped hands to be the only barrier between them. His strong frame was close enough to lean on. She closed her eyes to keep from staring at his chest.

For several breaths, he held her hands against him, until her breathing calmed. How could he comfort her, after what she'd done to him?

The door to the library burst open and King Alexander stormed in.

"Liar," he sneered.

Lordan strolled in behind him, looking smug.

Elise and Seb hopped apart, but there was little point. Lordan stepped forward, clapping his hands dramatically, in an *I-told-you-so* way that boiled Elise's blood.

"How dare you betray me," Alexander sneered. "I should have thrown you to the streets weeks ago." His bald head gleamed under his golden coronet. "You claim to hate your brother, but you are in love with his best friend? Pah! You are full of lies."

Elise's stomach dropped. He had said *love*. She glanced at Seb. His brow was both angry and expectant, a storm cloud before the deluge.

All her work to gain Alexander's trust had flown out the window when she'd shoved Lordan and yelled at him. Now, she was left with nothing. She doubted there was little she could now do to serve Tandera.

"And you," Alexander continued, one finger jabbed in Seb's direction, "one beating was not enough to staunch your treachery. This time, you will not survive. Tomorrow, at noon, you will be given forty lashes, then delivered on a cart to our approaching enemies. They may do with you as they wish."

Before Elise could collect her thoughts enough to speak, Alexander whirled back to Elise. "Your selfishness astounds me. You will marry King Lordan, and we will have his sorcerers at our side when those armies attack. I will arrange for a ceremony at dawn. Until then, you are forbidden from leaving the grounds. The matter is concluded."

Alexander spun, hands cupped neatly at his back, and marched out.

15

RED

Red ripped his knife out of the side of a woodwolf, one half the size of a grown man. Ignoring the howls of the animal, he spun and kicked the jaw of a foxblood cresting the ledge at his feet. They were coming in waves, rising straight up like spiders scrambling up a wall.

Grey shouted. Jakes shot flaming rocks from the path down into the darkness, picking off the beasts as they climbed. Antony hovered above the melee, hurling magic at the Canyon beasts.

It wasn't enough.

Amos fell on the gravelly path. A snarling woodwolf descended on him.

Red couldn't reach him. The path was too narrow and a foxblood stood in the way. Red grabbed the furry neck of the foxblood as it leaped and rammed its head into the stone wall beside him. The animal flopped on its back, giving Red time to drive his blade into its belly. He shoved the animal off the ledge and rushed to help Amos.

With a bolt of bright light, Antony killed the beast attacking Amos. The wolf collapsed onto Amos' chest.

"Amos!"

Red rolled the beast off the cliff and sucked in a breath at the sight of his friend's mangled face. *No.* "No!"

When Red pressed his fingers into Amos' throat, there was no pulse.

A growl pulled his attention away from his friend. Red turned just in time to punch the next beast in the snout, not caring that the animal's fang pierced his skin. He screamed a foul sound into the whirling mist as the loss of his friend tore at his insides.

"Behind you!" shouted Grey.

Red couldn't turn fast enough. He sensed a looming shadow, then heard a *thump* as something collided with the beast.

Grey tipped sideways and fell off the path. His bearded face stared blankly up at Red and Jakes as he plunged over the edge of the precipice.

"Grey!"

Then Antony was diving into the mist.

Red whooped as Antony flew after Grey, but his hope splintered as another monster charged. This one, a large panther, shifted as it crested the edge of the small path. "Lyth," Red shouted at Jakes, who battled something behind him.

Taking on the form of a badger, the beast darted for Red's ankles with uncanny swiftness. But before his knife could plunge into its back, it changed its shape again. Now as a mouse, it skittered away then quickly became a ferret, launching up Red's leg. He howled as it bit his wrist.

Jakes shouted spells behind him. Red groaned and bent over double as a shard of ice sank into his shoulder, but finally was able to yank the ferret off him. He slung the animal into the void, watching as it shifted into a bat and departed.

Not fair.

He slumped against the rock and clasped his shoulder.

"Sorry!" Jakes shouted, hands shaking. "I tried to hit the animal."

"Can you stop the bleeding?" Red asked, even as the bat fluttered back into view. It shouldn't be able to shift much more—lyths only had so many shifts in them before they needed to remain in one form for a while.

A searing pain in Red's shoulder answered his question. Jakes closed the wound with a rock so hot it glowed orange.

He tried to grit his teeth but a yell escaped. As the bat circled around, heading straight for them, Antony's white cloak rose in the fog with Weston Grey in his arms. Antony landed on the rock ledge, setting his employer down carefully. The bat attacked the sorcerer's ear, destroying it in seconds.

Antony's scream iced Red's blood. Before Red could swat the animal or Antony could bespell the beast, it changed again.

Taking the form of a wolf, it toppled Antony, its fangs finding Antony's throat. In the struggle, the beast slipped over the edge, dragging Antony with it, jaws still locked in a death hold.

"No!" Red lurched, but his hand grasped nothing but air.

Antony's limp frame fell into darkness with the wolf. A pulse of energy rippled in the air, and there were no more sounds of claws on rock. A deep silence settled over the Canyon.

On his hands and knees, Red stared after the sorcerer, assuming he would rise any second. Grey sat on the path beside him, eyes watching the abyss. Jakes leaned back against the rock, breathing loudly like a winded racehorse.

After several minutes, Red leaned back, trying to process what had happened, who they had lost.

Grey stared blankly out at the dark depths, but said nothing.

Red stood, turning to avoid seeing Amos' body. "We can't stay here," he said to Grey, offering him a hand.

Grey's eyes, always so hard and distant, were rimmed with tears. Red hid his surprise and gripped hard as he helped Grey stand. For a moment, Grey didn't release Red's arm. Red nodded at him, a silent acknowledgment that they had both lost someone.

After a moment, Red announced, "We will return the body to camp, then return to complete our mission."

Grey responded by smearing his hand across his cheek.

"We can't continue," Jakes muttered.

"Sure we will. We've got you," Grey answered with a wink.

And just like that, Grey had slipped back into his masked self, the man who never let anyone see beyond his constructed persona. Jakes didn't reply, but he bent down to collect Amos' arms. Red waved him away. He would carry his friend.

It was only four hours until nightfall when they returned to the place Amos and Antony had died.

Jakes had grown considerably more fidgety as the daylight waned. "Can't we just come back tomorrow?" he pleaded, glimpsing the blood still staining the rocks on the path.

"Daniels was clear," Red responded. "We're to conduct as thorough a search as we can. We haven't even reached the river. We can hardly say we've searched at all."

Jakes grumbled something.

They walked in silence for hours, grateful for the reprieve from attacks. Despite the small flicker of hope that still burned within Red that the man had survived, Antony never returned.

By the time they reached the bottom, little light fell into the depths of the Deep. Mist obscured their sight as the three men finally set foot on the sloping floor of the Canyon.

"We made it down, gentlemen," Red declared, ignoring as best he could the throbbing pain in his hand and shoulder. Jakes used a cooling spell to numb the wounds, and the ointments they'd hastily applied were doing their part to slow the poison.

Thought the poison sank in slowly, Red knew it would soon begin to affect his mind, as would the Canyon.

"Now the fun begins," whispered Grey as they spread out on the misty floor of the Deep.

"One sweep of the area, then back to the path. We will not spend the entire night down here," Red reminded them.

An hour later, Jakes and Grey still walked on either side of Red, insisting that Red remain in a protected position, despite the fact that none of them was safe down here.

The beasts had left them more or less alone since the massive attack on the walls above. Jakes had killed a lone foxblood before it had reached them, which had given the Comforter a needed boost of confidence. Red still hoped to discover what Ondorian was looking for—a new truth about the Black River—and he needed Jakes to be able to bring that truth back, should he and Grey not survive.

Red would have to tell Amos' children that their father was not coming home. He would have to tell Amos' wife that the man she loved, the man who provided for her family's wellbeing, was gone. Red couldn't shut down the emotions that crashed through him even as he tried to shove these thoughts away and stay alert for danger. He needed to save these men and extract them from the Deep—and investigate the river, whatever that would entail.

He hadn't actually thought about *how* he might uncover some lost truth about a river feared by most individuals. As they walked cautiously through the mists, he sifted through everything he'd ever heard or learned about the Black River. All the lore, all the poems, all the historical accounts pointed to the river as a source of power. Most considered its power to be evil, but, not everyone, as evidenced by the Bulvarnans in the Forgotten Cities.

The river had been uncovered when Usrich split the earth centuries ago, unleashing the water's evil into the world. But Ondorian believed there was something about the river that had been lost to history. Lies obscured the truth, and the river was a known source of lies, whispering falsehoods into the minds of those who sought its power. What if the river itself had propagated a lie that now the entire world held as truth?

It's not the water, Red corrected, recalling Ondorian's words. *It's something in the water.* He determined to discover what it was.

Soon, they reached the banks of the Black River.

"Over there!" Jakes hissed, pointing up ahead.

A small fire burned in the distance. The three men approached warily, knowing that the Canyon could lie to them in many ways, even visually.

Two men in crimson uniforms huddled near the fire, but leaped up with rocks in hand at the sound of Red and the others approaching. Excepting the rocks, they appeared to be weaponless.

Red lifted his hands. "State your names, soldiers," he said. Then, at their silence, he added, "I am Frederick Windon, son of the late King Gevar, and this is Lord Weston Grey and Private Jakes. We are here to help you return to Caridan."

The men exchanged a glance. One spoke. "The king? Here. A strange lie for the Deep to throw at us now, after all the others."

Red sighed, but internally, his chest surged with hope. These were two of the lost soldiers, he was certain. "I am no longer the king. Lord Benedict Alexander was crowned weeks ago at the official coronation."

The soldiers looked confused. "Lyths don't talk. They can't be lyths."

"We are not. We are really here," Red replied.

"Don't come any closer!" the two soldiers warned. "We've seen all manner of people down here, and every one of them turned out to be a vision or a lyth."

Jakes stepped forward. "I'll show you we are real." He knelt beside the river and a perfectly round sheet of ice the shape of a plate formed in the water. He reached down and grabbed it.

"Don't!" Grey and Red and the soldiers shouted at once.

Jakes held up the sheet of ice. "See? I can do magic. We are real. Lyths can't do this."

The hand that held the ice was already turning black.

Jakes dropped the plate of ice, where it shattered at his feet. He examined his hand, as black, snaking lines reached toward his wrist.

"You can't touch the water!" One of the soldiers ran toward him. Apparently, Jakes stunt had at least convinced the men they weren't having more visions.

Jakes trembled.

"We need to get out of here." This kind of poison couldn't be healed by antidotes or medicine or even magic. Ondorian's darkened hand was proof of that.

The taller soldier added, "After we saw them, we knew not to touch the water. I mean, we knew before that, but after what happened..." He trailed off, his gaze drifting as if seeing ghosts.

"Saw who?" asked Red.

One with a balding head and Esvedaran accent answered, "We were captured and brought here by the very Protectors who'd vowed to keep us safe. They looked different, as if their minds had been taken over completely. It was—" the man shivered, "—unsettling to say the least. They took us, and they brought us to the river, almost like sacrifices. The others, they shoved them in the water. Dropped them from above, actually. We saw them turn black and drown. Then we watched as the

Protectors walked into the water, muttering something. They went in and never came out."

Red cringed. The Protectors who'd left Caridan had indeed tossed themselves into the Deep. He'd thought those who could Truthpull were more immune to the lies of the Canyon, but apparently that was no longer true, if it ever had been.

He needed to find out what the river had been hiding from them. What lie had it bled into the world?

How can a river lie? Red wondered, backing closer to the bank. This was the issue that had always bothered him, though he'd never voiced it, never given it much consideration, until Ondorian voiced the very same idea. The Black River was the source of lies, but water was only water—wasn't it? A shiver of fear coursed through him, but he shook it off.

"How did you two survive?" Grey asked the men.

They glanced at each other again. "When we saw what happened to the others, we killed the Protector holding us."

Grey rubbed his arm, where a small rip in his sleeve was soaked with blood. He hadn't even spoken of his wound. "I see. But how have you survived without drinking the water?"

"We only drank from the puddles beside the banks. When we ran, we splashed through enough of those to know they were harmless."

"Interesting," Grey said, looking down at one such puddle.

Red knelt beside Grey, inches from the river's edge. "Ondorian said the water isn't evil," he muttered in hushed tones. "Something *in* the river is evil. I need to find out what." This puddle was safe to drink, proving the priest's point. Red dipped his hand into the puddle. Nothing happened. *Strange.* He spun on his ankles and glanced at the choppy river water. What was in the river that called grown men to sacrifice their friends and then themselves to it?

The water harmed Jakes. It had also harmed Ondorian, but

perhaps not as much. It had, in a strange way, saved Red's life by absorbing his death curse. Then, when he'd plunged his foot into it after the curse had left him, the water had not left Red with any noticeable damage or changes at all. And the Protectors who'd left Caridan had willingly drowned in the water, as if called to it. The river certainly seemed to have *preferences*, even agency. It did what it wanted, harmed who it willed, and affected the minds of people in varying ways.

There was one way to find out if Red's previous encounter with the river had been a fluke. He moved to catch his balance with his hand, dipping only his fingertips in the water.

No one behind him appeared to notice.

The cold water stung him. He jerked his hand away, but the tingling sensation remained in the ends of his fingers. He stared at his darkening skin with horror.

Why had the river left him unharmed before? What had been different then?

Aly.

He'd been Bound to her magic. Now, he was not protected by her.

He stood and shivered inadvertently in the cool air, shoving his hand into his uniform's pocket. The river contained something wicked. He couldn't conjure magic to peer into the water's energy.

A line from the *Verad* sounded in his mind. *Shadows lengthen and stretch toward the dark, seeking night's embrace and the removal of their bounds.* Only at night were shadows one with their surroundings. It spoke of the way evil sought company and multiplied when among more wickedness.

The river was calling more wickedness to itself. And there was only one way to do that—with a voice.

Red's fingers pulsed where the water had touched his skin. Now, more than ever, Red was certain there was an entity in the river, using the water as a host, of sorts. How this was possible, he had no idea, but nothing that happened in the bottom of the Canyon ever made sense.

The river was the darkness, pulling shadows toward it. The Protectors, who'd once held to the light, had somehow been enticed into the river's embrace, perhaps seeking a power that was not theirs to claim, a removal of their bounds, so to speak. Red shuddered at the thought. Could the river truly be multiplying its power as it drew sorcerers to its dark depths?

"Every time we try to leave, the animals hem us in," said the Esvedaran soldier, drawing Red's attention back to the scene. "It's like they want us to stay. They haven't attacked since the last time we tried to find a way out."

Red looked at Grey. This could be why the animals hadn't attacked since they reached the Canyon floor. Unease flickered in Red's stomach.

He wasn't certain if what he'd discovered was enough. But short of jumping in the river, Red wasn't sure he could determine the nature of the entity in the river. These men needed to reach safety, and night was swiftly approaching.

Grey looked at Jakes. "We have a Comforter with us."

The soldiers exchanged wary glances but nodded.

"There is a path an hour's walk that way," Red said, pointing back the way they'd come. But suddenly, the area around him looked entirely different. The rocks hadn't been like that before, had they? "Or maybe it is that way." He pointed a little to the left.

Grey cleared his throat. "I think we came from that direction." He pointed far to the right. Even as he pointed, Red's mind played tricks on him, causing the scenery to shift as the mist hovered all around them.

"Great," Jakes mumbled. "We're lost in the Deep."

16

ELISE

Elise slipped out of bed and padded across her empty sitting room to press her ear against the external door of her suite. Boots still marched the hall outside. She'd expected as much. A shimmering spell had been placed over her window, though it was much too high to contemplate leaping to freedom. Suppressing excitement, she tried the secret passage tucked into her bookcase.

It clunked like it too was barred.

With a small huff of annoyance, Elise spun toward her bedchamber. There was one other option.

Elise hurried into the small alcove that housed her armoire. She could only barely squeeze behind the massive piece of furniture. Her fingers trailed the paneling for the small notch.

"My lady, your dress has returned from pressing."

Greta's voice startled Elise, and she scrambled out of the small space as the woman entered Elise's bedchamber.

Greta attempted a small smile but erased it when she saw Elise's wild expression. "I apologize, my lady, but I saw your door was open, and I wanted to ensure the gown was hung up. I thought you would be sleeping." She quickly hung the gown in the armoire and curtsied. "I will return at dawn to arrange your hair."

When Greta left, Elise exhaled loudly.

She listened for the outer door to click shut, then she shuffled back to the armoire and squeezed behind it. A clunk sounded softly, signally the release of the latch on the secret passage hidden behind one wall panel.

Another relieved breath hissed from Elise's open mouth. This passage wasn't on any palace maps. The other one was the official escape route, which enough staff members knew about to make it less than secret, but this passage was the one her father had instructed her to use, should she truly ever desire to disappear. She drew in a steadying breath and slipped inside the stone passage.

There was a reason she'd only entered this passage once.

Her shoulders scraped the cobwebbed walls as she spun to close the door behind her. Her gossamer gown snagged on the rough texture. But the nightgown was part of her ruse, should she be caught. A ruse she hated, but one she needed nonetheless.

Walking sideways, one hand out to bat away the spiderwebs and the other hand feeling along the wall in the pitch dark, she hurried toward the door that would lead to a forgotten drawing room along her hall. From there, she would need to be quick and careful to reach her destination without being seen. Leaving the palace altogether was out of the question, considering every gate and the entire grounds were sealed against her exit—as Alexander had informed her via Greta.

The darkness made every step feel perilous. For the past two hours, her thoughts had drifted through ways to avoid what she was about to do. Seb's face peppered her thoughts, but she couldn't afford to dwell on him, or the way he'd held her hands, until she'd found a way to resolve this farce of a marriage. Seb would face more beatings because of her, and he didn't deserve such.

She'd vowed to be a storm, but she'd been no more than rainless clouds drifting about with the wind. It was time she picked a target and struck with all the force at her disposal. The dagger sheathed at her thigh felt foreign and the leather rubbed her soft skin.

A pang of sadness twisted in her chest as she thought of all the times she and Red had played hide and seek. In a way, she was still playing that game. But the consequences were much higher now.

After what felt like the hundredth cobweb, the wall beside her ended and her fingers bumped a wooden surface. She fumbled over the edges of the door, frantic to find the latch. Finally, her knuckle struck against it and she was spilling into a narrow stairwell that creaked with her arrival.

She took three deep breaths, grateful for the space.

Soon, she was back in the main palace hall, slinking along as silent as a cat. She grabbed a candle from a burning candelabra and slipped behind a large tapestry, into the main system of hidden passages. These were wider, less cobwebbed. She raced quietly along, counting the wooden beams.

After eight, she was fairly certain she was at the right room.

Her blood pounded in her ears and thrummed in her chest. She eased the panel open that led into a gold-hued bedroom.

Wrong room.

She eased the panel closed and moved down a little farther, to the next hidden door. This time, the room before her was decorated in blues, lit only by the moonlight outside. If Lordan had his sorcerer searching for Truthwells, she didn't have long.

The massive bed was dwarfed by the enormity of the room and the arched ceiling. Lordan's deep breathing was the only sound. How helpless he appeared in sleep.

She eased her nightgown up and gripped the handle of her dagger, padding to the edge of the bed.

The Referen king lay squarely in the middle of the mattress, which meant she would need to climb on top of the bed to reach him. With a quiet inhale, she pressed one knee into the covers and launched herself—as quietly as possible—toward his throat. The cool blade of the dagger landed against his skin and his eyes popped open.

"Nice to see you, my dear," he muttered. "I didn't realize that you had taken to politics so well." His handsome face flashed a wicked smile. "Do it," he snapped.

"I am not here to hurt you," she hissed.

"Your actions suggest the contrary."

The door to the anteroom burst open.

"Sire!"

"Tell him you invited me," Elise whispered through clenched teeth. From the door, the guards might believe she was merely a guest here. The dagger was lodged against the king's neck at an angle that no intruders could see.

Lordan's blue eyes pierced her even in the dim light. Without taking his eyes off her, he snarled at the sorcerer in the doorway. "Leave us!"

The sorcerer blurted an apology and closed the door.

"I need to know what Alexander promised you," Elise said.

Lordan snorted. "Why?"

Elise answered by pressing the blade a little harder against his neck.

"This little game is nice and all, Elise, but why does it matter what he said to me?"

"You would not have agreed to this. I know you. I called your bluff in Vona, and now this? He offered you something."

Lordan narrowed his eyes and leaned into her blade. "Why

do you care, Elise? What are you going to do with this information, should you obtain it?"

She hated how he was asking the questions. "I want to ruin Alexander. I will do whatever it takes, and whatever he offered you could be a—"

He shifted quickly, grasping Elise's wrist with a firm hand. She resisted, and the knife nicked his neck.

"Stop it, woman, or I won't be able to tell you anything." He pressed two fingers into the cut, pushing her weapon away as her eyes widened. "Yes, I'll tell you."

Lordan extricated himself from underneath her and sat up, his nightshirt annoyingly loose and open. Suddenly she realized she was in bed with a man, and in a nightgown no less. She scrambled backward, nearly falling as she stepped onto the floor.

"He's blackmailing me," Lordan said matter-of-factly. "He knows I was involved in your brother's poisoning. That's the kind of knowledge that can rip a man off his throne, even in a country that loves their sovereign."

Elise blinked in surprise. "How does he know?"

"Kings have knowledge of things they shouldn't know," Lordan retorted with a shrug.

"But only Kassia and her little puppets knew anything about that handkerchief."

"Ouch. Are you calling me a puppet of the Lady Wolf?"

Elise's expression soured. "You claimed you did not know it was cursed."

"I didn't. I promise. I have no desire to off any of you Tanderans." He tilted his head in a somewhat condescending way. "So, the only ones who knew were Kassia's people. Does that mean Alexander has Kassia's people in his midst? In his confidence?"

Elise tapped her lips with a finger. "He seems to receive mental messages from someone other than the Royal Sorcerer. It could be that he is receiving intelligence from one of Kassia's puppets, perhaps one who has turned against her?" This was a stretch, but how else did Alexander know about Lordan's involvement with the handkerchief?

Lordan stroked his smooth chin. "But he's using that information against me, which is a strange move for a man with a desire to create alliances and build a strong foundation for his own stolen throne."

Elise nodded. "So, he is not smart."

Lordan laughed. "Indeed. Or..." He scooted to the edge of the bed and flipped the covers off. Pacing in his nightclothes, he continued. "Or, he's working *with* Kassia. Intentionally or... under compulsion. Think of it," he said at Elise's bewildered expression. "He condemns Red after what happened in the north. He ousts your brother, then immediately turns on me as well with this blackmail scheme. Tandera and Refere have always been allies. I haven't perhaps upheld that relationship as well as I could have, but Alexander's utterly ruining it. What if, in his travels to Bulvarna, he incurred some sort of curse as well, and he's being manipulated by Kassia even now."

The possibility danced in Elise's head. If Tandera's king was under Kassia's direct control, the looming battle was sure to be a bloodbath for Mardon. They had to discover the truth if they had any hope of victory against Bulvarna.

Elise tapped the dagger still in her hand against her leg. "Why did you tell me all this?"

Lordan leaned forward. "Because you said you want to ruin Alexander." He flashed a joyless smile. "No one blackmails me and gets away with it. Now, come. We don't have long to plot this man's demise."

17

ALY

"Hold it," Aly called, darting toward Igor, who held a trembling ball of light in front of his face. Darkness made his light all the more impressive to behold. They'd agreed to practice late into the night and rise before dawn, given how quickly the army bore down on Mardon. If Aly was to have any soldiers at her side when she was called back to the capital, they had much work to do.

"That's it!" She circled Igor with her arms out, in case his magic went awry. Her stomach danced with delight at the sight. *Naia, I wish you could see this,* she mused. She'd send Naia a message later. Flying required unwavering concentration, and Naia was still a novice. She hoped Naia would reach Caridan sometime the following day.

It had been three days since Naia departed, and Red's Well was surrounded by a pitch darkness that could only mean he'd already descended into the Canyon. But a most surprising addition to his party eased Aly's constant worry over Red's safety: Grey and his Protector had descended with Red. This information left Aly better able to concentrate on teaching the Zealots how to hone their erratic magic by employing words and mental focus.

She'd promised to devote her entire attention to her students during the day and only check on Red before or after their practice sessions. The wait was agonizing, but watching her three students provided ample distraction.

"Now, see if you can move it," Aly prompted her pupil. Rainbow and Zoraiya were practicing simple cooling spells on a pile of dead leaves, cocooned in separate, glowing shield spells to contain the occasional dramatic explosion of unintentional magic.

The ball of light in Igor's hands fizzled. He looked at her with tired eyes, sweat dripping down his wrinkled face. She blinked in surprise at how exhausted he appeared. Magic wasn't physically difficult, only mentally taxing, and the cooler evenings of early fall were already upon them. Aly had to dispel an occasional shiver with her magic.

"Are you straining your muscles when you move your arms?" she asked.

He looked at his hands. They were calloused and scarred. Igor was missing the smallest finger on his left hand. "I don't mean to," he said, looking utterly defeated.

Aly offered him a weak smile. "It's all right. The forcefulness of your motions doesn't increase the effectiveness of your magic. The movements simply help us stay focused."

He sat down on a large log. Aly sat down beside him in the dim light from the shield encompassing them.

"I'm sorry," he said. "It is difficult."

"I don't think I'm the best teacher," she admitted.

Igor shrugged. "This magic is easy for you to do, which makes it hard for you to break it down and explain it to those of us who don't understand it."

Aly chewed her lips. He was right. She was good at Truthpulling, but she had no idea how to teach others how to master their magic, especially when their understanding of it was so very different from her own. Naia, despite her distractibility, had been an exceptional student, hardly asking for her to repeat lines from the *Verad* and shaping them to her own spells after the first week of practice.

Igor continued, "We didn't grow up with controlled magic the way you did. It was very different for us."

Aly closed her eyes and saw her adoptive mother's face. She missed her mother every single day, but when she allowed her mind to travel back to their cabin in the woods, the pain pricked sharper, so she seldom revisited these memories.

"Tell me about how you grew up," he said. "You asked how we learned magic. Tell me about how you learned it. Start from the beginning. Then maybe I can learn it the way you did."

Caught off guard by her sudden wave of emotion and his insightful words, she inhaled a sharp breath. "That's a great idea," she agreed, but a flicker of reluctance gnawed at her. Dark memories lurked in her past, sad memories, of loss and fear and loneliness. But there were also memories of love and family and finding her place in this world.

Her bad memories were nothing compared to Igor's. To Rainbow's.

Aly leaned forward, settled her elbows on her knees, and inhaled. The night creatures croaked and hummed all around. Lightning bugs blinked in and out among the trees.

"You told me that you grew up thinking of magic as sentient, as having a will of its own," she said, trying to connect with what Igor had told her days ago. "That whatever magic accomplished, whether painful or scary or good, was meant to be. I grew up not fully understanding what magic *was*. I was told by my mother that it was bad, that it corrupted people by the power it supplied. She'd seen that firsthand, and I'd almost died as a baby as a result." Aly rubbed her neck absently, fighting down the sadness of discussing her mother. "My mother wasn't wrong, but she wasn't fully right either. I heard from the priest in my town that magic was a gift. I had a hard time reconciling those two ideas for a very long time. I hid my magic. I shoved down the temptation to use it."

Igor groaned. "Ah, I know how stifling that is. I too quell my desire for magic at all times." He shrugged. "Until this week, that is. I find it safer that way, but it is a view many here disapprove of."

Aly looked into his eyes and saw the weight of restraint pulling at his aging face. She had to teach him that ignoring his magic wasn't the answer. "Even from a young age, I saw ways to help with my magic. I healed my mother of her pains, kept our cabin warm in winter, and helped lift heavy items." A smile broke on Aly's lips at the memories. "My mother never wanted me using magic, though I think she turned a blind eye in the winter. Eventually, I started trying my magic on others, healing them. It worked. I always thought of magic as good. As useful." She sighed. "And when I finally learned that Theod gave us magic for those very reasons, it was like I'd discovered a truth buried deep inside me that I'd always known was there."

Igor stared at his scarred hands. "I can see now why you like magic so much. For you, it has been a beautiful thing. For me..." He didn't finish his sentence.

Aly looked away from his hands, too afraid to ask about his past. She shifted her body to face him. "But the interesting thing is, we both think of magic as having divine purpose. You were taught that magic has a will, and you are the vessels of that will. I was taught that magic is a vessel to accomplish Theod's will. I'm merely meant to carry out what he's told us to do. I was taught that truth is what lights the world, and that lies have brought darkness into every place. Magic is Theod's gift to us to dispel the darkness."

It was several moments before Igor spoke. When he did, his voice rattled slightly, as if shaken deeply. "All I know of magic is darkness." After a few heartbeats, he added, "Do you know what Naia said when she found me? She said, 'Do you want to live free from fear?' I have no idea what it feels like to live life unafraid." He looked at Aly with a flash of clarity in his tired blue eyes.

A wave of compassion surged through Aly. Her fears while growing up were nothing compared to this man's.

"These shackles—" Igor lifted up his hands "—have held me for long enough. I want to let them go, but I fear I'm going to hurt you. I fear I'm going to hurt anyone I come in contact with. If there is a way to free me from this fear, then I want it."

Words evaded Aly as she stared at Igor. She understood now why Naia never spoke of her past. She didn't want to talk about the harms she had inflicted or those inflicted by others. These people offered praise for both wonderful and terrible things, believing magic itself to be a god. There was no sense of right and wrong for them. And yet, Naia had known something was wrong with her former way of life. Igor knew it too—as if the truth was inside of him, buried beneath the weight of a lifetime of lies.

Aly swept a small tear away. "I can teach you." She grabbed his hand. "You can be free."

Zoraiya let out a feral scream that made Aly's heart leap. She lunged for her other pupil, who stood inside Aly's protective barrier, dancing over a pile of hot coals.

With two great sweeping movements, Aly disabled the shield, lifted Zoraiya, and swept a heap of dirt over the burning coals.

"Hold still!" Aly yelled over Zoraiya's continued screams. When she managed to place a hand on Zoraiya's arm, a healing spell quickly restored Zoraiya's burned skin.

As the pain vanished, Zoraiya straightened and swatted Aly's hand off her arm. "Don't touch me."

Igor and Rainbow shuffled closer. Aly sighed. "Does it still hurt?"

"No," grunted Zoraiya. She picked up her burned sandals and tossed them aside into the night.

"Magic can heal as well as harm," Aly said.

With a grunt, Zoraiya crossed her arms and turned aside. "You asked us the other day what we know of magic. We know it is powerful. It can heal. It can kill." She shrugged, as if speaking of killing were no large matter. "It can immortalize too. Something you, with all your book knowledge, seem to have forgotten."

Aly froze. "What do you mean, immortalize?"

But instead of answering, Zoraiya merely picked at her dirty fingernails.

Rainbow, however, provided the answer. "Magic, it gives us what we want, whatever we want." Aly cringed at the misunderstanding but didn't interrupt as the older woman continued. "Some of us want strength, it gives us strength. Some want to live forever. Magic, it can do that too."

Zoraiya hissed at Rainbow, but the older woman wasn't deterred by the warning.

"Go on," Aly encouraged. "Magic heals, but it can't erase the approach of death altogether."

"I've seen the River Keepers—selfish lot—talking to the river like it has some sort of feelings. They say the river that created the Canyon flows with feelings all its own, and they treat our river like it's no different." Rainbow scoffed. "But they blooming crazy. I've been in that river myself, sneaked there one night, and I got to see that there is nothing in that river but water. I used it for magic, but that's when they found me." She shrugged. "They like to chop me in pieces for using their river, but I told them the river flows and nobody's going to miss the tiny bit of energy I took from it."

For several moments, Aly stared wide-eyed at her student. She'd said many things that hinted at the hidden histories of the Zealots, but the one that stood out the most was the line *the river that created the Canyon*. Aly had always been taught that the wicked sorcerer, Usrich, had blasted open a great fissure in the earth, uncovering the evil river that had once flowed far underground, unable to leech its lies into the world. Usrich died when he descended into the Canyon, and most assume he was swallowed by the very river he uncovered.

"You say the river created the Canyon?" Aly prodded. "That would have taken a long time. But the Canyon appeared overnight."

Igor nodded. "It did create the Canyon in one night."

"How?" asked Aly, incredulous.

"Magic." Rainbow lifted one shoulder nonchalantly.

"But that would mean the river was already there. Why would our accounts not tell it that way?" Aly wasn't ready to doubt her own histories, but she wanted to glean all she could from the one she was hearing now.

Zoraiya finally snapped her attention from digging at her nails. "Your precious histories can't possibly contain all there is to know."

She was right. Aly must admit that, at least.

"Usrich was a River Keeper, you see," Igor explained. "The first River Keeper. He started the community that became this." He lifted his arms at his sides. "He lived in a place far from here, a desert, but his ideas spread and the people here revere him for teaching that magic is our god. Or rather, a master to whom we all must bow."

"The Candul region," Aly whispered. Usrich had indeed been from the Candul region. She'd never known he had been the father of the Zealots. How had Tanderan sorcerers lost this crucial piece of information over the years? Was it simply because Zealots and the trained sorcerers had so little to do with each other?

Zoraiya frowned at Igor but didn't say anything more.

Aly needed to process everything she'd just learned, but she still had the job of teaching her students how to control their magic. She walked over to pick up the ruined shoes and handed them to Igor. "I'd like you to fix these." At his befuddled stare, she told him the words to say to craft the spell.

Igor held the melted shoes and repeated the words Aly had spoken. "What is broken shall be mended," he muttered.

The shoes twitched a little as the magic reworked the soles. Igor yelped and dropped them.

"It's safe," Aly whispered, again taking the shoes from the forest floor. "Look." She handed the mended shoes back to Igor. "You did it."

Zoraiya stomped over to where Igor stood, staring down at the sandals in his hands. Snatching them away, she tossed the sandals to the ground with a snort before slipping them back on.

Aly rushed to Igor, a broad smile on her face. Then she noticed the tears leaking down his cheeks. "What's wrong?" she asked.

He closed his eyes, pressing more tears down his face. "Bless you, child." His hands, clasped in hers, shook so hard she worried he was on the brink of accidental magic.

But then he straightened to his full height, his back no longer hunched, and his wrinkled face appeared to shed a decade of life as his expression relaxed. His hands stopped shaking, and he opened his eyes. He looked at Aly with a watery gaze.

In his aging eyes, Aly saw a fresh determination, a youthful energy that surprised her. "I knew you could do it."

He squeezed her hands and then released them. "Thank you."

He laughed as he smeared away his tears. "That was the first time I've done anything useful with magic."

Suddenly, a strange voice invaded her head.

Disoriented by the voice , she blinked at all three of her students before realizing it wasn't any of them.

The army is drawing near. Your defenses will fail. You will surrender.

Closing her eyes, she concentrated on the soft, slightly garbled sound of Kassia's voice. Aly's connection to Alexander's mind, while not her top priority right now, was still operating as a window into Kassia's thoughts. Aly wished she could hear what Alexander was thinking.

What was Kassia's game? She could have been telling Alexander not to worry, not to build up defenses at all. She could have whispered any lie to him, but she was goading his own fears.

Aly recalled something Gevar had told her once. *Those with power are most exposed when afraid. How they respond to fear reveals their true nature.* Kassia was perhaps trying to press Alexander into some action.

Kassia's words slithered through Aly's mind once more. *Accept the help offered to you. Your city will fall. Darkness is coming. Only magic can save you.*

Aly steadied herself on the nearest tree. Her students stared at her with wide eyes.

A shiver raced down Aly's back as she considered what sort of help Kassia would want her enemy to accept. Whatever it was, it was sure to be a trap.

Now, more than ever, Aly needed to attempt to fulfill Alexander's wishes and bring him a few more sorcerers to help defend the city—and soon. With renewed purpose, Aly turned back to her students, arms lifted.

"Let's try one more spell tonight," she said.

18

ELISE

The palace chapel was unadorned. Arthur Ondorian stood at the head of the short aisle, dark, priestly robes stark against the pale walls and altar. Honey-colored light poured in from the stained-glass on the chapel's east side.

Walking down the aisle, Elise spotted Carolyn standing in the front row with Edward Alexander. The thin grip she had on her composure slipped when she noticed her sister's shuttered expression. She could not recall the last time Carolyn had donned such a mask.

Reluctantly pulling her eyes from her sister, Elise looked at the King of Refere. He stood stiff and regal, hands rigid at his sides. He didn't even glance at her as she approached, but kept his gaze on the side wall of the chapel.

For a brief moment, she wondered if he'd changed his mind since their late-night discussion. She hoped Lordan would hold up his end of their plan.

She scanned the faces in the vaulted chapel. Two armies

approached, and Mardon was low on sorcerers, yet here stood the King of Tandera, the King of Refere, and those Elise assumed were important enough to witness this farce of a union. The councilmen were all present, save Lord Grey. *Not surprising. That man is part-ghost.* Elise spotted Seb's father, the former Chancellor of Trade, with a veiled frown on his bearded face. Her muscles twitched at his likeness to Seb's. He had remained within the king's good graces only by disavowing his son—not unlike Elise's own behavior.

Then, as her eyes settled again on the high priest, she noticed one more face, hidden in the shadows created by the early morning light that only reached halfway across the angular room. He sat to the side of the altar, cuffed to a guard.

Her heart lurched at the sight of Seb. Alexander had brought Seb to witness the event as punishment, and the look on his face proved his night had been worse than hers.

Elise forced herself to breathe. She hoped hers and Lordan's plan would work.

Staring hard at Arthur Ondorian, Elise took her place beside the Referen king. It was unbearable to think she'd spent so many days dreaming of marrying this man.

As Ondorian opened the ceremony with a prayer, Elise cringed internally. She begged Theod's forgiveness and darted a glance at Seb, whose eyes were still fixed on her with terrifying intensity. With a slow blink, she tore her attention away from him, ignoring the way her heart drummed against her ribs at his presence.

"Two great nations come together on this day," Ondorian began, breaking from the traditional ceremony to add a few words of his own, as was his custom at weddings, but Elise wished he would limit his chatter to the scripted lines. "The King of Refere gains a precious gift today, a bride, the steady companion of his life from this day forward."

Elise's hand resting on Lordan's forearm twitched at those words.

Ondorian rattled on, as if delaying the inevitable, but Elise stopped listening. She allowed herself one more glance at Seb. His eyes looked swollen—more wounds he'd taken because of her—and her heart stung at the knowledge that she had caused him more pain. But in his gaze, beneath the intensity of his stare, was a startling softness that made Elise's chest ache.

She was set to marry another man, and all Seb could do was love her enough to forgive her for it. He'd never spoken that word, nor had she realized it until this moment, but Sebastian Thorin was in love with her, despite the wounds she'd inflicted on him. Blinking back her shock, her composure faltered and her hand slipped. Lordan captured her hand, resettling it on his arm with a tight grip. Was he nervous?

After too many agonizing minutes, Ondorian turned to Elise. "Theod has gifted us with the blessing of marriage. This day you will bind yourself to your husband with the words you will now speak." He offered her a thin smile.

As was customary, Ondorian waited for Elise to recite the wedding vows.

Her plan raced through her mind one last time.

"My lady?" Ondorian pressed. "Your vows?"

Reckoners could discern the truth to any direct question. The trick was in asking the right question—and it must be a yes or no question.

After a deep inhale, Elise asked Ondorian, "Is King Alexander working with Queen Kassia of Bulvarna?"

Gasps rustled through the crowd, and Lordan turned so violently to face them that her arm wrenched away.

"He has information we believe to have come directly from Kassia or her court. Hear the man's answer." He glanced back at Ondorian.

Ondorian's brows rose, clearly startled by this turn of events.

"Wait! Stop him!" shouted Alexander.

It was too late. The Reckoner opened his mouth. "No."

Elise gasped. Lordan stiffened beside her and let out a quiet curse.

Members of the crowd were mumbling their confusion or shouting their anger at the accusations.

Elise's mind spun. They were certain this would pin Alexander. They'd placed their bet, and they had been wrong.

This was Elise's chance to finally be useful, to serve her brother and the Tandera she loved. She *had* to bring down Alexander. Her eyes narrowed as she recalled his outburst right before Ondorian answered. He was hiding something.

The wording of the question must be precise.

Whirling to face Alexander, she yelled another question for the Reckoner at the altar. "Is Alexander under Kassia's control in some way?"

"Yes." Ondorian's brows lifted and his mouth curled into a surprised smile, as if he'd been trying to work out this very problem and was now faced with the solution. Reckoners had a strange magic of their own, being able to speak truth even when they didn't know it before the question was posed.

Chaos erupted in the small chapel as men shouted, Alexander cursed and started for Elise, but his guards, who sensed danger, converged on him.

Over the guards' shoulders, he shouted, "Arrest her! Arrest the high priest!"

A few guards shuffled toward the altar, uncertain expressions on their faces. Lordan nodded to Elise and stepped away, vanishing from sight as his Protector slipped a shroud over him.

Women added shrieks of surprise and fear to the mix. At least one person was laughing, but it took Elise a moment to discover it was Sebastian Thorin.

Ondorian leaned forward, urgency in his dark eyes. "My lady, it might be best if you leave now. You will find the key to Mr. Thorin's shackles on the guard's belt. Theod be with you."

As Elise bolted toward Seb, the guard restraining him jerked Seb's arm to an uncomfortable angle.

"Get out of my way," Elise snarled at the guard.

The man dropped Seb's arm and backed away, tossing her a key.

Her fingers shook as she unfastened Seb's shackles. He said nothing.

"What are you doing? Stop her!" Alexander's voice boomed in the vaulted room.

As Elise and Seb raced toward the external door leading to the gardens, Alexander shouted, "My sorcerer will prove they are lying!"

If anything, Aly would be able to prove, once and for all, that Alexander was a pawn in Kassia's hands.

They raced into the palace gardens, heading directly for the nearest gate. Elise welcomed the sunlight on her face, praying her actions would finally turn out for the good of Tandera.

19

ALY

Aly stood before her three students, observing as they each ignited a single blade of grass. Shields glowed faintly in the air around each of them.

She cast her awareness outward, to the faintly glowing Truthwell that had been standing in the early morning shadows for some time. Another Zealot was watching them, and for the present, he or she appeared content to remain out of sight.

Aly refocused on her students and stepped closer to Zor, watching her hands and listening to her words. The woman snarled the words of the *Verad*, always cutting syllables or rearranging the lines to unintelligible invocations. She flashed a mocking smile at Aly's scrutiny.

"Why do you keep coming back every day if you hate this so much?" asked Aly.

Zor's hands twirled in the air. "So I can prove you wrong. I can do all the magic you can do, but I don't need your little ball and chain to make it happen."

Aly sighed and shoved down her rebuttal. Zoraiya was older

by a decade, and it would do no good to snap back at her. "You are using the words I taught you."

Zor shrugged. "Not in the way you taught them."

Aly wondered why it mattered so much to Zoraiya to antagonize her. Zor was certainly powerful enough to be a Master, if she could embrace the words of truth and the beauty of control. Rainbow was likely only a Comforter, and Igor had already proven himself capable of greater magic than merely heating and cooling.

"It's okay to learn we were wrong about something we always thought was right," Aly said, voice calm and measured. "I think that's part of what it means to be wise, leaving behind the lies we once believed."

Her pupil snorted. "And you? Are you wise enough to leave behind the lies you so dearly love?"

Before Aly could answer, the blade of grass hovering before them burst into flame and disintegrated.

"Good!" Aly clapped. "That showed great control!"

Zor turned a fierce scowl at Aly, her face bright behind the magical shield. "Magic doesn't want to be bound. It wants to cover the whole earth!"

The words shook Aly. She searched for a response but could think of nothing to say. Inside her mind, she repeated the phrase that kept her going every day: *Truth will rise.* Eventually, even if in a thousand years, the truth would prevail. Aly only hoped it would prevail here, in this woman's heart.

"I'd like you to try again," Aly said, stepping away from Zoraiya to observe Rainbow. As she did so, she sent a quick message to Naia. *I hope all is well. Send update when you can.*

According to Naia's last update, she was almost to Luxler, which meant she would reach Red today. The flight was taxing her mind, but she hadn't given up yet. Naia had grit, and that made up for her lack of formal training.

Brush crashed to her left as someone hacked a way through twisted, hanging vines. Aly's defensive shields would protect them, but she lifted her hands, just in case. A young boy with long, mousy hair leaped over a fallen log and stood just outside the twinkling shield, a broad smile on his face.

Aly and her students stopped to stare at him.

"Can I try, too?" he asked. He had a high-pitched voice, but he was taller than Aly. His limbs were so thin they might snap in a high wind. "I've been watching you for a while and I think I can do that."

A smile grew on Aly's face. "I'm delighted you want to try. What is your name?"

"Quince. I know that one's name is Zoraiya, and he's Igor, I think. I haven't heard you say her name much." He pointed at Rainbow, then lifted a hand toward the shield. "Will this hurt me if I touch it?"

The answer was most likely no, considering this young boy didn't appear to be much of a threat, but Aly held out a cautious hand nonetheless. "I wouldn't touch it, just in case. Do you want to learn how to control your magic?"

The boy looked at her with a strange expression. "Control? I guess that's one way to look at it." He shrugged. "I assumed you were teaching them how to do small magic."

"Small magic?"

"I've never been able to do something as small as light a blade of grass on fire. For me, it's usually an entire tree or meadow."

And with that introduction, Aly welcomed her fourth student.

After getting Quince settled under a shield, she set him to work on the same spells Igor and Rainbow had already mastered. The boy stood off to the side, in his own cocoon of protection, occasionally igniting a flurry of sparks around his head in frustration.

Meanwhile, Rainbow tossed spell after spell at the blade of grass, all with no effect whatsoever. As she walked among her students, Aly broke her rule and did a quick mental search for Red. He'd been in the Canyon all night, a feat in itself. He was alive, but she sensed more poison in his body. Grey was also alive, but there were two new Truthwells with them, and two had gone missing. Aly wasn't sure if one of the Wells that had vanished was that of Grey's Protector or merely another soldier. If they were in the Deep without a Protector, they wouldn't survive long. Aly yearned to go to him, but her work was here, with these students. She'd sent Naia, who would have to be enough.

Into Aly's mind came a fierce and jarring message. She braced against a tree.

Scepter, you are ordered to return to Mardon immediately by order of the king.

Blinking in confusion, Aly repeated the words in a small whisper. Scepter was the king's personal code word for her. The message had definitely come from him.

A jolt shot through Aly as she turned back toward camp. *Has Mardon been attacked?*

She planted her feet and shoved one arm toward the south. With eyes closed, she stretched her awareness back toward the capital, honing in on Alexander's Well. When she found it, she expanded outward, searching for the mass of Wells that indicated the approaching army.

They were not yet on top of Mardon, but they were right outside the city.

She exhaled and opened her eyes.

All four students were watching her.

"Message from Mardon," she explained. "I've been called back. I'm to leave as soon as possible." Alexander would expect her within hours, given that's how long it would take to fly back from the Crescent.

"You're leaving us?" Rainbow asked, a jarring note of sadness in her voice.

Aly stared at her students, her face slack and her breaths quick. She couldn't just leave them. She hadn't left to go to Red, why should she leave to go to Alexander?

She rubbed her hands down her face. She'd vowed to protect Alexander. Perhaps he was in some other kind of danger. There were still those loyal to Red in the city, and there was still Kassia to consider. *What if Kassia has turned on Alexander and he is in mortal danger even now?*

With a deep inhale, she dispelled all the shields around her students. "I need to return to Mardon, but I do not wish for your studies to end. I must leave soon, but I will be back."

Zoraiya swiped a dismissive hand through the air. "No, you won't. You're giving up. I see it on your face."

Quince, who'd only been her student for a quarter hour, cringed at those words. Igor's expression sagged.

Aly stormed up to Zor. "No, I'm not. Come with me if you wish. I am *not* giving up on you."

For a second, Zor's brows remained pinched and her mouth hard. But then she blinked and said, "All right."

"All right, what?" Igor prodded.

"All right, let's go to the capital."

Aly's eyes narrowed. "You want to go? To a city? Full of people?"

Zoraiya sniffed. "Sure. Why not?"

"You live here because you dislike society, correct?"

"I'm training with you to *change*, am I not?"

Based on what Zor had said minutes ago, she wasn't here to change her own mind, but to change Aly's. Could she be trusted in Mardon?

Aly tilted her head. To gain Zoraiya's full trust, she should bestow a little trust of her own. "Fine. You'll be shielded the entire time, to keep your magic contained. Still want to go?"

"I do," Igor said.

"I sure don't want to stay here by myself," Rainbow added. "They're going to kill me soon as you leave."

Quince raised his hand. "I'll go."

Zor picked at her nails with her teeth. When everyone looked at her, she said, "Yes, I'm coming."

Aly paced the clearing behind the small cookhouse, rehearsing in her mind the newly altered spells for flight that would take all four of her students to Mardon with her.

She had never flown four other people alongside her before, but the magic was the same no matter the payload. The mental effort and concentration, however, would be much more intense.

"You sure this will work?" Quince asked, his voice a little shaky. Igor and Rainbow were inside the cabin, preparing rations for their short trip.

Aly gave him a half-smile. "The magic won't fail. It's the source I'm a little worried about."

Quince's brown eyes grew large. "Will it give out?"

Aly shook her head. "No, a human Truthwell never really runs out of energy, not when it's employed correctly. But some Wells are polluted, and they don't give power as easily."

"I thought you said you pulled from the King of Tandera? Is he polluted?"

Aly gave him a weak smile. "Yes. Very much so."

Quince considered this. "How do you teach someone who can't see the truth that they are polluted?"

"That's a very good question."

Zoraiya stomped up with a small satchel over her shoulder.

"For a minute, I thought you'd run off," Rainbow commented, coming out of the cookhouse carrying a small, wrapped parcel. "Should last us all a day or so."

Aly nodded. "The trip will only take four hours, five at most." She wasn't sure how fast Alexander's energy would fuel the flight of five people, or how well her mind would hold up to the concentration necessary for such a feat. She wasn't leaving them behind, not when they appeared so eager to keep learning.

Quince hopped up, his skinny legs bouncing underneath him. "I can't believe you can really fly us all to Mardon. Igor was right—you're incredible."

Shaking her head slightly, she he looked at each of them in turn. Her little army. Alexander would laugh at her efforts, but she was quite proud of them, even Zor, for agreeing to come.

"Try to stay stable in the air. So, no flipping or rolling. It's best to just lie flat. I have a place in mind that will house you until I'm certain the king is ready to meet you." With that, she shrugged her shoulders and said, "Let's go."

Aside from Quince vomiting and Rainbow having to stop their flight to relieve herself, the trip was fairly smooth. Zoraiya tried out several bird calls, all of which grated Aly's nerves, before falling blissfully silent. Igor was the most at home zipping through the air, his white hair pressed back against his head, a small smile on his lips.

Mardon's skyline rose on the horizon as night fell. The sunset was no more than a flash of pale yellow before the heavy shadows of night painted the city in gray.

"Wow," whispered Quince, his tired eyes no longer drooping as he took in the city. "It's huge."

Aly initiated a spell that cloaked their Truthwells, not

wanting any trouble from scouts watching the skies. She hoped their focus would be to the east, where the Zealot army was already visible.

A weight dropped in Aly's chest as she observed with her eyes what her magical senses had already seen: a blanket of soldiers descending on Mardon. If Mardon was still low on Protectors, this battle would result in great loss.

With a stab of sadness, she thought of Red and wished he could be here to lead his people. Sustaining flight for five people made it impossible to search for him with her magic. She hoped he was still all right.

The New Moon Tavern sat below three floors of small apartments. When they drifted quietly into the alley behind the building, one man smoking a pipe on his balcony startled at the inexplicable breeze that blew his smoke into tiny whorls.

Quince chuckled, and the man leaped backward at the sound, slamming into the wall of his apartment.

Aly shoved a finger over her mouth. With all the spells for flight and the one to shroud their Wells, she hadn't bothered to shroud their sound.

Rainbow, looking like she was holding back tears, crouched down and patted the alley floor when her feet touched the ground. Igor patted her on the shoulder.

Zoraiya shuddered, then recomposed herself into her natural, icy demeanor. "This place stinks," she observed.

For a moment, Aly stared blankly past Zor's shoulder. When Zor snapped her fingers, Aly blinked. "We're in an alley behind a tavern," she explained. "But let's be quick. I need to reach the palace." Her legs wobbled underneath her but she ignored the sensation.

Inside, Aly walked the narrow hallway with one hand against the wall. She took three deep breaths before entering the mostly empty tavern. Not many people were out tonight. Aly flagged down the one waitress she recognized, the one who'd been at work the night she and Red had come here to meet Grey. The woman knew her instantly.

"My lady, what can I do for you? Bishop isn't in town. He's been gone a while."

"You mean Grey?" When the woman nodded, Aly shrugged. It wasn't her place to tell this woman that Grey was in the Canyon with the dethroned sovereign. "I need two rooms." She almost said three, but Alexander was waiting for her. Sleep must wait.

"Certainly."

The rooms were small but clean. Bare but comfortable. The beds looked like the most inviting ones Aly had ever seen, but she shook her head. *Focus*, she told herself as she left Igor and Quince in their room. Igor could keep an eye on Quince. Aly wasn't worried about them.

When she looked between Rainbow and Zoraiya, however, she bit her lip. "You'll be under two shields. One to keep you from harming yourself. Another to keep you from harming anyone else. The shields will be visible, so people might ask questions. Try to ignore them. Pretend you don't speak the language if necessary."

Zor snorted. "Go on, we'll be fine."

Rainbow smiled, showing off the gap where a tooth should have been. "I'm glad you brought us. I'm right pleased to be out of that place."

Aly nodded at her. Naia had once expressed similar feelings. Aly hesitated before turning to the door, not sure if it was wise to leave them here. She trusted Igor—and Rainbow too, though she hadn't developed the same level of control yet. Quince was young and still a complete wild card, but he at least seemed thankful to be here and eager to learn more from Aly.

It was Zor she didn't trust. But she must be willing to admit she was wrong about this student. After all, Aly was hoping Zor would admit to being wrong about magic.

With another brief smile, she walked out of the room.

The air around the palace shimmered with a shield spell Aly didn't recognize. She stopped short as she approached the eastern garden gate on foot. She had enjoyed the break from magic as she strolled through Mardon, her mind disengaged and rather hazy. But seeing the palace and the unfamiliar shield refocused her mind and helped dispel some of the exhaustion still lingering from the intense concentration of the flight.

Her own defenses, which had protected the palace for the past six years, still sat quietly beneath this new enchantment. Why would Alexander add another?

The king's Well burned dimly in the vast back gardens. Since he moved into the palace, he was in the habit of taking evening walks for the fresh air, after the heat of the day had dissipated.

From outside the grounds, Aly pushed into his Truthwell, searching his depths as she rarely had before. As expected, his energy was polluted with shadows like ink spots, but they ran deep, stains of black dripping down into what should have been almost pure, white light. Nothing felt or looked different than it had since the coronation, other than the lies within his mind had sunk deeper.

He had no idea that the army heading for him was likely sent by the very woman controlling his mind. He'd denied Kassia's control over him each time Aly had brought it up. The man was utterly blind to what Aly could see so clearly.

With a sharp inhale, Aly lifted herself over the garden wall, angling toward the king. When she passed through the foreign shield, she let out a yelp of pain. The shield stung her skin like the brief touch of a hot pan.

"Ah!" Aly flung a quick jet of water, using the moisture in the air, at the shield. It sizzled and evaporated. "Hmm, what are you up to?"

She deposited herself right behind the king and yawned. Her tiredness would have to wait. Two guards walked a stone's throw away, but she didn't sense any nearby sorcerers.

She removed her shroud.

When she cleared her throat, Alexander startled so violently, Aly suppressed a chuckle.

"You!" he barked, whirling on her. "Finally. I have been waiting all day." For a moment, his expression flickered between anger and desperation, settling into a stark frown.

"Why is there a foreign shield around the palace?"

He scoffed at her abruptness. "What are you talking about?"

"Did you not order a second shield?"

He glanced around, as if someone would pop out and explain that Aly was playing a trick on him. "I did not call you here so you could badger me with questions. Shroud us."

She obliged, shrouding only their voices, as was customary when walking with the king in the sight of his other guards. For him to vanish would only incite worry from the guards.

If he didn't order another shield, then who did? But to appease him, she shoved away her desire to ask him more questions.

He frowned at her. "Is this what you wear to meet with your sovereign?"

Her gray dress was rather dirty and rumpled. Red had never cared what she wore. With a grunt, she flicked her wrist and altered her dress into a sleek, green gown. She lifted her brows but kept back her sharp retort.

The king huffed, and a shadow darkened his features. "Your friend, Arthur Ondorian, colluded with the former princess to tell lies about me."

"Sir, that isn't poss—"

"Do not interrupt. At the wedding, the Reckoner said that I am under the influence of Queen Kassia. I brought you here to repudiate those preposterous claims."

Aly's mouth fell open. *What wedding?* she wanted to ask, but she discarded the irrelevant question. Into his mind, she said, *This is what I've been telling you.*

He spat and turned away. "You are in cohorts with them. You all want me off the throne."

She followed him down the gravel path. "I swore to protect you. But you have rejected my protection. If a Reckoner said it, you know it is true. Your mind is not your own."

"Nonsense! A Reckoner can lie as well as any man."

Aly scoffed. "Not when someone invokes the truth. Sire, you know that."

"That deceiving daughter of Gevar," he spat. "You should have warned me of her schemes."

Between Elise and Carolyn, only one of them seemed capable of *schemes. Has Elise worked out that Alexander's mind is being manipulated? Did she try to expose him? That would mean she betrayed him as well.* But maybe Aly wasn't interpreting the king correctly.

"You forget I cannot read people's minds," Aly said through gritted teeth. "I do not know of what you speak."

"She turned Mardon against me!" he bellowed. "On the eve of battle, my own council has refused to meet with me. I secured her the wedding she wanted, and she turned them all against me."

At once, Aly wanted to both cheer and cry. Elise had proven her true loyalties, albeit too late, and the result was that Mardon now faced battle with no clear leader at all. If the troops couldn't look to the king, even a usurper, their defenses would fall all the sooner.

The palace blocked the light of the rising moon, and the

gardens were lit only by the pale gas lamps near the building. Flowers perfumed the air. The king's troubled face caught the distant light, making him look every bit an old, tired man. This was no battle-ready general.

"Sire, Kassia is a skilled manipulator. Her lies will be hard to detect." Her voice held pity.

Alexander huffed and waved a hand. "I cannot trust you either. You are working with your lover's sister. I should have expected you would do something like this."

He really had no idea Kassia was controlling him. Aly's pity washed away as a jolt of clarity flashed through her. She must purge Kassia from his mind. She didn't know if it was even possible, but she had to try.

Glancing at the two guards standing nearby, she considered how long she would have before someone intervened. The king's other Protectors were within the palace, their Wells easy to identify as they shone with fewer lies darkening their energy.

The one Well Aly wished she could pinpoint was Kassia's. If only Aly had memorized her enemy's energy signature when they'd battled.

Aly exhaled, thinking fast. Now was not the time to worry about Kassia's whereabouts. The enemy queen wouldn't be able to penetrate the palace grounds, not with Aly's shields intact.

But Red had circumvented her shields once by inviting the enemy inside. If Alexander invited Kassia in, she could walk straight through the otherwise impassible shields.

A brief moment of terror overtook Aly as she considered the fact that Kassia might be inside the palace walls even now. But short of searching every room with her own eyes, Aly would never know. There was only one thing to do: Aly needed to reach inside of Alexander's Well and yank Kassia out, without hurting him and without the other sorcerers sensing any danger.

"I need to speak with you," she said, stepping closer. For this magic to work, she would need to touch him.

"We are speaking," he replied.

Perhaps now was the time to take a page out of Red's book. Being rash didn't need to equate to being foolish.

She lunged forward and grabbed Alexander's wrist, confining him with a binding spell before plunging into his energy Well.

She must discover the extent of Kassia's hold on him. Like Red's death curse, Kassia's infection of Alexander's mind would have a visible end. If Aly could find that end, she could set him free. But how would the grip of a liar appear inside of the mind of a king?

As her awareness fell into the power of his Well, her hold on reality slackened. She hoped she could maintain her binding spell long enough to accomplish what she needed. Aly ignored the slight dizziness that came from losing her grasp on the world around her and clamped a hand on Alexander's forehead. Her magic surged into him, reaching deeper.

She needed to finish before the guards came asking questions.

With all of her concentration, she poured herself into his Well, trying to find the deepest point she could reach. It was unlike searching Red's Well—the energy didn't respond to her the same way. It was like diving through murky water rather than clear, crisp mountain air.

She pressed and she pressed, digging into his light, letting herself be consumed by it. Her desire increased the deeper she went. This was dangerous territory, but she knew her limits and she knew control. She must do this to save him.

The spell to restrict his movements would soon be too complex for her to maintain while diving deeper and deeper into his Well. At last, she released of all other spells—her shroud, her protective shields around her students, and the spell that bound the king's limbs. Something shook her, but she couldn't stop now. Deep in his Well, her mind barely registered the lurch and sudden tumbling of her body.

The sensation of swimming in an ocean of mottled light overpowered Aly's thoughts. Darkness swirled all around, and as she dove deeper, the shadows reached for her mind, as if they could leap from one Well to the next. The fringes of darkness lessened as she stretched farther into his light, brushing against the echoes of the Maker. Buried in his Well, deeper than she had ever been, was a small, single thread of black, snarled and knotted in a swirling eddy of light. That must be Kassia's hold— Aly had never seen anything like it.

She pushed all of her attention toward this tiny fingernail of darkness. She wrapped her magic around it and yanked, pulling up, up, as she withdrew her mind from the king's pulsing energy. The darkness resisted, but it came with her, somehow moving as she moved, though there was no movement at all, only the sensation of it, as she lifted up and away from his Well.

With a scream, she ripped her consciousness away from Alexander's Well, pulling with it what she hoped were Kassia's lies. Aly's mind awoke to the world around them as the guards descended upon them, wrenching Aly off the fallen body of the king.

Alexander, no longer magically bound, scrambled up.

The two guards grabbed her by the arms, pulling her away from the king.

Alexander brushed off the dirt and mud from his suit as best he could, then stared at Aly with a confused expression. "What just happened?" He glanced around, brows knitting. "Why are we at the palace? Where is the..." He trailed off, his pinched brows rising.

Aly spluttered and collapsed against her captors with a sigh of relief. She hadn't known the extent of Kassia's control over him, but it appeared his mind was now free.

The two guards holding her faltered at the king's strange words, and she ripped her arms free.

"He's been manipulated," she shouted, pointing at the king. The guards lifted their weapons, but she cast a gleaming shield between herself and them. She looked at Alexander.

Aly sensed a strangeness in the air, as if a great amount of energy had been expended somewhere far away. Magic, *big* magic, sent a ripple through the world of light only sorcerers could see.

"She knows," Aly muttered. The magic she sensed felt nearby, in Mardon somewhere.

Kassia certainly had felt the break in her Binding to Alexander, as Aly had felt the tearing of her magic from Red when her Binding to him had severed. Aly had no idea how the queen might retaliate, but Aly wasn't looking forward to finding out.

Alexander stared blankly off to the left. "Why can I not remember walking out here?" he asked again. He spotted the coronet on the ground near his feet, then touched his bald head with a strained expression. A look of panic swept over his face. "I am the King of Tandera," he said, as if shocked by this revelation.

"Yes," she said. She wondered what kind of control Kassia had had on his mind if he wasn't certain of his own sovereignty. What part had he even played in gaining the crown?

"I stole it from—" the words exited his mouth before he snapped his jaw shut. "I am the King of Tandera," he said, more confidently. "I was crowned. I said the vows." He narrowed his eyes at Aly. "You are the Royal Sorcerer. What in Theod's name is wrong with me?" He asked, mustache twitching.

Pity flooded Aly's heart once again as she stared at the king. "These past weeks, you have been under the control of Queen

Kassia of Bulvarna," Aly declared. "She's been manipulating you with falsehoods, speaking them directly to your mind and likely using those around you to confirm the lies."

Alexander scoffed. "Not possible. I could not have been *controlled* by her. It is simply ridiculous." His arms swung at his sides. Eventually, he hugged them around himself, as if trying to hold himself together. She'd never seen this arrogant older man look so frail. His gaze fell to the ground, then flickered angrily. "There's no way I could possibly have been controlled by someone like her. I refuse to believe it."

"Sir," Aly said, stepping carefully toward him. "It's true. But she no longer has any hold on you."

"No," he shouted, turning toward her with vitriol in his eyes. "I was never controlled!"

Stepping backward to avoid the spit flying from his mouth, she said, "The sorcerer who wore the wolf mask, *that* was Kassia. When I Bound to you, I sensed that there was someone else Pulling from your Well, and it led me to her. When I fought her, I saw her face. I know it was her."

Alexander scoffed. "How do I know you are not lying?"

Aly shook her head. "You know I don't."

"Convenient excuse," he barked, spinning away, his heel crunching the gravel path.

The guards exchanged worried glances but followed their king. Aly marched along beside him.

Alexander held his breath, his entire body rigid as he stormed toward the palace. Then, his shoulders sank as he let out a long breath. "It cannot be true. I will not believe that my crowning, my reign—" he pointed vehemently at the ground "— is a lie. I won the crown from Frederick, and I will not give it back." After a pause, his eyes flashed at Aly, and in them, she saw a note of panic. "I cannot have won it on a lie."

He needed to come to terms with this on his own. What he

would do when he finally admitted the truth, Aly had no idea. Here was a man who had gained the throne via a sorcerer's manipulation; however, he'd still been the one to pollute Red's reputation, dismissed him as a poor leader, moved into his house, and banished him from his own city. Kassia may have planted the lies in his mind, but he had still usurped a throne that rightfully belonged to Red.

"Sir," she said, "Kassia likely knows—"

"Get out of my way." He fisted his hands and walked up the wide steps to the palace's grand terrace. "I will hear no more from you tonight. I have a battle to prepare for." He spun on the top step. "Where is my army?"

Aly blinked at him. She couldn't believe he was still clinging to that. Even with Kassia's hold on his mind broken, he still clung to that wretched desire. Somewhere underneath Kassia's manipulation was his own deep fear that Mardon wasn't going to survive the oncoming attack. The two guards glanced at her.

Ignoring his question, she pressed on. "She will have felt the breach. She won't be happy." Aly whispered a protective spell and pushed a palm outward toward the usurper. "She will likely come searching for you."

Fists by his side, he said again, voice urgent and threatening, "Where is my army?"

She fixed him with a determined scowl. "She will try to Bind with you again as soon as you leave the palace grounds."

"You will not tell me what I can and cannot do. Enough of your lies! *Where is my army?*" he yelled.

Aly let out a slow, calming breath. "I brought them to Mardon with me."

His face lit up slightly. "Well, now. That wasn't so hard." He paused, then descended the steps once more, a slight bounce in his gait now. "I shall meet them."

"Sir, you are not safe out there," she pleaded, returning to her argument.

"You are trying to prevent me from leading our troops. You want our city to fall! Cease these persuasions or I will order Frederick killed at once."

She closed her eyes briefly, a stab of pain in her chest at his threat. "Yes, sire." Perhaps Alexander didn't know Red was in the Canyon. Either way, should Red survive the Deep, she couldn't very well have him killed on her account. She didn't want to frustrate Alexander further, but he'd become angry all over again when he learned this army he hoped in was composed of four barely-trained sorcerers.

Aly remembered the words Kassia had spoken to his mind yesterday. The Bulvarnan queen could have sent someone under her control to do her bidding, like she had with the ambassador at Red's coronation ball. "Sir, has anyone come to our aid recently?"

"Enough questions. Leave me." He huffed and strode toward two tall glass doors. The guards marched behind him.

Pressing back her annoyance, she restated all of her protective spells that he would carry with him when he left the palace. She added a few additional spells, hoping that her efforts would protect him against Kassia, whenever she found him.

The words of her vows echoed in her mind and she rushed forward. "Sir, I believe Kassia may be in Mardon, and it is my duty to protect you. Let me remain until dawn." They both knew Aly would be necessary in the fight to save Mardon.

"I desire to meet with the generals before dawn. I will require neither your magic nor your opinion until tomorrow." With that, the door was opened for him and he swept into the palace.

The generals needed sleep on the eve of battle, but there was no deterring the king now. He had his mind back, and she had to at least let him try to manufacture some sort of plan before the enemy attacked. She feared his efforts would be too little too late, given the army would likely attack at dawn.

Theod, help us, Aly pleaded as she stepped through the palace gate.

On the sidewalk outside the gate, Aly gripped fistfuls of her hair and let out a small, angry scream. She was so *tired*. She wanted to sleep for a couple of hours in order to have the strength to fight whatever was coming their way.

She walked toward the New Moon Tavern without bothering to shroud herself. Red was still in the Canyon, and she yearned to search out his Well, but her mind needed respite. Naia might already have reached him in the hours since was last able to search out Red's Well. It was the only thought that kept her from crumpling under the fear of losing him to the Deep.

Focusing instead on the here and now, Aly angled toward the tavern, avoiding the busier roads and the oddly bustling side-walks. People had more business than she'd imagined on the night before a known invasion. She hoped her students were safe—and that everyone in the tavern was safe from them.

To heal Alexander, she'd been forced to drop her other ongoing spells, and she couldn't reestablish her students' shields as well from a distance, as she wasn't as familiar with their energy signatures as she was with the king's. When she searched for their Wells, however, she stopped short.

They were close. All four of her students were moving closer, as if running.

A blast of light burst toward them in the darkened city street. Zoraiya rushed from between two buildings into the light of the gas lamps.

Aly screamed and diverted the flaming ball. It billowed over the cobblestones before dissipating. Pebbles shot at her, then two arrows, but she blasted them all away. From behind Zor rushed at least a dozen men and women in plain brown robes. Sparks ignited in the air all around them. Several carried spears.

These were Canduli Zealots. Too stunned to attack her student, Aly leaped once more to dodge a spear. Before her feet touched ground, the pavement beneath her crumbled away, revealing a deep hole.

A cavernous maw opened up in the earth, and as Aly fell, she sensed a great weight pushing her down, down. She fell, screaming as the air above her became impressively heavy and her spells to lift herself did nothing but squeeze her like a vice against the invisible force.

In seconds, she was surrounded by darkness, walls of earth rising around her as the tiny circle of light above her shrank. Then the sky above her disappeared and the earth closed around her.

20

RED

The men shuffled single file through the damp Canyon bottom as they searched for a way out. False visions danced in the darkness all around. Their second night in the Canyon was dropping, and the thin light of day was vanishing once again, as was their hope of finding a path out. From the shadows, shapes snuffled and prowled, but the animals only attacked when the men dared to approach the Canyon walls.

Red had not anticipated how difficult it would be to leave this place.

He tucked his back against a giant boulder and peered around the side, but visibility was too poor to decipher what lay ahead. Jakes struck up a conversation with the boulder, but Red reached for his friend and clapped and hand over his mouth.

Shaking his head, Red removed his hand slowly. "It's not real," he reminded Jakes.

Jakes touched the rock, then cursed quietly. He grabbed a strip of fabric from his jacket pocket and wrapped it around a small stone, his hands fumbling. The hand that had touched the

Black River shook violently, making the movement onerous and slow. Red held his breath as Jakes completed the simple task. Red's fingers were blackened by the river, but his hands hadn't yet begun to shake.

Then Jakes hurled the rock into the darkness, and as it sailed away, the fabric around it caught fire, illuminating what waited directly ahead. Three foxbloods scattered out of the way.

"Three," Red announced, his heart pounding.

Jakes clutched his trembling hand against his chest, continuously glancing down at his blackened skin. Red nodded to him, offering a bit of hope, which they would need if they were to escape this place alive.

They'd wandered in the Canyon too long. Red didn't recognize any of the terrain, but he didn't fully trust his memories or his sight. Their plan was to reach the Canyon wall, then walk along it until they found a path out.

Only trouble was, the beasts had prevented it—for an entire day.

Without Antony, the only magic they had was from Jakes, and while he could kill single beasts quite well, he couldn't protect a group this large from attacks on all sides.

"We can't seriously be trying this again?" asked the Esvedaran soldier. He kept glancing around with twitching motions, perhaps watching ghosts no one else could see.

Red spun on his knees and stared at the small group. "Madness can only be held off so long." These men had been down here so long that they floated in and out of rationality, occasionally talking to the darkness or muttering strange things under their breath. It was a wonder they'd survived at all, given the nature of the beasts, though Red was beginning to wonder if the beasts had other plans than simply eating the soldiers.

Grey, who knelt beside him behind the boulder, coughed and

nodded. "We can't keep playing cat and mouse with these creatures. I'm with Red."

There was nothing to do but to run for it. The longer they waited, the more animals would come for them, the deeper the madness would infect their minds, and the hungrier they would all become. They'd given nearly all their combined rations to the starving men they'd found, which had given them some much-needed strength for the hike out. Red's right arm tingled with partial numbness as the poison of both the bites and the water's evil worked its way toward his shoulder.

Jakes launched into incoherent mumblings. The other soldier, a Private Cooper, shook with fever and cast Jake a haunted look. These men were not going to survive another night here.

Using his good arm, Red tugged Jakes' collar, wrenching him from the hysteria. "Listen carefully. All of you. No matter what happens to me, you get to the rim and you find a way to send a message, securely, to Aly—to Tandera's Royal Sorcerer. If you can't send one to her, send one to Arthur Ondorian, the high priest in Mardon. Tell them the river is gaining power. Tell them it is not a 'what' but a 'who'. Ondorian can figure out who it is. The river has a mind capable of acting. Tell them."

Jakes' wide eyes betrayed only confusion and fear. When Red shook him, he spluttered out an affirmation. The two soldiers muttered their assent as well.

Red spun to face Grey. Grey was the only person with ammunition left—two bullets. "I will run ahead, draw the beasts' attention. Clear a way through, and reach that path." He held Grey's stare, daring him to try to call him off. Grey looked about to protest, but gave a small nod.

Theod, help us, Red prayed, charging into the night.

The beasts lunged for him, as he hoped, and turned away from the others. His arms and legs pumped as fast as they could, but the poison coursing through his blood slowed him slightly.

One bullet fired.

Whimpers echoed in the darkness, and at least one beast still pursued him. He waited until he could see the shape right over his shoulder, then he turned and, holding the knife blade out at his chest, took the beast in the throat as it lunged at him. This one was smaller than the others, but it still took him down. His forward momentum carried the beast over his head. Red pushed it against the rocks and scrambled back to his feet.

The beast couldn't stand, but it snarled at him, scrabbling against the rocks with its teeth and claws to reach Red, even as the blade still protruded from its fur.

What was it about these animals that they pursued death so intensely?

Its mane bristled and its fangs dripped saliva. Red drew his other blade out of his boot and flipped it down into the fox's side. Only then was he willing to reach forward and grab the hilt lodged in the fox's chest.

At that moment, he felt a wretched pain searing his ankle. When he turned around, a giant white cat had its teeth in his ankle right above his boot. The pain made his vision blur. This was a venom like he had never felt before.

Writhing on the ground, he kicked at the cat with his free foot. Suddenly, the cat's tail caught fire, and the cat released his ankle and slunk into the darkness.

Grey rushed up and knelt beside him. Finding the wound, he shoved Red's pant leg up his calf and ripped off his boot, then his sock, and cradled Red's foot in his lap. All the while, Red's head rocked back and forth over the rocky ground as he moaned.

"They made it," Grey said. "They're headed up the path now."

Red's sacrifice had made it possible for his men to reach the path. At least they were out of the depths of the Canyon, heading home. Jakes could keep them safe on the path—he would have to.

Grey took Red's two blades, wiped the blood off on his pants, and handed them back. "These are for you."

A knot of panic formed in Red's throat. "You're going to leave me here."

"Never." Grey crammed an arm under Red's back and helped him stand.

Red settled his weight on his injured ankle and hissed in pain. Grey adjusted Red's arm over his shoulder.

He would never be able to walk out of the Canyon now.

The way was blocked, as if every beast of the Deep had come out to stop them from rising and returning to the world above. There was an odd *oneness* to these snarling creatures as they stared at Red and Grey from the shadows. There were foxbloods and woodwolves, and at least one garland cat, but there were smaller creatures that scampered among them, and one hulking frame that looked like it might be a bear. Something was causing these beasts to wait.

"Why don't they attack?" Grey whispered, knife in one hand, pistol in the other.

"Something is controlling them. Look at how they pace."

The beasts pressed the men back toward the river. With their small blades and only one bullet, there was no way they could fight their way out. Only death awaited them if the beasts attacked.

Red's heel struck a loose rock, which tumbled into the rushing waters. They could travel no farther.

"They're pushing us into the river," Grey hissed.

Red's blackened fingers throbbed.

"It's almost as if they're waiting on someone's command," Grey said, brandishing his knife at the encroaching animals.

Who could command all the beasts the Deep? The only person who seemed capable of such magic was Aly's father, but they had killed and buried him.

Aly had been certain Kassia was merely a Comforter—unless Kassia had been masking her true power. But that seemed unlikely considering she'd battled Aly with the intent to kill, using all the magic at her disposal. Someone else was enchanting these creatures.

Red's stomach tightened. If there was a foe more wicked than Kassia and more powerful than Aly's father, he never wanted to face that person.

A thought slammed into Red's mind so forcefully he nearly toppled over. "You said someone is commanding the beasts." He took a few deep breaths. "The river has not only energy but also a *will*. It drew those Protectors into the water."

Grey glanced down at the river. "You think the river is controlling them?" Grey scratched his head, the cool and collected spy more agitated than Red had ever seen him. "There's definitely a reason they pushed us here. I don't like it."

One woodwolf stepped forward and snapped at Grey's ankle. He shouted and waved his knife. The wolf jumped back. Grey swallowed and looked at Red. "I didn't want it to end this way, brother."

Red nodded, unsure how to respond. He didn't want this to be the end.

His fingers throbbed, his arm was almost entirely useless, and his ankle screamed with pain. He was a goner.

"You must get out," he whispered to Grey, unable to fully override the lump forming in his throat.

"I'm not leaving you here." He gestured at the beasts. "Besides, I wouldn't make it far."

Red edged closer to the river. It splashed up at his boots.

It hadn't harmed him the first time he'd touched the water.

Whatever sentient being lurked somewhere in the water might not kill him. The beasts certainly would.

A strange, low whistling sound jerked his attention up and away from the water. Light zoomed overhead in a bizarre, zigzag fashion. Whatever was hurtling through the air was also *on fire*. It almost had a human shape. A lyth? Or was the Canyon playing more tricks on their eyes?

Grey aimed high, but as he did so, a wolf slunk closer. He pointed his blade at the wolf, and fired into the air at this new threat.

The screeching, flaming thing fell straight toward them, falling fast through the air, arms flapping, fabric snapping.

The flames were *around* the person, like an orb.

As the figure slammed ungracefully to the ground, the flames petered out, and the wolf launched at Grey. Screaming obscenities, Grey fell beneath the massive animal.

Before Red could stumble two steps toward Grey, the figure —a woman, by her high-pitched, hollering voice—leaped into the air and slammed into the wolf attacking Grey.

Blinking in surprise, Red stared at Naia as she scrambled to her feet, huffing and puffing and shouting at the now dead wolf. Her hair billowed around her face.

"Oy, you're alive!" she called, hurrying toward him. Then she looked down at Grey. "And who are you?"

Grey groaned and sat up. There was no blood. *Thank Theod.* "Name's Grey," he said, pushing himself to his feet.

"Naia."

Grey stared at the dead wolf. "I think you crushed its lungs with that hit."

Naia pursed her lips. "I take it you are against animal cruelty?"

Tilting his head, Grey lifted a brow. He likely couldn't tell if she was joking or not. Her tone suggested she was not.

Red, however, had heard her dry humor a handful of times on the road from the Crescent Forest. "Naia, thank you for coming."

"Do I curtsey in a place like this?" she asked. Now Red was the one confused about whether or not she was serious. She looked dreadfully concerned about it, clutching her skirts with her hands and darting strange looks all around. "I suppose Grey doesn't mind if I don't. Do you?"

Grey shook his head.

"Hey," Naia said, stepping closer to Grey. "You have scars." Her eyes raked up and down his face. "Like me." She glanced at her hands and arms. "Were you a Zealot once?"

He stared down at her, perplexed. "I'm not a sorcerer, if that's what you mean, but I suppose I'm a zealot for what I believe in."

"Oh? And what is that?" Naia's hands planted on her hips like they had all the time in the world to discuss personal philosophies.

"Now isn't really the best time to chat. We have a parade of death behind us that way, and a river that wants to melt our flesh that way. I'd prefer a third option. That way." He pointed straight up.

Naia let out an angry wheeze and stomped in a circle. "I *told* her I wasn't good enough at this. I don't even know the *Verad* yet. I only know three verses!"

Red scanned the shadows for the waiting beasts. For now, they appeared content to hold them at the river's edge. But they didn't know for how long.

"You can get us out of here," Red said. "You flew in, you can fly out."

"Not holding *you two*." Naia waved her arms. "I barely flew, to be exact. I tried what he suggested and sort of caught on fire at one point, and the flying spell was too tricky to maintain while trying to put the flames out, so I stopped." She took a few quick breaths.

Grey and Red stared at her with lifted brows.

"It was rather alarming to see you headed toward us," Red admitted.

"Was that why he *shot* me?"

"I missed, didn't I?"

Naia *humphed*. She crossed her arms. "I'm not Aly."

Red stepped forward. "But you're here."

Naia let out an exaggerated sigh. "I can't do it. I can't fly you both out. It takes a strength spell as well as the flying spell, and I can barely maintain the flying one."

Red and Grey exchanged a glance. At the same time, they said, "Take him."

Lifting both arms, Naia silenced them. "I'm not here to play favorites. I won't leave one of you to die down here. Now, what was your plan for—"

A foxblood charged from Red's left. Unprepared for the sudden attack, he lost his balance. His injured ankle buckled under the weight of his body, and he fell.

Grey lunged, tackling the animal. Naia screamed again, and the air crackled with sparks of blueish lightning leaping between herself and the rocks. Grey grunted as he stabbed his knife into the foxblood.

When Red scrambled away from the fight, he saw blood spattering the rocks. Grey's entire front, from his collar to his belt, was soaked with red.

An explosion of blue light blasted the beast off of Grey, but it wasn't precise enough, and part of the shock knocked Grey backwards.

Naia yelped and dove for Grey. He didn't respond to her prodding, then her yelling, then her violent shaking.

Red's entire body froze as he stared at Grey's unmoving

body. "Save him, Naia," he said, voice low and firm despite the turmoil inside him.

Naia's hair blew around her face, obscuring her look of wild terror. "He's alive. I think I...oh Aly, why did you send me?" Naia rocked forward and put her ear against Grey's chest. She came away with blood on her cheek.

The animals became restless, moving about in quick movements right out of arm's reach.

"Get him out of here. Take him, now."

Naia shot Red a tear-streaked glower. "I'm not the one for this. I'm nowhere near ready for this kind of magic. She shouldn't have trusted me."

In Naia's voice, Red heard the same self-doubt he had felt right after his father had died. He'd wept for the loss of his father, but he'd also spilled tears of anger at being left an impossible task. He'd wilted under the sudden pressure of running a country, and his entire demeanor, his manners, and his ability to make wise decisions had suffered as a result. He regretted allowing himself to sink so low, but grief and fear did unimaginable things to the mind.

He scooted toward Naia and crouched beside her. "You can do this. Aly wouldn't have sent you if you were not capable of accomplishing what needs to be done." He remembered that touch frightened her, so he kept one hand on the rocks for balance, and the other on his knee, ignoring his own pain for the moment. "You can save him."

She shook her head fast. "I can't. I might hurt him even more."

Her spell to kill the foxblood had injured Grey. Perhaps she *shouldn't* attempt to heal him, especially not in such an agitated state. He nodded. "Can you fly him out?"

She sucked in a breath, steeling herself. "I can try."

Grey moaned.

"Grey!" Red shuffled to his side. "Grey, it's going to be all right. We're going to get you out of here."

"Don't save me," Grey rasped, looking up at Naia. "Save the king."

Red stared hard at Naia and shook his head. "I have commanded her to take you to safety."

"Idiot," hissed Grey, eyes drifting closed.

"Well, come on then." Naia leaned over Grey, shimmied one arm under his back, and pried his torso off the ground with Red's help. "No sense waiting for the rest of those animals to attack."

Red glanced at the snout of a woodwolf that was an arm's length from his face. The beast's yellow eyes stared with a hungry satisfaction, as if aware of the approaching meal. Red swallowed and pushed the fear aside.

When Grey was mostly standing, leaning on Naia for support, two wolves snapped at them, then danced back to the shadows as Naia's hands crackled with energy.

Grey cursed under his breath as the sparking energy stung him.

"Sorry!" barked Naia, nearly dropping Grey.

"Can you do this?" he asked, skepticism heavy in his rasping voice.

"There aren't many Wells down here. Not good ones, anyway. Except yours."

Grey sighed. "Use mine, then."

Naia shifted uncomfortably.

Red, sensing her hesitation, said, "Do it and get him out of here."

She spat, "I haven't tried flying a heavy man straight up out of a deep canyon before."

Grey moaned with pain. "I know...plenty of truth to get us out of here. Now...listen to me." He spoke slowly and deliberately through pained breaths. "Repeat what you need for your spells."

With careful, whispered words, he began reciting verses from the *Verad* like he was a schoolboy being quizzed on his lessons. As he spoke, his skin emitted an odd blueish glow. Naia's face scrunched and twisted, and her skin reflected the faint blue glow, but she never looked away from Grey.

Grey's eyes never closed, his words never ceased, even as Naia's magic Bound to his Well.

The beasts recoiled as if a force had knocked them backward. Naia's eyes popped open.

She repeated one line and her body lifted off the ground. Grey sagged, and she quickly looped both arms around his middle. He grunted, but his feet rose off the canyon floor. In this way, with Grey reciting truth, pausing every few seconds for Naia to repeat what he'd said, they lifted into the darkness and out of sight.

As the sound of their voices faded, the animals charged.

All of them converged on Red at once, as if he had been their true target all along.

Theod, help, was all he could think before one solution presented itself: the river.

Without thought to the consequences, he dove.

21

ALY

Dirt tumbled onto Aly's body, filling every space and pressing against her clothing, her skin, her hair. In minutes, she wouldn't be able to breathe. She squeezed her eyes shut.

Even as the earth threatened to bury her alive, a strange, ripping sensation tore at her insides. It was the same feeling she'd had when Red's Well had been stripped away from her during the coronation.

In seconds, the feeling ceased, and an emptiness remained. In her mind's eye, a light had blinked out.

Aly gasped, inhaling clumps of dirt, sending her into a fit of choking coughs stifled by the weight of earth suffocating her.

But the truth screamed at her. She'd experienced this twice before: when Gevar had died and when her bond with Red had been severed.

Alexander is dead, she thought.

But how? She'd just left him.

Drowning in the earth, Aly had no human Truthwell to pull from to save herself. All she had was the soil around her, which was whirling and swirling as if it had a life of its own, crushing her with its increasing weight.

There was little air left to breathe in this earthen tomb.

Panic seized her. She grasped for the Truthwells of the world above. The dirt offered little energy—not nearly as much as she needed to maneuver her way out of this.

Aly tried to tuck her hands over her face to keep the dirt away from her nose and mouth. With her mind, she searched for something, anything, she could use, for a Well strong enough to pull her body from the earth.

Red, I wish I had never—Aly's thought cut off. If she was no longer Bound to Alexander, she was free to Bind again.

"Red!" she shouted, making the mistake of opening her mouth. Dirt flew in. Her arms and legs could no longer move.

She pushed her awareness out, using what tiny energy she could glean from the dirt. *Red!* She searched and she searched, her awareness not able to reach as far or as fast or as wide as she hoped.

Red!

In her mind, she screamed. In her mind, she saw Red's face. In her mind, she kissed him one last time.

Red, I need you.

Red...

Her mind brushed against the darkness of the Canyon, then the familiar pattern she sought played its rhythm at the edges of her consciousness.

Red's light was dim, as if covered with a thin blanket.

Aly's body flared with heat as her magic sank once more into the familiar, blinding depths of Red's Well.

The earth will change, the sky will fall, but your truth will rise above it all.

The earth shook.

Mountains bow their mighty heads to the one who made the stars.

Light poured down through a fissure as it widened. She heaved a breath of fresh air.

Lift your face, O downcast ones. Light will show the way.

Aly wrenched her body from the earthen tomb and shot toward the sky above.

Cease your striving, men of dust, and know that power alone belongs to the Maker.

She screamed in delight at the sight of the sun, the air in her lungs, and the warmth crackling in her veins as the magic of the Binding wore off.

Dirt fell from her clothes and hair, and the scene below her came into focus.

A swarm of Zealots peeled away from the palace gates, like scattering beetles. In the street lay Zoraiya, arms bent awkwardly at her sides. Blood darkened the pavement around her torso. Her mouth was open and her eyes stared up at Aly. A guard from the palace gate stood with weapon drawn, staring down his barrel at the fleeing Zealots.

A gasp escaped Aly's lips and the feeling of a fist in her chest made it hard to breathe for a moment. Zor was dead. One palace guard had also fallen, halfway onto the road. A spear stuck out of his chest.

A white-haired man rushed to Zoraiya's side. Igor. Rainbow crept into the yellow glow of a gas lamp, her hands raised for magic. Quince hunched beside her.

Aly descended and ran to Igor. The Canduli Zealots had all vanished, leaving it eerily quiet. The palace guard glanced at Aly, nodded once, then hefted his companion's body inside the grounds and closed the gate.

Heart pounding like mad, Aly stared down at Zor. "She's gone."

Her voice startled Igor. He stood with a few grunts and placed a comforting hand on Aly's cheek. "She turned on us.

When our shields fell away, she ran. Like she knew exactly where to go."

Rainbow and Quince walked up. Aly offered them a weak smile. Quince wrapped her in a brief, tight hug, then released her and looked away sheepishly.

Aly inhaled, trying to catch her breath. Bits of dirt crunched between her teeth. She glanced at the deep hole she'd just risen from, and terror gripped her heart once more.

Before she could speak, Igor lifted a shaky hand. "Go. I sense you are eager to depart. I will watch over these two." He rested a hand on the others' shoulders.

"The king is dead," Aly whispered. The truth was strange to say aloud. *And I'm Bound once more to Red.*

Red's light was dimmer than it should be. It had saved her, but it was diminishing even as she held on to it with her magical awareness. One thing was clear: *Red was dying.*

She pressed a dirt-streaked hand to her mouth, shoving down the scream she wanted to let loose. Her students needed her protection, Mardon needed her magic, but Red would die if she didn't reach him soon.

"Dead?" Igor repeated. "Didn't you just speak with him?"

Aly nodded, overcome with the reality that she'd failed to do her duty. The king had died while she was *right here.* She pressed her palms against her eyes. "I healed him. I gave him his mind back, but then he sent me away. He was so angry." Strange tears rose up in her eyes. She hated Alexander for what he'd done to Red, but he had been hers to protect. Someone inside the palace had killed him, as soon as Zoraiya had attacked Aly.

Rainbow stopped chewing a fingernail. "Right before you showed up at the forest, she'd been talking with someone from your city, and I thought that meant she wanted to change." Rainbow shrugged. "I didn't know she was getting orders to kill you."

"Orders?" Aly trembled with adrenaline and the desire to leave and reach Red. Whatever Zor had done, it appeared to have been coordinated with Alexander's assassination.

Aly squatted to the ground and rocked on her heels. "How?" she repeated several times. Nearly dying had invigorated her and pushed her exhaustion away, but her mind scrambled at the weight of Alexander's death.

Igor dropped his gaze. "Neither of us saw it coming."

She stood and touched Igor's shoulder. "You are not responsible for her actions. And I think I know who has been giving her orders. Someone has wanted me dead for a very long time, someone who also no longer had reason to keep Alexander alive." With one more deep breath, she said, "But the king is dying—the true king. I must go to him. I trust you both to keep Quince safe. Likely, a battle will break out here tomorrow. You should be safe enough in your rooms. They are far from the city's eastern side."

With a firm nod at her students, she leaped once more into the air. She called on the power inside of Red's Well, Pulling it to her as she flew, crafting spell after spell for speed, flight, and shields.

Theod, I know there are limits to the magic you've given us, but if ever I could move fast, let it be now.

Soon, she was arcing up over the city, flying north to avoid a direct route over the Zealot army. Within minutes, she was moving so fast that the air against her head began to hurt, threatening to snap her neck. Even her spells for aerodynamics were failing as she pushed past the boundaries for flight.

The Maker of man established his boundaries. Aly recited the words, using her gift to find the extremes of magic's capabilities. Magic couldn't rewrite physics—not really—and it couldn't truly take the place of the Maker in creation or destruction. But as Aly flew, she wondered if the boundaries she faced were really her own walls, built to guard against disappointment, should her magic not do what she hoped it could.

She sensed Red was in danger, that he needed her *now*.

Altering time and space were not within her power.

Igor's words to Naia coursed through her raging thoughts. *You could try burning.*

Aly had once seen a comet streaking through the evening sky, visible even before sunset. People in Kitrel had talked of it for weeks, and Aly had questioned the priest at the abbey about it. He'd explained to her that rocks occasionally fell from the sky, and they burned with fire as they fell as a result of moving so quickly through the air.

I can break a rock into dust. I can shape the earth into a crown. Those were spells any skilled sorcerer could accomplish. *I made a dagger out of ash and transformed a bullet into a flower.* These were Aly's own, unique spells, ones she still didn't fully understand. There was more to magic than Aly had been taught. There was more to magic than what most people believed.

Beacon and Beholder could do more than the average pair. She wished now that she and Red had had more time to explore this concept.

Red, she called in her mind. *I'm coming.* He couldn't answer, but she wanted him to know. To hold on. To fight.

I love you, she said, knowing this time that her voice carried far enough. She could have called to him from among the stars, and he would have heard her.

She only hoped she'd reach him fast enough to say it out loud.

On the fringes of her awareness, a shadowy Truthwell prickled her mind. Now that Aly sensed the Truthwell following her, she did recognize it. She'd fought against the queen before.

Aly carefully crafted the spell she hoped would ignite her body like a comet from the heavens, but before casting it, she waited one moment and called out to Naia. *Where are you? Is Red all right?*

Naia's voice quickly returned, agitated and winded. *Caridan. Grey is injured. Red is in the Canyon. Alone.*

Aly nearly dropped out of the sky. Her concentration cracked and her spells fractured. Within seconds of faltering, her spells were recast and she was again shooting through the air toward the Canyon.

If Red was alone in the Deep, he didn't have long.

"May the Maker guide me," Aly intoned before whispering a new spell for speed.

Fire erupted all around her. Her stomach lurched with the sudden burst in speed. She was grateful she'd woven in protections for her skin and hair and clothing and a way to breathe amid the flames. The land beneath her blurred and she could no longer keep her eyes open. She used her magical awareness to sense her surroundings. The Wells of trees became a dull golden gleam below her. The Well of a nearby river burned bright white in her mind. Tanderan villages and towns flashed by as solid pools of light.

Flying like a shooting star, Aly smiled at what the Maker had allowed. *This* was what magic could do.

In less than an hour, she reached the Canyon.

Aly hadn't prepared herself for slowing down from such speeds. When the spells dropped, she screamed with dizziness, cartwheeling through the air and crashing through trees as she hurtled toward the ground.

A quick spell cushioned her fall, but her impact still carved a mark in the earth. Her shoulders ached. Her body trembled. Lodged in the dirt once again, Aly wanted more than anything to be free of her confines.

But her mind had turned to pudding. She stared up at the stars peeking through the tree branches and took several steadying breaths. Her mind refused to focus. *Get up*, she commanded herself, but her muscles rejected her request.

Finally, she focused enough to mutter another spell, lifting her body off the ground and slapping a cold breeze across her face.

Blinking and alert, Aly assessed her surroundings. She'd taken out several trees in her crash. She sensed several hundred Truthwells a short distance to her left. Caridan. Red's Well still burned from within the Canyon.

Grey's Well was in Caridan, as was Naia's.

Aly ran toward the Canyon's edge with all the speed she could muster. Her lungs ached within minutes. She slowed to a jog, then finally a walk. At the rim, she dropped her hands to her knees and heaved air. The flight had taken so much from her mentally that her muscles and bones felt like they were turning to stone, like her brain was shutting down all bodily functions in order to sleep.

"No!" she yelled to herself, pouring a jolt of energy into her body. It was a risky spell, considering it would make her even more tired later, but it was a worry for a few hours from now. She launched again into the air and relished the feeling of lightness and swiftness that accompanied flight.

The misty depths of the Canyon rushed into view. The air sizzled with magic, and a strangeness clawed at Aly's magical senses. The river was raging, its wickedness like writhing shadows in Aly's mind.

Red's Well had darkened even more.

Energy hummed in the air. The tiny Wells of each drop of mist manifested like hands reaching for her. She shook away the illogical visions.

But there *was* something in the distance, coming faster than Aly would have thought possible for a mere Comforter.

Kassia.

22

RED

A power gripped Red's mind as cold water stung his skin. Pressure built in his head, like an unseen hand squeezed his skull.

The rushing water pushed against his body, slamming him into a rock. He spun away, his shoulder bouncing off another rock as he spun into the heart of the tumultuous Black River.

Red sucked down water, cursing himself for being such an idiot. He finally raised his head above the river and started kicking as hard as he could toward shore.

His head dipped below the fast waters. He couldn't draw enough air. Something was pulling him down. Every inch of his body burned, then ached from the inside. He'd experienced this sensation once before, when a sorcerer not as talented as Aly had almost Stripped him of his energy. The *river* was attempting to steal the energy from his Truthwell.

But that wasn't possible.

Determination raged inside of him as he kicked and pushed, throwing his arms forward and forward and forward. The greedy river curled over his flailing body. Red howled in anger.

His strength was leaving his body as the river yanked on his Well. This river was alive in more ways than one.

He drew one last quick breath before his face was dragged beneath the waves, his hands trailing after him, reaching for the sky.

Down, down, he sank, no more powerful to rise than an anvil tossed into the sea. Water stung his eyes, but he forced them open, watching as his world disappeared above him.

Aly, I love you. And Theod, I'm sorry.

Out of all he could possibly hope to say again, these were the only important words left inside him.

He kicked again.

His vision purpled.

He had one aim: to fill his lungs with sweet breath.

Water stung as it crashed into his desperate lungs.

A strange warming from within accompanied the sensation of drowning. A moment ago, he'd felt his life's energy draining away, but now, he felt it returning, as if someone were filling him up. *Is this what it feels like to die?* His eyes were scrunched shut, but he could almost see light behind his eyelids. The feeling became almost intoxicatingly blissful.

He'd felt this way once before. He thrashed in the water, prying his eyes open to gaze at his skin. It was glowing.

Red.

It was Aly's voice.

A furious, wild hope awoke inside him. He kicked and thrashed against the power pulling him toward the grave. He couldn't breathe, but his mind sharpened and he recalled Veeter Yin's last words: *Rise with her.*

Red had assumed Yin had meant Tandera, but in these seconds before death claimed him, Red saw Aly in his mind's eye and could only think: *Rise with her.*

Red's face broke the waves, and he choked as air and water mingled in his throat.

The light emitting from his body pierced the darkness all around him. He could see the shore and willed his body toward it, revitalized with a new energy. As his glowing hands tore through the waves, he saw tendrils of darkness curling within the water.

The water raged, slapping at his face but no longer burning his skin. The current tugged harder, trying to bring him down. Whatever was in the river was angry.

Red!

Aly's voice cut through his near-death panic. He could hear her as if she swam beside him.

Somehow, she had Bound to him once again.

The very world shook as the light faded from Red's skin and his feet touched the river bottom before he propelled himself to shore.

He scrambled free of the hungry waters and lay for a moment, breathing heavily on the damp rocks as the ground trembled beneath him. Surely it was only the Canyon twisting his understanding of reality.

When he glanced at his feet to ensure they were clear of the water's reach, he noted that the river rose in little agitated waves that never crashed, as if repelled by a force not unlike a strong wind, blowing the water back from Red.

"Aly!" He knew she couldn't hear him, but it felt good to say her name aloud, to know that she was alive and *with him*, even if still far away. Pushing himself up, he hobbled along the river's edge, completely uncertain of what to do next.

He had no plan. He only had one blade left—the other had sunk in the river.

If Aly had Bound to him once again, it meant Alexander was dead. Had the army attacked Mardon already?

He must get out. But as he moved along the river bank, the beasts emerged from the shadows once again, their fangs bared, their hair on end.

Into Red's mind came a familiar voice.

I'm coming.

He stumbled over the uneven ground and caught himself, landing hard with his wrists. A smile broke across his face as he spotted a tall boulder nearby.

His ankle throbbed and his injured arm burned, but he finally reached the top. Drawing his knife, he shouted at the beasts drawing near the boulder, "She's coming, and you won't survive her."

23

ALY

The shadows in the air danced, as if excited. Then the river *leaped*.

Aly sensed the ground rushing up to meet her as she slowed her descent. She honed in on Red's location, her green skirts flapping.

"Aly!" Red's voice rose up out of the mists.

Her heart jumped inside her chest as she alighted beside him on a large boulder. He was favoring one leg, and his right arm hung limp at his side.

When she landed, a dozen beasts from below snapped hungry jaws at their ankles.

Arms arcing overhead, she spun, slicing her hands like daggers through the air. Each beast fell with a forceful *thud* against the stone.

Red pulled her into an embrace. She fell into him, choking back a sob that he was all right. He held her so tightly that she felt his ribs against her own.

Her mouth uttered healing spells as she clung to him, a pale light glowing as her magic sank into his body.

No part of her wanted to release him, but they needed to escape this place.

"Kassia is coming," Aly mumbled against his chest. "We must go."

He cupped her face in his hands. "What happened?" His thumbs brushed dirt from under her eyes, along her cheeks, and off her lips.

Her entire body shook as his hands moved across her skin. Instead of speaking, she hooked her arms tightly around him once again and, with a string of spells, lifted them straight up like a firework exploding into the night.

The energy in the air crackled, almost as if in anticipation of Kassia's arrival. Like called to like, and Aly sensed the magnetism between the river and Kassia. As long Red and Aly were in this place, they were in danger.

"I need to keep Kassia away from the Canyon," Aly yelled to Red over the wind as they shot toward the sky. "I think the river is waiting for her."

Red grunted in agreement. "Ondorian was right. There is something in the river, Aly. It didn't want to let me go. I think it might be—"

"Usrich," they said at the same time.

Red smiled. "I just figured it out."

"Me too," Aly said, voice slightly muffled against Red's chest.

The river hummed with a strange, dark energy. Among the light of the water's natural Truthwell hovered a black cloud that flittered in and out of Aly's perception. She focused on the dust-like darkness. It slid among the pure, clear light of the water, but didn't flow away with the current.

It was true: *There were two entities in the river.* One was the Well of the water and the other was something else, an energy signature like she'd never seen before. It held the twisting, smoke-like shadows of a human Well, but devoid of all light.

And the shadows of that second Well had a distinct plurality to them. The darkness was a sickening cluster of energy signatures that made Aly's skin crawl.

It wasn't *only* Usrich in the river.

Red held her as hard as she held him—despite the fact that her magic wouldn't let him fall. She relished the feeling as they left the Black River behind.

Aly could see the top of the Canyon walls. Safety was drawing near.

A fierce, frozen wind began to blow down from above. Aly pressed into it, still rising.

The wind became a gale. A gust hit so hard that it slammed them against the Canyon wall. Red's head snapped sideways, crashing into hers so hard her vision danced with stars.

Her concentration broke, as did her hold on Red.

The harsh wind blasted them back toward the Canyon floor. Aly screamed in anger and reached for Red as they plummeted.

Kassia whirled into view, yanking Red away with a flash of her white cloak that faded into the milky fog.

"Red!"

Aly sliced her palms through the air, and a floor of ice stretched across the Canyon, stopping their descent. The sound of ice cracking and water sizzling brought another grunt of anger from Aly's lips, even as her next spell left her mouth.

With this one, she needed her hands even more than usual. Within seconds, she was diving alongside Kassia and Red toward the Black River. Aly curled her fingers into fists, watching as strings of small rocks broke free from the walls and looped around Kassia's ankles. Kassia shrieked in agony as the rocks squeezed her ankles, jerking her to a violent stop.

When Kassia released Red, throwing him toward the river, Aly yelped a spell that pushed him over the rocks and cushioned his fall. She quickly added another shield for him, but her distraction gave Kassia the opportunity to dissolve the rocks binding her ankles. She flipped and landed on the rocky ground.

Animals crept from every shadow and crevice to stand behind Kassia, awaiting her command. Nearby, Red scrambled for footing, the pale glow of a shield around him.

A cackle of laughter erupted from Kassia, and shards of ice lifted off the river and pelted toward Red and Aly.

Aly disintegrated them with a flick of her wrist. A Comforter was no match for a Master. Something else was at play here for Kassia to even *think* she had a chance. Perhaps Kassia had figured out how to burn like a comet as well, but her ability stopped with heating and cooling.

The river swelled, overflowing its banks and surging across the smooth rocks. With a small yelp, Aly jumped and hovered over the water.

Kassia and the river were fighting as a team.

The darkness Aly had seen in the river lurched into the air, its tentacles twining around Kassia's skirts and up her torso. Aly yelled several spells, but not one touched Kassia or the shadow.

As the living darkness reached Kassia's face, it wreathed her head and then dove into her open mouth. Kassia inhaled deeply, and the sight chilled Aly's blood.

When Kassia's eyes met Aly's, they glowed like embers. Even her skin radiated a deep, reddish light.

Kassia had just Bound herself to the river, Aly was certain of it. And whatever was in that water had made Kassia *much* stronger.

"You can't evade us forever!" Kassia bellowed, hurling flames at Aly.

Us. She and the river? Aly batted the flames away, but the energy necessary to combat Kassia's attacks was increasing.

The warmth of the flames countered the icy chill in the

Canyon's magic-cooled depths. *She's talking, which means she's worried,* Aly said silently to Red as she backed in front of him.

A flaming ball soared past Aly's head, crashing against the rocks behind her.

She lifted both hands out at her sides. This needed to end—now.

With her arms, she made a fluid motion, and the Canyon walls mimicked it, rippling like the surface of a pond. Rocks rained down, scattering the animals that circled them.

Over the noise, Red yelled, "I will fight alongside you, like we fought your father."

Aly pressed a hand to his chest. "You already are."

This was a battle between her and Kassia, and he needed to remain safe. If Aly lost Red's light, she'd lose this fight. "I'm sorry," she whispered, and her next spell caged him with the strongest shield she could conjure.

Kassia's white powdered face matched the ghostly mist.

"It's only you and me now," Aly yelled.

"It was never only me and you." Kassia shot a dart of ice at Aly.

Aly dissolved it with a word. But she needed to know what Kassia meant, and where this new power of hers came from. She was still only heating or cooling, to extreme degrees. The shadow in the river hadn't *changed* the Comforter's ability, only the *power* of her attacks.

Kassia shouted a spell and suddenly every beast in sight converged on Red.

Aly's stomach flipped, but her shield held as the animals dashed themselves against it, again and again, their snarling sounds rising above the sounds of magic and wind and waves. With a flip of her hand, Aly lifted Kassia and slammed her against the stones.

Kassia screamed in anger under the pressure of Aly's binding spell. "I will not fail."

Over the whipping wind and freezing temperature, a blast of heat knocked into Aly's chest. It wasn't visible, and she hadn't moved fast enough to counter it. Aly cringed in pain and smelled burning fabric.

Theod, help me, Aly muttered over and over again, hoping beyond hope that she had believed the right teachings in her life, that she had not been the one who had been deceived. Her magic was proof that she had believed the truth, and yet here was Kassia, a powerful sorcerer in her own right, but with a different motivation.

How could magic be so divided, if it originated with the Maker?

Whatever gift Kassia had received, she'd polluted it with a desire for power, a desire to lift herself over others and use them as tools. This was not what Theod had intended.

Aly shoved one palm forward, and her binding spell anchored Kassia's chest and hands to the stones. The Bulvarnan queen barely moved, but she managed to hiss out a spell and a thousand tiny ice darts sliced toward Aly's flesh.

With a grunt, Aly crossed her arms in front of her and flung them wide. A dome-like spell burst out around her and shattered the ice into tiny snow-like crystals that felt cold against her skin.

"You cannot win against a Master," Aly yelled over the howling wind. "Why are you doing this?" They could battle like this all day, and Kassia would never win. She was more adept at combat spells than any Comforter Aly had ever seen, but it was not enough to defeat Aly. Kassia fought with a wicked desperation, as if she knew she couldn't win, and the anger of it pushed her into a frenzy.

"My magic is not *lesser*," screamed Kassia as flames leaped up from the ground at Aly's ankles.

Was *this* what had angered Kassia?

Aly danced away from the heat, dousing the flames with a blanket of rock dust, but her focus had been snapped, and the binding spell fell away.

"You are a Comforter. Do not deny it!" Aly dissolved the rocks under Kassia's feet, shaping them like snow. Kassia yowled and leaped into the air, but the rocks hardened again, caging one of Kassia's legs from the knee down. *Try getting out of that one.*

"I despise that term." Kassia jerked and grunted as she tried to free her leg. Curses trailed out of Kassia's mouth alongside attack spells. "And you're wrong. You've all always been wrong. Those you call Comforters have never been *less* than the worshipped *Protectors*. I will show you what my magic can do."

Aly batted away Kassia's attack spells. The queen was stuck. Only one spell would end her.

Aly had a spell ready—one breath more and Kassia's terror would be over. Every warrior carried a weapon, and Aly's weapon was the truth. She would cut down this liar and end her reign of deception.

The rock moved at Aly's command. She curled her fist upward, and the rocks climbed over Kassia's legs, then her torso. As soon as they were around her chest, Aly would snap her fingers and the stones would crush the woman between them.

Death was never easy, even the death of a wicked enemy. Killing always stung. Aly braced for that sting.

Kassia's screams barely rattled Aly's thoughts as she recited the spell over and over so as not to lose concentration while maintaining a shield to deflect the shards of ice shooting toward her.

Then, in response to Aly's trap, Kassia played her last hand.

"You think I can die?" Her words were strained by the pain of the rocks encircling her body. "I belong to the river now. You will never defeat me. Not even with your precious Beacon."

With those words, the river leaped over its banks and crashed around the small prison holding Kassia captive. She sighed as if accepting the embrace of a lover, and within seconds, the water swirled over Kassia's head.

As soon as Kassia's head disappeared under the living waters, a pulse of energy thundered out of the river, knocking Aly down against the damp rocks. Before she could even scramble to her feet, a tower of water shot toward the sky, swirling like a hurricane.

Frozen droplets stung Aly's face. She pushed her hands up, casting a spell to shield her. The water roared as it reached for the heavens.

"Red!" Aly yelled, launching into the air as the banks overflowed.

When the water crashed back down, there was no Kassia. The small cone of rock that had been meant to be her tomb was empty.

Aly gaped at the scene.

A rumble sounded deep within the river.

Then a curling back shadow lifted from the surface of the waves.

It moved like a sentient creature, searching her out with quick hands.

Aly shot toward Red, eyes fixed on the black smoke and swirling waters rising beneath her.

From within the shadowy mass, a voice entered Aly's mind.

My magic is not lesser now.

The howls of the beasts of the Deep rose in answer.

24

ELISE

Elise and Seb raced down an alleyway in the heart of Mardon away from a pair of law enforcement officers they'd spotted in the street. Elise's blood pounded, her heart protesting the pace she was trying to keep.

Alexander hadn't lost any time marking her as a traitor, a liar, and a criminal. Elise and Seb had spent most of the previous day moving deeper into the city, peeking around corners and darting across roads.

Elise leaned against the bricks of the alleyway. "I can't do this," she wheezed, clutching at her chest.

Seb whipped around, his bruised and swollen face blazing with determination. "Yes, you can." His eyes searched wildly behind them, then he relaxed. "I don't think they're following us. Look." He pointed, and at the mouth of the alley, the two officers marched by, not even glancing their way.

The palace guards as well as the police had chased them for most of the day, but as night came on, the chase had died out, as if the bigger matter looming over them all had rendered two palace escapees insignificant.

The army was set to attack at first light, and Mardon was on the brink of war. Elise had no idea how Alexander was handling the mess she'd thrown him in the chapel, but all that mattered to her now was finding a safe place to wait out the attack—and a way to look Sebastian Thorin in the eye.

Since they'd left the palace, neither Seb nor Elise had spoken of what had transpired. Running for their lives had a way of postponing important conversations.

"Let's go," urged Seb.

They zigzagged up two more alleys. Quickly pivoting onto one of the broader streets, they slammed into a crowd of people, earning grumbles and a few curses.

"What are they doing? It's past midnight," Elise declared, clinging to Seb as the unusually busy streets of Mardon swept them along.

Everyone was hurrying. Few people spoke other than to push and yell for others to get out of their way. Most pedestrians had baskets under their arms or blankets. Several were carrying children. All wore grave expressions.

"People don't always do what's best, especially when they're scared," Seb replied between heavy breaths. "These people believed what Alexander told them, that the army would turn back. Or they believed their king would save them with a wall of magic or something. They put off preparations and are scrambling now."

One man nearly pushed Elise down as he raced.

Elise watched the faces of the people. "There is something else wrong," she heaved. "Something we have missed. The people have known the army was coming. Yesterday, they weren't out like this."

She tapped on one man's shoulder as he strode by with determined steps. He blinked at her. "Excuse me," she said, "What news?"

The man blinked again, as if shocked she was asking. As he hurried on, he said over his shoulder, "The king's dead. Battle's coming, and we have no king."

Elise choked on her next breath.

Seb grabbed her and pulled her toward him. "Come on, the people are panicking. We need to get off the streets."

As they hurried down the sidewalk, Elise watched as businesses shut and bolted their doors, locked against the hordes of refugees from the country. Many of those refugees had created makeshift shelters along the wide avenues or tucked into alleys. A child cried as one mother attempted to comfort her.

Elise scanned the faces with a concerned frown. "There is no more room. They shouldn't have come."

Seb grunted as they hurried around another building. "When two armies are headed toward my little wooden farmhouse and there's a fortified city nearby full of rich families with Protectors and a king with a powerful sorcerer, I'm heading to that city with my child in one hand and all my hope in the other." He stopped and stared at Elise, the glow from the gaslamps highlighting the sweat on his brow. "No one could have told them they'd be safer in their homes—they wouldn't have believed it. I don't blame them for coming."

Elise watched a man pound a fist on the door of a solicitor's office. No one answered. The door bore a hastily made sign: *No admittance*. A blond woman holding hands with two small children stood behind them. Strapped to her was a third child.

Elise's heart ached. All around her, the people of Tandera were terrified. There was no safe harbor here. Many of the wealthy families with Protectors had indeed left, though some had stayed after Alexander's edicts demanding all Protectors remain in the city. Now that he was dead, she wondered if the rest would flee. A gasp clawed from her throat and she clapped a hand over her lips, heaving at the despair and her lack of ability to help.

Seb looped a tentative arm around her. She grabbed his shirt and pressed her forehead against her fists, as if to shrink away from the awful scene around her. He brought his other arm around and squeezed her to his chest. For a moment, she relished the safety she felt in his strong arms. She didn't deserve him.

"I think we should try the cathedral," Seb muttered over her head. "Looks like the police are not worried about us anymore."

A block over, the cathedral was overrun, its doors open but the crowd pushing to gain cover had nowhere else to fit. Refugees huddled against the buildings and around the central fountain.

"I hate not knowing what's coming," Elise said, trembling. "At least the army can't enter the city. We have Protectors here to keep them at bay."

"Not enough," Seb said.

"Don't say that."

He chewed his lower lip and looked away. "I'm sorry. I'm not good at this either."

"We need Aly back," Elise muttered as she took in the crowded square.

"Alexander was a fool to send her away on the brink of war."

Elise inhaled sharply. "He advised my father and grandfather for years. But here at his end, he seemed to lose all reason."

"We have no king. We have no Royal Sorcerer." Seb ran a hand over the back of his neck.

"Wait," Elise paused. "If Alexander is dead, then Aly doesn't need to protect him anymore."

"Astute conclusion."

"That means she isn't Bound to him anymore."

Seb's eyes widened. "So she could come back here and save

us all, is that what you're saying?"

"No," Elise replied, eyes searching the skies as if she might glimpse a cannonball plummeting toward them. "It means she'll find Red. I know she will."

Seb made a contemplative expression but did not respond. "There," he said, pointing to the top of the cathedral's tower. "I bet from up there we can see what's happening."

The cathedral was packed with people, but they weren't turning anyone away. Seb and Elise squeezed and elbowed their way through the tight crowd toward the stairwells tucked away in a side room along the nave. One led up to the tower, another to the rotunda.

They climbed a thousand steps and popped out a door that opened onto a tiny balcony along the inside of the rotunda. Elise's stomach climbed into her throat as she followed Seb onto the terrifying walkway, toward a door set into the wall.

A tiny balcony circled the rotunda on the outside as well, but this one felt much higher, partly due to the strong breeze that set Elise off balance.

The roof was occupied by four other curious people. They nodded at Seb and Elise but said nothing. Elise crept behind Seb along the tiny ledge until they reached the easternmost corner of the building. They wedged themselves against the sloping roof, buttressing themselves with their feet against the small stone wall that separated them from a great fall to the square below.

Elise let out a small, desperate sound as she took in the view.

They couldn't see the city's edge, but they could see the fires of the army stretching across the plains outside of the city. It was far larger than she'd ever imagined.

Seb grabbed Elise's hand and squeezed, as if to say, perhaps, that he was sorry he brought her up here.

But she wanted the advantage of seeing what was coming.

Her fear rattled her bones, but the warmth of Seb's hand

around hers acted like a tether, keeping her from flying into fits of panic. She could sense his gaze, and knew he deserved answers. For several minutes, they remained silent. He seemed to be waiting for her to speak.

She couldn't bring herself to admit her mistakes. They were too awful, and she wasn't quite ready to see the anger in his face when she revealed them.

So for a time, they just sat there, staring out at the night.

"I wish we could do something," said finally Elise over the whistling wind. "We need Aly."

Elise's practiced composure was crumbling. Seb's sturdy arm around her shoulder was the only thing keeping her from falling completely to pieces.

"It'll be all right," Seb whispered against her hair.

She knew he didn't mean it. He had no better idea what would happen than she did, but she appreciated the words either way.

"Why are you...?" she began, her throat closing around her words. She shook her head, unable to voice her thoughts.

His brown eyes watched her. He didn't appear angry or eager, but rather patient. In his eyes burned his desire for an explanation.

She swallowed several times before speaking again. "How can you possibly forgive me?"

He exhaled. "You haven't actually apologized for anything yet."

Her eyes pinned on the flickering lights of the enemy soldiers, Elise whispered, "I'm so sorry. I was...I had..." No matter how she chose to explain it, the truth was too ugly.

He nudged her with his shoulder, his gaze mercifully angled away, as if he couldn't quite look at her as she fumbled through this apology. "I need to know why, Elise."

She nodded and pushed down the guilt that threatened to

bring on a flood of emotion. "I thought it would make Alexander trust me. That if I turned you two in, he would grant me into his confidences, and I could learn something of great value. Something that could eventually help."

She left out the part about wanting to spy on Lordan. It was too childish to admit, after everything. In the end, Lordan had come to her aid. She still disliked him for the way he'd so carelessly broken her heart, but he'd offered his help to her when she'd needed it most.

A lot of good it did. The king was dead, and her attempts to expose him were altogether worthless now. She wiped at the tears filling her eyes.

Seb remained silent a long while, the only sounds were the breeze whistling and the occasional crying of a frightened child in the square below. She waited for his response, every nerve on edge.

He propped his wrists on his knees and sighed. "Thank you for telling me."

That's it? Elise blinked at him. *What else?* She wanted him to say he forgave her, that it was all right and that he understood. She hung onto this possibility, like his forgiveness would absolve her of all wrongdoing.

Instead, he changed the subject. "I think I'm going to be optimistic about this," he said, jerking his head toward the army encamped outside their city.

She let out a small sound that was entirely too close to a whimper for a princess.

"Would you rather me be practical and forthright? Because I can be." He offered a small smile that thawed some of the frozen tension in her chest. "But I personally don't want to live in the land of *we're-all-going-to-die*."

Elise pushed against him with her shoulder. "I don't want to live there either. And I can't quite picture *practical* on you."

He leaned closer. "It never did suit me."

Elise's head snapped up. "That's it!"

Seb raised his brows.

"You are the least practical person I've ever met."

"Thanks."

"You build *trebuchets* in a time when castles no longer exist."

His lips twitched upward. "Indeed, I do. What did you have in mind, my ruthless one?"

Her chest hitched at the word *my*. Somehow, she warmed from toes to ears despite the chilly breeze and the icy fear in her veins. "I say we wheel that thing out of storage."

He shook his head in pleasant surprise. "A marvelous idea, but for the fact it is locked away in a palace we have been forbidden from entering."

She stood as best she could on the terrifying ledge and extended her hand. "Benedict Alexander is dead. As far as I'm concerned, that renders me royal again—and who's to say otherwise? It's my palace or no one's."

His eyes shone with wonder over a crisp smirk. He grabbed her hand. "Lead the way, Princess."

Elise ran as fast as she could in her heavy, beaded wedding dress. Every few minutes she needed to stop to breathe. Seb waited for her patiently each time, never hurrying her.

Having a plan made the streets seem less perilous, the crashes of magic less paralyzing. She could see now why Red had faced a death curse by forging wild plans. Action mollified fear.

"Come on," she hissed over heavy breaths. "The nearest entrance is the back garden gate. This way."

Trumpets sounded outside the city walls, and Elise froze. The battle had come. She peered up at Seb with terrified eyes.

People screamed. Children clung to their parents.

This was really happening. Mardon was going to be attacked, and they had nowhere to hide, no king to lead them to victory. Dawn's first light was rising in the east.

The first booms of the attack sounded.

Elise stumbled, caught off guard by the deep, bone-rattling sound and the screams that followed. Her hands began to shake. The people here were not in the line of fire, but that sound was enough to make the very stones quake. The fear here was palpable.

Seb grabbed Elise and leaned up against the wall of the university library, whose façade had already been rebuilt since the coronation debacle. He cradled her head against his chest. "It'll be all right," he said, stroking her hair over and over again as they felt the impact of a cannonball as though it had hit in the cathedral's square rather than at the city's edge.

"They're using artillery," she said, her mouth against his neck. "I expected magic."

"Maybe that was magic."

They looked at each other. Neither of them had witnessed war. They'd been the happy offspring of a peaceful generation, sequestered away in palaces while any skirmishes were handled by the skilled soldiers and trained sorcerers who defended the kingdom.

"Come on," he urged. "To the palace."

Minutes later, Elise caught her breath one final time and walked casually around a corner only to stop short at what she saw at the rear palace gate.

A swarm of Mardonians, clamoring for entrance.

Elise pressed a hand to her mouth. She could hear shouts from several of the men and women shaking the iron fence around the palace perimeter.

"They know it's enchanted," she breathed, pity crashing over her. "They think it's safe."

Seb looked at Elise. "It is. Aly's enchantments protect that place."

"If she's still alive, you're right. It's the safest place in the city." She stepped toward the crowd.

"And it's practically empty," Seb grumbled, following.

Carolyn would still be at the palace, tucked away in some safe room with Edward. Elise smirked at the memories of Carolyn and Seb hurling sacks of flour over the vast garden. A sting of guilt pricked Elise, too, knowing that the flour they'd so easily exploded for sport was now in such short supply.

"The magic of our Protectors will hold," she said, mostly to assure herself. "If we could take out some of the Zealots, I would feel a lot better."

Seb guffawed. "Elise, the warrior princess. Where did this bloodlust come from?"

She pushed his shoulder. "If I could do anything to slow that army, I would do it."

He smiled at her, then he stepped toward the crowd and shouted. "Make way for the Princess Elise."

His deep voice cut through the commotion, and people turned, hesitant at first, then confused. Some stepped aside with quick bows or hasty curtsies. Others hurled insults at them and refused to move away from the gates.

"All right, then." Elise sighed and employed her elbow to relocate one stubborn man in her path. At a surprised look from Seb, she grunted, "A princess will do what a princess must do to obtain an old, rickety piece of ancient weaponry."

"Wait, wait," Seb said, arms out. "It's anything but *rickety*."

She grinned and trod on another man's foot. Soon, they'd pushed their way to the palace gate.

The garden gate was guarded by two men with rifles. Their resolve looked like it was already cracking.

Elise was instantly grateful for the gown and the tiara, which both sparkled in the first rays of morning sun. She straightened her posture and announced, "Let me through."

The guards ignored her.

"In case you are not informed, your late king, the usurper, has died. I, Elise Windon, retain my status as royal, and you will let me in to my home."

The guards glanced at each other, unsure what to do. Then one spoke. "We were told not to let you in."

"By whom? Alexander's men? They have no authority here now. We are under attack. I have a way to help. Let me in."

The other guard snarled. "You only want to be in here because it's safer."

Elise sighed, ready for her next move. She had seen this tactic work many times before with her father and with Alexander. Red had never used this method, to her knowledge, but perhaps that was only because he hadn't been king long enough.

"If you let me in and we survive this, I will grant each of you title and lands. Think now about your future, gentleman."

Seb covered a smile with his knuckles.

The first guard eventually unlocked the gate.

Elise's lips curled into a satisfied smile. "Your names, so I may reward you when this is over."

The guards spoke their names, and the gate swung open.

"Only you two," growled one of the guards.

The people burst into angry protests.

Elise held up a hand as she stepped through the gate. "You will let the people in."

The guards exchanged one more worried glance, then nodded and stepped aside. The people flooded in to the gardens behind Seb and Elise, several whooping with shouts of joy.

As soon as they rounded a row of tall, neatly trimmed hedges, Elise and Seb broke into a run once more.

"Carolyn would want to help," Elise noted as they wove

through the hedges.

"Considering the trebuchet was her idea, I wouldn't be surprised if she's already wheeling it out," Seb replied with a half grin.

"If she's not, I will go find her," Elise decided.

Just then, Elise spotted the tall wooden frame of the trebuchet peeking out above the hedges. She yelled in delight as she started up the sloping green to where Seb and Carolyn and Edward were pushing the giant weapon into place on the highest point in the garden.

Carolyn ran into her sister's embrace.

Edward bowed politely to Elise, in this one motion, showing his respect for the old Tandera, the *true* Tandera, and his place in it. In his eyes was an unspoken apology, and also sadness at losing an uncle. She nodded briefly back to him, accepting his help, for Carolyn's sake.

While Seb placed the wheel braces, Edward examined the contraption. "How will the magicians not see the stones and push them back toward us?"

Carolyn pouted and stuck her hands on her hips. "I don't know."

Edward glanced tentatively at Elise. "I think I have an idea for that. Elise, you're a painter."

Elise tilted her head. "Yes, but what does—"

"I apologize, Your Highness, for many things, and for my uncle's actions, but we can discuss that later. Can you fetch us some blue paint?" He pointed upward at the sky. "Preferably that color?"

Carolyn jumped up and planted a kiss on his cheek. "Brilliant! Elise, come, let's paint some rocks."

"I will bring you a bucket," Edward said and took off toward the gardener's house.

Inside the solarium, where Elise had dragged all her jars of blue and white, Edward leaned over the bucket. "Can you mix a bright blue to match the sky? We need a lot of it," he said.

"Fortunately, my father misjudged how much one person can paint, and he bought me more paint than I could ever use in a lifetime." Elise's chest pinched at the sweet memory of her father, but she felt a calm wash over her as the scent of her paints met her nose.

Carolyn poured one blue jar in the bucket. "Too dark." She poured in a white. "This will take forever. I wish we had magic."

Elise scoffed. "Says the girl who said she would defy magic and do everything on her own."

Carolyn waved a hand to silence her sister and continued pouring paint in the bucket.

Elise mixed and mixed until they created a color that was similar to the sky outside, the crisp blue of early fall.

"Will this work?" Carolyn asked, staring down at the sloshing bucket as Edward placed it beside the trebuchet. "Zealots might be wild, but they're not stupid."

"They are not going to be thinking about rocks flying in from above, I hope," said Elise. "And this won't prevent them from seeing it, but just make it more difficult for them to comprehend what is happening."

Seb gently placed a large sack at his feet and dusted off his hands. "This garden isn't exactly bursting with boulders."

Elise lifted a brow. "What's that?"

Seb rubbed his chin and looked down at the bag. "Sand bag."

Carolyn made a disappointed huff. "Well, no one will write of us, 'They defeated an army with a bag of sand.'"

"Ah, but I made a small addition."

Elise stared expectantly at Seb.

"What? *Explosive* sand?" Carolyn quipped, sarcasm oozing off her tongue.

"Precisely."

"Wait, seriously?" Carolyn stepped away from the sandbag.

"I found my stash of old explosives. No one had touched them."

"I don't blame them," whispered Carolyn.

"And I added a stick of dynamite to the top of this bag." Seb beamed at Elise.

Edward clapped his hands, impressed. "This sounds promising."

Seb lifted his brows at Edward, then flashed an amused smile at Elise. The scholar looked entirely too eager to load up that sand bag.

"Who's going to paint it?" Carolyn asked, clutching Edward's arm.

Seb knelt beside the bag. "I'll turn the bag. Someone else can pour on the paint."

Edward nodded and picked up the bucket. His pant leg was already smeared with blue paint.

Elise accepted Carolyn's nervous embrace as the boys coated the bag, very carefully, with blue paint. It was a messy, splotchy thing when it was finished.

Seb tenderly hefted the bag into the trebuchet's sling. "Well, here goes." His hands were entirely blue, and his clothes had a large blue stain from where he'd held the painted bag. He wiped sweat from his forehead, leaving a blue line.

Elise covered a small laugh. "Who will light it?"

Seb laughed. "I forgot. I put some matches in my jacket pocket." He lifted his blue hands. "Grab them for me?" he asked Elise.

She gawked at him a moment. "Oh, fine!" she said, waving a hand in the air. War was upon them, what difference did it make? She pulled open his jacket and slid her hand into his inner pocket, grabbing the box of matches.

"Are we certain this will reach the enemy soldiers?" she asked, mostly to divert Carolyn's knowing smirk.

"It'll reach," Seb affirmed.

Edward lit the fuse of the dynamite, and Carolyn had the honor of releasing the counterweight. All four of them scrambled away and hid behind a pair of statues.

Elise grabbed Seb's hand and squeezed as the giant machine creaked, the counterweight swinging down as the sling leapt into the air. The blue sandbag flung drops of paint as it soared up over the palace garden toward the edge of the city.

"There's no way they won't see that," hissed Carolyn, her hands tapping against her lips in worry.

"I wish we could see it hit," said Elise.

Carolyn lifted eyebrows at her. Seb poked a thumb in Elise's direction and said to Carolyn, "Brutal, this one."

A boom shook the gardens. Then a plume of smoke rose up.

"Did it make it far enough?" Elise wondered, suddenly worried they'd bombed their own men.

Seb cleared his throat. "I've shot this thing many times. I know its range. It made it."

After a moment of watching the smoke rise, Elise released Seb's hand. She glanced at the blue on her skin, then rubbed her hand down Seb's already ruined shirt.

"Oh, I see," he said. He grabbed her face with both of his blue hands and planted a quick kiss in front of everyone.

Elise's skin burned as embarrassment and shock flooded her cheeks, but the feelings quickly blazed into desire. Her mouth curled into a grin. It was all the encouragement he needed. His hands pulled her face to him once more, this time, his kiss slower, harder. She melted against him.

Carolyn gasped, but then broke into a giggle that wouldn't stop.

Edward rubbed his hands together. "Got any more sandbags?"

Seb pulled away, smiling down at Elise. "Several."

25

RED

Aly swooped toward Red with both arms out, cloak torn and flapping. She scooped him up and pressed him to her side right as the strange black fog curled toward his ankles. Aly grunted out the words of her spells. One for flight. One for strength. One for speed.

Red was grateful for the speed.

The black fog closed over the space where he'd just been standing. The beasts vanished, but their howls still reached his ears.

Below the shadowy mist, the sound of the waters crashed and whistled through crevices in the rock walls. The river was climbing too. Aly screamed as the black mist licked at their heels.

Wind snapped her hair all around her face and Red's. He reached up and pulled her hair away from her eyes, pressing his cheek against hers as they flew.

Soon, they broke over the rim of the Canyon. Dawn had broken in the east, and beneath them, the darkness roiled, contained, for now, within the tall rock walls—but it was still rising. Beasts like startled ants rushed over the rim and into the forests beyond.

To their right, Caridan was in flames.

"No!" yelled Red.

She dropped down outside the camp's border, and Red took off at a sprint toward the inferno.

"Red, no!"

A strange sound turned his eyes back to Aly. She lay flat on the ground.

He dove for her prostrate body and rolled her over. "Aly!"

Her eyes searched vaguely for his face. "I'm...all right."

"No, you're not. What's wrong?" His hands shook slightly. If Aly was hurt, there was little he could do.

"Tired," she mumbled, her eyes drifting shut.

He glanced over his shoulder at Caridan.

With closed eyes, she answered his unspoken question. "I see no Wells there."

Tipping his head down over Aly, he squeezed his eyes shut and fisted his hand.

Then he stood and released a guttural yell.

Aly flinched, but then lay still, her mouth parted in sleep.

A moment ago, she'd conducted powerful magic with her fingertips, and now she looked utterly harmless, helpless. He scooped her up in his arms, cradling her limp form against his chest. He kissed her head, amazed at the woman in his arms. "I've got you," he whispered. He didn't know where to go, only that they couldn't stay here.

Rushing wind and a woman's hollering voice rose over the sound of Caridan's flames. Naia and Grey crashed to the ground beside them.

After a moment of rolling limbs and tangled garments, Naia and Grey hopped up and leaped apart.

"Landing is still a little tricky for me," Naia admitted, staring back at Grey, as if apologizing to him. "Came as soon as I saw— Oh." She finally looked at Red holding Aly.

Grey stared at Aly. "Is she all right?"

Naia waved a hand at him. "She just flew across the country. She's utterly drained."

Grey shot her a narrow look. "You didn't collapse after flying that far."

"I took longer to get here. And I *am* tired. I'm simply denying it to keep your bleeding hide alive."

Grey stared at Naia a moment with an unreadable expression, perhaps somewhere between gratefulness and fear. Instead of responding, he turned to the burning camp, and his face slackened as he took in the sight. "The entire perimeter caught fire at once. Naia lifted me to safety, then returned to douse the flames enough to let the men out."

"Kassia must have set it ablaze," Aly whispered, drawing everyone's attention. She lifted her head and smiled weakly at Red. "I think I can stand."

Red set Aly down gently, keeping one arm wrapped around her waist. "Where are the men?" he asked Naia.

"Heading for Luxler."

Red's heart surged with relief. "Thank you," he said to Naia. "You saved them. And you healed him," Red said, nodding at Grey. "I knew you could do it."

Naia tucked her hair behind her ears and glanced at Grey. "Turns out you were right, Pulling from a human Truthwell is… more powerful." She appeared almost ashamed to admit it.

Grey's expression hardened once again. "We shouldn't linger." He turned back to Red.

The burning remains of Caridan pumped black smoke into the air, and the Canyon emitted strange cracks and groans.

Naia walked up to Aly. "What happened down there?"

"Kassia disappeared into the water. I think she's part of the river now." Aly leaned against Red for support. "And now there's a black fog rising from the depths that acts as if it is almost alive."

When Red exchanged a glance with Grey, the spymaster grunted. "If Kassia has transformed into a living shadow, I think it would behoove us to leave this place."

"I must stop her," hissed Aly, stepping away from Red. She gave a small shake of her head as he reached for her. "I'm fine. I need to try to stop that fog from rising."

Grey turned away in frustration. Red sensed that he, too, disliked being idle.

Red wanted to help Aly, but the best way to help to her was the energy he supplied for her magic. All he needed to do was remain *still* and let her do her magic—and that felt wrong.

"Naia, can you help me?" Aly turned to explain a spell to Naia. The two women soon were lost in casting spells at the Canyon. The ground shook once, but nothing visible happened.

Tilting his head at Aly, Red muttered to Grey, "It isn't fair."

"What isn't?"

"I am a king, and I can't even be of use."

Grey snorted in amusement. "You're of use to her."

A strange feeling prickled Red's skin. "Only because I have a bright Well. I want to *act*."

Grey cut him a flat look. "I didn't mean in that way." He dropped his crossed arms. "You compel her. It is more than magic, my friend."

Red lifted his brows as he stared at Aly. She'd dropped her cloak beneath a tree and her thin arms waved madly as she hurled magic with all her heart at the darkening Canyon.

In the middle of swinging her hands over her head, Aly's movement stopped suddenly and she stumbled into Naia.

Red ran forward. "What happened?"

Aly held on to Naia's shoulders a moment, breathing deeply.

"Message," Aly panted, eyes flickering as if seeing something not there. "Mardon has been attacked."

Dread sank in Red's chest.

There was no king in the city, and a city under attack with no leader was a defeat waiting to happen.

"I should be there," he huffed.

Grey cursed and started pacing. "What are your orders, my king?" Grey asked, his eyes fierce with the passion of a warrior held back from battle.

Red glanced at the Canyon, then at Aly. Mardon needed them both—Mardon needed Aly's power and Red's leadership. Tandera needed her scepter and her crown.

Red knew what he wanted to do. Lives were ending, and he was *here*, standing in a forest. But whatever was happening in the Canyon was ominous, and he didn't want to turn away from here if this was fog was a threat they could contain. "Aly?" he pressed. He needed her confirmation, her support. Going to Mardon would take them away from the Canyon, and he needed to know it was the right thing to do. "Can you contain it?"

She looked at him with a pained expression. This wasn't as easy a choice for her. She fought against foes he couldn't see and would never fully understand. Biting her top lip in apparent consternation, Aly again looked to the dark depths of the Canyon. "This shadow is unlike anything I've seen. I don't know what it wants, but it will not stop until it acquires what it seeks."

"At least it moves slowly?" Naia offered, voice rising as if uncertain her words were any comfort.

"It gains power as it grows. We can't assume it will move slowly forever."

Grey stepped forward. "Send me back, then. I can be of no use here. If you must stay, I will return." He sounded almost desperate for battle. His fingers twitched at his sides. "Naia, can you fly me to Mardon?"

Naia coughed and her eyes widened. "I—er—maybe?"

"She can do it," Aly cut in. "Remember what Igor said about burning?"

"Igor?" asked Red.

Aly smiled at Red. "One of my students. He is particularly skilled at bursting into flame, and he managed once to ignite himself as he shot across the forest. It worked to propel him." She shrugged. "I tried it on the way here. I've never flown so fast in my life, though I can't say it was an enjoyable experience."

Naia twisted her face in an ugly cringe. "I tried it, too." She shuddered. "I'm not a fan of burning."

The edges of Aly's mouth curled up. "Well, at least it worked." Aly turned from Naia to Red. "And we should all go. Mardon needs her king. Besides, I can't contain that." She turned to stare at the Canyon's dark depths.

Naia frowned. "Fine. But what about Igor and the others? Your little army? Are we going to leave them in the Crescent?"

Red shot Aly an impressed expression. "You have an army?"

"Not exactly." Aly placed a hand on Red's arm. Just her touch sent a wave of warmth through him. "I have three barely trained students." Her eyes closed briefly. "Zor is dead," she whispered.

A small gasp escaped Naia's lips.

"She tried to kill me. I think she might have been working with Kassia, but I may never know for sure." Aly leaned her face against Red's arm. "She attacked me as I left the palace, at the exact same time someone assassinated Alexander." Aly ran a hand down her face, aware that dirt still stuck to her hair and she likely looked a terrible mess. "I had just freed Alexander from Kassia's control."

At the mention of the usurper king's death, no one spoke.

Finally, Naia broke the silence,

snarling her next words. "That nasty little sneak. I knew she couldn't be trusted."

"And my students are already in Mardon," Aly added.

"Then what are we waiting for?" Grey asked. "Let's go home."

Aly and Naia exchanged a glance.

"It's not exactly as simple as flying into battle from here and saving the day," Naia began, her voice a little cautious, almost conciliatory, as she spoke to Grey. "We're both already tired from flying *to* the Canyon. To fly immediately back across the country, carrying you two? It'll knock us both out."

Aly nodded. "I know we need to leave, but if you think either of us will be able to fight when we arrive, you're mistaken. If we go now, you'll be fighting without us."

Grey stared at Red, as if he might have some way around this. Red hissed a long exhale and studied the smoke rising against a misty dawn.

Finally, he said, "Okay, here's what we'll do."

Minutes later, they had a thin plan and high hopes.

To Red's surprise, Grey lifted his arms in dramatic fashion, waiting for Naia. With an overly exasperated sigh, he beckoned her, "My lady chariot."

She pursed her lips and stomped up to him. She was small next to him, but she was just as fierce as the spymaster. Naia boasted more scars than Grey, and together, they made a fearsome pair. Aly chuckled as Naia crushed him with a violent embrace.

"To Mardon," Red said, and they rose into the brightening sky.

Red's stomach soured as they lifted over the forest. From so high, he could see the scorched camp with its burning remnants. Then the black scar of the Canyon sharpened into focus as they lifted even higher. It was so wide, and the bridge across it appeared no more substantial than a spider's web.

Aly's body tucked tightly against his ribs was his only comfort. Everything inside him was buzzing with fear at this deadly height.

"I'm going to do it now," Aly shouted to all of them.

He wasn't afraid of Aly or of what she could do with the energy inside him, but flying was his least favorite mode of transportation, and she was about to light them on fire.

When magical words left her mouth, Red's body lurched, but only briefly. Within seconds, the gut-churning sensation of speed had diminished and a quiet enveloped them even as flames licked at an invisible barrier right beyond their skin. Red's blood ignited with adrenaline, and it was all he could do to remain still.

Their closeness suddenly felt much more intimate. Before, flying had been so marvelously terrifying that hugging Aly barely registered in his mind. Now that the ground below them was obscured by bright flames and the sounds of their breathing were amplified in silent bubble of magic around them, he could fully appreciate his arms wrapped around Aly, hers around him. He tucked his head against her shoulder, and she hummed into his chest.

He wanted to whisper his affection, but she'd said once that his love distracted her. In his mind, he sang of his love for Aly, wishing for the day he could say all that was on his mind without fear of breaking her magic. Until that day, he would offer her what he could: his nearness and his trust. Despite her determination to keep him from distracting her, he recalled the way she had kissed him, the way she had melted into him when he held her. And as she'd flown to save him in the Canyon, she'd spoken into his mind the words *I love you.* Perhaps one day her love for him wouldn't negatively affect her magic.

"We're here," she whispered after a short time.

How could they possibly have traveled so far already?

Sure enough, when the propulsion spell fell away, Mardon's skyline rushed toward them.

Smoke rose in columns from several places along the city's eastern side. Booms shook the air and bright flashes of light sparked both outside the city and within its streets.

Mardon's defenses were scattered everywhere. Tanderan soldiers in their crimson uniforms dotted the field outside of Mardon, battling enemies in brown tunics and Bulvarnan troops in blue. Aly and Naia swooped in a large circle, giving them a full view of the situation. Throughout the easternmost quarter of the city, almost to the cathedral's spire, more small battles raged.

Red's breathing increased. He'd expected a dismal sight, but it crushed his heart to see Mardon under fire.

"There," said Grey.

At first, Red assumed he meant the battle.

Then he knew Grey's attention was not focused on the city but on the snaking, thick shadow hanging low over the land to the left of Mardon. Over the neat rows of troops' tents came a velvet darkness, creeping over the hills like someone was pulling a blanket over the scene.

It looked exactly like the hungry shadows from the Canyon.

"Aly," he whispered, too shocked to form a sentence.

How could it have traveled so far in mere hours?

Then again, he had traveled that far. Aly said the shadow gained power as it grew. Now, it was a massive cloud stretching back over the horizon to the northeast.

Aly twisted her head and whimpered at the sight. Naia saw it too and spluttered a few incoherent words. They drifted down toward the buildings.

Would this cloud change things? Their plan had sounded good, but had assumed the enemy was on the ground.

As they dropped over the city, Red spotted the palace, wondering where Carolyn and Elise might be. The city's outer buildings passed underneath Red as Aly's magic maneuvered them directly into position.

This close, Red's eyes could discern shapes below. Men were fighting in the streets. His throat clamped shut as he tried to swallow. No skirmish he'd witnessed during his father's reign held a candle to what lay before him now. This was his true crucible.

He exchanged a look with Grey as the magic propelling them slowed their motion. The plan was in place and, despite the strange shadow he did not understand, the attack would proceed —he prayed it would work.

"The sun rises on another fine day in Mardon," Grey intoned as their feet descended toward the battle.

He hoped one of the buildings that burned had been a butcher shop, for the smell of charred meat was strong in the air, mixed with the smell of gunpowder.

"Are you ready?" he asked Aly, his mouth against her hair.

"Mm."

She dropped the propulsion spell and slowed their flight, expertly landing them in the alley behind the New Moon Tavern with the same impact as if they'd merely jumped. But as soon as their feet were firmly planted, Aly's body fell limp.

Red readily scooped her into his arms. She breathed evenly, face slack. Red pressed a kiss to her forehead as he cradled her in his arms. A white-haired man rushed from the tavern door, while a woman behind him held the door open.

Naia and Grey smashed uncomfortably into the pavement beside Red. Grey rolled off Naia, who was also already asleep. He lifted her with little effort and nodded at the white-haired man.

"You must be Igor," Red said.

Igor bowed awkwardly and rushed back toward the woman at the door. Red and Grey carried the two exhausted women into the back room marked with a small sliver of moon. Two chairs and two couches filled the space before a lit fire. A bowl full of white powder sat beside the fireplace. Two glasses of water stood on the center table along with a bowl of fruit and brown muffins. Aly's students had received her messages and prepared as best they could.

Red maneuvered Aly onto one of the couches. He kissed her before stepping away. Grey knelt and gently placed Naia on the other couch. Before he stood, he took a moment to gather her dangling arm and tuck it gently beside her body.

Red tilted his brows but stilled his expression as soon as Grey turned to him.

Grey moved to a painting hanging in the room, took it off the wall, and spun the dial of a large safe. A few seconds later, he withdrew two pistols and handed them to Red, along with a box of bullets. Grey slung a belt around his waist fitted with two holsters, then shoved a gun in each.

"Let's go," Grey said, his voice deep and official. He marched past Red and exited the room so fast Red nearly chuckled.

Back in the alley, Igor motioned to the woman who'd held the door for them. She was short and somewhat bedraggled-looking, missing a tooth and wearing a strange assortment of cloth.

"This is Rainbow," Igor announced. "And Quince." He motioned to a young boy with long hair standing against the wall of the tavern. Red hadn't noticed the boy hiding in the shadows. "They will watch over Aly and Naia. I will accompany you."

Red had listened as Aly had told him about her students. She'd said Igor was the strongest of them, and that despite his appearance, he would be an asset in battle. She'd admitted Quince was too new at controlling his magic to be helpful in a scenario where aim was important, but she believed Quince to be a fine person to help Rainbow stand watch.

Grey handed Rainbow his pocket watch. "One hour."

She nodded, running a thumb over the smooth metal.

Red and Grey exchanged another meaningful glance. This was it—they were headed to war.

Without a word, Red nodded at Igor and Grey. "Follow me."

They raced through Mardon's streets, past families huddled against buildings, past broken windows and boarded up doors. They heard fighting before they saw it.

Igor kept pace better than Red had expected, and the sorcerer barely seemed winded as they approached the final corner. Red and Grey drew their weapons and burst around the building.

As soon as the soldiers came into view, so did the dense, black cloud that they'd seen as they'd approached the city. The hungry shadow curled toward them, tendrils reaching for them with predatory accuracy.

Red aimed at a soldier in Bulvarnan blue, taking him down with a bullet to the shoulder. His veins ran electric. Gunpowder and the spray of magic hung in the air.

Rocks crumbled beneath his feet and he hopped sideways to avoid being dropped into a hole that opened up as a Zealot in a Canduli tunic ran at him with arms flailing. The shadowy cloud hovered directly over the man's bald head, drawn forward as the man charged Red.

A bullet flattened the Zealot, and the shadow paused, reaching but unable to come closer.

Between Grey's gun firing and the booms of Igor's magic, Red yelled to Grey, "The shadow travels with the soldiers."

Grey nodded and fired.

A stinging breeze nearly swept Red off his feet, but a wall of ice briefly formed in front of him before melting into a tiny deluge in the street. Igor was defending him.

His pistol took out two Zealots shoving loose boards at Tanderan soldiers.

"The king!" Shouted someone nearby. "The king has returned!"

Whoops and hollers rose from the soldiers wearing crimson. A renewed vigor pulsed down the entire street as this news spread.

Grey flashed a smile and ran with Red toward a pair of fleeing Zealots. Grey fired and one of the Zealots fell, while Red took aim and brought down the other. A blast of cold air alerted Red to magic behind him, and when he spun, he saw Igor snatching a spear from the air and whirling it over his head before smashing it into smithereens against a charging Zealot's head.

Together, they marched farther down the street. Igor walked a step behind them, and Red was glad for the man's presence.

A chant broke out among the Tanderan soldiers. "Long live the king!"

The words echoed down the street as more soldiers took up the sound.

As they marched, the shadow withdrew.

ELISE

Elise wove through a crowded hallway, nodding politely at anyone who bowed or curtsied, which was only a handful of people. Most of these citizens didn't know her face, and her disheveled appearance brought more than a few questioning looks. Another boom sounded, closer, and everyone in the hallway ducked. Elise's heart skipped a beat.

A messenger had brought word that the armies had broken through the city's outer defenses.

But the Protectors and soldiers were holding them a few streets away—for now. The black cloud that hung over the attackers drifted over the first rows of buildings, pressed back by magic as long as the line of defense held.

The palace's back gate, where Elise and Seb had entered, had been wrenched off one hinge with the crazed surge of Mardonians desperate for shelter. Seb had launched his final explosive sandbag, abandoning the trebuchet as the influx of bodies pressed around the outdated weapon.

Elise and Carolyn stood at an upstairs window watching as fires engulfed the streets beneath the strange black cloud edging into the city. Seb sat at a desk, an array of small bottles before him, and Edward paced the room behind them.

"The fires are spreading," Elise whispered. Despite the shortage, Mardon would need even more wood to rebuild.

Frightened citizens banged on the doors below. Soon, glass shattered. Seb cursed and wiped sweat from his brow, bending down to check the level of liquid in a clear vial.

"Can that shadow breach the magic around the palace?" asked Carolyn.

"No," Elise mumbled, shaking her head. It must be true, because if that terrifying shadow broke over the grounds, then she had put thousands of people in danger by letting them in. She couldn't accept that.

Carolyn tore her eyes from the wicked sight and walked away from the window. "Where is Aly? Where is Red?"

The last Elise had heard of her brother, he'd survived the attack at Caridan that had sent Seb to Chesterton's estate. On the way back to Mardon, Seb had told her that before the attack, Red had volunteered to descend into the Canyon on a risky rescue mission. Since then, there had been no word.

Aly had been ordered to the Crescent Forest. Now that Alexander was dead, what did that mean for the Royal Sorcerer? Elise didn't have all the facts, but she knew Aly's magic bid her protect the king—and now the king was dead. The only other person who'd spoken the vows to serve and lead this country was Red. If he was still alive, Aly would find him.

If he was not alive, who would rule Tandera?

Her father had always spoken to her of the possibility that, should tragedy strike, Elise would be in line for the throne after her brother. He'd impressed upon her, and even Carolyn to some extent, the need for readiness, should the crown fall to one of them. She'd always considered her father and brother to be immortal, invincible, and the crown to be forever on someone else's head.

Gevar's funeral had proven her wrong. Red's death curse had almost taken him, too.

Theod, don't let Red be dead. Elise shivered, but all the same, she lifted her shoulders and stood tall. Her father might be ashamed of her recent actions, but moving forward, she would make him proud.

Dense silence hung after Carolyn's question. Finally, Elise said, "We can't wait for them save us. Someone must lead this city or it will surely fall."

Seb's eyes widened even as Carolyn covered her mouth with both hands.

"You?" he asked, standing.

Elise blushed. "We have no sovereign. We do not know where my brother is. Believe me, I wish there was another option."

"This place has so many enchantments on it, certainly Aly's magic is still intact," Carolyn spluttered, her voice thick with emotion.

"Perhaps," replied Elise. "But the army out there is not benefiting from those enchantments. Without orders, they will eventually disband."

"Surely a general or someone has taken up command," offered Carolyn.

Elise peered out the window. Black plumes of smoke rose up through the twisting cloud that hovered over the enemy soldiers. "One can hope. But what if there are two generals giving contradicting commands? What they need is a unified authority."

"But Elise, it's *war!*"

Her sister's desperation made Elise's next words difficult. "Crowns weren't won in times of peace."

Seb's mouth hardened into a look she'd rarely seen on him, a look of respect. "What do you need?"

She flinched a little at being asked this question, like she truly was in command. She wasn't ready for this, but she had little choice. "I need to reach the generals in command out there."

Carolyn wailed, "You don't even have a plan! Going out there will only get you killed!"

Elise turned a loving smile on her sister. "I do have a plan. Red wasn't the only one to study military tactics." She had studied battle strategy and military history, as had they all. She'd always added in her own fantasies—a princess needing rescuing or a queen awaiting her king's return. But in real life, battle wasn't romantic; no one was coming to save the princess. "I may not be a warrior, but I know how to read a situation, and I can provide the unified leadership they need—but only if I can get them all together, or enough of them, to discuss strategy and release orders back out to all the men."

Carolyn's jaw fell open. She leaned into Edward and watched her sister with wide eyes.

"How is it coming?" Elise asked Seb, glancing at his project on the table.

He held up the now-corked vial. "I think this will work. It's not much, but it's fairly potent."

"Good. I will be glad of an escort to the battle. And I think I know how best to use that." She nodded at the explosive in Seb's hand. "Come, let's get to the armory."

In the hall, Seb turned one way and Elise the other. Elise quirked a grin at him. "Not that armory. I mean the one where we keep *my* armor."

Elise's hands quivered slightly as she waited for Seb to fasten her elaborate breastplate. His fingers brushed tender places by her ribs as he secured the straps over the simpler dress she'd donned. Her father had ordered custom armor designed for all his children, even his wife, though he'd told them that he hoped they'd never need it.

When Seb finished, he stood but did not step away. "You are terrifying," he said in a low tone that made the hairs along Elise's arms stand tall. His fingers traveled down her arm and caught her hand. He'd donned one of Gevar's old breastplates, which fit him better than any of Red's would have. "Terrifying and beautiful."

The tension between them crackled and raced across her skin. But did he feel it? This was Sebastian Thorin, after all. He'd kissed her, but he'd kissed so many women. Surely she was nothing different to him than all the rest. "We must go," she said.

He nodded and stepped away, following her out the door.

The most direct route to battle was through the palace's front gates. The long, wide avenue leading from the palace was already filling with soldiers as they pressed in from side streets. The attack was almost upon the royal residence.

A flood of people pressed themselves against the enchanted gate. Whatever guards might have been stationed there had already fled. Women pushed their children onto their shoulders, attempting to help them grasp the top of the iron fence and climb over.

Elise's chest ached at the sight.

Several people rattled the lock from the inside, even swung an axe at it, but it was no use. No petty attempts to open the gate would work, enchanted as it was to withstand force.

Holding the large, iron key in one hand, Elise marched purposefully across the wide palace courtyard, crowded along the edges with people already inside the grounds. She had never worn her armor, but it didn't feel too different from to the bodice of a tight-fitting dress. People began pointing.

Her cheeks blazed, but it wasn't embarrassment that colored her fair skin this time—it was fear. She was marching into war. She might not have any experience in battle, but she did have sense—and it was time she did something good for Tandera.

Elise visualized herself walking out toward the battle. She knew where the commanding officers would be stationed, more or less, based on her lessons. They would be behind the men, shielded by Protectors, at a height advantage, able to move quickly.

She spotted a man wearing a soldier's uniform, only the jacket was missing. He was attempting to hoist a child over the palace fence. She rushed to the deserter and asked through the bars, "Where are the officers?"

But it was Seb who answered. He pointed at a building near the end of the street. "Up there."

Her eyes found a glowing magical dome. Whoever stood under it was shrouded, so they couldn't be seen, but the vast quantity of magical shields protecting them had a sparkly sheen to them that caught the sunlight. That was likely where the strategizing officers now stood, watching the battle unfold below.

The soldier scoffed. "They're tossing everywhere. It's chaos out there."

Elise bit her lip and closed her eyes. It was worse than she'd expected. To Seb, she said, "We only need to reach one. Then Protectors can spread the orders to all the officers."

It was all she could hope for.

As they neared the gate, people stepped out of their path. The Mardonians on the other side cheered when they saw what was in her hand.

Elise scanned the faces, holding a practiced smile on her frightened face. Then, above their heads, she saw a flash of light.

When her eyes registered what it was, she dropped the key in shock.

A wall of fire exploded down the wide avenue.

A moment ago, soldiers in Tanderan red had been firing rifles down side streets. Now, all that occupied the corridor was flame. Within that flame, a dark shape, almost serpentine in its movements.

Elise pressed her hand to her mouth, the key forgotten on the stones. Terror seized her.

The flame was heading right for them.

"What is *that*?" Seb rasped.

The screams of the people threatened Elise's grip on rationality. They were trapped out there. The flames would consume every person standing outside the palace gates.

And possibly every person within.

Could Aly's magic protect them from *this*?

There was no longer a battle at the end of the lane. The building holding the officers was lost in flame. There was no way this magic was from the Zealots. This was something bigger, fouler, as if the Deep had come to consume Mardon.

Elise knelt and grabbed the key. "We must let them in."

"Toss it," Seb yelled over the chaos around them.

Smoke from the massive burning monster was beginning to obscure the sky. Mardon was on fire. Arms reached through the fence with desperate hands.

She jogged the rest of the way to the massive iron gate. Seb didn't miss a step beside her, but his wide eyes were pinned on the approaching fire.

Her hands shook as she fit the key in the lock. Heat from the fire-beast already warmed her face. It was moving too fast. To live, they would have to be *inside* the palace, because the heat could pass through the shields.

The lock clunked as it opened. She was breathing so hard

that her hands couldn't unhook the lock. Seb yanked off the lock with one swift move and tossed it aside, pulling Elise behind him as the gates burst inward.

If Seb hadn't sheltered her, she would have been trampled. He spun her around and pushed her hard, forcing her into a run. The people swarmed into the courtyard. Heat intensified at their backs, as did the screams of those not close enough to the gate.

Elise couldn't think of that now. All that mattered in this moment was the palace entrance. Her shoes slapped the pavement as she moved as fast as she could manage, but it wasn't fast enough.

Her body burned as the intense heat grew ever hotter. Seb kept one hand on her back, pushing her pace. Then his hand fell away.

"Seb!" Elise spun, but the crowd carried her toward the palace. She grunted and shoved her way back to where Seb had fallen. People were running right over his body. "Get off!" she screamed.

One woman who blasted past Elise was shouting, "He's here, he'll save us! The king is here!"

Elise was saddened to think the woman was still placing her hope in a dead sovereign—that news of Alexander's death had not spread. It didn't matter now.

The heat made her eyes water. Fire licked at the edges of the buildings nearest the palace. It had only one more street to cross and it would reach the gates. People still streamed in through the gate. She hoped the enchantments would hold.

Elise scooped up Seb's head, then his chest. It was no use. He was much too heavy. She tucked herself over his face and covered her head with her hands. Her armor would have to be enough.

"Elise! Take his feet."

Edward Alexander snaked his way through the panicked

crowd. He grabbed Seb under his shoulders. Elise scrambled to take hold of his feet. She turned her face from the blistering heat and ran.

"Let me, Princess," offered a stranger who stepped in to take Seb's feet. Together, he and Edward ferried Seb toward the palace steps.

With one last glance at the approaching flames, Elise let out a muffled prayer. She spun back and shuffled up the stairs with the last of the frenzied citizens.

Edward and the stranger placed Seb's body against the wall right inside the front door. Edward looked up at the stairs, where Carolyn stood leaning over the railing, shouting Edward's name. Without a word, he ran toward her.

It was every man for himself now. If that beastly fire could burn through the enchantments, they were all dead.

Seb's body tipped sideways. Elise dropped to her knees and caught his head before it hit the marble. If they were about to be consumed, what happened next wouldn't matter at all. She leaned down and pressed a hard kiss to his unconscious face. Her skin was warm from the fire's heat, but kissing him made her cheeks burn even hotter.

The screams from the courtyard grew louder. Elise inhaled and leaned around the doorframe. Her breath caught.

The fire formed a towering wall at the palace gate. Its smoke and its heat alone reached past the entrance.

Elise wasn't sure if she was choking on the smoky air or her own relief. She began to cry and laugh at the same time. As she leaned happily against Seb, he woke with a start and collapsed sideways against the floor. She tumbled with him.

"What happened?" His hand found her face.

"It stopped," she sobbed.

He carefully sat up and leaned around the doorframe. He

spat out a happy laugh and pressed a fist to his mouth. "It worked. We're all safe."

Elise took his hand and stood with him. "Only the ones who made it," she whispered. "So many did not."

He squeezed her hand, pulling her to him. "But so many did. Thanks to you."

27

ALY

As soon as her eyes popped open, Aly became aware of two things: Rainbow's face lit by firelight, and the presence of the black, writhing mass pressing against Aly's magical senses.

She sat up abruptly on the couch. Naia groaned and rocked back and forth on the couch across from her. Rainbow stood and tossed a handful of something into the fire.

"Eat," she told them.

Aly's head throbbed. She rubbed her eyes. The plan had been to sleep for one hour. But her body raged at being wrenched from sleep so soon. The feel of that black monster against her consciousness, however, brought her quickly to her feet.

"Naia, get up." Aly bent and grabbed a muffin. After two bites, she crammed a handful of raisins in her mouth and drained a cup of water.

To keep from feeling idle as she ate, Aly tried to recall the accounts of strange evils recorded in the Canticles. Surely someone had dealt with a similar cloud-creature. She'd read of a tornado composed of skulls, and it had haunted her thoughts for months. A sorcerer had once smothered an entire village with dense smoke. Her own father had unleashed plumes of poison gas upon citizens who disobeyed their queen. She shook off the thought.

Augustus Penwater had told her of his personal encounter with a strange moving shadow. It had no living form, yet it could take a life as easily as a bullet. It was as large as a house and traveled rather quickly. He'd defeated it by Stripping an entire swath of forest, killing every tree and drying up a mountain stream. He had been too afraid to Pull from the king for this endeavor, afraid of Stripping his sovereign of life.

This shadow was much larger than a house. Then a realization struck her that knocked her back down to the couch. The half-eaten muffin in her hand tumbled to the floor.

The formless evil that swarmed around Mardon blocked all light behind it.

"Naia," she breathed. "Can you see it from here?"

Naia looked up from an apple. "See what?"

Aly stood once more, her appetite gone. "The fog from the Canyon. I can't see behind it. I can't even see *through* it. In the Canyon, I didn't realize…" Her heartrate tripled as she raced for the door. "We must reach Red. If that cloud gets to him first…"

Naia sprang to her feet. "You won't be able to see his Well!"

Red, I'm coming.

In the hallway, she braced her tired body against the wall, breathing heavily. Naia sagged against the doorframe, looking no better than Aly felt.

They shared a knowing glance. The only way to get through what lay ahead was to steal a little more energy for themselves. It wasn't magic Aly liked using, as she'd pay for it later, but she didn't see a way around it.

When she uttered the words of the spell, her eyes brightened but her heart sank a little. Naia repeated them, and instantly she bounded for the tavern's back door.

"When the exhaustion comes again," Aly warned as they raced into the daylight, "We likely won't be able to push it back."

Rainbow and Quince followed without question. Aly turned to Quince, an apologetic look in her eye.

"Quince," she began, but he cut her off.

"I know what you're going to say. You don't trust me out there. My magic is still too unpredictable." His face reddened and his spritely countenance fell.

Aly didn't have time to discuss it, so she simply nodded.

"Can you shield me? Can I come and watch what your magic can do?"

Aly sighed. "It's still too dangerous. I can't take you to battle only to watch."

"It's not a sport," Naia snapped.

The boy winced. "I know. But I want to see your magic win."

Aly glanced quickly at Naia. "Thank you, Quince, but war is never decided before it's over. We really must leave now."

He shook a little, like a child about to launch into a tantrum. "Please, I can't stay here." He paused. "I'm afraid."

His terrified face broke Aly's heart. Finally, she said, "Can you find the palace? Go there. See what is happening, then send me word. That would be very helpful, Quince." She gave him a firm nod. "And tell any sorcerers you encounter that the black cloud will shroud their ability to see energy signatures. If they don't know this already, that will be crucial information for them."

Already, Quince looked eager, his frown replaced by a tentative smile. "I will do it."

After dousing him with a shield that would both protect him from direct attacks and contain any erratic spells of his own, she pointed him in the direction of the palace, then took off down a street headed toward Red's Well.

She and Naia raced through the streets, allowing their minds a few more minutes of rest from conducting magic. As they ran, Aly pieced together a new spell, what she hoped was a weapon powerful enough to crack through that awful black cloud.

Sunlight shone bright as they neared the street where Grey and Red fought, illuminating the wall of thick fog, giving it an almost tangible façade. Already, Aly sensed that the Tanderan troops were pushing back the Zealots and the Bulvarnans, based on the movement of the burning Truthwells up ahead.

Booms echoed down the street. Smoke spewed up in an alarming fashion a few streets to the right, perhaps near the palace. It was as if a massive freight train barreled down the city's avenues, filling the sky with a plume of black steam. Aly focused instead on the swirling darkness up ahead, trying to define its epicenter. Beneath the writhing black cloud, the streets were dark as dusk.

Red's Well glowed at the edge of the dark mass. Her shields still held around him.

"Now," she whispered to Naia.

Adrenaline took over and she launched into the air to soar over the final building separating her from Red. She speared down through the air like a hawk toward her prey. With a flick of her wrist, she pushed a powerful spell at the shadow, a hurricane-force wind snapping to life at her command. The shadow shuddered but otherwise remained unmoved by the wind.

It isn't affected by physical force, she mentally explained to Naia.

She prepared another spell, inspired by the magic she'd seen her father conduct in Bulvarna. The words brought lightning out of the clear sky, nailing it straight through the shadow to the cathedral's spire. This time, the shadow curled back and away from the lightning strike.

Was it the heat or the light or the electricity? Aly wished she knew.

Bulvarnan and Canduli soldiers rushed from beneath the cloud toward Red and the others.

Aly landed beside Red, who tossed a rifle aside and took a sword from a soldier in crimson as more Bulvarnans descended upon them. Nearby, Grey fired a pistol from a kneeling position.

She moved so fast no one saw her approach. No one, that is, but the shadow, which recoiled from her like smoke from a bullet.

When her feet slapped the stones, she didn't pause to even look at Red, but hurled a trio of quick spells: a spray of sand that bit at the enemy soldiers like hornets, a flaming canopy that pressed back the shadow-beast, and an icy gust that ripped through the streets, so sudden and so cold that it stopped all movement as it passed.

The battle paused for the blink of an eye. Everyone on the streets knew something had changed.

Red fought with a borrowed blade, swinging with well-trained blows at a Bulvarnan soldier. He shouted, but Aly's mind was full of magic, her purpose singular: destroy the cloud.

Out of nowhere, Igor thudded to the ground beside her, his staff whirling over his head before words left his mouth. With magic, he wrenched a windowpane from a nearby building to stop a spell from a charging Zealot. The glass shattered, then the shards took shape and arrowed their way toward the enemy soldier. When the Zealot fell, Igor turned flaming darts toward the black shadow, shredding through it like a cat's nails through a silk curtain.

"Light and heat," he shouted to her, pointing his staff—which was actually a spear—at the black cloud.

She nodded, thankful for the tip. "Naia, can you—"

"Already on it!"

Naia lifted to a balcony halfway up a nearby building, and as Aly turned her attention back to the soldiers on the ground, she saw flashes of light coming from Naia's position.

Crimson uniforms flashed all around. Swords glinted. Pistols and rifles fired. Magic whispered in the air, a frigid breeze whirling all around.

Rainbow had remained where she'd touched down in the street, frozen in fear. Aly threw her one sympathetic look, then whirled back to the battle. If Rainbow wasn't able to handle war, she should retreat and find safety. Aly hoped the woman would make the wise choice.

Ahead, a soldier in crimson raced beneath the cloud, chasing a Zealot who had lit himself on fire. The sight was so horrifying it stole Aly's gaze away from the shadow. The blazing man smashed himself through a window of the nearest building as the Tanderan soldier aimed and fired. Aly gagged but managed to scream out the words of her next spell.

As he entered the cloud, the Tanderan soldier clawed at his face. Before she could utter a healing spell, the soldier fell, his face and hands already turning black.

It was then she noticed the other bodies.

The fallen soldiers in crimson had skin blackened as if by fire. Those in Bulvarnan blue or desert tan had no such markings.

Red yelled across to her, "The shadow is poison to us. Not to them."

It is sentient, then. If she'd had any doubt, Aly knew now that the shadow was the true foe. It was the enemy to be defeated if this battle was to be won.

Soon, she became aware of an increase in enemy soldiers

pouring in from every side street. She'd expected them to flee, not converge upon her.

She swung both arms out, then pulled her fists down toward her hips. With the motion, she yanked down the partially charred façades of two empty buildings on either side of the approaching soldiers. Their screams were lost under the sound of bricks crashing to the cobblestones. The sting of death was countered by the pulse of fear over what she stood to lose.

"They're still coming," she whispered, dumbfounded, as the dust cleared and more enemy soldiers crawled over the rubble toward her. Their faces were set with a blank determination, almost as if unphased by the destruction all around. Her hand shot to her mouth.

Could it be?

Igor was again beside her. "They are controlled by something," he spat, hurrying his words.

Aly nodded. He'd realized it too.

"Alexander was controlled by Kassia," she mused aloud, watching the rush of enemy soldiers. "And Kassia was consumed by that shadow creature in the Black River." It appeared the shadow creature had followed them to Mardon.

As she blasted a wave of air that knocked down the soldiers, Aly cringed. The cloud hovering over the enemy soldiers *was* Kassia, at least in part. "The cloud controls them."

But the cloud hadn't left Candul with these Zealots; it hadn't traveled south with Bulvarna's soldiers. The shadow-beast had only risen from the Canyon when Kassia had entered the river. It had come to them, though, as if the army had simply been paving the way for the shadow beast all along.

Not possible, Aly growled to herself.

Kassia had given herself to the river like it had been her plan all along. She'd given up her body to take the form of this shadow, growing more powerful with each Well it drank in along its path. When the enemy soldier's Wells extinguished, their minds became the shadow-beast's puppets.

Zoraiya had said magic wanted to cover the whole earth. Kassia had immortalized herself in the river, as Usrich had done, and was now spreading her shadow over vast distances, consuming the world in darkness.

Aly screamed in rage.

This may have been Kassia's plan, but she *hadn't* planned on having Red and Aly here for this fight.

Aly bent down, placed both hands on the cobblestones, and pressed hard against the road. The stones ahead rippled like seawater, coursing between the buildings, and every enemy soldier toppled. When she stood, she lifted both hands. The cobblestones rose with her silent command, piling in heaps on top of the squirming soldiers.

Swallowing her unease, she shouted to Red, "They won't stop unless they're dead. We need to move away from that shadow."

"Can you defeat it?"

"Not until I find its source."

Red nodded in Aly's periphery. "To the palace, then."

Aly snapped her fingers and lightning crashed to the ground mere steps before her feet. The shadow slithered back. "To the palace."

Aly tossed out a spell that lifted the rubble to form a wall behind them. The Zealots would blast through it soon enough, but it would give Aly and the others time to retreat. She and Igor followed Red and the other Tanderan soldiers back through the streets toward the palace. Naia was nowhere in sight.

Only when the fighting was at her back did Aly search for Naia's Well. She found it a few streets over. "What happened to Naia? And where is Grey?"

Red jogged beside her, wiping away sweat. "Got separated in the fight. Naia went after him."

Aly lifted her brows and reached outward with her magic, quickly scanning the surrounding streets for Grey's energy. She sighed with relief. "Alive," she murmured. But for how long? That shadow-beast had a seemingly endless supply of soldiers to throw at Mardon. Grey and Naia and the others needed to retreat to the palace to regroup. But they didn't have long if they cared about the lives of everyone still on the streets and sheltered in unprotected buildings.

As they raced by, Rainbow darted out from behind an abandoned carriage. She tried to speak, but her words fumbled out through trembling lips. Aly waved her along with them.

Despite her hatred at running away, Aly clenched her fists and made for the palace. They must find a way to defeat the shadow, or the battle would never be won.

Naia, Aly called out with her mind, *find Grey and head to the palace.*

It was dangerous to withdraw all magic from the battle, but that shadow was going to kill anyone it touched. Surely it was better to save lives than to lose them.

As they charged away from the cloud, a voice entered Aly's mind. It was Quince. *Palace overwhelmed. Fire at the gates!*

Aly stumbled over a discarded rifle. Red caught her arm.

"We need to hurry."

Every step she took, Aly's chest tightened until she could barely draw breath. This battle—and likely the future state of the continent—hinged on whether or not she could bring down this strange shadow beast. The weight of this truth was almost too much to bear.

Hearing her belabored breathing, Red glanced over at her as they rounded a corner. When he caught her eye, the flash of warmth there, of complete trust, renewed her confidence.

She was the Beholder, and she had *him.* Was this the moment they'd been made for?

A boom from a street to the left fractured her hopeful thought. Magic was still active there, which meant her friends were likely trapped in combat and couldn't retreat. Aly curled her fingers into fists, then launched herself into the air.

From this height, she saw curling plumes of smoke where the palace gates stood. Her heart constricted, but she must help Naia.

With each fist, she called down one lightning bolt from the clear, blue sky, directing them into the fringes of the shadow lurking over the streets where Naia's and Grey's Wells burned.

Thanks, Naia's voice cut through Aly's concentration. She wobbled slightly in the air. *You'll need to teach me that one*, Naia added.

Aly touched back down on the stones beside Red and her two students. Together, they raced toward the palace gates. As they neared, an awful burnt smell polluted the air.

Rounding one last corner, Aly recoiled at the sight of a wall of flame licking at her defensive shields around the palace grounds. The fire snapped outward with tongues of flame, but everywhere it reached, the shield held it back.

Aly's heart skipped a beat as she let out a small gasp.

Red's mouth fell open at the sight.

"Help me," Aly shouted to Igor and Rainbow. "Call down a wall of water. Push that flame back."

Igor's hands shot up, one still holding the spear. To her right, Rainbow's shaking hands lifted as well. Aly drew on Red's bright Well. "Repeat after me," she snapped. *"The rain falls and the sun shines by the word of the Maker."*

Soon, an acute rainstorm, pouring down from a sudden, lone cloud, doused the fire-beast lapping at the palace gates. A great hissing accompanied an explosion of steam as the flames retreated.

Minutes later, the fire-beast was all but extinguished. The

final curls of flame slithered back down the street as the rainstorm chased it away. Aly shoved the rain cloud after the retreating flames and raced again toward the palace.

Tens of thousands of bright Truthwells sparkled within the palace grounds. There were people everywhere, draped around the columns, crammed in doorways, huddled against topiaries and statues. Aly's jaw fell open as they hurried across the main courtyard toward the front steps. So many had come here—and how smart! The black fog couldn't pass the barriers of Aly's own shields, set up ages ago to protect the royal family.

Red hurried up the steps. Aly quickly checked and, as she'd sensed earlier, his sisters were both here. And Seb.

She wanted to tell him, but he would find out soon enough.

Igor hobbled as he tried to hurry, his hand pressed to his side. Aly whispered a spell to relieve his pain. He straightened and dropped his arm. "Thank you," he said without looking over at her as they jogged up the steps. "I was enjoying a moment of no magic."

Aly understood. Igor was powerful, but he was still so new at controlling his magic. His mind could benefit from a break from intense concentration. Aly looked forward to a moment of rest —if there was one waiting for her in the future. Rainbow ran along behind Igor.

Passing through the front doors of the palace, Aly breathed a sigh of relief as she watched Red step into the foyer. After fighting so hard to get here, Red was finally *home*.

But the battle wasn't over, and the faces peering at them from every inch of the palace grounds confirmed that they had much work left to do.

28

RED

Red passed through the doorway and, though he'd wanted so badly to return here, a heavy weight tugged at his chest. Memories bombarded him: of his mother, elegant as a snowflake, descending the front stair; of his father offering him a seat on his council; of Elise sneaking up on him during hide and seek; of Carolyn lifting books up a back stairwell with a pulley she made; of Seb running down the hall, fleeing from the goat he'd let in as a prank.

Red caught himself against the banister. *Are my sisters even alive? Is Seb?*

Aly stepped up beside him, her hand light on his back. "They're here," she whispered.

His eyes closed and the weight fell away. He jogged up the stairs, allowing Aly to lead the way. She hurried toward the looping stair that took them to the living quarters. Igor fell behind after two flights, due to his slower pace.

People lined every level: sitting against the walls, pacing the corridors, perched in windows. Women cuddled children. Others sat weeping on the cold wooden floor. Aly and Red stopped climbing when they reached the sorcerer's hall, which was as crowded as the rest. Red's stomach knotted at the sight. So many had made it to the palace, but so many had not. He wondered if many other homes protected by magic had become refuges.

As they neared the room with an enchanted door—Aly's living quarters—Red slowed. "How would they be in there, if no one can get in?"

Aly spun, her hair a mess. She looked tired. He'd never seen her tired before. "They must have known the password."

Red nearly tripped he stopped so fast. "There's a *password?*" His jaw hung open. "After all this time…"

Aly didn't look amused. "Your father only told one person, and it was only in case of the worst kind of tragedy."

"Who?"

"Elise," Aly said. "She was only to use it if you…if you died."

Red blinked as he processed this. "No one told me the password."

Aly blushed. "You would have used it—before it was time."

He scoffed and looked away. She was right, of course. He shook his head. "But not Elise."

"She was never curious, like you were. If anything, she was afraid to ever have to use that password, because of what it meant." Aly turned toward her door.

He brushed past Aly toward the door.

From behind Red, Aly opened the door with a whispered word, allowing him to be the first to enter the room.

He raced forward.

"Red!"

Carolyn scrambled up from Aly's armchair to pounce on him with a crushing hug. Seb hovered behind her, ready for his own back-slapping embrace. Looking past his friend, he found Elise standing at Aly's desk, her face entirely inscrutable and wearing her armor.

Carolyn's weeping joy dissolved into blubbering and an altogether too-fast account of everything that had happened. Red nodded but stepped forward to greet Elise.

"You're alive," she breathed. Her hands trembled as she reached out to him, but something held her back. "Oh, Red, I...I am so sorry."

"Why, Elise?" he croaked.

She sniffed and looked quickly away. "I will explain. But we do not have time now."

He leaned forward, anger blazing. "I know we don't have time, Elise. I was out there. People are dying. But I need to know."

Her pale face blanched. "It was...I thought I could garner Alexander's trust. Learn his ways." Her eyes fell to the floor. "I was trying to be a spy."

More footsteps entered the room, but Red couldn't tear his gaze away from his sister.

"She's telling the truth," Grey's deep voice intoned from behind him. Grey placed a hand on Red's shoulder and moved around him. "I employed your sister at her request, to maintain favor with Alexander. Her actions against you are my responsibility. And against you." He bowed stiffly at Red and Seb in turn.

"A spy?" Seb asked, staring wide-eyed at Elise.

She pressed fingers to her mouth and turned away, apparently unable to bear their scrutiny. In a way, she deserved to feel uncomfortable. Red's breathing hadn't slowed even though he'd left battle. Instead, it still raced as he stood watching his sister.

Grey moved away, giving Red space. The explanation didn't change the pain he'd felt or the injury Seb had received when she'd betrayed them, but it proved she had acted—at least in her own mind—in a way she thought might help.

Red let out an overwhelmed guffaw, pent-up anger mixed with relief bursting from him. The truth, and perhaps the battle raging outside, made it easier to look his sister in the eye and feel a surge of love. He shook his head, still angry, but grateful she was alive.

Seb pulled Elise into a hug and whispered something in her ear. Red balked the intimacy. Apparently, Seb had already forgiven her.

Elise's quiet crying was muffled against Seb's shoulder. Watching his friend hold his little sister, Red realized that something had changed since he'd last seen them. He blinked and looked away.

Seb released Elise, but kept one arm looped around her waist. He flashed an almost embarrassed smile at Red. "Your sister is the most ruthless woman I've ever met."

From across the room, Grey stifled a cough. "Who would have known *ruthless* was the quality to bring down Sebastian Thorin?"

Seb shrugged, but Elise stepped out of his arm. "Red, can you forgive me?" she asked.

For a moment, he recalled the sight of Seb's back, bleeding and puffy, as his friend had lain in the barracks after they'd been forced to join the army. Red had told himself Elise had been coerced into her betrayal, that she'd done it to save Carolyn or their mother. Instead, she had chosen it. She had thought it *worth* the intelligence she might gain afterward. Red's throat threatened to close up, so he shoved away those awful memories, knowing there was a battle to win, and chose the answer that came easily but felt partly untrue, as if not yet fully realized. "Already have," he said, dragging her into an embrace.

It would take time to understand what she'd done, but Elise was his sister, his best friend. Forgiveness was the only way to mend their relationship. He hugged her tightly.

Carolyn whispered from behind them, "It was Elise who exposed Alexander as a fraud. She found out he was under Kassia's control, and she told everyone."

Elise stepped back and delicately wiped the corner of one eye.

Red studied his sister. So, in the end, she had discovered something worthy. Aly had tried to tell Alexander of Kassia's control, but he'd ignored her warnings.

"That's when he called Aly back, after the wedding. Well, it wasn't really a wedding," Carolyn corrected, though Red still didn't understand. "Alexander wanted to prove Elise wrong, but...he died." Carolyn looked horrified as she relayed the news.

Aly and Red shared a glance. So it had been Elise, in the end, who'd exposed Alexander's corruption and set in motion the events that brought Aly back to Red.

"I came here, hoping to find some way of contacting Aly," Elise said. "I knew we needed her to defeat that shadow."

At the mention of the word *shadow*, the room fell silent. Red's eyes traveled out the window. Smoke polluted the sky over his beloved city. How would they ever rebuild after this?

After would only arrive if they won.

"That cloud is controlling the enemy soldiers," Aly informed the others.

"It can do that?" asked Seb.

Aly nodded. She walked past Red to the window and dismissed the glass with a flick of her wrist. A fierce, cold wind sawed through the room, but Aly stood there, unphased. She stepped into the window frame.

"What is she doing?" Seb asked, pointing with his thumb.

Aly's clothes rippled in the cold breeze. "I would like to examine our foe."

Red stepped toward Aly. "While you're out there, find the

officers. Call our men back. We need all our forces united for our next move."

After a quick nod, she leapt from the window ledge, like a crow taking flight.

"How do you get accustomed to a woman who can *jump out of windows?*" Seb asked, shaking his head at Red. When no one responded, he added, "Now what?"

"Now, we coordinate our next moves. To take down that shadow, we'll likely need all the magic we can garner, which means the rest of us will be left to manage the ground battle without Protectors, or without as many. When the officers return, we'll form a plan." Red nodded at the place where Aly had vanished. She would need him for this, his powerful light. Would his light, a power he still didn't fully grasp, be enough to defeat the shadow? What if his Well, despite her claims, wasn't bright enough to push back this strange darkness?

Or what if it was? What if, as he feared, it would take *all* his light to defeat the shadow? Deep down, he knew this was the likely scenario, but he couldn't dwell on that now. If that was what it would take, then that was the reason Theod had crafted his bright Well.

Red glanced at Grey, who'd taken a seat in a high-back chair and crossed his legs, perfectly at ease. His sleeves were pushed back to his elbows, and he picked at the skin around a bleeding cut.

Naia bustled over to him and crossed her arms. "You like to bleed, or do you want me to fix that?"

He shrugged. She huffed and bent down to place a hand on his arm, right above the wound. In seconds, the skin healed over. She snapped her hand away and Grey's arm slithered down into his lap.

"Carolyn, Elise, can you two see that the people here have

food and water?" Red asked. His sisters nodded. "Rainbow, can you help them?"

The woman stepped into the room from where she'd been hovering outside the door. She squatted strangely, and Red realized she might be trying to curtsey. Red smiled at her.

"Where is Quince?" Naia asked, hands on her hips. "Aly sent him here."

Carolyn and Elise shared a glance before Elise said, "Young boy? Zealot, by his appearance?"

Naia nodded.

Carolyn stepped forward. "The people were too afraid to let him in. He said he was sent by Aly, but it was hard to know for sure. The people assumed he was the enemy."

"Where is he?" Red asked, his voice commanding.

Carolyn shrugged. "The people barred him from entering the gate. We didn't know what to do. The fire came, and we ran up here."

Just then Igor hobbled into the room, the spear acting like a walking stick now. No one would know he was a warrior by the look of him right now.

"Igor, find Quince. He's likely outside the grounds. Seb, give me your coat."

Seb obliged, tossing it across the sitting space.

Red in turn handed it to Igor. "Tell him to wear this."

When his sisters, Rainbow, and Igor had left the room, Red flopped heavily into the other armchair, his legs splayed out in what was decidedly un-regal posture. In this space, he had learned to be his true self. For a brief moment, no more than a handful of breaths, his mind flashed with memories of the nights he spent in here when he first met Aly.

Grey's voice snapped Red from his thoughts. "It pains you to sit here, does it not, when the enemy is still out there?"

Red's tired eyes flickered with renewed energy. "Yes."

Grey steepled his fingers. "I hate it too. Warriors need to fight."

Red nodded. Perhaps now he understood at least a little why Grey had spent so many years at the Canyon's edge.

Seb wandered over and rested an arm on the mantle. "You might want to fight, but that mist is consuming everything in its path."

For a moment, no one said anything. Naia shuffled off into Aly's bedchamber and the wooden four-poster bed creaked. The sorcerers were clearly tired, minds taxed by their magic.

Red craned his neck to look out the window. How was Aly faring?

His knees jiggled as he waited. Then he heard a whistling sound, like a strong wind through a keyhole.

He was at the window in a breath. Aly, all fluttering fabric and billowing hair, blazed toward the open window.

"Aly!"

A pulse of energy radiated outward from Aly and she darted into the room, crashing into Red and taking him to the floor.

"Are you all right?"

Ignoring him, she rolled off him and leaned back on her elbows. "She didn't like me searching out her shadow, but I found her source."

"Her?" asked Elise.

Wind still whipped through the open window, but no magic passed through the shield.

Aly turned and looked up at Elise. "Kassia. She's the one controlling that shadow. She's the one we must kill."

Grey offered Red and Aly each a hand and pulled them both up. "If she's already dead, how exactly do we kill her again?"

All eyes turned to Aly.

"She's one with the Black River now. That's her source. To defeat her, I must sever her connection to the river."

29

ALY

Aly took in the crowded sitting space. These rooms had been Aly's haven, the place she could drop her magical shroud and be completely *free*, but they had also been the rooms where she'd felt most alone. Visible but with no one to see her, save the king.

An incredulous smile flickered across her face despite the knot of fear in her stomach and the aching exhaustion creeping into her bones. Even if she couldn't change the world with her magic, *her* world had changed when Red stepped into it, and the faces staring at her—truly seeing her—were the evidence.

The wind howled through the open window, chilled by the vast amount of magic being continuously consumed by the shadow. The cloud hovering over the city had begun to thicken as it drew power from yet more victims, casting everything underneath it in the gloom of midnight.

Sounds of battle continued to trickle in with the breeze. Not all had received the message to regroup at the palace—or they hadn't yet been able to retreat.

The longer it took Aly to dispel this evil, the more people would die. Rest would have to wait.

And she could think of only one way to rip Kassia's remaining power apart from the source that fueled her.

She inhaled slowly and turned to Red, her heart unwilling to accept what she needed to say.

Kassia had been trying to separate Aly from Red for as long as Aly had been alive. All the Bulvarnan queen's actions had been to keep the Beholder from her Beacon. Somehow, Kassia had known Aly was a Beholder. Perhaps a Reckoner had discerned this truth for her, but how she'd acquired the information didn't matter now.

This—this deathly cloud—had been Kassia's aim all along: to consume all the light in its path, perhaps even all the light in the world.

Of course Kassia had wanted to rid the world of Beacon and Beholder before her final act. But she had failed.

Red touched Aly's shoulder. She hadn't realized she'd started shaking until his hand steadied her. He didn't say anything, didn't ask her any questions, simply stood there, beside her.

She gripped his hand and said what couldn't be avoided any longer. "It will take every bit of energy I can Pull from you."

His voice was close when he whispered back, "I'm not afraid."

She blinked back the emotion welling inside her. "It might hurt." *It might kill you*, she said in her mind, not to him, not to anyone, but the words resounded in her head as loud as cannon fire.

"Tell me what to do." His face cemented with iron resolve, as if he'd known this would take every bit of his light.

She turned and stood close to him, thankful for the support as her energy flagged. "I need to be able to focus entirely on this one spell. I will not be able to defend myself or you." In a lower voice, she added, "And I'm starting to become very tired—we don't have long." Her eyes drifted absently and her body slumped against Red. He held her tightly.

Seb perked up. "I will defend you."

Grey stood. "As will I."

Edward faltered before adding, "And I."

"We're going to need Naia and the others," Aly said, pointing to her room, where Naia snored softly. At least she was getting a few minutes of much-needed rest.

"What, exactly, do you need?" asked Seb with a tilt of his head.

Aly sighed. "Time. But we don't have that. I need to reach the Black River."

Red's shoulders sank and Edward spun to look out the window. Disappointment settled like glue in the room.

"No, you don't," Grey said. Everyone turned to him. He scratched his head a moment, appearing lost in thought, then he fixed his gaze on Aly. "You Pulled from a river once to save a town, and that was well before your Mastery."

He looked at her the way he had that first day she had conjured magic in his house, a spark of amazement in his eyes. This time, however, it wasn't the fiery admiration that had once lit her own heart ablaze, but the quiet challenge of a former tutor to his former student. He was giving her one last test.

She uttered a small, disbelieving laugh. "The Black River is on the other side of the *continent*."

Red broke his stare from Grey and turned to Aly. "He's right." His enthusiasm surprised Aly. "You found me when I was on the other side of the continent. You Pulled from me all the way from Mardon to fuel your flight."

"That was different." Aly pressed her hands to her face, but she couldn't hide from their piercing gazes. They expected too much of her. "I don't want to Pull from the Black River. I want to destroy it."

Red gently tugged her hands down and held them. His eyes locked on hers, and she felt a flicker of his mad hope inside her. "You don't have to destroy the river. It's not the water that's the problem—it's Kassia."

Aly blinked at him, turning it over in her mind. "Come, it's time to get rid of her. For good."

Seb spoke up, his voice shakier than normal. "Where are you going? I thought Grey said you could fight her from here?"

With a heavy sigh, Aly said, "Perhaps, but when I fight that shadow, it will throw everything it has at me, and I imagine that will be enough to break any shields I can compose. It won't be defeated easily, and I can't put all these people at risk by bringing that kind of attack to the palace." She lifted her hand toward the door. "We will fight outside the grounds. At least that way, everyone inside my shields will be safe."

Aly's gaze traveled back out the window, where the darkness hovered over the edge of the city. To fight this darkness, she would have to take the light to it.

To reach the dawn, we must press through the night, advised a familiar song from the Canticles. It was time to do just that.

Her heart weighed heavy as she grabbed Red's hand and squeezed. Theod might have crafted him for this very moment, but it didn't guarantee he was meant to survive. What if, to crack this false night, she would have to expend *all* of Red's light?

30

ELISE

The king's office still smelled of Alexander's lingering pipe smoke, a different weed than Gevar had smoked, and Red had never taken up the habit. Elise ran her hand along the smooth wood of her father's huge desk, searching for the drawer with a keyhole.

Over the past seventeen years, there had been a time or two she'd barged into her father's office while he worked and sat in his lap as he signed papers or scribbled out what she imagined to be edicts of grand scope.

Once or twice, her father had stood to move about the room, and she'd sat in this chair, her little legs not yet touching the floor, her hands running along the sculpted wood trim that edged the workspace.

"You would make a fine queen, my daughter," Gevar had said to her, staring over at her small frame in his massive chair. "But let us pray to Theod it never comes to pass." In his eyes had been the pain of a father's worst fear—that of losing a child. She'd always cowered away from this strange compliment, knowing that for her to be queen would mean her brother would be dead.

Still, she'd cherished his praise, fantasizing about ordering all wars to end and all soldiers to come home.

She pinched her lips and shook her head. She was no ruler. Red and Aly were going to survive—they must.

The key to the palace's massive emergency storage pantry was in the king's desk. She slid a tiny key out from her pocket and opened the locked desk drawer.

A soft knock startled Elise, and she looked up to see Seb stepping through the cracked door.

"Did you find it?"

She nodded at him as he boldly walked up and perched on the king's desk, leaning over it toward her. She held up a large, metal key and relocked the desk drawer with the smaller one.

"They are ready," he said.

As she opened her mouth to respond, her throat closed over unsaid words. He touched her chin with a finger, and she froze.

"We'll be all right," he said gently.

He couldn't make promises like that. They were impractical and only knifed more pain into Elise's heart. She was not one for mad hope, like her brother, as much as she wanted to be.

"Theod, help," was all she could whisper in reply. Then she leaned forward and kissed him.

He scooped her head against his, encouraged by her action, and she stumbled against the wooden desk. Then she was scooting across it as he pulled her to him.

Something heavy hit the floor, breaking the moment. She breathlessly pushed herself off the desk, and looked down at the inkpot they'd upended. A black stain spread across the beautiful patterned rug.

"Leave it," Seb said, tugging her by the waist. She bumped against him and the world disappeared for the flash of a moment as she spun in his arms. "There are more important things than spilled ink."

She nodded, and they walked out of the office into the teeming hallways. In one hand was the key to the emergency stores of food; in the other, Seb's fingers linked with hers. They hurried toward the front courtyard, where her brother and the others waited in a tight circle.

"I will create a distraction," said Grey as they approached. Shadows darkened the blue sky and crept ever nearer.

Aly crossed her arms. "I don't like it, but we can't risk a full-on attack. I won't be able to protect you," she said to Red. "My mind will be entirely lost to this spell."

Seb's face brightened. "What sort of distraction did you have in mind?" He lifted the vial from his pocket. "I have this, if it will help."

"I want to release a pack of woodwolves into the city," Grey stated, as if discussing which theater show to attend.

Elise covered a surprised cough. Naia gaped at him.

Shaking his head, Seb said, "And just how do you have a pack of woodwolves on hand?"

Grey looked at Red with a pained, almost apologetic expression. "I have been capturing and selling Canyon beasts for nearly a year."

Red coughed, shattering the awkwardness into uncomfortable splinters. He appeared at a loss for words. This was something he'd assumed a spy would tell his sovereign, but apparently Grey had plenty of secrets, even from his king.

Shaking his head, Red glanced at Aly, then back to Grey. "Whatever your past actions, they matter little now. Whether we succeed or fail, in a short time, the world will be in need of leaders to put back the broken pieces. And whether I live or die, we need men like you to stand watch as Tandera, or whatever is left of her, begins again."

"The gang I run," Grey continued, "sold a lyth I captured last spring to our rivals to avoid a bloodbath among our members.

They, in turn, sold it to the Bulvarnans. It showed up at your coronation ball and nearly killed you." He matched Red's iron stare.

It was *Grey* who'd caught that lyth, who'd sold it to the enemy. Everyone in the small group fidgeted slightly as they processed this revelation. Although there was sincerity, possibly even apology in Grey's expression, he never voiced any remorse. Elise wondered how he could believe in his role so fiercely as to live without regret.

Finally, Red said, "You've saved my life enough times to make up for it. Now, come, we don't have long."

The white-haired Igor jogged across the courtyard alongside a young boy with lanky limbs and shoulder-length hair.

As the others welcomed them and explained the plan, Seb leaned over and whispered in Elise's ear. "Since you're a spy, does that mean you are good at hiding things?" His fingers nipped playfully at her ribcage.

"Scandalous!" she hissed quietly at him, glancing madly about, but no one seemed to have noticed.

Against her hair, he said, "*Pah.* I can show you scandalous, my dear."

Elise disguised a twisted smile as her once-shattered heart now soared. Seb was a wonder, and she did not deserve him. When she looked at him, he grinned with all the silliness of a wide-eyed child. He was utterly smitten and she had no idea how or why, but only that in this moment she was free from the shackles of her secrets and the burden of her betrayal.

She shuddered a little to think of what his words meant, but she didn't care how many other women he'd loved. All that mattered was that he had brought back to life the heart she'd thought was dead.

Now, they simply needed to survive what loomed before them.

31

ALY

The fighting had died down as word of the king's retreat filtered through the streets. Soldiers and officers formed up in lines in front of the palace's front gates, ready to do as their king commanded.

They'd accepted his orders with almost pleased expressions, perhaps glad that someone was finally planning an attack aimed at *winning* this fight.

As Aly walked ahead of Red and the others toward the palace gate, the city beyond seemed eerily quiet. Only the black shadow curled and twisted in the air, never still, and the crash of distant fires rumbled in the air. The enemy soldiers lurked in the darkness, too far back to see but nonetheless a threat. They weren't attacking for now, but Aly knew it was only because she and Red remained within the shielded palace grounds. As soon as they set foot outside, the enemy would charge.

At the gate, Aly paused. Grey stepped up beside her. Red drew near on her other side. Naia and Igor and Seb surrounded them.

Aly waited for Grey to speak, to say something that would

make her feel better about what he was going to do. When she could stand the silence no longer, she said, "Thank you. For everything."

He cocked a sideways grin at her, defying the danger ahead with his easy swagger. "Remember that painting? The one in the hall?"

Visions of death personified filled Aly's mind.

"Many people think the man on the ship is oblivious to his doom, but I think perhaps he knows death comes for him, and he smiles all the same. After all, there's no sense fearing what will come for us all."

He glanced back at Naia, who nodded solemnly. "Let's go."

With that, he jogged through the gate and into the shadow. Naia took off after him, spells blazing as she hit the wall of darkness.

Within seconds, they were too far to see.

Aly bit her lip and hoped Naia's shields held against the dark fog.

Red grasped her hand, squeezing hard. "They'll make it," he said.

After the agonizing five-minute head-start they'd agreed upon, Aly said, "Now, it's our turn."

As soon as Aly and the others crossed her magical barrier, the shadow pressed against her shield like a mountain caving down on an ant hill.

With a scream of both shock and fear, Aly yanked lightning from the sky and speared it at the heart of the shadow. The darkness shrank back, but quickly returned. It had gained power even in the past hour.

As expected, a wave of enemy soldiers charged at them from the gloom. With ferocious howls, they swarmed the Tanderan forces as Red, Aly, Igor, and Seb moved into position. The soldiers obeyed the command issued by their king and formed up around the five of them, creating a small pocket of space where Aly could conduct her magic.

Aly's shields were the strongest she'd ever composed, but within seconds outside the gate, all her shields failed and the stinging black fog descended on them all.

Seb hollered in pain. Several soldiers collapsed at once as the fog initiated its attack—it too had been waiting. Igor called down water from the air, misting them all. The burning lessened.

Aly needed to remain focused. She was not here to combat the shadow or the soldiers. She was here to destroy the shadow's source—energy from the Black River. But if the soldiers and her friends fell, no one would be there to defend her and Red against attacks.

Another of Aly's shields erupted around them, and the stinging ceased as the fog was momentarily pressed back.

Moving with the plan, Seb withdrew his two vials, poured them together, then hurled the explosive through Aly's shield toward the heart of the shadow-beast.

Aly scraped the skies for power. Her breathing turned to a gritty yell as she struck the vial with a bolt of lightning.

Seb's mixture broke half the block. Those under her shield were unharmed. Even the shadow recoiled, and sunlight peeked down into the small crater strewn with bodies. She hated that war involved so much death, but these soldiers were not in their right minds. As Alexander's mind had been warped, so had theirs. They were bent on death, and they wouldn't stop until she defeated the one ruling their minds.

She must end this shadow.

Kneeling on the stones, she closed her eyes and pressed her awareness to the north, quickly finding the Well of the Black

River. She had never let her mind lose it, not after realizing what needed to be done.

As she prepared to gather every bit of energy in Red's Well, the sounds of approaching feet, gunfire, and snarling beasts wrenched her eyes open.

Three woodwolves barreled down the street, blue sparks exploding near their tails. Naia came into view first, arms and hair flapping. Grey sprinted right behind her, staying clear of her magic. The wolves charged past Aly's shield dome and ran straight for the Bulvarnan soldiers already climbing through the crater toward the line of Tanderans.

Naia and Grey ran to Aly and the others, but a Canduli Zealot leaped from the top of a nearby building and rained rubble down on them as he fell.

Naia, occupied directing the beasts with her magic, didn't notice. Aly opened her mouth to voice a spell at the same moment Grey lunged for Naia, wrapping her in a protective embrace. The rubble bounced off Aly's sparkling shield and Grey and Naia were again racing toward them. Grey held two pistols and Naia kept her arms lifted in front of her.

As planned, a dozen enemy soldiers broke off to fight the approaching beasts.

If Aly kept opening her eyes to watch the battle around her, she'd never accomplish the magic necessary to end the shadow-beast. Red fired a rifle and an approaching soldier went down. She needed to trust that the plan would work.

She closed her eyes, but the sounds were too chaotic. How could she ever concentrate like this?

Even with her eyes closed, she could see the shadow-beast, its magic as visible to her as its cloudy form. The darkness contorted into the shape of a wolf's open fangs and reached around Aly's shield. Aly hissed a spell that kept the wolf's jaws from snapping shut, but the shadow did not dissolve. Instead, it deepened and crushed from all directions.

It squeezed. It pricked. It stung. The shadow broke through her shield—again.

Her mind became a whirlwind of light and shadow. The fog had thickened and turned vicious, taking on a life of its own. Within the fog, Aly sensed the dim Wells of her friends, but their light was shrinking away. If the fog managed to creep between her and Red, she would lose sight of him. He'd promised to stay close, but they hadn't expected the shadow to bite like this, to press so hard and move so fast.

The cloud's force became so great that her arms buckled at her sides and her face hit the ground.

Her fingernails dug into the grit between stones. Inside her mind, a battle raged. Angry shadows clawed at Red's light, threatening to cover it entirely. Woodwolves and foxbloods were nothing compared to the shadow creatures she now saw raking at the edges of his Truthwell.

With a shout, she lunged forward off the ground, and in her mind's eye, she slung blades of pure light at the creature of darkness nipping at his Truthwell. This was the battle only she could see—the battle for Red's energy.

Phrases of the *Verad* acted as blades of truth, swords of light that sliced the shadow creature licking at Red's Well.

Soon, she lost the edges between reality and her magical sight. What she saw was real, if only to her. She stormed forward, hurling verses of the *Verad* as fast as she could think of them, and with this weapon, she advanced into the heart of the shadow.

She sensed a hand grasping for her, but she was too far into her own fight that she couldn't stop now.

Red's Well burned like an inferno made only for her. She

relished the sensation of Pulling from it, her appetite for its beauty only increased the more energy she gathered.

The shadow didn't like it.

Aly's body shook with a blow that toppled her again to the hard road.

Her mind, anchored as it was to Red's Well, held fast, but her body was beginning to break. The shadow-beast wanted her flesh.

She drew power for her next spell and cast a solid beam of light into the shadow-beast. In her mind, she saw tongues of black smoke peeling away from the light.

The pressure crushing her body released. She opened her eyes briefly and stood. Her friends battled with pistols and blades and magic. Too many Tanderan soldiers had fallen, their skin blackened by the stinging fog. Aly gasped.

Naia pushed a column of fire into a violent spin, then shoved it toward the still-charging Canduli soldiers. Grey swung a sword, stopping a Bulvarnan from stabbing Naia in the back. Igor whirled his staff over his head, a disc of small rocks arcing after the spearhead and pelting into the enemy line.

The shadow curled back on Aly's beam of light.

With a pained moan, she watched as the shadow closed over the light that moments ago had pushed it back. It was still gaining strength.

She yelled as another wave of pressure slammed into her, knocking her to the pavement. Red's presence beside her slipped away.

In that moment, the shadow swallowed Red.

The world turned dark and the shadow swaddled her like a babe.

Instead of screaming, Aly's heart cracked inside her chest and she let out a silent *oh*.

This was what she'd feared.

Cut off from her source, Aly's spells ceased at once. The pressure on her body became so great she could barely draw breath. Her bones crushed against the pavement.

No!

As Aly drew on the energy of the ground around her and the stones beneath her feet, another lightning bolt split the black cloud, releasing the pressure on Aly once more. Naia screamed as she held the spell, drawing another crackling bolt into the heart of the beast.

Igor aimed his staff at the sky, and fire poured from the tip. With their help, enough pressure released that Aly could breathe.

The crack of electricity rent the shadow, revealing Red a few steps away.

But her mind was spent, her energy entirely gone. She'd pushed back her exhaustion too long, and when her spells had cut off, all of the stress she'd put on her mind imploded in a sudden wave. Tears leaked out of her eyes onto the road as she stared at Red, who was swinging a sword at a man in blue.

She couldn't even call out to him. Her mind was in a tunnel, and the world was shrinking.

"Red!" Someone shouted. It might have been Grey.

Red turned, spotted Aly, and rushed to her. A Canduli Zealot leaped, a spiral of purple magic about to consume the king. She couldn't lift her hand to warn him, couldn't speak into his mind. Her body and her faculties were shutting down.

The purple magic was almost upon Red's back when another figure dove across Aly's narrowing line of sight and took the hit full in his chest. Igor's white hair reflected the purple glow. She heard Igor's body flump against the stones, but she didn't see him get up. His Well blinked out in her mind's eye.

Her eyes drifted shut as a wave of sadness and fear coursed

through her body. Then Red's strong hands scooped under her shoulders and legs, lifting her off the ground.

She couldn't hear what he was yelling at her. All she cared about was that his Truthwell again burned in her mind's eye. Her head lolled backward, her mind slipping into sleep in the midst of battle.

"Stay with me," he whispered to her. "Stay with me, Little Fire."

She tried to nod, but all her strength was gone. She took one more breath and sleep took her.

"No, you don't!" Naia's hands were ice and steam as they slapped each of Aly's cheeks.

Aly lifted her head, a splitting headache already muddying her thoughts.

"Take my energy," Naia said, clamping a hand on Aly's wrist. "I'm not sure if this is how you do it, but here."

A jolt shot through Aly. It only lasted a second, and again she slumped in Red's arms.

Guns fired and frigid air whirled around them. She didn't have time to fall asleep!

Magic had stolen so much heat from the air that tiny ice crystals clung to Red's eyelashes and brows. "Can you walk?"

She shook her head. "No. I need to go higher. To a rooftop."

Red began to move as the words left her mouth. He shouted to the others to clear a safe path to the nearest building. Bullets fired, the breeze rattled windows, but Aly's eyes drifted shut.

He moved up the stairs, and Aly was asleep by the time they reached the top.

She woke to him shaking her and calling her name. "Aly, I will hold you, but it's now or never."

It was time for her final spell. The Truthwells of Grey, Naia, and Seb burned in a small circle around them, but all other Wells had disappeared from her sight. The shadow obscured every other light.

This fiendish shadow wanted to plunge the world into a new night, a night so deep no one would have the power to destroy the darkness.

With truth magic cut off, people would become the shadow's slaves, as so many had already. The darkness was going to blind them all.

In her mind, Aly recited the familiar words: *Truth will rise.*

To end the darkness, Aly would have to Pull every bit of light inside of Red. He'd offered it to her once, but she hadn't needed to use it. This time, she would.

Aly squeezed Red around the middle and pressed her face into the hollow at his neck. It wasn't fair. Theod had crafted Red the way a master smith crafts the perfect sword: expertly balanced and sharp enough to end even the strongest enemy.

And Aly was the one to whom the sword had been given.

She reached into his Well. The spell was ready on her tongue, but heavy on her heart.

"I love you," she whispered.

He moved his hand up to cup the back of her head amid her windswept hair. After a moment, he said, "I love you too."

She Pulled.

Diving into his Well, she aimed herself like a bullet to the brightest depth he possessed. Infinite light spread out around her, erasing all else. She closed her mind to all other realities save this one.

Energy raced to her. She felt it building in every inch of her body, dancing like lightning down her skin and raging like floodwaters in her veins.

Aly began to lose herself in the light.

Sharp jabs pricked her skin and an insufferable weight dragged her downward. Though her mind could only see Red's light, her body felt the shadow's attack. Red groaned in pain, his body twisting and jerking.

She should expend the energy now.

No, just a little more.

A part of her mind said *enough* and another part said *more*. It was like drinking the very sun.

Snippets of a poem flashed into her thoughts as she pressed farther into the exquisite light.

Suns to drink.

The world to brink.

Aly was on the brink of the world, the energy at her disposal enough to rip the foundations of the earth apart and toss them all to pieces at Theod's feet.

The poem echoed in her ear.

Press, O world, into the dawn alight with songs of joy,

She was going to remake the world with Red's light. But what kind of dawn would it be without him there by her side?

When night lies down and breathes its last,

She would end the darkness. Not only *this* darkness, but all shadows. All lies. She hadn't seen the truth so plainly until now. The writers of the Canticles had known this day would come. The *Verad* spoke of this dawn like it was a certainty, but Aly had never expected it to come like this.

The faces shine that once were cast.

No one will be bound by darkness.

And none within can e'er destroy.

Whatever was about to happen couldn't be undone.

Red's bright Well poured more power into her than she'd ever felt. It was now, perhaps, that she understood how the Canyon had been created in a day. With this much energy, she could lift a mountain and throw it into the sea. She could reach the moon with no more than a word.

Maker, guide me, she thought, trembling at the power Theod'd allowed her to touch.

Every tangible, accessible spark of Red's light was at her command. *I love you*, she thought one last time.

For Tandera. For truth. For freedom.

She voiced her final spell, driving every bit of power into the darkness engulfing her.

Energy fired outward, and her body rocked with the force of it. Wind gusted. Her stomach knocked into her throat. They were hurtling through the air by a wind stronger than a hurricane, Red's strong arms still wrapped around her.

Her voice rattled as she screamed the last words of her magic, ripping every last fringe of this black beast from the river in the Deep.

When the spell ended, her muscles turned limp and her arms fell away from Red. She became weightless, unaware of whether she stood or lay sprawled on the ground.

Aly opened her eyes.

The light had seared her natural vision, and she couldn't see Red's face in front of her own. In seconds, her vision returned as flecks of purple sparked across her open eyes. Red fell beside her, his body unmoving.

How were they falling? When had she leaped into the air?

She tried to reach for him, but her muscles were too spent to obey. Red's face was perfectly still, his hair a mad tangle on top of his head.

The earth rumbled beneath them, though her eyes remained on Red as they crashed toward the ground. She must have flown while Pulling on his energy. Or had the shadow moved them in one last attempt to defeat them?

She hoped her friends had survived. They had fought to the end.

Aly's limp arms hung in the air slightly above her. She eyed her finger where her Master's ring had been. Even that spell had ceased, and the ring was gone.

Tingles ran along her arms and legs. Sensation trickled back to her, and she again reached for Red, this time looping her arms and legs around his body, content to fall with him to whatever end. Magic couldn't save her now.

Aly looked with her mind for Red's energy signature. It was not there. Nothing was. No light anywhere, not in the rocks, not in the Cresen River below, not in the sky above.

Save him, she pleaded.

There was no light at all in her mind's eye.

Not me. Save him.

Nor was there darkness.

Up above, a blue sky shone down on the crumbling city.

"From the ashes, truth will rise," Aly said aloud as she stared up at the sun-bright sky.

Then her body pierced water and jerked away from Red.

32

GREY

The small skiff Grey'd borrowed at the river's wharf peeled silently through the gentle water. Several abandoned boats bumped hopelessly against the grassy banks.

An oar floated by Grey's hand as he rowed quietly, scanning the water for signs of life.

Naia slept on the opposite end of the skiff. Her demeanor had changed since that blinding light shattered the darkness, leaving them all both blind and deaf for several minutes. She had a strange ease about her movements now—less twitching and fidgeting. It made little sense to Grey, but he didn't question it.

Naia had also followed, wordlessly, as he'd marched off, heading in the direction to where two figures had fallen from the sky. She claimed she couldn't see their Truthwells anywhere, that she couldn't see anyone's Truthwells anymore. When he inquired of several scared Mardonians creeping out into the now silent streets, he discovered the falling figures had landed in the river.

A strange mercy.

He would not stop searching until he found them.

Neither would Naia, though she hadn't been able to fend off sleep once they'd set out on the river. He watched her sleeping, breaths coming steadily. It was odd how magic taxed their minds so much that it shut down their entire bodies as well. She'd saved his life several times during the battle. He wouldn't be here without her.

The wounds he'd incurred defending Aly and Red throbbed, but Naia no longer had the ability to heal him.

The last of the sun glinted off the water, making it hard on the eyes as Grey stared at the wake created by his oars. Aly had said she might have to Strip Red to defeat the darkness. It had always been a possibility, but Red had never once wavered. He'd gone with her to the death as readily as a river to the sea.

He had surprised them all.

"Long live the king," Grey said to the slapping waves. *He would have made a fine sovereign.*

Grey stopped himself. Red had indeed been a fine sovereign. In the mere months he'd worn the crown, he had saved Tandera —and maybe even the world—from a shadow that would have consumed all light. No other king would leave such a legacy.

Naia groaned and sat up, her skin pinched around squinting eyes. A crease from her sleeve left a line on her brown skin. She looked at him expectantly. He shook his head, and tears sprang from the corners of her eyes.

To Grey's infinite surprise, at the sight of her tears, his throat constricted. He hadn't felt emotion this sharp in *years,* not since his boyhood, when he'd watched his father turn away from him yet again with disinterested eyes.

Aly and Red deserved to live. Grey had wanted them to live, to be the ones to see Tandera happily restored. *I should have been the one to die, to end with the darkness.*

He turned away so Naia wouldn't see his struggle.

The boat rocked slightly as Naia moved. He felt her when she settled on the nearest plank bench across from him, but he did not face her.

"Weston."

He recovered himself, steeled his expression, and swallowed. He still couldn't look at her but kept his eyes out on the water.

"Don't carry this with you," she said in her rough accent. Her voice fascinated him, the way it shaped vowels and rasped as if snagging on something in her throat. "It isn't your burden to bear." When he didn't respond, she added, "You seem like a man who carries burdens he should have left behind long ago."

His eyes snapped to hers, which were rimmed with red.

"It's okay to mourn them. And it's okay to let them go." She pressed her lips into a tight smile and turned away, as if to move back to her original seat.

"Wait."

He couldn't reach out to her. It was pointless. He lowered his hand. *Fool.*

She narrowed her eyes and scrutinized him. "Let it go, Weston. Let it *all* go."

"I can't." His father's coldness. His sisters' indifference. His mother's selfishness. He shook his head. "I've tried." Years of living at the Canyon. Hurting Aly when he'd known better. Living a lie. Burying himself under so many masks he wasn't even sure who he was underneath it all.

Naia huffed. "Don't you say *I can't.* If I can let go of the horrors my magic has done, you can let go of your ghosts too. They can't be as bad as what I've done."

He shot her a skeptical glance.

"You think there's a limit to our redemption? If that were so, we'd all be lost." She pointed forcefully down the river. "She taught me the truth always rises. Either we rise with it, or we're as dead as the demons in that shadow."

For someone who grew up without the truth, she clung to it tighter than anyone he knew. He'd lived with the truths of the *Verad* etched in his mind for years, and he'd never believed them like that.

When she shook her head, her curls tossed about wildly. "Don't you claim to be too broken for the truth to fix. I was broken once too, but now I'm..." She cast about for the right word. "Now I'm restored."

He couldn't help himself. Desperate for the mending she spoke of, he tilted his head down, his forehead so close to hers he could feel her warmth. "Fix me," he whispered. But inside, the one truth he'd internalized yelled over his own desires: *I am unlovable.*

Her breath quickened, and electric tension radiated off of her.

"I can't fix you." She trembled as the boat drifted with the current. Finally, she lifted her chin and met his gaze. Fear shone out of her brown eyes. Apparently, she was afraid of this as much as he was.

"You don't want this. I'm not what you want." It was the only truth he knew, and yet he hated it. With Red and Aly gone, his brokenness was even worse. If they had survived, maybe he could have found a way to see it all as worth it.

"You don't know what I want." She hesitated, then, "Would you like to know?"

She was extending him an opportunity. He'd been given a similar opportunity once, by a woman he'd come to admire. He knew then that he shouldn't have taken the chance to dance with Aly, to give her hope where none should exist.

If he had learned anything since that day, it was to ignore hope.

He closed his eyes and exhaled. "No, Naia." *Save yourself from me.*

A prickly moment passed.

"I want you to open your eyes."

He obeyed. She stared at him with eyes so wide it was nearly comical. The edge of his lip curled up. "What?"

"Me." She grabbed his shirt with a fist, startling him. "I'm right here. I'm not sure how this will work. I'm not sure how to even touch another person without getting the shivers. But I'm ready to try it. We both have our ghosts. Maybe all that means is we'll understand each other better. Maybe it means we'll point each other back to the truth. Back to the light. What do you say? Are you going to keep pretending to be immune to emotion, or are you going to finally let go of all that plagues you?"

He reached for her with nerves ablaze. When his hand slid into her hair, he smiled at the texture of it. Her body shook with a sudden tremor. "You weren't kidding," he teased. More terrified than he'd ever been, he couldn't bring himself to kiss her.

Killing Canyon beasts wasn't as frightening as kissing a woman. It signified a beginning rather than an ending, and he was good at endings. They were all he'd ever known.

She sensed his struggle. "It's not easy for me either."

Her acknowledgement loosened something stiff inside him. He pulled her to him and pressed his lips to hers.

Briefly, she held his kiss. Then it was over—too soon, he decided.

"See, that wasn't so hard," she muttered, voice softer than usual. When he tensed to pull his arm away, she touched him with delicate fingers. "Not yet." Boldly, she spun to sit on the bench beside him. "There's only one way to get better at this." She turned her face up and whispered, "Practice."

He held her tightly as the boat swayed from her movement. To him, it was better than all the dances in all the ballrooms he'd ever entered.

"I think it's time we turned back for today," he said, finally brave enough to face the pain of losing Aly and Red. Naia had lent him the courage he needed. She'd done more than that, too, but it would take years to understand everything she'd done in this one moment.

As he regripped the oars, something on the bank caught his eye. In among the low branches of a riverside tree was a dark shape curled right above the water's edge.

"Over there!" Grey yelled, pointing at the figure.

He barely dared to hope.

As the skiff drew nearer, he saw it was a woman.

"Aly!" Naia yelled, scrambling into the shallow water and over to Aly. "She's breathing!" Naia covered her mouth, where happy sobs burst out.

Grey's chest swelled with pride and hope and a rare joy. A pang of sadness tempered his mood as he and Naia hauled Aly's limp body into the boat. They should be hauling two people aboard. But that was wishful thinking.

Aly flopped like a wet doll onto the boards, but the small crash shocked her body out of sleep and she coughed several times. She didn't make eye contact with either of them, only curled into herself, shivering uncontrollably.

Grey leaned into the oars, ready to propel them quickly back to the wharf. He would come back tomorrow to search for Red. Now, Aly needed help.

He exchanged a worried glance with Naia. She nodded and awkwardly snuggled up to Aly's side in the bottom of the small skiff.

33

ALY

Aly awoke to the sound of crows. Her body trembled with a deep chill, souring her empty stomach. She instinctively reached for the energy around her, but it was like reaching with bound hands. Her eyes popped open.

Dingy boards and the smell of fish greeted her.

Her mind could no longer see the light of Truthwells. She sat up with a start, rocking the small boat and the person pressed against her side.

"Naia?" Aly's voice croaked from her dry throat.

Naia attempted to disentangle herself from Aly, and someone helped her up from the cramped space.

"Aly."

It was dark, but Aly knew the face and voice of Lord Weston Grey. Naia and Grey had survived. Aly shivered, her clothes damp and clingy.

Red. Losing him was unbearable, but to lose him *and* her magic was unthinkable. One more time she tried to access the light of truth that lit the magical world only sorcerers could see.

Nothing.

Aly lay back down, exhausted, her mind searching, searching. The only thing that she could see were the memories inside her head. Red falling beside her. The water sloshing, endlessly, over her head as her tired body barely fought the current until she bumped into the shore.

Aly's gaze passed over Naia and Grey without really seeing them. No Truthwells burned within her friends, though there they were, alive and well. Nothing made sense.

No comforting glow emitted from the water beneath her. No twinkling energy sparkled in the air around her.

The world had gone dark.

She'd meant to dispel the darkness, not swallow herself within it.

Naia knelt beside Aly. "You slept. That's good. How are you feeling?" Her tone was apologetic. She didn't need to mention the dead weight hanging off every syllable.

Dead. He was, certainly. Aly had known it before they'd hit the water. His Truthwell had gone dark. But so had Naia's. And Grey's. And the world's.

Aly couldn't answer. She closed her eyes and fought back the poisonous grief that wanted to strangle her.

"We'll be at the wharf soon."

Aly sat up. "No."

Naia arched her brows.

"I can't—I will—We must search for him." Her throat closed, and she gasped for air. "I can't return without him."

He, at least, deserved that much.

Naia sighed and scooted back onto the bench beside Grey. "It's dark, Aly. We have no light to see by, save the stars. And you're freezing. Let's come back tomorrow."

"No, I can fly on my own. I can..." But she couldn't. Magic was no longer tangible, no longer *there*. She looked down at her hands, as if they could somehow still direct a spell. "Is it gone for you too?"

Naia nodded. "Thank you."

Aly couldn't imagine being happy about this. But then again, that had been Naia's wish the first day they had met.

"Don't you miss it?" asked Aly. "It feels like going blind."

Naia waved a hand dismissively. "I don't. I like the world better without the shadows that haunted me."

Aly hadn't thought of it like that. She instinctively tried to reach out with her mind to see the Truthwells that should surely be burning in the outskirts of Mardon. Nothing happened. She felt small, smaller than she'd ever felt in her life.

"I will still search for him. If it takes me months, I will drag his body from the depths of the river." She tucked her head on her crossed arms and tried to ignore the fishy smell of the little boat.

Then her head popped up. "What of the war?" she asked.

Grey rowed quietly, his movements a steady rhythm. "The shadow is gone. Almost as suddenly as the shadow disappeared, the enemy soldiers under its control returned to their right minds. They were very confused. There was still some fighting, but by the time I left the city to search for you, I heard the horn signaling their retreat."

Aly nodded but she wasn't as happy as she should have been at the news.

"I don't want to go back," she said.

"The city needs you."

She scoffed. "No, it doesn't need me. I am nothing now."

He leaned forward with his next row, his tone sharp, like he was again her tutor. "Aly, you know more about statecraft than many people. Elise will want you by her side, even without magic."

So he knew. Naia must have told him magic was no more. His words stung, despite his attempted compliment. *Without magic* had a nasty ring to it. Glancing at her fingers, she drummed them along the wooden rail. No Master's ring flickered on her middle finger.

The poem in the Canticles spoke of a dawn alight with songs of joy. This felt more like walking into an eternal night.

"I hate this," she admitted.

The poem spoke of shining faces, and Aly had always assigned that line to mean the light of Truthwells.

As if noticing for the first time, Aly glanced from Grey to Naia, who sat particularly close to Grey. With each revolution of his hands, the oar almost scraped over Naia's lap.

Aly stared for several long seconds.

Her heart swelled and she couldn't keep down a small chuckle. *Of course.* She wasn't the only person in the world. The world was now free of a powerful evil. People would live to see another day—another love. Perhaps good things were all around her, if she took the time to look.

She smiled up at Grey, who pointedly avoided her gaze. Finally, she looked back to the water. "I will return to Mardon. But not without him."

Grey only nodded and turned his gaze back over his shoulder a moment. "We will return at dawn."

She didn't want to wait, but without light, searching for Red would be nearly impossible. And the shivers had returned, shaking Aly's entire body. Trying to ignore the pain in her own heart, Aly lifted a knowing half-smile at Naia, relishing the distraction from her heavy sadness.

Naia pursed her lips in her typical annoyed fashion. "What?"

Leave it to the wild one to break the stonehearted spy. Aly was thrilled with the prospect of Naia and Grey, happier than she'd assumed possible after waking up to a dark world devoid of Red's light. She wasn't exactly singing songs of joy, but Aly delighted in the glow on her friend's face.

Chill air and swirling columns of white mist hovered over the river as sunlight broke through the trees. Aly wore a fur coat from Elise's closet. She'd never needed a warm coat before, and she tugged it around her as if it might hold her together.

The enemy army was disbanding, the wounded and dead being removed from the city streets. Mardon still burned in places, and there was no magic to put out the fires.

Arthur Ondorian stood beside her, his priestly robes replaced with a woolen suit and long coat.

Overnight, a band of angry nobles and former sorcerers had tried to storm the palace, enraged that magic had vanished, but the crowded grounds had made for a poor target. There were too many civilians crammed in the palace to make an attack on the royal family feasible. Aly slept through it all, hoping she might wake to find Red's disappearance had been a dream.

She had not.

Now, from the prow of a small clipper ship, the pride of Mardon's shipping industry, Aly and Naia stared out at the Cresen River. A dozen smaller boats had dispersed over the water to search for the man everyone now assumed to be dead.

Aly had poured Red's light into the shadow, then directed it to the waters of the Black River. It had taken every bit of his light to separate the shadow from its source. His light had been powerful enough to isolate the Wells of Kassia, Usrich, and the others who'd given themselves to the river, from the energy signature of the water.

Ondorian looked over at Aly. "You did it, you know."

"Ripped the world apart? Yes, I know."

The priest sighed. "No, Aly. You and Red changed the world,

C. F. E. BLACK

yes, but it is still whole. More so, perhaps, if we take the time to think about it."

She shrugged away his optimism and shivered. She hated the cold.

"You and Red uncovered what we had all missed," he continued, his breath darting out in small gray swirls. "For so many generations, the Black River poured evil into the world, but the biggest lie of all was *how* it did so. Everyone believed it was the water. Perhaps at one time, people knew the truth, but over time, and as fear of the river grew, the truth was buried under myths and false understandings and outright lies. The evil never came from the water, but the dark magic of sorcerers who'd given themselves to the river, like Kassia. Usrich immortalized himself by merging his Well with the water's energy, choosing one of man's most deceptive temptations. His darkness, visible only to the gifted few, drew the minds of some sorcerers the way the light drew your mind, Aly."

"And now they're both gone. Light and darkness."

Ondorian tapped the ship's railing. "Oh, you are smarter than that, Aly. You may not have the special ability to see them as you once did, but light and darkness are a part of our world, as are truth and lies."

The explosion of energy at Aly's final spell had returned the river to nothing more than flowing water. But this tearing apart of darkness and light had ripped the very fabric of the world. Aly had ripped out the seams that had held magic together.

The angry mob that attacked the palace hated her for removing their power, their comfort.

Aly pressed her fingers to her eyes. "It was the only way. They'll never accept that, but it's true. It was that or live as slaves of that shadow."

She dreaded searching the bottom of the river, but it was the necessary next step.

314

A shudder raced down her spine as men unfurled nets.

Ondorian nodded. "Many will suffer at the loss of magic, including you. But it is a suffering we shall endure. History will write you as a hero, Aly."

She huffed. "Not the historians from this generation."

"Perhaps not," Ondorian agreed, surprising Aly. "But remember not everyone lauds Theod as they should. What people believe and what is true are not always the same." He bumped her shoulder with his. "Isn't it good that we don't build our faith based on what people already believe? You know the truth of your actions. Let that be enough."

Another boat, a skiff much like the one Grey had taken to search for her, trolled up the river toward the clipper, steering well to the side of the deep center channel to let the larger boat pass.

"Fine morning!" called the fisherman at the oars.

She nodded but did not look over at the boat, her eyes raking the river banks.

A strange sensation caused Aly to turn toward the skiff as they sailed by.

There, on the other boat, stood a dark silhouette outlined by the rising sun. She was certain he was staring at her. She could feel his gaze across the water.

It lit her skin on fire, even from this distance.

Her heart stumbled in her chest as she crashed against the ship's railing. Ondorian steadied her with a tentative hand.

In her mind, she dared to hope. After all, she'd been picked up by a similar boat. Her throat closed up and she couldn't cry out. What if it wasn't him?

He was dead—she'd watched his Truthwell go dark. One hand clapped to her mouth. *All* Truthwells were dark to her now.

Emotion clogged her throat as she swatted at Naia's arm.

"There," she said, pointing at the lone figure standing in the small boat. It was the only syllable Aly could speak. Her hands trembled.

"Hey, sailor!" yelled Naia, voicing what Aly could not. "Tell me your name."

"Naia?"

A familiar voice.

Aly collapsed to the deck, everything inside her pooling into uncontrollable sobs.

"That's my name, you idiot," Naia yelled back, her voice buoyant with happiness.

Shuffling steps, quick orders, and the sailors aboard Grey's clipper ship slowed, the boat already tipping as it turned around in the wide river.

She had imagined Red's voice, surely. It was what her mind wanted to hear. It was too good to be true. A mad hope.

The sound of heavy boots on the deck brought her back to the moment. Red raced toward her.

She couldn't scramble up fast enough. When he caught her in his arms, the world melted away. She was flying again, but not by magic.

He held her until her sobs subsided.

"How are you alive?" he asked, his thumb stroking her cheek.

"How are *you* alive?" She wanted to hold him forever.

"When I hit the water, I woke. I felt stronger than I ever had before. It was strange, like I had magic in me. It was *your* magic."

Aly laughed, still so happy to see him that she didn't care that his words made no sense. "I don't have magic anymore."

His brow wrinkled. "Really? I was like a bullet in the water, Aly. I was definitely enchanted in some way, considering I'm a terrible swimmer. I reached shore and, before I even spoke to anyone, a fisherman ran up to me and offered to take his boat out and search the river for you. Like he could read my mind."

She shook her head, enjoying the warmth of his hand on her skin. "But you died. I saw your Well vanish."

"I'm right here," he said, tipping his forehead against hers. "Whatever you did there at the end, it gave me the power I needed to survive that fall and swim to shore. I'd bet it's also what caused us to conveniently land in the river," he said with a smile. "What happened to you after we hit? I never saw you."

She shrugged. "I don't know." She hadn't seen him either, though her mind had been so warped from exhaustion that she couldn't recall anything after the impact with the water.

He sighed, incredulous. "It's a miracle we both survived."

She thought back to her final spell. Her words had been shaped for the purpose of tearing the darkness from the river's light, but no matter how hard she'd tried to concentrate on that spell, her heart had been focused on Red. Diving into his Well was intoxicating, but even his blinding light hadn't fully eclipsed her own love for him. When she'd said the spell, her heart had yearned for him.

When she'd made the ash blade, her magic had provided the item she'd needed, acting almost on its own, as if the words of the *Verad* knew better than her own mind what was necessary to defeat her father.

When she'd created the peony from the bullet, her magic had responded in a similar fashion, crafting a lovely flower from a deadly weapon in a moment when she was trapped between worlds, worried that her growing affection for Red would prove his undoing.

Perhaps when she'd released that final spell, her magic had crafted one last thing: a way to save Red.

Her love for him hadn't been her undoing, nor his. Instead, it had saved him.

She stared at him, shocked at the notion that he was her ash blade, her peony, her...*What is he?*

Tracing his face with a finger, she whispered, "Can you still swim like a bullet?"

He chuckled softly. "Haven't tried. But the boat we were on moved…I know it doesn't make sense, but it moved where I wanted it to go, without oars."

Her eyes widened. "You have magic now!"

"I can't figure it out. It's not like I'm using spells."

"*You* are magic, then," she said, bewildered. "You're the phoenix. Magic isn't gone, not if it's in you!"

"That sounds preposterous." He tucked her against his chest. "What matters is that you are here." He glanced around. "Grey and Naia too. Thank Theod."

He accepted pats on the back from Grey and Ondorian, and an awkward fist to the shoulder from Naia, but he never released Aly.

She leaned into his warmth, enjoying the small thud of his heart against her ear. "You're my ash blade now. My only magic left."

Sailing back into Mardon took only a quarter hour, as they hadn't made it far, but it felt so slow without magic aiding the sails. Moving without magic would change the world. The shipping industry would have to completely realign. *Everything* would have to realign.

But there was the mystery of Red and the magic inside of him. It gave Aly hope. A mad hope that maybe, in time, they would discover that magic hadn't really perished for good.

She pushed aside these thoughts and settled for handling the immediate needs.

Mardon needed to be rebuilt. And there was the issue of the failed crop. All of the problems they'd faced before still waited to be solved. And now they didn't have magic to help.

By the time they reached the docks, Elise was there, regal in her fine gown and small, glittering tiara. She'd been alerted to their return by the criers assigned to watch for them. Seb stood at her side. She'd been optimistic to dress for the occasion, given what could have transpired, and Aly beamed at her for her dash of wild hope. Maybe Elise was a bit more like her brother than Aly realized.

This time, trumpets blared at the return of the king, an impressive display considering how quickly they'd returned. Elise must have prepared all night for this possibility. Aly smiled and squeezed Red's hand before disembarking after the king.

Elise's eyes were rimmed with tears, but she maintained her practiced composure. A strained expression tugged at her mouth, however, and Aly sensed there was much Red's sister itched to say.

It was then that Aly noticed the Tanderan soldiers lined up along the river bank and along the road leading into the city. They were not facing the king. Instead, their weapons were held at the ready, their faces toward Mardon.

The crowd behind the soldiers swayed with agitation, their shouts drowned out by the victorious trumpets.

Aly had taken magic from these people. They would have to redefine their lives without its comforts.

Aly leveled her breathing and lifted her chin. One way or another, magic was not going to exist in this world in the way they'd always known. They'd come to the very brink, the crux of what was to be.

Darkness had tried to consume the light. If it had won, these people would still be without magic, but perhaps they wouldn't know it, lost in the distorted reality of a lie. Instead, they were privy to the truth: that magic was gone—or at least *Truthpulling* was gone.

Red proved it wasn't fully gone.

Everything would change, in the days going forward. The wealthy, most of all, would feel the lack of magic. Until they could figure out how to do everything without magic, the world would experience a pinch like never before. And the change would be agonizing.

Amid the screamed curses and wailed laments of the gathered nobility, Aly detected loud cheers from the west side of the street.

Citizens from the Creaks pumped fists in the air, shouting their approval of the destruction of magic. They were the ones who'd never felt the comfort of a cool room on a hot day or the bliss of a hot bath warmed by nothing more than a spoken word.

They'd lived their lives without magic, and they had survived. Aly suppressed a grin. It would be to these citizens that Mardon would now turn. Life without magic would be difficult for the wealthy to accept, but plenty of Tanderans—most, really—would return to life as normal.

As Aly accepted a crushing hug from Carolyn, the princess hissed into Aly's ear, "They hate you for what you did, for taking magic away. But," she leaned back, smiling at Aly, "the rest of the city is singing your praises for saving their lives. Don't listen to the angry ones. Listen to the joyful ones."

Aly had only seen Carolyn briefly that morning, right before they had departed for the wharf. She hadn't had a chance to speak to the younger princess, and she was startled by a realization. She leaned forward and spoke loudly into Carolyn's ear over the commotion. "You always said you could do everything magic could do. Now's your chance. Show the world we don't need magic to thrive."

Carolyn beamed as Aly bobbed a small curtsey.

Aly wanted to tell Carolyn that magic might not be fully erased, that Red still contained some, but she felt it wasn't her place to tell Red's sister. They knew very little about what he was capable of, and if it would even last. Best to let Red tell his family, when he was ready.

And as they walked toward the palace, escorted by soldiers in crimson, Aly heard the exuberant joy Carolyn had mentioned.

Aside from a select few, Mardon was rejoicing at the victory. They had lost magic, but they had gained their freedom from the tyranny of that consuming shadow.

The sunlight reflected off the palace windows, and Aly squeezed Red's hand a little harder. People tossed flowers at them and sang songs. It was indeed a dawn alight with songs of joy.

The angry crowds of noblemen and former sorcerers, with their pistols and their fire pokers and their swords, attempted to storm the palace during the entire next week, but with each nightly attack, their numbers dwindled. The palace gates held, and the guards remained loyal to the royal family, defending Red from these attacks. The soldiers had witnessed what the shadow had done to the enemy and the way it had twisted the minds of the sorcerers who'd fallen victim to it. They knew that the alternative to this new reality, however uncomfortable it felt for now, would have been far worse.

Several nobles took up the banner of defending Red and Aly. Lord Chesterton, who had arrived in Mardon with one Protector the day before the attack, cheerfully took up the work of cleaning up the streets of Mardon alongside shop owners and mill workers alike. At his example, many other nobles and former sorcerers, engaged in repairing their city. They had no magic, only their hands.

Aly had spent two days mostly asleep, her body still recovering from that final spell and the hours spent shivering on the shore. Red had passed those two days in meetings and signing papers. One of those papers was a purchase agreement for wheat from Esvedara. The colony was preparing to declare its independence from Bulvarna, and Tandera pledged her support as they sought their freedom. Mardonians wouldn't starve this winter, after all, thanks to Red.

He had requested Elise organize much of the clean-up efforts in the city, her expertise in handling details perfectly suited to the task. Rainbow, after a heart-felt thank you to Aly for teaching her, slipped out of the city, claiming the bustling place wasn't the life for her. Seb was reinstated as a member of Red's council, and Grey, after considerable persuasion from Red, departed for a much-needed holiday on the Sapphire Coast. A few days later, Naia said she'd always wanted to see the ocean, and she too left for Virienne's famed southern coast.

Aly and Red daily left the palace to help with the cleanup effort. Aly found the work distracted her from the loss of magic. She had splinters in her hands from picking up debris, and her feet ached from hours on foot, but she found joy in simply standing beside Red as they pieced together their broken city.

One afternoon, as Red helped Chesterton load up a wheelbarrow full of charred wood, the lord wiped sweat off his brow and paused for a rest.

"You know, sire," Chesterton said, "I've never seen so many people from varying walks of life out in the streets, working together." He had ash smeared across his face in several places. "You two did more than take away the darkness."

Perhaps Chesterton was right. Mardon was coming together to rebuild, but they had lost many to the shadow, and they still did not have enough wood to replace all that had been burned. At least, not yet.

A man with long, knotted hair crept past the people working, eyeing the scene with lifted brows. Red nodded at the former Zealot, but the man only shuffled down the street.

Several of the Canduli Zealots who had lost their magic in the blink of an eye still wandered about Mardon, mesmerized by its grandeur. Many of them had asked to remain, to learn to live without magic, as most of the Mardonians already did. The ones who weren't ready to live among society had left after a few days. Still, a small band of former Zealots, led by none other than young Quince, had volunteered to go to the Crescent Forest and restart the lumber yard there. Experienced men from other lumber yards also agreed to go, now that there was no longer a threat of magic in the forest.

In some ways, the world had improved when magic had vanished. But there was still the mystery of Red's new abilities.

A week later, a familiar knock sounded at Aly's chamber door.

Red was early.

Aly jumped up from sipping her coffee by the fire as the season's first gold and orange leaves waved softly outside. Her coffee was cold now anyway, and she never liked cold coffee. Stashing her cup on a side table, she rushed to her room to change from her nightgown and robe to a proper dress.

He was never early.

In the mornings, usually after breakfast, they had been trying to learn about Red's strange magic.

Their practice sessions had been another welcome distraction as Aly adjusted to the world without light at her fingertips —as he had his particular way of hanging onto her every word, of holding her gaze in ways that shouldn't be allowed in public.

She fumbled with her dress, not yet accustomed to the kinds of dresses most women wore about the palace. She'd been so accustomed to her plain dresses and white cloak.

The loss of her magic weighed on her, and every day without it felt like living in a maze she could never escape. She didn't *know* the world without the light of Truthwells. She needed to relearn her routine, and practicing with Red had become the reason she looked forward to each new day. There was still magic in the world, if only in him.

She was sorry she'd taken the light from those who could see it—she'd stolen something beautiful from the world. But she'd also taken the darkness.

It had to be worth it. The *Verad* spoke of a dawn, and she'd always pictured it as bringing *more* light, not less. She wasn't sure what she and Red had created was the dawn everyone had waited for.

"I'm coming in!"

She smiled and yelped as she darted out of his view and closed her bedroom door.

"You're early!"

"I have something for you."

She tied the sash behind her back and was easing tangles from her hair as she stepped into her sitting room. She stopped short.

A massive bouquet of mixed blooms sat on the small table beside her abandoned coffee cup. There were peonies falling lazily over the sides and many other flowers she couldn't name or didn't recognize. Poking out of the top were purple irises.

Red stood in his finest navy suit, gold collar crisp and tall. He wore the golden coronet.

"It's not my birthday," she said, eying him with a skeptical grin.

"No." He watched her like she was the moon come to greet him. "You never told me your favorite flower, so I told the florist to include every bloom in the solarium."

Aly blushed. She'd only ever fixated on peonies because of the painting Grey had given her. She glanced at it now. The painting was lovely, but those flowers had never really lived. The flowers exploding out of the vase on her table were fresh, soft, and smelled like springtime.

Many of them had been cultivated with magic, and though they still bloomed, once the plants died, that would be the end of them in the palace solarium. They represented some of the last living things to be touched by the world's former magic. Loss pricked at Aly's chest. Once, she would have been able to see the tiny glowing light inside these blooms.

She knelt and touched them, inhaling their sweetness. "They're beautiful." Tears welled up, and she couldn't shake the sudden sadness clamping her throat into a knot.

Red dropped to a knee before her, his hand moving across her back. He let her cry, never making her feel bad for mourning the loss of magic.

When she had mostly recovered, she finally met his warm gaze. There was no judgment in his eyes. "I miss it. The light."

He nodded. "I suppose truth will be less tangible now."

She discreetly tried to wipe her nose with the back of her arm. He offered her a handkerchief. "I hate these, you know." She playfully tossed the cloth at his face. "I'm surprised you don't."

Picking up the cloth, he offered it once more. "They remind me of how you saved me."

Eyes wide, she took the handkerchief.

"And because of you, I'll never have to face a death curse again. No one will. You saved every Zealot in the forest and the desert. Every soul lost to the power of magic created by lies."

Aly stood. Red remained on his knee.

She looked at the flowers and back at his smiling face. Her mouth fell open.

He held up a small box. "The world might be a different place now, but some things haven't changed, Aly. I love you. I can't rule this country without you, magic or no magic. Stay by my side. Marry me."

She half-laughed, half-cried as he opened the box to reveal a massive emerald surrounded by diamonds. Words failed her, so she nodded and grabbed his hands, pulling him up.

He kissed her with enthusiasm, with joy. She kept breaking the kiss to laugh. Eventually he joined in, his hand tucked around the side of her head.

"Truth may not move mountains anymore," she said, the words weighty on the otherwise happy moment. "But at least we still have the *Verad*. I guess that, at least, will never change."

Red grinned. "Truth will always move mountains. Maybe just not in the literal sense. Igor would agree, don't you think?"

The mention of her student brought more quick tears. He should have lived. So many lives were lost to the darkness. But no more. Truth and lies still existed, but their power would be different now. Men would still be lured by the darkness, and the light would still fight against it. But it was a battlefield Aly could no longer see. A battlefield within men's hearts.

The power Theod had gifted them through magic had remade the world. Magic as they knew it had burst to flames, and whatever magic Red now possessed was the small phoenix rising from those ashes. It gave her hope that Theod had a new plan, a new way of orchestrating his power in the world of men.

"You're the scepter now, Red," she said, wiping a stray tear.

He laughed quietly. "We'll see about that."

"The dawn," she whispered, words of the *Verad* echoing in her memory. "It's not a physical dawn." She breathed an incredulous laugh. "Light will shine in new ways. Inside of us, rather than visibly."

"*I* never could see that light. Most people never saw it. *And those without can ne'er enjoy.*" He quoted the very idea the poem was contemplating. "You'll simply have to enjoy the light as I see it. As we all now see it." His smile was impossible not to mirror, though she would miss the sparkling beauty of his Truthwell.

There would no longer be any faces cast in shadow, any chosen children gifted with the ability to see truth and lies. There would be only the truth, and those willing to live by it.

And none within can e'er destroy.

No longer would there be a power of darkness strong enough to blot out the light.

She kissed him again, longer and slower, letting her tears rub off on his warm skin. As her tears wiped away, so did the ache of losing what she'd once held so dear. Though it would be a strange new world for her, a thrill of joy danced through her. Night had breathed its last, and the power of the magic of lies was no more.

Even though Aly couldn't see her face, she knew it was shining like the poem described. Red was right. Truth still had power, and nothing would ever change that.

ALSO BY C. F. E. BLACK

Scepter and Crown series:

Shield of Shadow

Blade of Ash

Crown of Dust

Scepter of Fire

Other titles:

The Veritas Project

To read Lord Weston Grey's backstory, sign up to be a reader VIP at

vip.cfeblack.com/join

If you enjoyed this book, please consider leaving a review. It helps more than you know.

ACKNOWLEDGMENTS

Guys, we did it! The Scepter and Crown series is finally complete. There's no way I could have written an entire series while parenting two small boys without lots of help.

First, to Will, for understanding how much this dream means to me. I couldn't do this writer thing without your support. And truthfully, you've taught me what it actually means to work hard and be efficient. So, thanks for being such a great example to follow!

To Dad, for being the best dev editor in the world. Now I know how your students feel when you shred their hard work and tell them how to improve. Don't worry, I can take it. My stories thank you, and my readers thank you.

To Mom, for being there when I needed a little more time or a little more gushing enthusiasm. Every writer needs these things in vast quantities.

To my two boys, for napping at the same time, and for getting me outside as much as possible. You two help me keep my work in perspective. I hope one day you appreciate that.

Also, Hannah. This book is as much for you and because of

you as it is any other single person. Your friendship and encouragement along the way have meant so much.

I wouldn't have made it this far without my street team. You people keep me going and bring a smile to my face. Like I said, every author needs heaps of encouragement, and you guys are the best.

To Sarah Wilson, Constance Lopez, and Anastasis Blythe, thank you for talking me down from my ledges, for helping with blurbs, for being my friend, for spilling your heart about art, and for being generally awesome. I'm so glad to have you as friends.

For everyone who has made it this far in the series, thank you! I hope you have enjoyed this adventure as much as I have.

And thank you, Lord, for allowing me this incredible dream come true.

As always, soli Deo gloria.

ABOUT THE AUTHOR

C. F. E. Black loves to get swept away in books, both reading and writing them. Fantasy and science fiction have been her bread and butter since childhood, and she can't imagine life without her beloved fictional worlds. She lives in beautiful north Alabama with her superhero husband, sons, and fur-family. Connect with her and find free stories at www.cfeblack.com.

Printed in the USA
CPSIA information can be obtained
at www.ICGtesting.com
LVHW04052522210231023
761592LV00034B/397/J